David Tory (signature)

DAVID TORY

Exploration

THE STANFIELD CHRONICLES

RIVER GROVE
BOOKS

This is a work of fiction. Although most of the characters, organizations, and events portrayed in the novel are based on actual historical counterparts, the dialogue and thoughts of these characters are products of the author's imagination.

Published by River Grove Books
Austin, TX
www.rivergrovebooks.com

Distributed by River Grove Books

Design and composition by Greenleaf Book Group and Brian Phillips
Cover design by Greenleaf Book Group and Brian Phillips
Cover images: © Everett Collection, Morphart Creation.
Used under license from Shutterstock.com

Publisher's Cataloging-in-Publication data is available.

Print ISBN: 978-1-63299-331-1

eBook ISBN: 978-1-63299-332-8

First Edition

This book is dedicated to Helen.

―――― ACKNOWLEDGMENTS ――――

In addition to the wonderful team at Greenleaf, I have many people to thank who have guided me through the development of the Chronicles. Jack Armitage, who made the suggestion I should write the book and has encouraged and supported me ever since; Tom Vowler and Martha Bustin for their editorial advice; Brian Lavery, who introduced me to the *Susan Constant*, which became the *Sweet Rose*; family and friends, always appreciative, but most of all, my wife, Helen, a constant advisor, brainstormer, critic, and editor.

—— AUTHOR'S NOTE ——

This is the story of the opening up of New England, prior to the arrival of the Pilgrims, as seen through the eyes of a young man called Isaac Stanfield. While he and others in his circle are imaginary, his life intersects with some real people, such as Reverend John White, rector of Holy Trinity Church, Dorchester, Dorset, and Sir Ferdinando Gorges, governor of Plymouth Fort in Devon, England. When characters are added to a historical narrative, they tend to develop lives of their own over which the author has little control, but the essential historical facts are there.

Part 1

CHAPTER 1

Letter to Isaac Stanfield—*12 August 1613*

Dear Isaac,

Chaos here. Most of Dorchester is consumed. The George gutted, so Silas is out of a job. I was out harvesting with everyone else when we first saw the smoke. By the time I got back to town it was an inferno. Silas said you and some horses went to Weymouth. What?

Silas taking this letter down to Weymouth, looking for a job with Adam's help.

Will

Letter to Will—*15 August 1613*

Dear Will,

On August 9, the Patriarch sent me to get some more church candles from Old Man Baker. Aby was in the kitchen preparing a meal. I took advantage to share it. Old Man Baker came in and told Aby he had a big cauldron of tallow being heated in the shop. He had to go to make a delivery, so told her to watch the fire and keep it stoked. After he left, Aby and I went to check the fire. Alone in the shop together, we quickly settled down for some cozies . . .

Next thing I knew Aby was screaming in my ear, leaping to her feet. The cauldron had boiled over and tallow was in the fire. The fire exploded, walls quickly alighting. We were like madmen trying to beat out the flames with anything to hand.

I was running out to find water and help just as Aby's father came back, yelling at me for burning his shop down. In the street, I bounced off Bailiff

Vawter, who had seen the smoke. By this time the flames were already to the roof; Bingham's shop was alight. Vawter grabbed me and shouted, "Shit, gunpowder!" He dragged me next door to the Shire Hall and said: "Get sacks, wet them, and help me move the barrels—quick, before they blow us all up."

I froze, terrified. But Vawter, cool headed, grabbed some sacks that were stacked against the wall, pushed them into my hands, pointed at the horse trough, and slapped me on the shoulder. By this time the smoke was intense, and the fire had made it to the roof of the warehouse. I stumbled to the trough and wet the sacks, feeling I was in some waking dream state. Didn't have time to think. Sack to a barrel, wrapped, and rolled out the door. Some-one, I couldn't see who, helped me lift the barrel onto a cart and I went back for the next one. Vawter was doing the same.

Will, I can't describe well enough the heat, flames, smoke, the noise of the fire, the shouting, and the terror that a burning beam from the ceiling—now aflame—would drop onto the barrels to blow us to kingdom come.

Bailiff Spicer arrived, and between us we were able to move the barrels up West Street to the fields upwind of the fire. At least I did until the people harvesting in the fields ran back to town to lend a hand. Spicer told me to get some rest. I was replaced by newcomers. I bumped into Aby, scorched but all right. She grabbed me, shouting that the flames were already down South Street to the George. I ran there, worried about Silas. The wind was pushing the fire forward faster than I could run. As the flames touched each roof there was an explosion, as if the thatch were covered in gunpowder, and instantly the house was ablaze. Then, the smoke—blue, black, and yellow—was pouring out of the houses and hurled sideways by the force of the wind. Sparks being blasted down the street onto me. My clothes were smoldering. I had to keep beating myself with my cap as I ran.

I found Silas. He and the other ostlers were leading the horses out of the stable. I shouted at him, giving him the briefest of details. Quick as a ferret, he gave me the reins of three horses and told me to take them back to the King's Arms in Weymouth where they belonged. He would follow on later with a cartload of rescued belongings from the George. Once in Weymouth, I should tell Adam Trescothick what happened.

What happened after I left? Is Aby all right? Stories coming in say that most of Dorchester has burned down, as far as Fordingham.

I am boarding the *Sweet Rose* this afternoon for France, to La Rochelle in the Bay of Biscay. I won't be around for a while. I'll explain how that came about when I have a moment. Adam has Silas working in the stable, and they will get my note to you.

Isaac

Letter to Will—*17 August 1613*

Dear Will,

I met Silas at the King's Arms when he arrived with a cartload of bits and pieces saved from the George. We were standing in the stable yard talking when a man came in. I recognized him with a great lurch in my stomach.

You probably don't remember, but shortly after the plague took my parents in 1607, I was badly beaten up by some idiot behind the George. Silas found me, bandaged me up, and became my mentor. That's why he taught me all he knew about fighting, including how to fight down-and-dirty, not just to defend myself. "Take it to the enemy," he'd said. Silas also taught me to use the dirk and anything else useable as a weapon, as you have been known to comment. I learned to fence, too, with the help of his fencing-master friend, the one you took an instant dislike to. Anyway, I never told anyone the circumstances.

What follows is for your ears only. That idiot, I never knew his name, must have been about eighteen years old. He came out of the George for a piss and saw me stripped, washing in a horse trough. Before I knew it, he had grabbed me and slapped a hand over my mouth. With the other he started fondling my privies. For pity's sake I was only ten years old. I managed to kick him in the goolies, but he got mad, punched and kicked the hell out of me, and left me behind the trough for Silas to find shortly afterward. I never saw the bastard again until now.

I told Silas and he said we should follow him, so we did. The man walked down to the quayside holding a canvas bag and looked like he was preparing to board a ship. As we approached, he dropped down into a boat and was rowed away. At that moment, Silas was hailed by a sailor. Silas introduced me to him, an old friend called Tiny Hadfield. He was an enormous man, a sailor on the *Sweet Rose*. After some rough pleasantries he asked Silas if I was the new ship's boy for the *Sweet Rose*. Before I could say anything, Silas, with a wicked gleam in his eye, said yes—at least for a proving trip. If I was no good, they could throw me overboard.

I grabbed Silas's arm, moved him out of hearing, and asked what he was playing at. He laughed and said being such an adventurous lad it would be a good experience for me and there was nothing for me back in Dorchester at the moment. It would keep me out of mischief now I'm no longer a schoolboy. Time for me to start earning my living. If I didn't like it, no harm done. Silas knew the skipper and had absolute trust he would look after me. I shrugged, Silas handed me over, Tiny ordered me into a waiting boat, and we were rowed out to my new home.

A new adventure for sure, and no more thoughts of the bastard who had attacked me—well not until I boarded the *Sweet Rose*. There he was, Second Mate Tred Gunt. He didn't recognize me, and I sure as hell wasn't going to introduce myself. We shall see what we shall see.

I have had a day on board the *Sweet Rose*, and it has been an overwhelming experience. I am scribbling down the bits I remember, but I need to start a journal that I will send you pages from, for safekeeping. It will keep you up-to-date with my activities, and it will keep my memories fresh. We are about to sail, so I will get this last letter to Adam for you.

Isaac

Journal entry—*17 to 22 August 1613*

As promised to Will, I am starting a journal. This is the first entry.

As soon as I went aboard, I was hauled up onto the quarterdeck by the First Mate, Mr. Andrew Jones—called "Peg" for his wooden leg. He brought me before the captain, Mr. Isaiah Brown, whom everyone calls "skipper," although not to his face. The captain interrogated me, declaring that he didn't trust that rogue Silas Beale (he meant our Silas, though it took me a moment to realize), and thus was disinclined to trust me. I must have looked startled. When a flicker of a smile appeared on the captain's face, I understood it to mean his remark was not to be taken seriously.

He quickly found out I had finished my schooling at Reverend Cheeke's establishment, as he called it. He seemed impressed that I could read, write, and spell "trigonometry." He wasn't that interested in my Latin or Greek, but he perked up to know I had a few words of French. The captain didn't care to know how I came to be on his ship and, as he didn't throw me off, I supposed I would be staying. He did kick me off his piece of the deck, which is apparently sacred to skippers, and gave instructions to Peg about my future. Seems I am in possession of some talents not typically found in a ship's boy with not one jot of sailing experience. However, I must start from scratch learning one end of the ship from the other. He said that on this first trip—which was interesting, since I hadn't realized he thought there would be more than one—I was to be one of two ship's boys. This is a bottom-end job normally given to a ten- or twelve-year-old. The other boy is called Johnny Dawkins.

The skipper put me under the charge of Peg, who, in turn, put me under the charge of James Braddock—an able seaman known as "J.B." His job was to provide me with suitable clothing and help familiarize me with the ship, its layout, rigging, watch system, and crew. Around twenty years old, J.B. is tall and clean shaven with long brown hair, a lean face, bushy eyebrows, brown eyes, and large ears pierced with small gold rings. A calm, laconic man, he told me he had been with the skipper for ten years and had started on the *Sweet Rose* as a ship's boy.

The ship in motion was a new experience. J.B. advised sea air, then, more urgently, the proximity of a bucket. Mr. Glynn, boatswain (bosun), would have my hide if vomit touched any part of the ship. Concentration was difficult. We went to the slop chest for clothing, where I was given britches, jacket, as well as an oilskin; payment due when I receive pay. I received a canvas bag to keep my personal belongings in, with the possibility of a chest with my name on it if I lasted long enough. A corner was found for me way for'ard on the lower deck, where I could sleep on a straw-filled palliasse wedged among numerous other palliasses.

J.B. introduced me to the head, with which he thought I might soon develop an intimate understanding, given my seasickness. It is a deck under the bowsprit with gratings at the bows. It is exposed, swept regularly by the water surging past the bows. I had immediate use of it. My bowels, bladder, and stomach relieved themselves of their contents as J.B. watched, unconcerned. From the head we climbed steps up to the forecastle (focsle) where the foremast rose from the deck. Hundreds of ropes were all fastened or belayed to numerous points around the foot of the mast, as well as on the rails. J.B. went through them, telling me I was expected to learn where each was located and what they were used for by the time we reached La Rochelle. My head reeled from the names. How the hell would I remember them, let alone where they were belayed and what they did?

Bowlines—foretopmast, main, and fore. Stays, halyards, downhauls, sheets, leach-lines, tack-lines, buntlines, clew-lines, lifts, and braces. I was informed that the *Sweet Rose* was referred to with great affection by the crew as simply *Rosie*, because—like a buxom barmaid—she was all sweetness and light under a fair wind, but had a mind of her own once roused. Then we descended to the main deck, the "waist" between focsle and quarterdeck. It was a good name, I thought, for a ship called *Rosie* with an ample bosom for'ard, bum aft. The main mast rose from the deck. More hundreds of ropes. Similar names and functions for the main mast's sails and spars. We didn't climb back onto the quarterdeck, but I presumed a like number and uses for the mizzen mast as well.

J.B. told me I was being added to a crew of sixteen and gave me a quick description of the key members:

THE SKIPPER, ISAIAH BROWN

A dour man, not given to conversation, the skipper is a stern but fair disciplinarian. Excellent seaman and navigator. Born to a sailing family, he'd been at sea thirty years before I came aboard *Rosie*. He is highly respected by the crew, most of whom have sailed with him for years. Forty years old, the skipper was Dorset born and bred and shorter than average in height, with a wiry frame, clean-shaven face, close-cropped gray hair, and brown eyes. A scar wound down his left cheek, his left ear partially missing—marks left by an old pirate cutlass. Part-owner—with Richard Bushrode, of the *Sweet Rose*—the skipper knows the Patriarch, whom he refers to respectfully as the Reverend John White. Bushrode and the skipper have strong business links to Sir Ferdinando Gorges, the Governor of Plymouth Fort.

FIRST MATE ANDREW "PEG" JONES

Lost his leg in 1588 at the time of the Armada. Served with Silas before Silas's age caused him to be paid off. Bosun's mate in the English Navy. Another Dorset man, he was a childhood friend of the skipper, who recruited Peg after the Navy discarded him. A devoted first mate, he is a talker and a wonderful storyteller who is naturally cheerful but quick to anger when crossed. Highly skilled seaman. Forty-four years old, he is clean shaven, above average height, broad-shouldered, immensely strong, and agile on his wooden leg.

SECOND MATE TRED GUNT

A recent addition to the crew. Rumor has it that Sir Ferdinando asked the skipper to take him on as a replacement for the previous second mate, whom Captain John Smith recruited for a voyage across the Atlantic Ocean to Newfoundland and Northern Virginia. Comes from Bristol. An experienced seaman, but not much known about him. Crew is wary of him. Twenty-four years old and of medium height, he is overweight with long blond hair, a walrus moustache, and a short beard.

GUNNER JEREMIAH BABBS

Gunner Babbs loves his guns. Came from an iron foundry in Woolwich that made ordnance for the Navy. Recruited by the skipper after a run-in with the pirates who gave the skipper his cutlass wound. The skipper decided to invest in suitable armament with a skilled gunnery officer to be better able to defend himself. Babbs is old at forty-eight—hoarse of voice, bald, deaf, bow-legged, and bent of back—though he is strong. Babbs is skilled at maneuvering, sighting his falcon, and minion guns.

BOSUN DAI GLYNN

Mr. Glynn is in charge of the crewmen, a Welshman from Penarth. He is taciturn, and a strong disciplinarian. Crew respects and is a little frightened of him. He has a serious bark and a mean demeanor. Rumor has it that he is descended from Penarth pirates. An experienced seaman, he has served with the skipper for years. Aged about thirty, bearded, with grizzled gray hair.

COOK DUSTY CATTIGAN

Dusty is the long-time cook. Large, bald, with bushy white eyebrows. Aged about forty with a round, pink face and twinkling blue eyes. Huge hands but gentle and soft spoken. He comes from Somerset with a deep burr. Keeps to himself but is much respected and appreciated by the crew. I was advised to establish close and friendly relations with Dusty. He dispenses food and hot drinks on cold nights, as well as cures for any injuries.

Letter to Isaac—*20 August 1613*

Dear Isaac,

Thanks for your notes—it must have been terrifying. Saw the smoke and we all came running, but not much we could do. Everything was dry and the wind, unbelievable. You are in the clear. Aby told her father you both had arrived in the shop just as the cauldron boiled over. You were running out to get help. He admitted to her he had overfilled the cauldron. Not sure he would tell anyone else, though—accident waiting to happen. Seems the authorities have decided it was an accident, too. Not sure how they came to that conclusion. Maybe Old Man Baker has a patron somewhere. Bailiff Vawter confirmed you had helped him move the gunpowder. He said you were a hero. There's a turnaround—you, a hero.

Anyway, Dorchester is a mess. Initially, most of it seemed to have been burned down. Holy Trinity Church and the Patriarch's house escaped with little damage. I still have a roof over my head. All Saints was badly damaged. The School is destroyed, and Reverend Cheeke is beside himself as a result. I am gut-sick at the destruction. Only the stone buildings survived, although the roofs are gone. West Street right down to the bridge is smoldering ruins. South Street the same. Nothing much left of the George. The stench of burning, charred buildings is strong, with everything in them destroyed— food, animals, and bedding alike. Even now, ten days later, the smell seems as bad. People have been wandering around, poking through the remains, looking for something to rescue.

The Patriarch's house is now the center for all aid, with him and Reverend Cheeke very much running things. People are raising money to support those who are newly homeless. Mothers and daughters are cooking and sharing food with others every day. Able-bodied men from the congregation are helping to clear, repair, and rebuild, with me and the gang boarding with the Patriarch and roped in as errand boys. By nightfall we are covered with black soot and exhausted. I have never seen anyone charged as the Patriarch—pleading, threatening, and comforting. He has everyone focused on recovery. The bailiffs and town elders, under his inspired leadership, are the steel that is bringing back strong discipline, structure, and order. Those with the resources are reaching out to those who have lost everything. P. is ensuring good Christian charity is in full flood.

Sadly, Mrs. Bingham died clearing out her stock room. The roof fell in on her. Incredibly, no other deaths. A blessing that almost everyone was helping with the harvest. The fire started in the early afternoon, not in the evening when everyone would have been home, trapped in their houses like poor Mrs. Bingham. There were lots of burns, some broken bones. P. wanted to know where you were. Reverend Cheeke did too, not yet accustomed to you no longer being under his charge (and cane). He is trying to gather his students together, but P. finds us all too useful and needed. I told him that you had been called away to Weymouth, but I didn't know where you were now. He gave me that knowing look, the one that says, "God moves in mysterious ways." You were sent to get candles, and you ended up saving the town from a gunpowder explosion.

He asked me to tell you to contact him if I happened to be in touch with you. Message delivered. I'm envious you escaped the aftermath of the fire. I can't believe you are sailing to France. Watch the m'selles. Shall I tell Aby you are facing distractions? I suspect a fierce reaction. Perhaps not. I'm pleased you are going to keep a journal, as I will try to do. We can share our adventures.

Will

Journal entry—*23 August to 3 September 1613*

After my initial introduction to *Rosie* by J.B., I hardly remember the trip to La Rochelle. I was warned the Bay of Biscay could be rough. I was as sick as a dog. When I wasn't huddled over the gratings at the head, I was moaning in my berth. I was made to get up to work after twenty-four hours, though I tripped or stumbled over everything and everyone and J.B. was given the task of looking after me. The rest of the crew were either exasperated by or laughed at my total inadequacy. J.B., bless him, stuck with me. He only cuffed me a couple of times an hour. The only person who really sympathized was the other boy, Johnny Dawkins. We are on separate watches and don't have much time to talk, but it seems that I have taken his place as the newest, and therefore most wretched piece of humanity that ever existed. I'm pleased to be of some value to *someone*. Johnny is bright, open, and friendly—small for a twelve-year-old, with blond hair, blue-green eyes, and a happy countenance. He is naturally popular.

23 August, we arrived in the port called La Rochelle. I was told to keep out of the way, as *Rosie* worked her way into the inner harbor between two towers that marked the entrance. It gave me a chance to savor the port. Fishing boats abounded, double- and even triple-berthed with brown sails and hulls painted in brightly colored patchworks. I saw wide quays of white stone with tightly packed houses—some up to five stories—set back. The roads ran around the harbor-side, cobbled and filled with throngs of people. Arcades on the ground floors of the houses, made of the same stone, stretched the whole way around the harbor. They contained shops, bars, and gathering places on the western side of the harbor, while to the east, where we were berthed, they were for storage or the entries to warehouses.

All sorts of activity burst out on deck and in the rigging. I kept being shouted at to "mind my head," or "get out of the way, you stupid numbskull," and the like. By the time the chaos was sorted out we were nestled up to a quay, offloading our cargo. A man at the quayside seemed to be in charge of something or other, because the skipper was quite deferential to him—even doffed his hat. At one point as the man was about to leave, Peg Jones shouted at me.

"Stanfield, stop standing there gawking and make yourself useful! Go with

Monsieur Giradeau, here. He needs to fetch some papers. He will give them to you to bring back. Now, move."

By this time, M. Giradeau was on his way. I jumped off *Rosie* and ran after him to a big house with fancy carvings and balconies. It overlooked the street not far from the harbor. He opened the door, glancing back at me as I followed him like a puppy dog.

"Come," he said.

We entered his house. With cap clutched in hand, I gazed about, much impressed.

"Wait here."

He disappeared. I was alone in the front hall. A few moments later, a vision appeared. The vision spoke.

"Bonjour."

I stuttered a response. Can't remember what I said. She giggled, and the spell was broken.

"Je suis Vivienne."

"Je suis Isaac."

Will, I have to tell you Vivienne is stunningly, mouth-wateringly, stomach knot-makingly beautiful. Her French accent is utterly captivating. I was dazzled. I couldn't speak. She took my hand, led me to a small walled garden, sat me down, and started to talk to me. I didn't catch a word she said. I was drowning in her eyes. Suddenly, she jumped up as M. Giradeau appeared with a package in his hands.

"Come, no time for this, Vivienne,"he said. *"Va t'en."*

We went our separate ways, me back to *Rosie,* carrying the package. It appears that M. Giradeau is Bushrode's La Rochelle business partner. We were in La Rochelle for about a week. When our holds were refilled on 30 August, we sailed away from Vivienne. All the while in harbor, I was confined to *Rosie,* unable to see her or stop thinking about her. She was so close, but untouchable. Once at sea, I was able to think more rationally, and as we approached England, I found Aby back in my thoughts.

The return journey was different. The weather was good, and I wasn't sick. I could find my way round *Rosie.* I remembered what J.B. had told me. I began to understand and obey the commands thrown at me, and—I have to say—I started to enjoy myself. *Rosie* moved at a great pace through the water, and the crew were inclined to treat me more like a human being. J.B. even complimented me for something I did. We arrived back in Weymouth, on Saturday, 4 September.

Letter to Will—*Saturday, 4 September, 1613*

Dear Will,

I am including pages of the journal entries I have written with this letter and will continue to send subsequent entries to you for safekeeping.

To your note of 20 August—Silas gave it to me when I got back to Weymouth from La Rochelle. I am sad to hear about Mrs. Bingham. She must have been in the storeroom when I was dragged off to the gunpowder store. She was always kind to me, unlike her bloody husband, who was a mean old sod. Trust him to leave her to fend for herself while all hell broke loose.

Tell Aby I can't wait to see her. I will be in Weymouth a while unloading—picking up another cargo, then straight back to La Rochelle, probably in ten days or so. I wanted to go ashore to make a quick trip to Dorchester, especially having been given the clear regarding the fire. Sadly, I am required to stay aboard, ordered to work, as well as continue to learn being a seaman. I am being tested on my knowledge and competence every day. I must learn to be useful, as I have been promoted. On this next trip I will be a seaman. Rumor has it that we will be going directly to Plymouth from La Rochelle. Seeing as how we seem to be working for Mr. Bushrode, at some point I assume we will be back in Weymouth.

I am leaving this letter and packet with Silas at the King's Arms. He says he has a safe courier.

Isaac

Journal entry—*4 to 23 September 1613*

At the start of the return trip to La Rochelle on Thursday, 16 September, Peg Jones took me aside to ask if I had noticed anything wrong with Johnny Dawkins. I said that as I was on starboard watch, I hadn't had any opportunity. Peg told me he was putting me on larboard watch under Mr. Gunt, and that I should keep my eyes open. I realized I might have overlooked Johnny as he had become withdrawn as of late. Now on larboard watch, I took to observing him. I quickly saw Johnny was a different boy than I had known—quiet, his spark gone, trying to make himself invisible. He was clearly terrified of Mr. Gunt. One night into the return passage to La Rochelle, larboard watch crew sleeping below, I had to visit the head. As I was coming back, I saw a small figure creeping toward and down the hatch to the for'ard hold. I hid. What was he doing? About fifteen minutes later Johnny came back out of the hold. He crept back to his palliasse. As I pondered what I had seen, another figure emerged out of the hatch, and I recognized the silhouette of Second Mate Tred Gunt—no doubt up to his old tricks. After some serious thought, I returned to my palliasse.

Next day, when we were again off watch, I cornered Johnny. After some heavy persuasion he said that on the previous passage back from La Rochelle, Gunt had one night ordered him to attend him in the hold to check stowage. When down there, Gunt grabbed and started pawing him like he had me those many years previously. Apparently, this practice had become a regular activity, with Johnny now an unwilling accomplice in sodomy—a hanging offense for both parties, willing or not. With this threat over him he was trapped, terrified, and lost. I told him I would tell no one, but asked him to give me fair warning of the next time he was summoned to the hold by Gunt.

Two nights later Johnny gave me the word. I hid myself, suitably armed, in the for'ard hold to await developments. The large shape of Gunt appeared, followed a short time later by the slight figure of Johnny. I could hear Gunt wheezing, Johnny whimpering. Gunt lit a stub of a candle, presumably to add to his enjoyment by seeing what he was doing. I saw him from the back, his britches round his ankles, forcing Johnny—likewise britchless—to bend over a barrel. Creeping up behind Gunt, who was too preoccupied to be aware of me, I gave him a sharp crack over his right ear with my heavy belaying pin. I told Johnny to scarper and rolled the unconscious Gunt over, marking his privates and stomach with my dirk. No serious damage but lots of blood. A clear sign that his unnatural acts were known, and any recurrence would result in castration or worse. I left him stunned.

Didn't see Gunt next day. His watch duties were taken on by the bosun. The following day we made La Rochelle by mid-afternoon. Gunt was helped ashore with a huge bandage round his head. Rumor had it that he'd badly damaged himself colliding with a beam in some rough seas and needed to be treated by the local physician. He appeared to me to be seriously overplaying the role of a wounded sailor, but it was clear that he couldn't stay aboard *Rosie* while an unnamed member of the crew was aware of his secret.

Bosun Glynn was promoted to second mate, Pete Couch to bosun, and J.B. to bosun's mate. I had the distinct feeling that I had not seen the last of Mr. Gunt. He was someone to be avoided, but my gut doubted that was possible. Johnny Dawkins was not noticeably recovering, either, after Gunt's departure. I needed to see what I could do to lift his spirits. Having thankfully never experienced what he'd been through, I was not sure what I could do. I would have to see. Apart from dealing with Gunt, the voyage down was relatively uneventful, under a fresh northeast wind. Still busy learning the ropes. Much else besides. The weather was kindly, but we were nearly into October. I was informed that our return trip could be brutal.

CHAPTER 2

Journal entry—*24 to 28 September 1613*

As I write this, it is afternoon and I'm off watch. We are sailing up the French coast after an early departure out of La Rochelle, heading for Plymouth. The wind is up from the east. I am told that we are going to have a time of it working our way back to Plymouth once we've passed Ushant.

We arrived at La Rochelle two days ago, Thursday, 23 September. After Mr. Gunt went ashore, we unloaded *Rosie*. The skipper supervised the unloading as I'm told there was some *precious cargo* that he watched over until it had been safely transferred to the wagons of M. Giradeau. He stayed thus occupied until first dog watch yesterday, Friday. Thereafter, M. Giradeau's wagons started returning with cargo for shipment back to England. Seemed like this trip was scheduled to be a quick turn 'round—not much time for Vivienne. As four bells struck, ending the second dog watch, the skipper grabbed his sword, coat, and hat. He left the boat and headed off the quay into town as evening darkened. He left instructions for Peg Jones to continue loading the cargo that had arrived by wagon onto the quay. As there wasn't much to load at the time, Peg released the off-watch crew. I saw J.B. and Tiny Hadfield leave, following the skipper, so with nothing else to do, I grabbed my cap and coat and went after them.

I was a short distance behind J.B. and Tiny and lost sight of them as they rounded a corner. When I got to the corner, I heard a shout from J.B. and saw that the skipper had been waylaid by a couple of ruffians. He was down, sword barely drawn, stunned from a blow to the head, and one of the men was trying to pull a packet out of his coat. J.B. and Tiny leapt at them with knives drawn, forcing them to back off. The two had cudgels that they used to regain the upper hand. Without thinking, I shouted and ran toward them, drawing my dirk. It was sufficient to distract the assailants, and as J.B. stuck one attacker in his shoulder—the man dropping to his knees cursing—Tiny skewered the other in the thigh. At that point, distracted as I bent down to pick up the skipper's sword, a third bastard crept up behind me and hammered me over the head. Luckily my cap took most of the blow, but I was stunned for a moment. Mercifully, J.B. and Tiny proved too much for the rogues, who ran off—one limping, both men carrying the third with them.

The skipper wasn't in good shape; blood all over his head. He was awake enough to give me a slight nod, hand me the packet the rogues had been after, and whisper I should take it to Henri Giradeau as quickly as possible. The skipper slumped back and J.B. said he and Tiny had to get him back to *Rosie* immediately and I should follow the skipper's orders. So I made my way to the Giradeau house. I wasn't in very good shape either. My head was pounding and when I felt under my cap, there was a lot of blood collecting—some of it smeared down my face. At the Giradeau house I hammered on the door with the hilt of the skipper's sword. Next thing I knew I was on a couch with M. Giradeau asking me what had happened. He had recognized me from my last visit. I told him the story, passing over the skipper's packet, before taking my cap off—blood flowed.

Giradeau called for Vivienne, who must have been waiting outside the room. She took one look at me, gave a little cry, and left. Meantime, Giradeau clapped me on the shoulder and left with the packet. Vivienne returned with basin and cloth to begin swabbing my head. As I was half lying on the couch, she had me sit up and hold the basin so she could focus on the repair work. Gentle she was. My head bowed forward, I was within nuzzling distance of her mesmerizing body, but with my head still throbbing I was somewhat preoccupied. All fine until she started stitching up the wound. I was unaware until the needle first struck. I flinched, spilling the bloody water down the front of her dress. Dear Viv gave hardly a blink and continued stitching. Suddenly, the stitching stopped and I looked up to see Viv's eyes were closed. She pushed my hands away, whispering for me to lie down. Oh sweet Jesus, I raptured. *"Imbecile, c'est mon père! Dorme-toi."* I did, pretending to sleep on her command. M. Giradeau reappeared, and the two of them had a conversation too fast for me to follow, though Viv was obviously protesting at some point. Giradeau leaned over and shook my shoulder. In English, he told me to wake up, which I did.

"I am sorry," he continued. "It is vital you take this packet to someone who is waiting at the auberge with the sign of the Pewter Platter on Rue de Perrot. He is white-haired with a long white moustache and will have his left arm in a sling. Your Captain should have gone to meet him. He is a spy for Sir Ferdinando

Gorges, and neither I nor any of my servants can be seen to be involved. You must go; it is most urgent. Forgive me, but you look inconspicuous and no one will suspect you. No matter the risk, this package must be delivered, and you must obtain anything he has to give you. The password is 'Remember Agincourt.' You need to hide your wound, so I will give you a cloak and chevalier hat. Pull it down to cover your face. Perhaps you should take your Captain's sword as well. You need a scabbard. Vivienne—see to his head."

Equipped with disguise, sword, and directions—my head now bandaged and hidden under the chevalier—I ventured out, but not before a chaste kiss from Viv under her father's impatient glare. As I hurried across town, I puzzled over what had happened. My aching head did not help. What was in the packet? Why had it been valuable enough to inspire violent robbery? How did the ruffians know about it? How did they know the skipper would be carrying it, and when? Who were they? Who did they work for? I had many questions, but none with answers.

Meantime, I soldiered on, trusting no one, trying to appear as a local. With sufficient care, I was able to circle round the harbor to enter Rue de Perrot, where a bustling, noisy crowd hid my progress. As I approached the Pewter Platter, I saw a limping figure ahead of me, hurrying in the same direction. It was one of the three men who had attacked the skipper, the one Tiny had bloodied in the thigh. I held back a little as he entered the auberge. Approaching with care, my chevalier pulled well down, I ducked through the door into the bar and moved along against one wall. The tables were filled with groups of men talking loudly, washing the day's dust and salt from their throats. I slowly worked my way through the room, keeping to shadows and searching for my contact. I spotted him a table away, facing me with his head down and seemingly alone. I sat down beside him and muttered the password. Without glancing at me, he pushed a package under my thigh on the bench. Catching on, I followed suit and did likewise with my packet, which he took and hid, then stood and departed, while I slipped the new package into the inside pocket of my cloak.

The barmaid came over. Would I like a drink, she asked. I grinned my affirmation and she inclined her head in response. When she returned with a tankard of beer, she told me her name—Camille—and said to signal if I needed anything else.

Once she'd gone, I looked around, my eyes now accustomed to the gloom. In the far reaches of the room, I saw the attacker with the injured leg sitting at a table with two men who had their backs to me. They both seemed familiar, but from where I sat I couldn't make out their identities. I needed to know who they were. With my tankard in hand, I moved through the flow of bodies as casually as I could until I could see their profiles. It was still too dark. Suddenly, a match was struck to light a candle and the clear outline of Tred Gunt was revealed, minus the walrus moustache and bandages I'd last seen him in. The other man was David Searle, a seaman on the *Sweet Rose*. That solved one question, but I hadn't time to ponder further before Searle looked over in my direction. Puzzled, he turned to his two companions, who swung 'round to look at me. The attacker recognized me, muttered something, and vanished. By this time, I was moving as calmly as possible toward the door. Gunt and Searle started toward me. I needed reinforcements. At that moment, Camille, with a fist full of tankards, appeared at my elbow. In my fractured French I admitted to being in *"beaucoup de merde"* with bad men after me. I need to lose myself, or words to that effect. Smart girl, she set the tankards on the table, including mine, and put her hand under my elbow. She whisked me into the kitchen. I just had time to retrieve and pocket the package as she took my cloak and chevalier, jammed a beret on my head, draped a long coat over my shoulders, and shoved me through a side door, telling me to *"allez vite, mon jeune anglais."*

The alley connected Rue de Perrot to another road, farther west from the harbor. As I left the alley, I saw a man appear out of the kitchen door and start after me. I feared I was in for some bad encounters. I didn't want to appear to be in full flight but hurried on, intending to make a wide circuit around the town and back to the quay. As I crossed an intersection, I was grabbed around the waist and pushed against a wall by a young, blond giant. I couldn't move. Suddenly, his arms dropped and he fell to the ground. A shadowy figure leaned over the young giant, a small iron bar in his hand. He confirmed the giant was alive before telling me to *"vite, sauvez vous-même."* *"Qui êtes-vous?"* I asked. He glanced at me and moved off, saying *en passant,* *"C'est pour Camille Pils."* Not knowing how the young giant knew me, I was puzzled. Were Gunt and his cohorts somehow aware of the *new* package I was carrying? Had they seen me transfer it to my coat in the kitchen? I had not been entirely discreet. Or were they out to stop me from passing on what I had seen? I kept to my plan, hoping that by intercepting the young giant, a link had been broken in the chain connecting my enemies.

I hurried on. If the road ahead was clear or had pedestrians walking the same direction, I moved forward. I took care at intersections. My sword was unsheathed but hidden from sight under my cloak. I was not approached again as I worked my way north, then west past the Hotel de Ville, and south over the bridge onto Rue Saint Nicholas. I turned right on Rue d'Ablois, down to the southern end of the harbor, sneaking onto the quay as close as possible to *Rosie*. Only two hundred paces more. The quay was lined with ships tied up fore and aft of *Rosie*. It was getting late. I was tired, my headache had returned, and I was beginning to weaken.

The moon had risen. Low above the eastern horizon, it outlined the buildings in stark relief, providing some light to see down the quay. The harbor had settled for the night. Each ship had lit lanterns, and the quayside braziers were also burning, throwing flickering light around them. People were about, but for the most part they were wending their ways—some decidedly unsteady—back toward their ships. The air was still and I could hear the gentle lapping of the water against the many hulls, the muffled creaks of the hulls in response, occasional shouts, distant music, laughter, and singing. All seemed peaceful. I moved onto the quay, starting toward *Rosie,* my heart pounding. So close to safety, I had a premonition of danger. Just then, a long shadow materialized beside me. I turned my head and the shadow became a man in black holding a sword. Oh, angels protect me. I looked exactly like what I was—a boy, exhausted and apparently unarmed. I jumped back, swept my coat behind me, and raised my sword.

"Aha, the boy wishes to fight. So be it."

Then he knows I'm English, I thought. *And Gunt knows that.* Then back to matters in hand. Though I'm relatively proficient, thanks to Silas's fencing master, I was in deep trouble. I was fighting a grown man—a fresh, competent swordsman, dressed in black, at night. Not good.

"En garde!"

I brought my sword up and raised it in the proper fashion to salute my opponent. He smiled, nodded, and did likewise. Anything to gain me time while I slowly backed toward *Rosie*. We engaged. It was clear immediately that he was a much better swordsman and I was no match for him. He played with me. I gave ground toward safety step by step. He flicked my beret off with the tip of his sword and pricked my left shoulder. In fact, despite my entirely defensive fencing, he could do bloody well what he wanted to. Clearly enjoying himself, he almost forgot what he was there for. Was it me, the package, or both?

"The package, *monsieur*."

Who knows, he might have walked away if I'd given it to him. On the other hand, he could've skewered me at will. Almost on my knees by then, I had few options. A small, noisy crowd had gathered to watch, though they would not interfere. Some from the ships close by held flaming torches in their hands, blocking the view from *Rosie*. The crowd's enthusiastic commentary attracted the attention of one or two of *Rosie*'s crew, who had, at the direction of Peg

Jones, positioned themselves at the northern end of the quay, thinking I might be in need of help. They had expected me to come from that direction, with the possibility of a ravening wolf at my heels. Instead I had appeared at the other end with a ravening wolf having at me. My opponent must have realized he was out of time, and he slashed at me. All I could do was deflect his sword, which cut through the left side of my coat. The package fell to the ground. I dropped to one knee, too weak to stand. He approached, stamped on my lowered sword with his left foot, and transferred his sword to his left hand so he could grab the package with his right. I thought he would skewer me, too. I had drawn my dirk in my left hand, and with little time to think, I ducked under his sword and thrust the dirk into his stomach. He gasped and staggered back. Spent, I stayed where I was, but with the package firmly in my grasp. A pair of hands grabbed me under the armpits, another pair under my knees, and they carried me through the excited crowd back to *Rosie*.

"You've done enough, lad."

It was J.B.'s voice in my ear, at which point I knew no more. When I awoke, I was in J.B.'s box berth—no palliasse for a bosun's mate. I could see daylight, and we were under sail. I tried getting up but it was no good. I ached everywhere. My rebandaged head throbbed and my left shoulder stung like fire under its bloodied bandage. It seemed I had other damaged places as well. My groan signaled I was awake. Presumably, on command, Peg was alerted. He came down to me. I asked after the skipper.

"Sore head, incapacitated, but will recover. He wants to see you in his cabin as soon as you can walk. Take your time. J.B. will be keeping an eye on you. Stay off watch until further notice, but return to your duties before we leave the Bay of Biscay."

With that he left me, throwing a "well done, my lad" over his shoulder. J.B. was my next visitor, bringing food and a mug of ale. I was starving. He told me they had got the skipper back to *Rosie*. After that, following the skipper's instructions, they had gone looking for me as far as the Giradeau house. Informed that I was at the house, they returned to *Rosie* and reported to the skipper, who was confined to his berth in the great cabin.

"After we got you back to *Rosie*, the City Watch turned up wanting to know what the scuffle was all about and what had happened to the man who'd been carried on to the *Sweet Rose*. They asked about the other man in the duel. There was no sign of him. Everyone who had seen the fight played dumb and we did too. They weren't stupid. They advised us that they thought there was a threat to us, and they would try to contain it until we departed. Seems like you brought back cargo sufficiently important that the skipper felt we needed to leave as soon as possible heading for Plymouth. However, we had to wait till daybreak for the chain to be dropped before we could leave."

"Chain?" I echoed, befuddled.

"It's raised as a barrier overnight between the two towers that we sailed through at the mouth of the inner harbor," he replied. "As I was saying, that gave us time to load more cargo. We wouldn't want to leave entirely empty, which would have made Mr. Bushrode unhappy. We weren't bothered overnight. The City Watch did their job. In fact, it was on that basis that the skipper decided we could stay a day longer to finish loading Mr. Bushrode's cargo. The Watch continued to keep an eye on us all day."

This complicated explanation was too much for me, other than to realize I must have been unconscious or asleep for over a day. It must now be Saturday.

"You weren't in good shape when we got you back," J.B. continued. "Dusty took charge. He stripped you, washed and bandaged your wounds, and then tucked you up in my berth—would you believe it—and told us all to leave you to sleep. This morning, as soon as the chain was dropped, we sailed with a strong, ebbing tide. We are now heading northwest up the French coast with a strong easterly. At this rate we should make Ushant within two days, followed by a hard grind in open water north to Plymouth."

With that news, and filled with a good meal, I felt more comfortable and went back to sleep. When I awoke, I struggled to my feet, got myself back to the land of the living, and informed Peg I was ready to see the skipper. In no time I was shown into the great cabin. An equally bandaged Mr. Brown bid me sit by him.

"We make a pretty pair," he said as we sat looking out the stern windows.

A roiling wake streamed behind *Rosie*. We tore through the water, enjoying a great view of the coast of France some three miles off to starboard as we slid past at more than six knots. He thanked me for services rendered and asked me to give him a full explanation of my adventures, which I did. He told me messages had come from M. Giradeau that I'd been to the inn, had delivered the package, and was on my way back. So, M. Giradeau had had me followed. I wondered how far. Certainly no one had come to my aid, apart from Camille's friend . . . or had they? I'd survived after all, so perhaps they had. Presumably they'd left me as I'd approached the harbor, expecting me to arrive at the north end of the quay, as *Rosie*'s crew had. It had been a narrow escape. If the man in black had done his job, I'd have been dealt with and the package taken as soon as I'd made the quay. Gunt or someone else had seen me transfer the package to my coat at the Pewter Plate. The information I gave the skipper about Gunt and Searle resolved a number of issues he explained to me.

Sir Ferdinando Gorges had asked him to employ Gunt as second mate and was told Gunt had strong connections with Catholic interests in La Rochelle, a Huguenot town that had been given a great deal of independence to run its own affairs by a previous monarch. He had been led to believe that Gunt would provide useful intelligence back to Gorges about deteriorating relations between the Huguenots and the current king, Louis XIII, and his administration. Now, it turns out that Gunt was a double agent working to his own ends. It was even possible that his connections were to a group other than the Catholics. I said nothing of my previous experiences with Gunt; I needed to protect Johnny. I asked about Searle, and the skipper confirmed that, like Gunt, he was no longer a shipmate.

"It seems Gunt used Searle as an accomplice," the skipper said. "Somehow Searle had seen you with the package and gone to warn Gunt's men. The events have shown how naive we were."

I hoped that Gorges' spy, disguised though he undoubtedly would be, had gone to ground. He must be in grave danger.

"Thanks to you, Stanfield, we have survived, and Sir Ferdinando will receive his intelligence from the packet you brought back," the skipper added. "Now rest up. We will need all hands within twenty-four hours. When we get to Plymouth, I will have you take the packet to Sir Ferdinando. He will want a full report direct from you."

With that he dismissed me. J.B. had reclaimed his berth. I retired to a private corner to write this account in my now very secret journal.

Journal entry—*Wednesday 29 September to Saturday 2 October 1613*

I am now back on my feet, having stood my first watch—middle watch (12:00–4:00 a.m.) on 28 September. I had spent the previous two days recovering my strength and then returning to light duty and was well-rested. We cleared Ushant at around four bells of the morning watch, just after daybreak. My next watch was the forenoon starting eight a.m., which gave me time to worry about Johnny. As soon as he came off watch we spent time together, and he was clearly in a bad state mentally. Nothing I said settled the turmoil in his mind. His physical pain had eased and was less of a constant reminder, but he was lethargic and unable to focus on his work. His fellow seamen on our watch were giving him a hard time. They were already doing extra duty because of my injuries and they had no knowledge of Johnny's ordeal, so they chafed at their load increasing for no reason. I remained concerned.

Rosie moved well, sailing full and by (sails filled and drawing well). The wind was over her starboard quarter, *Rosie's* favorite point of sail. In the lee of the coast she had all sails set, including the "bonnets" (extra canvas attached to the bottom of the course sails) on fore and mizzen. The windward clew on the main course had been hauled up to the main yard. It looked odd and I asked why. A seaman explained that the fore course is the main driving sail. By lifting the sail, wind could drive the fore course uninterrupted. One pump was being worked but not vigorously. Coming on watch under Second Mate Glynn, I was assigned to support him in his capacity as watch officer. This job meant repeating instructions down to the steersman, turning the sandglass, and sounding the bell as required. For each turn of the sandglass, I also marked a chalkboard and sounded a bell. Half hour into the watch—one bell. One hour into the watch—two bells, continuing until the end of the watch—eight bells. My duties included supporting the "log-line" process to determine boat speed, as well as helping Mr. Glynn with the traverse board that marked our progress. It was not hard work, but the duty watch crew was not overly active anyway. With a steady wind over the quarter, no sail changes were required. The crew primarily worked the pumps and adjusted the brace, sheet, and tack lines as the wind backed and filled.

Once we rounded Ushant, I had the opportunity to ask Mr. Glynn about preparations for sailing. We were, at the time, sailing on a northwesterly and heading well clear of the French coast to avoid a line of rocks and islands that stretched the length of the coast from La Rochelle. Mr. Glynn told me that we would need to keep clear of the savage tidal races at Raz de Sein and Ile d'Ouessant (Ushant). With the tide running counter to the wind, the seas there would be too rough. The passages inside Raz de Sein and Ushant would have given us a better angle to make Plymouth, but it would be too dangerous for us to attempt, especially in bad light. A wide sweep 'round Ushant would ensure things become trickier. Assuming the wind stayed easterly, we would need to head up to nor' nor' east, but more likely due north. That's about as close to the wind as we can sail. Luckily, we would have the benefit of the current from the southwest to carry us further east to be able to make Plymouth. Otherwise, the wind would force us farther west than we wanted to go.

When the wind is abeam, *Rosie* is a handful. She has high freeboard, which results in a real windage problem, resulting in *Rosie* being pushed with much leeway to the west. We have to keep her as upright as possible. That way the keel can counteract the sideways slide through the water. The more heeled-over we are, the less the keel is able to keep us on track. To reduce heel, at some point we will need to furl the tops'ls and spill wind from the courses (bottom sails). This adjustment will reduce our speed and will mean a more difficult motion through the water, which will be rough and choppy with wind set against the prevailing current. To ease that motion, the main tops'l won't be furled until conditions dictate otherwise. It could take us more than two days to reach the English coastline. Possibly another day to make Plymouth, if the wind fills to the south. These facts were gradually explained to me in Mr. Glynn's terse style over the course of the watch.

Until sail had to be shortened, *Rosie* moved through the water like a coursing hound—eager and happy, with a good heel and spray flying. The roar of the waves raced past the hull, occasionally down the lee scuppers, and I heard the constant slapping of lines on mast, the crack of sails, and the wind whistling through the rigging. As darkness fell, the glow from the navigation lights gave the white maelstrom the appearance of a raging sea monster attempting to board us. Brushed aside, it growled its frustration.

Two exhilarating hours later, I was back on my palliasse sleeping in the lap of Triton.

At midnight I was roused for middle watch. Moving to my station, I was informed by Mr. Glynn that my previous duties had been assigned to Johnny Dawkins and that I was ordered to join the fellow members of my watch awaiting their orders in the waist of the main deck. I was greeted with the usual coarse banter, but all were quickly brought to heel as orders came down to make preparations for heavy weather. I was detailed to the gunroom. A fellow crewmember and I had to check the tiller, including the relieving block and tackle attached to each side. By the light of a flickering lantern, we had to ensure they were fully operational, greased, and ready for immediate use as emergency replacement for the whipstaff, should it become disabled. The constant movement of *Rosie* trying to buck us off our feet made scraped knuckles, bruised shins, and collisions between heads and overhead beams inevitable.

As soon as we cleared the gunroom we were ordered to the lower deck, main hatch, where a party of seamen were preparing to enter to move cargo in the hold to improve ballast. When we rounded Ushant to head north, the wind would move forward. *Rosie* would heel farther to leeward. We had left La Rochelle with barely a full load of cargo, and had to move what we had to the windward side to counter the heel, securing every item with no chance any might come loose. A few butts of wine on the loose could wreak havoc, even breaching the hull. While down there, we needed to make sure the limber holes were cleared. As I was the smallest, I was the one to scrabble forward to the for'ard end of the clearing line that ran through all the limber holes. I worked it while a shipmate worked the aft end—yanking backwards and forwards, the line's movement dislodging any blockage. After that, we had to check the well box, as well as the lower end of the two pump assemblies. *Rosie* ships a large amount of water when sailing jammed (close-hauled).

Meantime, above us we heard the intriguing rumble of the minions being secured, the hammering of the gun ports being barred and caulked. By the sounds, the lee guns were being secured amidships, as moving weight inboard helped to reduce heel. I was tired from heavy labor in dark, confined quarters, lifting, moving, and securing heavy objects in a smelly, noisy, heaving, battering black box. I was thankful to finish and go topside. Amazing how one watch could feel a kind of glorious world apart, while the next was spent down in a hell hole. My watch ended, I grabbed a mug of soup from the steaming cauldron Dusty kept filled in the cook room and went back to my palliasse.

I slept through the next watch, unaware of the clatter of feet and shouted orders as we rounded Ushant to come up to sail close-hauled. The wind increased as it came forward of the beam. Sprits'l (bowsprit sail) and Fore tops'l furled, bonnets off as fore and main courses (windward clew now dropped) braced round, leach lines reset to meet the changed apparent wind direction. My fore-noon watch was called. I woke and stumbled to my feet, noticing *Rosie's* angle and feel were different. The noise level had increased from a whistle to a howl. Every wooden beam and spar complained. In the storm, the lines hammered constantly against the masts. The rigging was taut, each shuddering and humming to a different note. The sails were braced to the wind and hard but still shimmering, cracking, like fusillades of muskets as the wind shifted and crew rebraced, leach and tacklines hauled tight and the helm adjusted. We gathered below deck to relieve the previous watch for breakfast and their palliasses.

I was in one of a pair of two-man teams assigned to operate the pumps, relieving the men who had been pumping constantly for the duration of their thirty-minute shift. To operate the pump, the pump handle—or brake—is moved up and down, causing the spear to pull water up inside the tube, which is discharged over the side. One man on one of the pumps can deal with the relatively small amount of water present in normal conditions but in these conditions, it took two pumps and two men, each pumping continuously, to keep up with the flow. At the end of our thirty-minute shift on the pump, we were relieved. We grabbed our oilskins and followed orders to go topside for clean air. Lifelines had been rigged fore and aft. Movement was high risk without hanging on for dear life.

Rosie was heeled far over. The lee scuppers in the waist were under a regular, bore-like torrent of water. Quicksaver lines had been rigged to support the main and fore courses but the main tops'l had yet to be furled. At this point, all hands were called aloft. I was up the ratline before I'd even thought about it. The world seemed to go mad. The main swayed through an enormous arc, trying to throw us off. We made it to main top, on up to the tops'l yard. I did not look down, only focused on moving out, straddling the yard or lying along it with my shipmates. I desperately hung on as I was pushed, pummeled, and pulled by a wind like enormous hands trying to drag me off the yardarm as it swung and plummeted. The wind seemed ferocious, snatching at our oilskins. My hat, the strap tied under my chin, was now off my head and 'round my neck, beating me across the face.

The topsail windward clew line was hauled pulling the lower windward corner of the clew (foresail) up toward the yard. We had to grab the sailcloth and pull it up to the yard before tying it down around the yard with the reefing tackle. The lee clew line pulled the rest of the sail up. The crew on the lee side captured and furled the remaining sail. I made it down to the deck, bruised about the body and fingers bloodied—but job done. *Rosie* lay more upright, but the motion had become more difficult. The noise of the wind, the sea, and *Rosie's* constant complaining made speech nearly impossible on deck. We were ordered below and informed that as long as the wind didn't freshen we would continue as is. But there was a danger if the weather worsened. We would be forced to scud—to run before the wind—which would take us down-channel. We would also have to reduce topside weight. The fore and main tops would need to be unshipped and brought down with the tops'ls, pushing us much farther to the west. We would have difficulty making landfall anywhere on the southwest coast of England.

Mr. Glynn called me to the quarterdeck, and informed me that although my assigned role was main top man, which I had worked on the trip down from Plymouth, the skipper wanted me back assisting him while he was officer of the watch. He didn't want me damaged before I was able to report directly to Sir Ferdinando on my excursion in La Rochelle. A more immediate problem: he had relieved Johnny Dawkins of his duties. Distracted and barely functioning, Johnny had been sent below. Skipper dropped the word to me that at the end of my watch I was to find out "what the hell was the matter with him" and whether he was recoverable. As of now he was no use as a crewman on the *Sweet Rose*. Watch ended and I went looking for Johnny, but found no sign of him on the lower deck or in the cook room, and none of the off-duty watch had seen him. One of the on-duty watches said they'd seen him working his way forward, looking like he was making his way to the head.

I climbed up to the foredeck and checked the head gratings. No place to be, with the bow constantly burying itself deep into oncoming waves, lurching up and over into the following trough. Looking up, I saw a figure up under the bowsprit, huddled in the belly of the furled sprits'l. It could only be Johnny. I turned, stumbling, to look down the main deck. In the waist I saw a crewman and screamed for his attention, waving like a madman. He dragged himself along a lifeline toward me as I shouted at him to inform the skipper that Dawkins was on the bowsprit and help was needed. I turned back to work out a way to get to Johnny. There was a mad scramble behind me as *Rosie*'s helm was eased. She fell off downwind with the main and fore courses loosened. Her movement steadied. The crew went aloft to furl the fore course, which further reduced pitching and slowed *Rosie* down.

J.B. joined me on the foredeck

"What the hell is the idiot doing?" he shouted.

"Don't know, but we have to get him back down," I shouted back. "We could haul the sprits'l spar down the length of the bowsprit, but it might tip Johnny out. We need to fetch him."

J.B. tied a line 'round my waist, me being the lighter and nimbler, with a spare for Johnny. I ventured down the ladder onto the beakhead and started up the bowsprit. Johnny had wedged himself into a pocket of canvas hard up against the sprits'l yard. His eyes were tight shut and he was trembling all over like he had the ague. I shouted at him to open his eyes, but he shook his head and squirmed away from me. Hanging on with one arm, I tied the spare line 'round his waist. He did not have his oilskins on and he was soaked, probably half frozen. I snatched my hat off my head and rammed it onto his; the distraction made him open his eyes. We went nose-to-nose.

"You're endangering others," I shouted. "You have to come down. We need to get you ashore. Your mother needs you at home. Your life is on land, not here in this maelstrom."

He didn't seem to be hearing me, but I was able to get an arm 'round him and work him away from his nest, pulling him up onto the bowsprit. Thank God for the line, as he almost went overboard. The shock spurred him into helping himself, his instinct for survival overcoming his lethargy. Once on the bowsprit, I rolled him face down. With me leading the way and dragging Johnny by his legs, we slid backwards slowly down the bowsprit. Arms reached out to grab us. J.B. lifted Johnny and took him to the cook room, where Dusty took charge. Johnny was quickly stripped, rubbed dry, wrapped in a blanket, and given a steaming tankard of cooking brandy. He wanted to collapse, but he was made to walk about in the heat. We headed back to the quarterdeck to report. By now, *Rosie* had been brought back to her previous heading, courses and lines reset, and sails braced accordingly. The skipper was on deck and gave me a bollocking for further risking my skin. He ordered me below to dry off and get some rest. J.B. gave me a wink behind the skipper's back. The rest of the trip was relatively uneventful. Wind continued from the east, gusting to gale force occasionally. Crew were kept busy trimming the courses and pumping. I checked on Johnny, but Dusty had him bedded down in the focsle next to the cook room. He wouldn't let me near the poor, sleeping fellow.

By the end of the middle watch on 2 October, we were approaching the English coastline. The skipper was pretty certain we were about twenty miles east of our intended heading, meaning we'd likely be making for Fowey in Cornwall. He would confirm that position at first light. In the meantime, the main course was furled to slow us down, as he didn't want to get too near to shore before daylight. Masthead lookout sighted land just after four bells in the morning watch. When I came on my watch (forenoon watch—eight a.m.), we had both courses reset. We were about six miles from Fowey. Mr. Glynn had the watch, but the skipper was on the quarterdeck with him. I was stationed to mark the time and record the log speeds on the traverse board. When we closed on Fowey, the skipper set our course heading nor'–nor'west, lined on the Castle on St. Catherine's Point. He had a lookout posted to keep a sharp eye on Punch Cross Rocks to starboard as we entered the mouth of the river. As soon as we passed between St. Catherine's Point and the Rocks, we headed up. Luffing, we pinched our way into Fowey harbor, anchoring a mile upriver opposite the Town Quay—a safe distance from Polruan Pool. The hourglass emptied and I sounded eight bells. The skipper called me to his cabin.

"The package you risked your life to retrieve in La Rochelle, and another package with additional letters, has to be carried to Sir Ferdinando Gorges in Plymouth as soon as possible," he said. "The wind has us pinned here for at least another twenty-four hours, possibly longer. Can you ride?"

"Yes, sir," I replied. "I have ridden almost as long as I have been able to walk."

"Good. I want you to be the carrier. Advise him of that fact and tell him I will report to him as soon as *Rosie* arrives in Plymouth. I know Sir Ferdinando will want to interrogate you himself. Gather some spare clothes; we go ashore in an hour. After a bite to eat at the Ship Inn we'll get you a horse from their livery. I'll explain the best route while we're eating."

I was dismissed. I will send Will this journal entry from Plymouth.

CHAPTER 3

Journal entry—*2 to 8 October 1613*

I went ashore with the skipper, to the Ship Inn for an ale and a bite to eat. I was given two months' wages—six crowns—which he said was well earned, as well as two additional crowns to cover immediate expenses in Plymouth. He said that Sir Ferdinando would cover any other legitimate costs I might have, requiring a detailed reckoning of all expenses incurred. As I was a full-time member of the crew of the *Sweet Rose*, my wages would continue to be paid. My course for Plymouth seemed straightforward—ferry from the Town Quay to Polruan with horse, then ride along the coast road to Looe. I would change horse at the Jolly Sailor before continuing along the coast road to Seaton, Portwrinkle, Crafthole, Millbrook, and Cremyll, where there was a ferry to Plymouth. I had to go to the Minerva to show the landlord an introductory letter from Mr. Brown. The landlord would then use the same letter to notify the office of Sir Ferdinando Gorges that packages awaited him in the hands of one Isaac Stanfield, a courier from La Rochelle.

"Word of warning," the skipper said to me in a low voice. "The Minerva is the focal point for English Navy impressment. Merchant sailors are much preferred. Be watchful you're not taken."

Mr. Brown also gave me a note to be shown to any impressment officer, vouching that I was an important member of his crew—the skipper had a powerful reputation. In addition, I was in the service of the Governor of Plymouth Fort, providing some additional protection. We hired a lively, young bay mare, Maddie, and with the packages safely stowed in one of my saddlebags, the horse and I were ferried across the harbor. By early afternoon I was on the road running along the clifftops of the Cornish coast. Higher up the wind continued strong, close to gale force from the northeast, with rain threatening. Maddie, keen for the exercise, seemed to relish the wind and sea air, and after initial attempts to shed her load she settled down to enjoy the journey. We made good time, and two hours later we were at the Jolly Sailor. I left Maddie with an ostler to rub her down and care for her. I intended to change horses, as advised by the skipper, but after a pie and ale I returned to the stables and found Maddie eager for more. The twelve miles we had traveled had not challenged her. With maybe two hours more daylight, I decided to push on to find an inn closer to Cremyll for the night, hoping to make Millbrook about fifteen miles away. The ride was uneventful to start with. Where the road allowed, we cantered into eye-watering, exhilaratingly strong headwinds. Maddie's long mane beat the rain from my face. Growing tired, wet, and cold, we left the coast at Portwrinkle. Millbrook was too far. The barman at the Jolly Sailor had suggested that as an alternative, we might want to head for the Finney-gook Inn at Crafthole. The signposted, grassy path to Crafthole disappeared into a glade of trees in the dim twilight. Giving Maddie her head, I was half asleep as we plodded along.

"Stand!" a voice shouted to my left, rousing me with a shock.

Maddie shied away from a dim figure on a horse by the side of the path. With Maddie unsettled, I was able to work my way closer. The figure was pointing what looked like a pistol.

"Thrown down your saddlebags," said the figure with a strained, gruff voice. "For any cause, I will shoot."

I hauled hard on Maddie's right rein as though trying to control her, while at the same time digging my left heel into her ribs. She bucked and threw me in a heap at the highwayman's feet. Rising, I grabbed the rider's left foot—no stirrup—and heaved him up over his horse, which, scared by the sudden movement, trotted away down the path. Before the rider had a chance to recover, I was on top of him, pinning his arms to the ground and sending the pistol flying. He was small and winded, if not bruised. Terrified eyes looked up at me from behind a scarf that covered his face. I relieved him of it and was surprised to recognize the man underneath.

"Hello, Isaac," the prone figure mumbled.

"Charlie Swain!" I exclaimed. "What the hell do you think you're doing? I could have killed you. More to the point, you could have been caught and hanged as a common thief!"

Charlie was an old acquaintance from Dorchester, a stable lad at one or other of the inns in town. I knew him as a harmless, unreliable sort, a year younger than me, small, underfed, and not very bright. His mother was a washerwoman and his older sister had an unsavory reputation.

Now I hauled him to his feet, at a loss to understand the depths to which he had sunk. He was risking his life on a foolhardy enterprise that could get him in real trouble, with those he attacked and with the law. When I let him go, he sat down hugging his knees to his chest, head bowed, and started to sob. I recovered his pistol, a wooden replica, and retrieved the horses that were cropping a short distance away. Charlie's horse was maybe fourteen hands, old, and ill-kempt, with a rope for a bridle and no saddle. I sat down next to Charlie and waited in the cold, driving rain till he calmed down. Then I proposed we travel on together. It was getting late, and I wanted to get to the Finnygook as soon as I could. I helped Charlie back to his feet, gave him a leg up onto his horse, and mounted mine. We started on the path, which was rising steeply now as we approached the village.

The Finnygook Inn had no beds available, but they offered us the hayloft above the stables. With horses rubbed down, watered, and fed, I took Charlie into the taproom, found a corner, and bought us both plates of roast beef and potatoes with flagons of ale. He hadn't eaten or drunk anything for a long while. By the time he had finished his second plate, Charlie felt able to start explaining his predicament. It seemed that the fire in Dorchester was the culmination of a series of catastrophes. He had been thrown out of his last job for causing a fight. His sister had been arrested and imprisoned for immoral behavior. His mother, Millie Swain, had fallen, broken her arm, and was unable to work. The fire had destroyed the house where they were living, so the two of them had gone down to Cawsand, to his mother's brother—a farm laborer who was, in fact, a smuggler. A week after they arrived, the brother was arrested by the customs in Cawsand Bay. As a result, they were destitute, with a roof but no food. That day, Charlie had taken his uncle's horse, aptly named Tatters, found himself a likely spot, and waited, terrified out of his wits. Three riders had passed before Charlie dared show himself. The fourth rider was me. Both of us tired, Charlie slightly the worse for the ale he'd consumed, we staggered off to our berths in the hay. I lay thinking about my course of action in the morning, the packages for Sir Ferdinando, and whether Charlie could be trusted. At some point, I fell asleep.

Next morning, 4 October, with no change in the weather and our clothes still damp, we set off toward Millbrook. I gave Charlie half a crown and told him that when we got to Millbrook he was to go on down to Cawsand and give the money to his mother. It seemed to me that there was no future for the two of them there. They should return to Dorchester. Charlie thought his sister was still in prison. I would write to the Patriarch to advise him of their need, putting their future in his hands. I explained my plan to Charlie, telling him that in return for the money I gave him, he was to fetch his mother and, by whatever means, he should bring her to the Minerva. From there we would work out how to get them both back up to Dorchester. At Millbrook, we parted ways. Charlie was relieved he no longer had to make decisions, and he promised to be at the Minerva as soon as he could. He said he might have a problem winkling his mother out of her abode, rough as it was, but he would get her to Plymouth within a few days. I wished him a good journey and rode on to the ferry at Cremyll.

The tide was at a fast ebb through the Narrows. It was making about three knots out of the Hamoaze into the sound. We had to wait several hours before the ferry was able to operate and take us to Stonehouse Pool in Plymouth. I rode around Mill Bay on to the Hoe where Sir Francis Drake left his game of bowls to beat the Spanish Armada twenty-five years since. It felt like hallowed ground, together with the mighty images of Gog and Magog cut in the turf. I hurried on, my journey's end in sight with the four towers of the fort ahead of me. Leaving the Hoe through the Little Hoe Gate, I made my way to the Minerva Inn, which had stable room for Maddie. I presented myself with my letter of introduction to the landlord, Mr. Alfred Potts, in the taproom. As I took off my wet oilskins and hat, he appeared more than a little surprised at my obvious youth. He read Mr. Brown's letter.

"Good man is Mr. Brown," he said. "Served with him many years since." He asked after Mr. Peg Jones. Having established Peg's health and my good standing with him, he shook my hand. "Call me Alfred," he said. I was ushered to a table, and a barmaid called Annie took my order. Alfred, meantime, disappeared to get the skipper's introductory letter to the Castle as quickly as possible.

Annie was attentive. I would have liked to think it was my irresistible charm, but the almost empty barroom must have had something to do with it, as well as Alfred's interest in me. With food and ale served, she sat down at the table and asked me who I was and where I had come from. Gazing at me with distracting blue eyes, she asked me why Alfred was attending to me, a mysterious stranger, especially considering my youth. The warmth of the room and the interest shown me by this rosy girl with auburn hair and a low-cut, well-filled dress beguiled me. However, Alfred was quick to return. A trusted servant had been sent to the office of Sir Ferdinando with my message, to await a response. I soon learned from Alfred that Annie was his sixteen-year-old niece, recently arrived from Weymouth. Keeping an avuncular eye on us, Alfred left to deal with a rapidly increasing trade. Annie was called away to serve, but she made regular trips back past my table, a most pleasant happening. I was much occupied.

A message came back that I was to stay where I was as Sir Ferdinando was away from the fort on a tour of inspection and not expected back for two days. A Captain Charles Turner would advise me when my appointment might be and would escort me to that appointment, which left me some freedom. My head was hurting and Annie was most solicitous. She led me to a scullery, sat me down, and examined my head. Unlike Viv, she stood behind me. Ah, well. With delicate fingers she probed my head, checked the wound, and bathed and bandaged it. I was allowed to go to my room to sleep, where I woke at regular intervals, my body conditioned to the watch system. After resting undisturbed till late in the morning, I awoke to a knock on the door, and Annie breezed in with a tray of food and drink. She insisted on checking my head again, unnecessary but pleasing. The day passed with me sleeping or being fed.

Next morning, 6 October, I was up, ready for action shortly after sun-up. A note came that Sir Ferdinando expected me at 8:00. Within thirty minutes, Captain Turner appeared wearing a red tunic. He was a tall, thin man with a large moustache and a disciplined posture, a smart, even immaculate uniform, and a ruddy complexion. He had a mole on his left cheek that seemed connected to the tip of his moustache, and a direct, clear-eyed look that quickly captured my attention.

We proceeded to a building adjacent to the fort, past sentries, and up flights of stairs busy with scurrying people. The noise and bustle of business was everywhere. Clearly, we were in a military headquarters where much was happening. In an anteroom, a functionary told me to wait. Presently, a door opened, and I was shown into a large room with a window that looked out over Sutton Pool. A broad expanse of table was covered in maps, documents, and books, with what looked like a globe in the corner. Behind this table sat a slim man with a dark complexion, deep-set brown eyes, a trimmed moustache, and a short beard. He looked up as I entered. I felt impaled by the most direct, piercing eyes I had ever encountered. Not normally overawed by any man, I stopped, waiting with some trepidation for him to speak.

"You are Mr. Isaac Stanfield?"

"Aye, sir," I said.

"Captain Brown speaks highly of you. How old are you?"

"Age sixteen, soon to be seventeen."

Sir Ferdinando looked startled. He said he thought me young but not that young and complimented me on how much I had done in such a short time. He asked me to tell him what happened in La Rochelle. I told him briefly. He asked a few keen questions, which I answered as best I could.

"You have packages for me," he said.

I handed over the packages with which I had been entrusted, relieved to be rid of them. He asked me what my plans were. I said I was to await the arrival of the *Sweet Rose*. My understanding was that Mr. Brown had duties in Plymouth, after which we were to sail on to Weymouth with Mr. Bushrode's cargo. The weather had continued contrary to Mr. Brown's intentions. As he still seemed weather-bound down in Fowey, it was likely I would be in Plymouth for several more days.

He said that was good, as he wanted to talk to me further in the company of other interested parties in a few days' time and would advise me of that event when details had been finalized. Now he had other matters more pressing to attend to. He dismissed me with a nod. I returned to the Minerva. Alfred was on hand, eager for a chat. He was most knowledgeable and enjoyed being the fount.

"You are most fortunate to have had the meeting with Sir Ferdinando," Alfred advised me. "He is a very busy man. He's having serious difficulties with the Plymouth City fathers. To maintain and man the fort, he needs resources, which are deemed vital to all but the city fathers, who are loath to provide any."

My hopes for a long discourse were interrupted by his customers' needs, so I took the opportunity to go for a stroll. I had hardly walked anywhere on dry land since disembarking from *Rosie*, and my sea legs were still evident. Minerva Inn is on Looe Street in the center of Plymouth. I walked east toward the quay, south through the Barbican around Sutton Pool toward the fort and through South Gate, out onto the Hoe. By late afternoon, the weather was moderating—the rain had stopped and the wind had calmed considerably, veering south. It was probable that the *Sweet Rose* would be making the transit to Plymouth tomorrow after all. I walked along beside the wall that extended west from the fort, surprised it did not go far, stopping at Little Hoe Gate at the south end of Castle Dyke Lane. Even in the fading light, it was disconcerting to see how the structure of the wall and the fort itself were in such bad repair. As I continued to walk along the Hoe beyond the wall fortification, there were mainly earthen defensive works in place, leaving the City exposed to the west. I hurried back by way of the West Gate into the city, to the Minerva, where I could waylay Mr. Potts and, I hoped, Annie. She was busy in the kitchen, but Mr. Potts was behind the bar setting up for the evening trade. He was happy to chat over an ale. I told him what I had seen and reminded him of his remarks earlier about Sir Ferdinando's problems with the City fathers.

Mr. Potts responded, "Sir Ferdinando is responsible for the defense of the realm in these parts. King James pursues a policy of peaceful co-existence with the three main rivals to England: France, Spain, and Holland. He appears unwilling or unable to provide the funds to do the necessary reconstruction or to expand the militia."

He was called away and then just as quickly returned and continued, "Earlier this year the new Spanish Ambassador landed in Plymouth. Forewarned, Sir F. had packed the fort with militia from elsewhere in the county, hoping to give the impression of a robust defensive force."

Alfred shook his head with a wry expression.

"He can do nothing to hide the fallen masonry and the cracks in the walls," he observed. "Merchants are becoming rich with the increased international trade. Sir F.'s only recourse, therefore, is to plead with the City merchants. It has to be in their interest to help defray the costs to maintain Plymouth's defenses."

He disappeared. I had only time for a quick pull at my ale before he reappeared. "Not seeing an immediate profit in such investments, the merchants aren't that interested," he went on as if without any interruption. "Another problem is the Barbary pirates."

That last fact surprised me. I was aware they were a menace in the Mediterranean and into the Bay of Biscay, but threatening Plymouth?

"These Barbary pirates are, in many cases, English sailors," Alfred explained. "When King James made the peace treaty with the Spanish, British privateers operating under license from the British Crown lost their livelihood. As a result, they've gone to offer their superior sailing skills to the Moroccans and Algerians. It's a funny thing, history."

I asked what he meant.

"When the Moors were kicked out of Spain in around 1500, they fled to places like Algiers and Morocco, swearing vengeance on the Spanish," he said. "Not surprising, as they had been living in Spain for about 700 years. They teamed up with the Turkish Barbary pirates and have been waging war against Spain and other Christian countries ever since. Now the British privateers have added an extra dimension to the pirates. They have become numerous and bold. At times they are able to base dozens of ships in the Scillies, attacking any vessels entering the Channel, including English ships. They've even come into Cawsand Bay."

Alfred left shaking his head, shocked and horrified at the temerity of it all. Annie came by with a fist of tankards. "How are you getting on with Uncle Alf?" she asked with a broad smile. "He loves an audience."

She left and Uncle Alf returned. Their alternations were becoming an entertainment.

"Plymouth is not a safe place to be as a result," Alfred stated in a most somber tone. "King James, by making peace, wants to reduce the threat of war. But with the reduced threat of war, he is unable to induce Parliament to provide tax revenue to maintain England's defenses, so the country has become more vulnerable to attack."

As I pondered such grave and complicated thoughts, the taproom filled and Alfred prepared to resume his duties, presumably leaving me for the evening. As the skipper had done, he advised me to keep my head down tomorrow— the press-gangs would be out. Defenses might be ill-maintained, but the Navy always needed men. As he departed, Alfred cheerfully threw over his shoulder these sobering cautionary words: "The letter of safe-passage from your skipper is some security, but not absolute."

His warning gave me a sudden jolt, bringing another thought to mind: Charlie. He and his mother were due here soon. Charlie could walk right into the arms of a press-gang. I had no idea when he was due, or even if they would be coming at all. His mother might not be moveable for reasons of poor health or transport. As for *Rosie*, I had no idea when she would reach port. I went to check on Maddie. Returning, I bumped into Annie coming from the kitchen carrying a tray laden with food. She smiled a promising smile again as we passed.

"Annie, what time do you work till?" I asked.

But she was gone. Traffic was too heavy to stand around. I resigned myself to a spare seat at a table and ordered sustenance from another barmaid. While I caught regular glimpses of Annie throughout the evening, I was too tired to wait the course and went to my room. Before I slept, I brought my journal up to date.

Journal entry—*9 to 10 October 1613*

9 October, up by dawn, down to the stable yard to wash my face in a water trough. I had got rid of Annie's bandage during the night, as it kept slipping over my eyes. Breakfast was ale, fishcakes, and a loaf of bread. Then, on this sparkling morning, I proceeded to the Barbican to check on movements in the Sutton Pool, which was filled with ships. A merchantman had come alongside. I hailed a deck seaman about the weather and sailing conditions outside. He told me there was a brisk southwesterly, ideal sailing from the west, about four hours from Fowey.

My plan was to make contact with the skipper as soon as *Rosie* arrived. My assumption was they would probably anchor in Sutton Pool. The skipper would not want his crew to be temptations for the press-gang either. He was likely to come ashore, without crew, to meet with Sir F. and within twenty-four hours be up and off to Weymouth with Mr. Bushrode's cargo. Whilst thinking about the press-gang, I worried about Charlie. I hoped that he and his mother would be here then, because the simplest—if not most direct—way to get them to Weymouth, and from thence onto Dorchester, was by *Rosie*. But how could I persuade the skipper to ship two passengers? Would Charlie arrive in time? He wouldn't be here at least until the afternoon, and *Rosie* could be here by midday. I walked up onto the Hoe to the cliffs looking over Plymouth Sound. I had guessed right. Within an hour of setting up my lookout spot, I spotted the unmistakable profile of *Rosie* scudding up the sound with all sails set—a wonderful sight. She had already passed St. Nicholas Island and was fast closing Fisher's Nose, the point where I stood. I waved when she passed, but the crew was busy preparing to enter the harbor and I was not noticed. I turned and ran back through the South Gate to the pier guarding the entrance to the pool. *Rosie* was just entering, passing close by the end of the pier. I hailed her again. J.B. looked up, saw me, and waved. He called to Peg Jones, pointing. The skipper, on the quarterdeck, was informed and looked over, raising a hand. I watched as *Rosie* worked her way through the thicket of ships to her chosen anchorage, and with main and fore courses furled, under tops'ls and mizzen course, rounding into wind, topsails backed, mizzen course flapping, she quickly slowed to lie dead in the water—anchor let go, tops'ls and mizzen course furled. It all looked very smart.

As *Rosie* was made shipshape, the ship's longboat, being towed behind her, was brought alongside. The skipper was rowed to the quayside. I was there to greet him as he came ashore. He nodded to me and sent the boat back with crew to be on alert for his return to the quay in two hours or so.

"Come with me, Stanfield," he said. "Did you deliver the packages to Sir Ferdinando?"

"Aye, sir."

He nodded. We proceeded at a brisk pace to the Minerva, where he was greeted with much warmth by Mr. Potts.

"Hello, Alf," the skipper returned the greeting, "How are you keeping? How's Miss Annie? Has young Stanfield been kept out of mischief?"

All answers in the affirmative.

"Good. Stanfield, you stay here," he ordered. "I have to find Sir Ferdinando now, and will need to speak with you on my return."

With that, he was off. Alfred winked at me and I went off to find Annie. The midday rush was on, but I was able to get her attention long enough to order a drink. When she returned with my order she grinned—it was not a smile, but a cheeky grin, as if she knew what was on my mind. She turned, waggled her bum as she strode off, and I did what I'd been told and stayed put. No hardship, with Annie enjoying the effect she was having. It might have been about two hours later that I heard a commotion outside. Several of us went to the windows to look out. A cart stood outside, surrounded by a press-gang of sailors. A woman with a heavily strapped arm was sobbing and wailing at them in anguish and fear. The sailors were attempting to grab some unfortunate lad squirming under the cart, close to the hooves of an old horse—the horse becoming increasingly agitated. Damn, it was Charlie, his mother Millie Swain, and Tatters.

From the door, Alfred warned me. "Careful, Isaac. You go out there, you will be nabbed too."

"It's a friend," I explained. "Can you distract them? There are only three. The impressment officer isn't there."

"I'll try."

Alfred strode out the door and grabbed the nearest sailor.

"Stop the hullabaloo. You're scaring my customers. It's too early to do your work," he scolded. "Anyway, where's your officer? Without him you have no authority. Lay off, come in, and wet your whistle."

The three sailors seemed relieved to leave the distraught woman, given the interested crowd gathering with no sympathy for what they were doing. I slipped out and hauled Charlie from under the cart. Telling him to follow me, I set off, and Charlie, back on the cart, his now-quiet but shaken mother by his side, urged the plodding Tatters forward. On the quay I left them in a bundle in a corner against a wall, their few possessions at their feet. I took Tatters and the cart back to the Minerva. In the stable yard, I told a lad to look after the horse and park the cart out of the way while I went in search of Alfred.

"Alfred, I need to settle my bill. I'll be off with the skipper. My horse, Maddie, is from the Ship Inn, Fowey. She should be returned. I have stabled a horse and cart with you. I imagine both can be sold as I doubt their owner will be back."

I settled my bill and told Alfred I would be back from Weymouth soon, in all probability. I was about to leave when Alfred stopped me. The impressment officer had turned up, angrily retrieved his press-gang, and stomped out of the Inn.

"Be careful," said Alfred.

"Tell Mr. Brown I will be on the quay."

I followed the press-gang, keeping well back, as they headed along Looe Street, down toward the Barbican. The crowds, especially the men, seemed to melt away before them. The press-gang preferred darkness, narrow streets, and an inebriated quarry, not the bright bustle of mid-afternoon. As they moved onto the quay, I prayed that Charlie was out of sight. It seemed they saw any man, seaman, or landlubber as fair game. One poor sod, well-oiled and half-witless, was scooped up. They had a whaler tied up alongside into which their prey was deposited. Another man put up a fight and was flattened by a belaying pin before being dropped into the boat. I thought they might miss the diminutive Charlie, but his mother looked up as the press-gang approached and renewed her whimpers of fear. Just as I started forward, I was grabbed from behind. It was the skipper, who told me to back off. I quickly explained about Charlie and his invalid mother and their dire straits. I said that Reverend White in Dorchester would be taking them in, but that they had to first travel to get there. The skipper gave me a quick, measuring look, then went to the quayside and blew a whistle. Instant action. *Rosie's* longboat was already working its way slowly back toward the quay when the rowers heard the whistle. They immediately redoubled their efforts. In no time they were alongside.

"You," he said to me. "Get aboard."

He strode over to the press-gang, which had surrounded Charlie and his mother, cowering against the wall with their ragged bundle of belongings. He called out to the officer, who, seeing the skipper, saluted him. In no time, Charlie, his mother, and their possessions were being escorted by the skipper back and into the longboat, and the longboat was heading back to *Rosie*. The skipper said nothing, but the way he looked at me, he didn't need to. Once back aboard *Rosie*, the two passengers were given over to J.B. to stow out of the way, and I was summoned to the skipper's cabin.

"I have the distinct feeling that in some way I have been hoodwinked into giving passage to two unfortunates," he said.

"Force of circumstances, sir, but thank you."

"Enough," he said. "We have more important things to discuss. I understand from Sir Ferdinando that he had asked you to stay close at hand, as he wanted to talk further with you about what had happened in La Rochelle."

"Aye, sir."

I had deserted my post. Now what kind of serious trouble was I in?

"The package you gave him has required him to leave for London. He has returned you to my charge. I am sailing for Weymouth. You are off the hook. However, we will be coming back within three weeks, by which time Sir Ferdinando will have returned, and he will want to talk to you then."

"Aye, sir. Will I be allowed to go to Dorchester?" I asked.

The skipper glared at me.

"I have letters for Reverend White," I added.

He glared at me still.

"I should escort our passengers to Dorchester, sir," I reasoned. "You will surely want them off your hands."

"Stanfield, you are incorrigible. On another matter, you need to offload Dawkins."

"Dawkins, sir?"

"Mr. Cattigan still has him under his wing. Dawkins needs to be off this ship and back with his family as soon as possible. I understand they live in Bincombe."

"Aye, sir."

"Mr. Cattigan says that something happened to Dawkins that has scrambled his mind. He has attempted to find out what happened, but all Dawkins will say is that you, Stanfield, will protect him. Protect him from what?"

I tried to look surprised, uncomprehending, but the skipper was not taken in.

"There is a serious matter on my ship, and you know something about it that I don't. That is unacceptable."

"It was Mr. Gunt, sir," I said. I explained what had happened, and how Dawkins feared he would be hanged for sodomy. The skipper was silent.

"So, you took it on yourself to sort this problem out."

"Aye, sir."

More silence.

"That explains something Sir Ferdinando told me," he said. "Mr. Gunt persuaded him that he had contacts in La Rochelle he could tap to gain valuable intelligence for Sir Ferdinando. I was persuaded to make Gunt my second mate. It now seems he was a double agent, and a bloody sodomite to boot."

"What about Dawkins, sir? Is he in danger of being accused?"

"No, he was assaulted and is a victim of a criminal. When the time is right, advise him so. I doubt he is capable of taking in that fact, at the moment, having been so unfortunately damaged."

I was given leave to escort three lost souls away from Weymouth. It meant I could go back to Dorchester, see Aby, catch up with Will, and learn how all were coping after the fire. It seemed an eternity ago, but it was, in fact, less than three months gone. After being dismissed by the skipper, I went in search of Charlie. He and his mother had been given a place to settle at the aft end of the lower deck on port side. A screen had been rigged to give Mrs. Swain some privacy. Exhausted, she had taken to bed and was already asleep. Charlie was grateful and told me he'd had a devil of a time convincing his mother to leave her brother's house, even though it was little more than a hovel. But when she realized that her brother would not be back, and that more likely than not he had been either hanged or offered employment in His Majesty's Navy, she accepted their new course as the only sensible one. He treated my promise that work would be found for her back in Dorchester with some skepticism, due to her broken arm and broken spirit, but perhaps he now saw some hope in the picture, too. I told him we would be in Weymouth by morning, then went to talk with Dusty. His charge, Johnny, spent most of his days in his berth in the focsle, uncommunicative. Dusty felt concerned, and that I knew a lot more about it than I was letting on. Telling the skipper had been a huge relief, but I was not going to tell anyone else. I sat down beside Johnny, who was curled into a ball, eyes shut tight.

"Johnny, it's me, Isaac," I said. "You're safe. I've got some good news."

He opened his eyes and stared at me. He looked like a frightened rabbit.

"Skipper's given me leave to take you back to Bincombe. You'll be home tomorrow."

As comprehension filtered through his confusion and self-loathing, Johnny buried his head and started to sob. I stayed with him awhile, then gently shook his shoulder and crept away.

Orders were made to prepare for sailing. I was rudely reminded that now I was safely back in the bosom of my sailing family, the larboard watch would be grateful for my company. We were on first dog watch. In fact, two bells sounded. I had one hour of the watch to go. I reported to my normal station on the quarterdeck but was ordered to the capstan in preparation for hoisting the anchor. It was my first time on the capstan, which was on the main deck for'ard of the main hatch. *Rosie* had been readied for sea while the skipper was ashore. Lines were on their belaying pins, ready for use. Decks were cleared, sails unstopped and ready to set. The light wind was from the southwest, and our passage out of Sutton Pool would be south. *Rosie* lay head to wind. Astern of *Rosie* was clear water. The anchor cable was let out, allowing *Rosie* to drift with some sternway, which would give her room to gather headway when the anchor was hoved up. With the order given to raise anchor, I and three other crewmen started pushing on the capstan bars to haul in the cable. The fore course, tops'l braced, tack line shortened, hauled hard to starboard, causing the wind to push the bows to larboard, bringing the wind onto her starboard bow. With the cable taut, her sternway was stopped and she started being pulled forward. When the anchor broke ground, the braces and tacklines were eased, the main tops'l was raised, and lines set. *Rosie* slowly gained headway and sailed toward the entrance to

Sutton Pool. The anchor was catted and fished to bring the shank horizontal. To secure the anchor for sea, the inboard fluke was lashed to a timberhead and the stock was lashed to the cathead. The main, mizzen courses, and sprits'l set, we headed south past Fisher's Nose and onward till we had to tack to round the peninsular guarding Cattwater. Closing in on St. Nicholas Island, we tacked back onto starboard on a course a point east of south. We headed out to sea around the Wembury peninsula, keeping the Mewstone Island to larboard. As we rounded Wembury the braces, leachlines were eased, all sails reset as we headed south east making for Prawle Point, some twenty miles away.

The later part of my watch was spent on main starboard braces, leach and tacklines, obeying a constant stream of orders from the quarterdeck as we maneuvered our way out of Plymouth Sound. Four bells sounded before we made Wembury. I went off watch when we were detailed to make *Rosie* shipshape. For me, these orders meant some serious holystoning, as all decks had to be restored to their pristine condition. After the storm, sailing conditions were ideal and it was wonderful to be out on the water. The hours of work both off and on watch slipped by, with *Rosie* charging through the water, the wind moving further aft as we followed the coastline to Prawle Point. Once night fell, we were scudding with a freshening breeze and our heading changed to east-nor'east, making for Portland Bill and Weymouth. My thoughts turned to Dorchester and Aby. With so many distractions, Aby had not been in the forefront of my mind. I was now able to enjoy the expectation of seeing her again, and I went to sleep with her much on my mind.

CHAPTER 4

Journal entry—*11 to 25 October 1613*

I am getting ready to return to Weymouth after a busy two weeks.

The weeks started with me being ferried ashore on the morning of 11 October, from *Rosie* in Weymouth harbor, together with Charlie, his mother, and a silent Johnny. I had Charlie hire a cart and horse, which he did from the King's Arms, with two shillings down and a promise to return it within a week. We set off immediately by way of Bincombe, just off the main highway and about halfway to Dorchester. Johnny's mother was working as a housekeeper for the vicar of Holy Trinity Church, so we went to the vicarage. I left Johnny in the cart with Charlie's mother trying to soothe him. He was in a dreadful state. His shakes had become more pronounced as we neared Bincombe. The vicar, Reverend Stoddard, came to the door. I asked whether I might have a word with him, and he invited me in. I explained that I was from the *Sweet Rose*, a shipmate of Johnny Dawkins, and there had been an unhappy incident that had upset Johnny to such an extent that the captain decided he'd needed to be sent home. Reverend Stoddard knew Johnny well. He had baptized him twelve years ago. Johnny had been sent to sea to "make a man of him" after his father had died some years past. The vicar asked me what had happened, what was wrong with Johnny. I said that it would be best for Johnny to be allowed to recover and tell the story himself, if he chose to. He came out to the cart with me. Charlie's mother gently helped Johnny, who had been clinging to her with his head buried in her arms, down off the cart. He turned, saw the vicar, cried out, and collapsed. The vicar knelt beside him.

"Father, I have sinned. I am damned forever."

"Johnny, Johnny, enough. You are not damned," the vicar said. "Get up and come inside. My sisters will look after you. I will fetch your mother. She's in the church cleaning."

He put his arm around Johnny for support and the two disappeared inside, shepherded by two elderly ladies who had appeared at the door. I climbed up onto the cart and the three of us continued our journey sadly, our thoughts unspoken.

We made good time to Dorchester. I had been away nearly three months. I felt, after my adventures, that I was a different Isaac from the one who rode away down this same road back in August. I thought about how I had left Aby, off on an unplanned adventure. Eager anticipation turned to guilt. How would she react when she saw me again? The first thing I had to do was to park Charlie and Mrs. Swain somewhere while I went to meet the Patriarch. It was Monday, and he would probably be at the Church or possibly at the rectory on Colliton Street, which had been sufficiently off the track of the fire to escape serious damage. I didn't know the state of repair of the inns in Dorchester after the fire, but I knew the Sun at Lower Burton was unscathed. I drove round Dorchester. I left Charlie and his mother to eat at the inn, along with their hired horse and cart, while I walked back down into Dorchester. I entered through West Gate and started down West Street. Even after three months, the smell of burnt wood and thatch was everywhere. In the empty spaces where houses had been demolished and cleared, much soot and burnt wood remained. It was evident that some houses had miraculously been spared. Some had been damaged but were still standing, roof thatching already patched or in progress. Walls had been repaired, cleaned, and re-whitewashed. The work had been bit hasty, as many sooty handprints showed clearly on the white walls. Some were small and childlike—clearly a new game to play. But the place was alive with townspeople and farm laborers still all working together to clear, demolish, and clean. Holy Trinity Church towered above the destruction. I headed for it, unrecognized, clothed as a seaman with cap pulled low. I needed to sort out Charlie and his mother before spending some time with P., as well as to see Silas, Will, and Aby. Silas had gone to Weymouth, but I was sure he'd have returned at the first prospect of paid work. Will would probably be at home, and Aby, doubtless with hammer in hand, working with her father to build new premises.

Entering Holy Trinity Church, I was told that P. was in a meeting at the rectory, so I went there. I was greeted by P.'s housekeeper, who asked me to wait in the kitchen. There, a tankard of ale, a loaf of bread, and a slab of cheese were put in front of me. I was being welcomed home, and it was good to be back. Some thirty minutes later, I heard P.'s voice saying goodbye to his visitors. He came into the kitchen.

"Ah! The prodigal returns," he said. "What have you been doing? By the looks of you, you are now a seafaring man."

"I have much to tell, sir. But I have an immediate problem that I need your help with."

I told him about Charlie Swain and the need to return him and his destitute mother to productive living. Apparently, she was known to P. Her family was somewhat notorious, although the lady herself was beyond reproach. Given the clean-up and reconstruction work at hand, I suggested to P. that surely there was gainful work for an able-bodied young man and his washerwoman mother. P. laughed. He said I was a good advocate. He was sure there was work available and he would take care of the matter. He told me to come back for supper that evening, and that he would invite Will Whiteway. I could tell them all what I had been doing, and they would bring me up to date with Dorchester happenings. It was possible Reverend Cheeke would join us. My bedroom was still available for my use, for which I thanked P.

Ahead of the supper, I said I wanted to meet with Will. P. told me he was almost certainly at school, in Cheeke's temporary school rooms farther down South Street. He wasn't sure when classes ended for the day. I went off to find him. I had forgotten that he was still a schoolboy, required to attend Cheeke's school for another two years. I was suddenly worried that if he saw me, Cheeke might grab me by the ear—as was his wont—and force me back into scholarly servitude. I found the temporary school building, at the end of South Street several hundred yards from the burnt-out shell of the old structure, where work had already started on clearing the site. The foundations still seemed sound, but the walls and roof were a heap of stones and ash. Mr. Hardy's school was no more.

I waited outside the school for classes to finish. It gave me time to ponder how my life had changed. Aby excepted, I couldn't see myself coming back to live in Dorchester on a permanent basis. I was committed to adventure and travel, fascinated by the intrigue I was becoming embroiled in.

How serious was I about Aby? Well, we had known each other a long time. Though we were both sixteen, she was much more mature. I was always into scrapes and eager to explore life. I felt I had been a problem for her. Wiser and more serene than me, she was a companion to her widowed father. At first, she must have found me a distraction, but we had grown up together, part of a tight-knit group of friends. Aby was somewhat aloof and always dressed soberly, a maid's cap covering her long brown hair. She was someone I had seen as a friend, nothing more. Matters changed when she suffered the unwanted attentions of an older man, a stranger visiting the Candlemas fair in February the previous year, 1612. He'd been chased off, but the incident had revealed a different, disheveled, more vulnerable side of Aby. Thereafter, I felt a sense of responsibility toward her and recognized the attractive woman previously unnoticed. Aby, in turn, paid me more attention and we became close. She found, under my devil-may-care appearance, someone she seemed attracted to. I wondered how serious she was.

I was leaning against the wall across the road from the school when I was woken from my reverie by a shout and grabbed in enthusiastic welcome by Will. We had much to talk about and were constantly interrupting each other. Eventually, as we sat on a couple of gravestones behind All Souls, I put a stop to the conversation, giving Will all my journal entries and the letters he had not yet received. I said we would be eating together at P.'s tonight and could talk about them then. We parted and I hurried back to the Sun, where I found Charlie's mother deep in conversation with another woman, an old friend of hers. They had arranged accommodation for themselves and didn't need my help. They told me where they would be and I said I would see them tomorrow. Back in Dorchester, by way of Glippath Bridge, I walked down South Street to the George. It was a shock to see it gutted, with only the stables standing. Looking at the destruction, I had difficulty imagining the building ever being rebuilt. However, it had been sold and the landlord had clearly received funds from the new owners to clean up the site and attempt to rebuild. There were a few undeniable signs of activity already.

I saw an old friend of Silas's and asked after him.

"Ah well, you missed him," he told me. "He was here earlier this week, up from Weymouth to talk to people about work. I think proper work details are being planned for rebuilding Dorchester, although I doubt much will happen till the spring. Best to talk to him at the King's Arms."

I thanked him and made a mental note to see Silas on my return to Weymouth. Next, I walked up West Street to where Old Man Baker had his chandlery. The warehouse made me pause, remembering the gunpowder and my terror. Old Man Baker's shop was gone but the cauldron and the brick fire pit were still there. Funny, they seemed to be in use. As I was investigating, there was an angry shout. It was Old Man Baker. He didn't recognize me at first and was all for having me clear off. I took my cap off, and things got easier.

"So, the hero returns."

I laughed, and he nodded a greeting and seemed not to be holding a grudge. I asked after Aby. He eyed me, now somewhat cooler. I just looked at him with a smile on my face. He relented and said she was home cooking. Apparently, they had rented accommodation just outside the West Gate. He was still making tallow in the ruins of his shop, but he'd heard that money might be available to help him rebuild from the funds being collected for Dorchester's restoration. Meantime, he had customers to serve, weather permitting. I left him and went searching. I found the house standing by itself and went round the back into a vegetable garden that looked decidedly autumnal. The door was open, leading directly into the kitchen. Aby was at the kitchen fire leaning over a steaming pot. I crept up behind her, accidentally knocking a metal ladle lying on a table, which fell to the floor with a clatter. Aby spun round and saw me. Her eyes lit up and she gave me an almighty slap across the face. I staggered back, fell over a stool, and hit my head on the floor. Stunned, I was dimly aware of footsteps as Old Man Baker came in. I played dead.

"What did you do that for? Was he being fresh? Looks like you did him some damage. There's blood on the floor."

Aby, now remorseful, knelt down by me, saying. "Sorry, sorry, sorry," and lifted my poor, bleeding head to lay it gently in her lap. I most definitely continued to play dead.

"Father, quick get me a cloth and a bowl of water."

She leaned over me and, with her father out of the room, kissed me on the mouth. Surprised, I opened my eyes. She started back and I grinned at her. She scrambled to her feet just as her father came in with a bowl and cloth, and my head banged back down to the floor again. I went back to my stunned state.

"Aby, are you trying to kill the poor boy?" he asked. "Have you gone crazy?"

Aby had her father lift me up into a chair, pushed my head forward, and began cleaning the wound. She tutted at the older wound, now scabbed over. I must have hit a corner because there was a loose flap of skin, which Aby cleaned none too gently. I yelped and opened my eyes. Blood stopped and wound cleaned, it disappeared underneath my thick mop. I sat back and Aby went over to the boiling pot. Her father left us, shaking his head.

"Now see what you did," she chided. "You've spoilt my broth, and look at your blood all over me."

"*Me?* I came hotfoot to see you the moment I got back and was beaten up for my pains. Aby, my love, why the friendly greeting?"

"One, you left without saying goodbye or where you were going. Two, you've been away for months with barely a word. And three, the one word I got was from Will, who showed me your letter. Why no letter to me, and more to the point, *who* is Vivienne?"

Oh no, what did Will show Aby? I couldn't remember exactly what I had written, but I was sure I had told Will not to say anything about Vivienne.

"Oh, Vivienne. She is the daughter of a friend of Mr. Bushrode in La Rochelle. Such a pretty girl."

I ducked and laughed as Aby swung a ladle at my head. Once she saw I was enjoying myself and clearly not feeling guilty about any wrongdoing, she calmed down. Meantime, Old Man Baker had returned in time to see his daughter again trying to do me an injury. This time he said nothing, simply stood watching us and then nodded to himself with a wry smile on his face. It seemed he had come to an understanding that Aby and I had a more serious relationship than he, or *I* for that matter—had realized. He eyed me thoughtfully. Before he started asking questions, I took my leave, as I was due to have supper with Reverend White. I promised Aby I would see her tomorrow. Aby hurried after me asking me what my plans were. Was I back for good? How long was I back for, if not? I gave her a quick peck on the cheek, said I would tell her all tomorrow, and fled leaving her arms akimbo, general demeanor cool.

I needed time to think through what Old Man Baker had seemed to understand. The day of the fire was the first time we had stepped over the threshold from close friendship to intimacy, and then I had gone. Old Man Baker had perceived Aby's reaction to be that of someone who cared deeply for me. It was his reaction that made me finally understand it, too. Thinking these thoughts, I hurried back to P.'s house. I saw that he had suffered some roof damage from the fire, which was being worked on. I came to Dorchester expecting total destruction and found part of the town destroyed, but it seemed that the damage hadn't been as bad as I'd thought. But as I started paying closer attention, I saw the ruin was widespread, with many more buildings in need of repair, if inhabitable. It was going to take great effort and sums of money to restore Dorchester, as everyone was affected. I wondered if and how the town would pull together. There was desperate poverty throughout the county and, I understood, in England as a whole. People were starving because there was no work. Small tenant farmers were being evicted, their land combined to form larger, apparently more efficient and productive farms. There was much wealth among the landed few in and around Dorchester and elsewhere in the county. Could those purse strings be loosened?

At P.'s table, I sat across from Reverend Cheeke. P. was at the head of the table, I was on his right, and Will on his left. Mrs. White was away with the boys in Wiltshire. Her place at the foot of the table was left vacant. After grace, food quickly covered the table and we set to. I was asked to describe my last few months, which I did between mouthfuls, glossing over much. Will said that he had already asked his father about La Rochelle. P. said he knew a Calvinist preacher there. Reverend Cheeke talked about the school and pointedly demanded to know what gainful employment I was contemplating now I had completed my education. I mumbled something with my mouth full, and P. changed the subject by asking how the temporary facilities were working and how the plans for the rebuilding were coming. Reverend Cheeke said he had gathered almost all his students, and that classes continued, with extra work to catch up on time missed. Will groaned in acknowledgment; theatrical, because I knew how much he was the scholar. Having the Free School back and operational, P. said, really brought home to the town that order was being restored. He said that housing the homeless had been a critical priority and the outlying citizens had opened their doors. The second priority had been clearing away the debris and cleaning up. This work was underway, with parallel efforts to rebuild and pay for it.

P. talked about the fire being a blessing, in a way, what he called a "Fire from Heaven," burning away the sins of the town. This is a new beginning. He had met with and organized meetings among the gentry—landowners, local aristocracy, and business owners. He led them to understand that God had delivered a fearful warning, and it must be heeded. He continued to preach this warning in every sermon. Collections had been started throughout the county and elsewhere in the country to help provide funds to rebuild. He said the king himself had been approached. The conversation, which bounced from Cheeke to P. and back again, was wide-ranging and enlightening. Will and I sat taking it all in. P. couldn't have welcomed me in a more gracious way. After everyone had left, I told him I felt humbled and honored to have been included.

"There is method to my madness," he replied. "Will showed me some of what you'd written. It's clear you are or will soon be part of Sir Ferdinando Gorges' circle. I want you to give him a good report of Dorchester's progress toward recovery and rebirth. He is an honorable man and God-fearing. Dorchester has had an unenviable reputation. I am determined to use this calamity to change all that.

"Sir Ferdinando has also been active in supporting settlements in Northern Virginia. In my communications with Pastor Robinson, whose Separatist group fled to Leiden in the Low Countries, he says they are worried about how much longer they can stay there. Might there be an opportunity to establish a God-fearing community in Northern Virginia of which they could be a part? I need to know what Sir Ferdinando is doing about those settlements. You can be a pair of ears for me."

I must have looked surprised and dismayed, because P. was quick to reassure me that he didn't want me to betray any trust. He admitted that he received regular reports from Mr. Bushrode. As I lay in bed that night, I tried to settle the many thoughts whirling around my poor brain: Dorchester and Aby, La Rochelle and spying for Sir F., Plymouth and spying for P. After struggling at length, my confused and troubled thoughts finally popped like soap bubbles, and I slept.

The days passed quickly. It was wet and windy, and autumn fast approached.

Wind from the southwest meant *Rosie* was harbor-bound with no chance to make for Plymouth. I felt more comfortable that my trip to Dorchester was not creating scheduling problems for the skipper. I met up with Charlie's mother, who had been offered the possibility of a job washing clothes once her arm was sufficiently mended. I told her of P.'s promise to find work for Charlie. The horse and cart I needed, both as transport back to Weymouth and to deliver them to the King's Arms, as promised. I left them at the Sun with the publican, who promised to keep them safe till I needed them—tuppence helped.

Most of my spare time I spent with Aby. We walked and talked, then walked some more. I had suddenly fallen into a serious relationship with clear, if unspoken, expectations. I was intrigued, proud, scared, and worried. It seemed we were now different around each other, with no casual intimacy. I tried on a couple of occasions and was firmly rebuffed. Aby's strong, independent spirit governed our behavior together. I had to explain Vivienne, which was difficult. Not being used to devotional honesty, I was somewhat circumspect. But then, little had happened—not for want of trying. I wondered whether this chastity would survive my next visit to La Rochelle. There was Annie in Plymouth, too—a relationship all promise and no action. Ah, well! We'll have to wait and see.

Saturday, 16 October, was a Puritan sabbath, and I was quickly made aware of P.'s religious conflict. Being a Church of England apparent conformist, Sunday was the day of worship. As a member of his household, I was invited to attend a Saturday evening sabbath service, which I was pleased to accept. I was thus able to witness his interest in "purifying" the Church of England of any residual Catholic practices. I was intrigued enough to attend the following Saturday sabbath service on 23 October, this time accompanied by Aby.

In private conversation, P. was a gentle and persuasive teacher, but in the pulpit he was like a man possessed with respect to his condemnation of the moral backsliding of the town, and his congregation in particular. The fire was a sign from God—Sodom and Gomorrah. He had a full church, possibly helped by the shilling fine levied on non-attendees. He spoke well and readily entertained his listeners, who for the most part were kept in rapt attention.

I was also able to spend time with Will, who showed me the extent of the work needed to restore Dorchester. The cost to repair was beyond my imagining, but Will acknowledged that Mr. White was a prodigious money raiser. Using guilt like cement, he was layering it thickly on merchants and gentry alike.

So, I complete this entry in late evening on the 25th, my last night under P.'s roof.

CHAPTER 5

Journal entry—*26 October to 7 November 1613*

I am now back at the Minerva Inn. It's late and we sail for La Rochelle on the tide tomorrow. There will not be many more trips *Rosie* takes down there this year, with winter soon arriving and bringing storms from the southwest. As it is, for now we have favorable weather and we hope it lasts long enough for our return voyage.

Sir Ferdinando had requested my attendance at the conference he'd planned to hold upon his return from London—today, Thursday—in the same room where I had met Sir F. two weeks ago. I was told by Captain Turner to sit at the back and wait until I was called on to answer any questions that Sir F. might wish to put to me. Some dozen people were seated in front of Sir F.'s table. Among them I recognized only the skipper and Mr. Bushrode. It seemed the purpose of the meeting was to determine what the consequences to English interests might be if the unrest in La Rochelle turned nasty. Sir F. had been in London, where he'd been told that La Rochelle was an important ally of England, as an independent, protestant enclave in Catholic France and a substantial trading partner, and should be supported.

I followed the proceedings as best I could. At one point I was asked to describe my adventures down there. Pointed and persistent questions were thrown at me, with the result that almost nothing was left unsaid. Tred Gunt's sodomy was not raised, thankfully, though his role as double agent was. What I had not known was the extent to which Sir F. has invested time, effort, and money in furthering England's (and his) interests in Northern Virginia. Most of the conversation was over my head, to such an extent I found it difficult to keep track. I must try to find someone, possibly Captain Turner, to brief me on the background of Sir F.'s Northern Virginia investments, as P. indicated he wants me to supply him with information on this subject. With respect to La Rochelle, it is a gateway for North American produce into England's western ports. While such commerce continues unabated, English traders such as Mr. Bushrode are rewarded. But Sir F. worries that unrest inside La Rochelle and the Catholic threat from outside will reduce or cut off that lucrative trade sooner or later. More reason, he believes, for England to establish its own commercial interests in Northern Virginia.

Finally, the conference disclosed the extent of the unrest in La Rochelle. Pierre Bernardeau, a rich merchant known to Mr. Bushrode, is leading a faction of fellow bourgeoisie merchants in demanding reform from the town council—a self-perpetuating government of senior and wealthy citizens, a de facto new aristocracy that have established permanent control of la Rochelle. The bourgeoise are no longer prepared to remain excluded. The town council is refusing to meet them, let alone negotiate. Things seem to be heading toward a crisis and open rebellion. Mr. Bushrode has a cargo of woolens that he wants shipped to La Rochelle straight away before that happens, and he expects to have a lucrative cargo, including wine and beaver pelts, waiting for him there. So, in spite of the danger, we are off to La Rochelle.

After the meeting ended, Sir F. took the opportunity to give the skipper instructions to deliver messages to his spies and to gather from them a detailed assessment of the situation in La Rochelle and the likely consequences. Sir F. thanked me for my previous assistance. He said that the skipper would be sure to find a use for me once back at La Rochelle, but that I should keep my head down and out of harm's way.

Journal entry—*8 to 14 November 1613*

The trip down was uneventful. Winds from the east and north blew cold and clear. We made La Rochelle harbor Sunday, 10 November, in late afternoon. We found a berth on the quayside, sandwiched among the late-in-season fishing fleet arriving from Newfoundland. Sunday, the day of rest, the skipper had us cleaning and scrubbing—both watches—on account of it being such an easy ride down, to make up for our perceived idleness. My off-duty watch was eventually allowed ashore for a few hours, though I was called to the skipper's cabin.

"Seeing as you know the streets of La Rochelle well, I want you to slip unobserved to deliver these packages and bring back any that are delivered to you. Keep out of trouble. I have a number of your fellow crew leaving in pairs at about the same time, all going in different directions to confuse any watchers. You will be accompanied by Mr. Braddock."

The first package was to M. Giradeau. J.B. and I set off in the evening twilight. Not too much foot traffic on the quay on this side of the harbor, which seemed a little strange. No one appeared overtly interested in us as we sauntered away from the harbor onto Rue de Pont. A short time later, we were on Rue de Merciers, approaching the Giradeau house. As we got nearer we noticed that there were some men from the City Watch clustered round a brazier on a road leading to his house. There was no way to pass them unnoticed. By their attitude they appeared to be on guard. I nudged J.B. and whispered to keep walking up Rue de Merciers. Not good, there were other guards farther up the street. We looked around and realized that we had stepped into a quagmire.

"Arretez!! Qui êtes vous?"

"Sorry, no French."

"Who are you?

"We are sailors looking for a drink."

"Go away. It is forbidden for you to be here. The bars for you are back 'round the harbor."

So we did. The return of the second package was dependent on the first being delivered, as M. Giradeau was to tell us where to go and to whom we were to deliver it. We went back to the harbor, found a tavern, had a drink, returned to *Rosie,* and reported to the skipper.

"Damn, Giradeau is a neighbor of Bernardeau. It seems the authorities have them in quarantine. This matter will have to wait till morning. You're dismissed."

We left the packages with the skipper and went topside. J.B. went for'ard about his own business. I stood on the main deck leaning over the rail, looking out across the harbor. I was curious. What was going on? I wanted to know. I'm much too impatient and hated not knowing. Still off-duty, I told the duty officer, Peg Jones, that I was going for a wander and went ashore. Having no secret papers, I needed no escort. I made a careful, seemingly careless circumnavigation of the harbor, keeping close to the numerous groups of animated seamen and townspeople talking amongst themselves. My French wasn't good enough to understand what they were saying, but everyone was voluble. Presumably the excitement was to do with the posted guards in town. I kept moving and made my way through the crowd to the Pewter Platter. It was packed, everyone shouting at the top of their voices trying to make themselves heard above the noise. Some of the conversations seemed to be verbal conflicts threatening to break out into physical altercations. Quantities of wine and beer were being consumed and used for Gallic emphasis, adding to the sense of barely controlled chaos. The smoke from tobacco and candles made the room even darker. I stood by the kitchen, hoping Camille was on duty. I didn't have long to wait. She came out of the kitchen carrying trays of food, looking hot and flustered. She glanced at me and then away as she hurried past, though she looked back over her shoulder at me before ploughing her way through the room. I waited. She came back with a tray of empty plates.

"*Mon jeune anglais, n'est-ce pas?*" she shouted as she passed.

"*Oui.* Do you speak English?" I shouted back.

"A little, but I am very busy."

With that she disappeared back into the kitchen. Serving wenches came and went. I stayed as clear away from the ever-swinging door as possible, but was in danger of being trampled underfoot. Traffic was brisk in all directions, as I was near the main door to the inn. After I watched her hurry to and from the kitchen several times, Camille grabbed my arm and dragged me to a distant empty table in the corner of the barroom.

She pushed me down and leaned over me. "Yes?"

"I went to Rue de Merciers to see a friend and got turned back. Why?"

"A friend?"

"Yes. Her name is Vivienne. She is almost as beautiful as you."

Camille smiled, then turned serious. In her limited English she said, or at least I think she said, that the watch fear an insurrection and have been sent to confine certain citizens to their homes. The citizens in question are popular in the town, and the authorities risk losing control.

"The people are in the streets," she concluded. "They are becoming angry."

Camille then jumped up and hurried off, returning with a foaming tankard for me. After securing my payment, she left again. While I couldn't understand the detail of what was being shouted all round me, I certainly picked up the gist. I hunched over my drink and wondered what to do, or, more to the point, what might happen next. A short time later, Camille returned, dragging a nondescript small boy behind her. His name, she said, was Yves Marceux. He was a pot-scrubber at the Pewter Platter. His mother worked in the kitchen in an inn off the Rue de Merciers, and they lived close by. Yves knew the area intimately.

"Is the name of your friend Vivienne Giradeau?" Camille asked.

"Yes." I was surprised.

"Yves knows this girl. I think he loves her . . . *de loin.*"

"*De loin?* Ah, from a distance?"

"*Oui. Il ne parle pas l'anglais. Mais, pour Vivienne, il dit qu'il vous conduira par une route secrète à sa maison.*"

"He'll take me to Vivienne, *pour quoi?*"

"*Tel est le jeune amour!*"

"*D'accord, Camille, je t'adore.*"

Camille smiled again, gave me a hug, wished me *bon chance*, and disappeared once more. Yves, keen to be off, tugged at my sleeve and headed for the door. Being small, he was in, around, and under the heaving throng in no time. I pushed my way through and met him outside on the street.

"*Suivez,*" he commanded.

So, I followed after him as fast as I could. In trying to keep up through the crush of humanity, I had no time to take an account of the route we were taking. Nor was I able to judge the changing mood of the crowd. As we moved north, I did realize that we were heading in a roundabout sort of way from the St. Jean de Perrott to the St. Sauveur district. We scuttled through a maze of alleyways and passages between buildings that seemed to lean in on us as if to block our way. At times we waded through muck or open sewers, which I didn't care to think about.

We came to a crossroads. Yves stopped me and investigated forward, returning when the coast was clear, beckoning me to follow. At one point as we rounded a corner, Yves bounced off a large night watchman who was pissing against a wall. With an oath, the man made a grab for Yves, who dodged him and ran down the alley, the night watchman chasing him and shouting abuse. I had ducked back behind the corner, then followed along the alley. Where it crossed another road, I waited. A short time later, Yves reappeared from farther down the road, waved at me, and ran into another alley. I followed. After several other near misses and close calls, Yves delivered me to the back door of a substantial house.

"*Chez Giradeau,*" he whispered, and then was gone in an instant.

I was left alone in a dark passageway in front of a small, unimposing door. With some trepidation, I knocked. Nothing. I knocked louder, worried that I would be overheard by the men guarding the house. I heard voices at the end of the alley, footsteps coming toward me. Oh, shit. Do I run or wait? Just as I turned to run, a voice came from behind the door.

"*Qui est là?*"

"*C'est moi, Isaac Stanfield de the* Sweet Rose, *bateau anglais.*"

A lock turned, a chain was undone, and the door opened enough for me to slip through—shutting in the faces of two night watchmen. I ignored their shouts and hammerings on the door as a servant took me through to the room I remembered from my last visit, when my head had been bleeding. He told me to wait and left to fetch M. Giradeau.

"Mr. Stanfield, what are you doing here?"

I explained that I had attempted to come earlier with packages for him and others from England but had been warned off. I had managed to find another way. Unfortunately, I had left the packages back with the skipper before setting out on my second attempt. I told him that I needed to report back to the skipper on what was happening in La Rochelle and to find another way to get the information from Sir Ferdinando to the right people.

"I've no idea how you got here, as we are currently locked up tight by orders of the authorities," he said. "We do have ways of coming and going, however. I must talk to your skipper. Go back to your ship and tell him to await my arrival. I will have someone take you beyond the ring of guards. You will be blindfolded before you leave. I do not want anyone to find out about our secret passageways. What you do not know you cannot tell."

With that, the servant returned. He tied a large sash around my eyes and led me along a passageway, down steps, and through a door that was opened and closed behind me with much turning of keys and creaking of hinges. We moved into a tight, dank passage. A hand pushed me forward. Another hand was on my head to keep it out of the way of obstacles. I stumbled my way onward, guided 'round corners, picked up on several occasions as I tripped over the uneven floor. All this, and I never got to see Vivienne. Ah, well, *c'est la vie!* Eventually, we climbed stairs and passed through a door down an echoing corridor. Another door opened and a chevalier was rammed down on my head. I was led down a street and another, bumping into people. At some point the sash was removed, and I was at the head of the harbor. I turned to thank my guide but he had gone. The crowds were thicker. Seemingly, they were too interested in other things to pay any attention to me. The hat had disguised the blindfold. I was just one more body milling around waiting for something to happen. Quickly, I made way onto the quay and back to the *Sweet Rose*. I had been away for about two hours. I was met by J.B. on board, who demanded to know where the hell I had been.

"I went for a stroll and a drink."

"You bugger. What's going on?"

"Much of interest. I need to report to the skipper."

A short time later I was in the skipper's cabin. No one had informed him of my absence until he was made aware I was back aboard with a tale to tell.

I told him that I had managed to get to M. Giradeau, and that he'd sent me ahead to warn the skipper of his intent to board the *Sweet Rose* this evening, as he needed to talk.

"How the hell did you get to Giradeau?"

I explained about my contact at the Pewter Platter, Camille, and Yves' help. The skipper raised his eyebrows.

"You never cease to amaze me. I think you should attend this upcoming meeting. Remain on board. I will call you when the meeting starts, if M. Giradeau approves. Now go."

J.B. was waiting for me on deck. Taking me with him up to a quiet corner on the focsle, he again demanded to know what was going on. I described my recent experience, and we discussed the state of unrest among the citizenry. There seemed to be no threat to the *Sweet Rose* or her crew. This turmoil was political and reflected anger against the authorities. If it came to open rebellion, J.B.'s humble opinion was the *Sweet Rose* should get out of there. I kept silent, though I was eager to be out in the midst of the impending tumult. As we talked, I noticed a dark, cloaked shape materialize out of the gloom on the quay, and M. Giradeau requested permission to come aboard. We returned to the main deck as he was escorted by Peg Jones to the skipper's cabin, under the curious eyes of many of the crew. A short time later, Peg came back and ordered me to attend the captain.

"Ah, Stanfield," the skipper said. "I have suggested to M. Giradeau that, unless there are other matters to be dealt with, discussion on the subject of delivery and receipt of information pertaining to Sir Ferdinando should have you present. M. Giradeau agrees."

"Thank you, sir. Good evening, again, monsieur."

M. Giradeau acknowledged me and started to explain the current situation in La Rochelle. The corps de ville, being the authority in power, had no interest in sharing that power with anyone else, as with power came influence and financial gain. There were a number of successful merchants who'd been excluded from membership of the corps de ville and, as a result, had been disadvantaged with regard to commercial and social opportunity. But, insisted M. Giradeau, who was now pacing in some agitation, it meant that the hundred members of the corps de ville were becoming increasingly isolated from the rest of the citizenry and were in a difficult position. The guards were on duty, but the militia, who were of the citizenry, were on standby and would not participate in any serious riot control if it came to that. Some members of the corps de ville were aware of the militia's divided loyalties, but the majority weren't. M. Bernardeau and a number of his colleagues were attempting to negotiate a compromise to reduce the tension and quiet the unsettled situation in the streets.

A more serious problem was that the tumult was being reported to the French government. Any sign of weakness on the part of La Rochelle to govern itself, and the king could be quickly persuaded to eliminate the city's independence. The basis of its wealth was that independence. The vultures were gathering. Those representing the wealth and prosperity of La Rochelle were fighting each other. The bourgeoisie were in some cases as blind to the risk as the corps de ville. The general rank and file, often Catholic, wanted stability, jobs, and a decent standard of living. They were siding with the bourgeoisie, though they distrusted the bourgeoisie's Calvinist influence. In turn, the city was surrounded by the people of the Banlieue, the countryside round La Rochelle, Catholics who felt they were being exploited into penury by the Rochelaise.

To my ears, it sounded as if M. Giradeau was frightened about the outcome. He was frightened for himself, as a merchant, and for his family. Sir F. had his own spies and his own instructions to be delivered to those spies. The first package, addressed to M. Giradeau, was handed to him by the skipper. Its contents were not for me to know, as was made clear. The second package needed to be delivered to the same spy I had met with previously. Unfortunately, M. Giradeau had lost contact with him, or so he claimed. The skipper pressed him for any information he might have. He was not forthcoming. I, on the other hand, would recognize him, though only if he wore the same long white moustache. Problem being that he was known to others in that disguise. I had been picked up quickly as his contact and, therefore, courier. I hoped that no one actually recognized me apart from Gunt and Dave Searle. I wondered if they were still around. Damn, there was the mysterious swordsman as well—who was he? Where was he? Perhaps I hadn't been as incognito as I'd thought. Perhaps I'd been foolish, as it turned out. However, I certainly wasn't going to say anything. I didn't want to disqualify myself from further action.

M. Giradeau said that the best he could do would be to let it be known among his reliable connections that this spy needed to make contact, as M. Giradeau had no interest in being involved himself. I said that we knew the spy frequented the Pewter Platter in one disguise or other. Could that be a contact point? M. Giradeau asked how that would help if we don't know what he looked like or if or when he might be there. The skipper kept quiet and looked at me. I felt I could trust Camille. If the spy gave a message to Camille addressed to J.A., I would get that message and that would be the start of establishing some kind of reliable contact.

"J.A.?"

I looked at the Skipper. He replied to M. Giradeau on my behalf, suggesting it was better not to know.

"*D'accord.*"

The skipper dismissed me. After M. Giradeau left, he called me back to his cabin.

"You do realize, don't you, that you are a marked man," he said. "There are a number of people in this town who know you are associated with intelligence gathering."

I told him I thought the restive crowds were cover enough. I could disguise myself and, if push came to shove, I could enlist the bosun's mate as a bodyguard. Without anything else to fall back on, he dismissed me. My watch had begun, anyway (first watch, starting 8:00 p.m.). I came on deck and was given a caustic welcome by Mr. Glynn. Watch was low key in harbor. The previous watch had been set to clear, coil, and make shipshape. My watch duties included trimming lights, keeping watch for quayside activity as well as all possible intrusions by land or sea, turning the half-hour glass, and sounding the bell at each turn. It gave me a chance to put my thoughts in order. Camille had the potential to be a useful ally. Her initial help had shown her initiative and her support. I was struck by the resourcefulness of Yves. I thought the three of us could make a successful team; I had only to enlist their willing help. During the forenoon watch tomorrow (8:00 a.m.–12:00 p.m.), I would be off duty. An ideal time to revisit the Pewter Platter. I hoped that the crowds would continue to provide cover.

At the end of my watch, late as it was, I requested a meeting with the skipper. I told him that I planned to set up my contacts in the morning, but I needed some backup. I was concerned that I might be followed or even accosted. Therefore, I asked if I could have a couple of men to help me. I didn't want to set out too early, as I wanted crowd cover, which meant I might not get back in time for the start of my next watch. The skipper suggested J.B. and Tiny Hadfield as being experienced and capable should there be trouble. They also probably knew more of my unpredictability than others in the crew. Tiny's size might be a problem, but his abilities were real assets. The skipper said that Mr. Glynn would be informed of our possible absence from duty. With that I was dismissed. I bedded down to catch what sleep I could before my next watch.

Over breakfast the next morning, I discussed my plan with J.B. and Tiny. They were pleased to have been nominated by the skipper and excited to be part of a caper ashore. Not least, a lot of cargo off-loading and on-loading had been detailed for the forenoon watch, a thankless, dirty job that they would be pleased to miss. My plan was to walk where the crowds were thickest 'round the harbor to the Pewter Platter. I wanted them to separate and head out before me to the Rue du Pont, keeping a distance from each other, then watch me pass them and wait to see if I was being followed. J.B. should follow me, staying well back, and Tiny should watch to see if J.B. was being followed. They should keep in the crowds and be as casual as possible. If I got into difficulties, they should intervene as necessary. I would be at the auberge for long enough only to get Camille on our side, I hoped, and then I would return to *Rosie*. J.B. and Tiny should follow me back in the same way to check for any suspicious activity.

They set off separately, quickly losing themselves in the throng of people already gathered at the head of the harbor. In fact, it seemed that many had stayed overnight drinking wine, and looked somewhat the worse for wear. A few minutes later I began my trip. The crowd was less noisy but surlier than it had been before. I walked leisurely through them and passed the end of Rue du Pont without catching sight of J.B. or Tiny. They were doing well. I continued 'round the harbor onto Rue de Perrot. I was undisguised, just a young, fresh-faced English sailor out for a stroll. To make it easier to flush out any unwelcome follower, I tacked back to the harbor a couple of times, aimless in direction, carefree in intent. My course to the Pewter Platter was uneventful. I wondered if J.B. or Tiny had noticed anything.

Entering the auberge, there were few patrons inside. The barroom had been cleared, scrubbed, and brushed down. Benches that had been put atop tables were now being moved back down onto the floor. I sat on a bench by the wall close to the door, watching the comings and goings. A passing barmaid looked at me. I asked for Camille. She nodded and left. A short time later, Camille appeared, bright and fresh for a new day. She greeted me with a peck on each cheek and asked how I was. In my poor French, I asked if she would be a contact point for me. She was hesitant and perturbed at the idea of becoming involved in dangerous activities. I told her that all I needed was for her to accept a message from a stranger addressed to J.A.

"J.A?"

"D'accord. Votre Jeune Anglais," I explained.

"Ah! Oui."

If and when the message arrived, I asked her to have Yves bring the message to me on the *Sweet Rose* by devious route, careful to elude potential watchers. It all seemed straightforward, especially when I promised payment for services provided. Camille agreed to help, after which, with another hug, I left. The discussion had taken no more than a few minutes. No one had entered while I was there. Any possible enemies were keeping their heads down. I returned in casual style to the *Sweet Rose,* to be followed by my two guardians some minutes apart. It seemed that both J.B. and I were followed. My aimless, apparently random journey had made it easy to spot the followers. A young woman had followed me. She appeared to be a flower-seller, but the basket she carried contained the same number of flowers at the start of the journey as at the end. On the other hand, J.B. was followed by two workmen, or at least they looked as if they were following him. While I was at the auberge, the young girl had taken up station in sight of the door, seemingly to establish her spot to sell flowers. There were no takers and she didn't try very hard. When I came back out, she abandoned her spot and followed me. The two workmen had split up when J.B. approached the auberge. One stayed watching the main door, and the other had moved round to the back to cover the kitchen door. They knew J.B. was with me. They were careful and prepared for someone to cover my back. It seemed they were aware that I had previously escaped by that same kitchen door. I asked if one of the workmen had been large and blond. Tiny, surprised, said yes. I explained my earlier dealings with him.

So, J.B. and I were known to whomever that team worked for, and the fact that I had protection meant that someone knew I warranted it. They weren't overly concerned about what I was doing in the Pewter Platter, perhaps because they knew that the person I was supposed to meet wasn't there or had not arrived—which meant they might know who that person was. I had no idea whether or not I had been followed the previous night, but it might have been too soon for them to have gathered their forces. J.B. and I had left *Rosie* soon after our arrival in La Rochelle to go for a stroll, a quick visit to a seaman's bar, and back to *Rosie.* Surely, they wouldn't have expected my second venture that evening out into the town. More likely, they would have set their watchers out the following morning. If they had followed me last night, both Camille and Yves would be at risk, which I fervently hoped was not the case. The only clear advantage we appeared to have was the knowledge that we'd been followed and by whom—unless they had a fourth who'd followed Tiny, which was doubtful.

At the heart of the matter, I realized that I didn't know which faction Sir F. was obtaining information about from his spy—the one I was supposed to meet up with. Perhaps the skipper knew. I thought that whoever was being spied on would want to know what we knew. Presumably, they would want to prevent us from learning any more. It seemed that through M. Giradeau, Sir F. would have access to everything he needed to know about the Huguenot faction and the internal strife in La Rochelle—unless he had other spies among the corps de ville. He needed to be able to measure the likely outcomes by receiving information from both sides. Then he might have additional spies who were keeping him abreast of the Catholic faction and what the king and the French government were doing and planning with respect to La Rochelle.

I asked to speak with the skipper. I had to admit to him that he was right. I had greatly underestimated the preparedness of the opposition. I described the journey to the Pewter Platter. I told him my conclusions. No, he didn't know who Sir F.'s spies were spying on. He did know that Sir F. was anxious to make contact with this particular one. Either the word being sent out by M. Giradeau would get to the right person or it wouldn't. If it didn't, we would be in a quandary. If it did, we would be able to plan our next step. We discussed my role going forward.

"Stanfield, I say again, you are a marked man. You are a risk to yourself and others. No reason for you to continue to be involved."

"Sir, they do not know that we know we are being watched and who those watchers are. They will assume that any movement ashore on my part will likely have something to do with Sir Ferdinando's intelligence gathering. They will follow me, especially if I am being shadowed by J.B."

The skipper nodded.

"If we do get a response via Camille, I assume it will be to arrange a time and place to exchange information—Sir Ferdinando's package for one from the spy," I said. "I can act as a decoy while someone else makes the contact."

"Dangerous for you and whoever makes that contact."

"No, sir. The more likely danger is when I have the package from the spy. Remember back in October, I was attacked on my way back to the *Sweet Rose* after I had been given the package. If I am a decoy, I won't be meeting anyone, won't have the package, and won't be attacked. I don't think they know who the spy is. And if they do, they will have taken him and we won't get a message."

"Hmm. We will await developments. Return to your duties."

Duty consisted of joining the work party in the hold as they completed off-loading the cargo of mainly bales of wool. Dusty but not too onerous. While engaged in the work, I had time to think more on the situation. I had forgotten something, which nagged at me. At one point, I bumped into Obediah Burch—called Obi—the new ship's boy to replace Johnny, who was trying in vain to be useful. A tall, thin, uncoordinated twelve-year-old boy with a shock of red hair and freckles all over his face. Then it hit me: Tred Gunt.

My problems had started when Gunt saw me back at the Pewter Platter last time. He had convinced Sir F. that he had contacts in La Rochelle that would provide important intelligence. Instead, he'd been a double agent. Which faction was he in league with? Sir F. would know the answer, but he wasn't here. I would have to work it out for myself. It was after Gunt saw me that I got waylaid by the blond giant and the swordsman. No, that wasn't right—it was the Frenchman Tiny had wounded over the body of the stunned skipper. He met up with Gunt at the Pewter Platter and left when he saw me. Gunt wouldn't have had time to organize an ambush, but the Frenchman certainly would have. Still, it meant that Gunt was part of the same faction.

I hadn't seen him since, nor Searle, nor the swordsman for that matter, but that didn't mean he wasn't around. Maybe I had damaged the swordsman more seriously than I remembered. Another thought struck me: If we had been followed as soon as we left *Rosie* after docking, they would have had to have been aware that *Rosie* was due to dock. The only person who knew we were coming was M. Giradeau and someone or other of the people working for him. That means there was a spy in his household, if it wasn't M. Giradeau himself. But they didn't know when we would arrive. It could have been any time within a week. Wouldn't it be more likely, in that case, that this faction would have been alerted only after *Rosie* arrived? In which case they would not have had time to organize anything before J.B. and I set off. If I was the trigger, it would most likely have been pulled by my turning up at M. Giradeau's house. M. Giradeau and his servant were the only ones to see me. One of them was the probable spy—hardly M. Giradeau. The prime suspect was the servant. That meant that Camille and Yves were in the clear.

Now, why would I have been the trigger? Because I had the package from Sir F. and delivered it to his spy at the Pewter Platter, and I took the package destined for Sir F., in doing so identifying myself as Sir F.'s courier. Not foolproof logic but feasible. If it was the servant, then this faction would know of M. Giradeau's secrets—and passage, incidentally. He needed to be told. Another thought, if the servant was the spy (he seemed close to M. Giradeau), he would have been able to hinder communications between M. Giradeau and his spies. The person I was to meet had either got wind of the spy in M. Giradeau's household or the communications to him had been intercepted and M. Giradeau would not have contacted him. It meant that the plan to have the message left with Camille for "J.A." would have been compromised. So, a good test for my theory would be to see if the message was left and, more importantly, if it was a trap of some kind. The skipper was obviously still concerned. He summoned me to his cabin, where he and Peg Jones had been plotting the next moves. They seemed very unhappy to have to depend on a boy in what was a dangerous enterprise. Permitted to speak, I told them my thoughts. The skipper was noncommittal, but he did agree that M. Giradeau should be informed. I was dismissed.

Over the course of the next two days, the skipper decided to make it as difficult for the watchers as possible by having members of the crew go ashore and scatter round the town. They would visit different taverns singly and in pairs at irregular but frequent intervals, including J.B., Tiny, and myself. The three of us split up and others among the crew followed at discreet distances. It all appeared somewhat random. When they returned, the skipper questioned them as to whether they noticed if they or those they watched over had been followed. The crew leaving early believed that there had been suspicious activity, but later on it seemed nothing untoward had occurred. These reassuring observations applied to my trips around town as well, although I didn't visit the Pewter Platter. After the second day ended without any message, the skipper called me to his cabin and gave me his thoughts on the situation.

"It seems that things have quietened down in town. The guards have been withdrawn from the neighborhood around M. Giradeau's house. I have had a meeting with him. He tells me that he has had no contact from his spy. I informed him of our suspicions regarding an informer among his people, which shook him. He is becoming increasingly uncomfortable with his present situation. For a simple merchant, he feels he is beyond being able to deal with the intrigue and its inherent dangers. I am aware that Sir Ferdinando requires us to do everything we can to make contact with his spy, but my primary responsibility is to Mr. Bushrode and the cargo we now have aboard. It should be transported back to Weymouth. It seems we need to make one final effort to make contact.

"Your most recent trip 'round town appeared not to rouse much interest. I would like you to make one more trip to the Pewter Platter, if for no other reason than to alert Camille that we are leaving. I'm inclined to believe you when you say that Mr. Gunt is somehow involved in all this. See if you can obtain some trace of his whereabouts. It will be dangerous. I have told Mr. Braddock to select sufficient members of the crew to be in the vicinity wherever you go. I don't want them too close. Watch yourself. If in trouble, blow this whistle. They have been briefed to respond accordingly."

The skipper gave me a silver bosun's whistle and told me to get J.B. to teach me how to use it. Not just a simple matter of blowing it, apparently. I reported to J.B. with my whistle, and he demonstrated and had me practice. I was dexterous enough to get the hang of it quickly. There were a number of different calls that could be played. I was only taught to make a long, loud, piercing call. J.B. told me it was my first serious step to becoming a bosun's mate. He urged me to get some sleep so we would be ready for tomorrow's caper.

Next morning, at four bells in the forenoon watch, J.B.'s team gathered on the main deck, all keen to be involved. With the relaxing of tensions in the town, the crowds had lessened, although there was much general traffic. *Rosie's* team was given orders to spread out and be in sight of Tiny, who would keep J.B. in sight, and J.B., me. In ones and twos they went ashore, scattering as they left the quay. They appeared to be looking for a drink or two, as they'd done a day or so earlier. Then it was J.B. and me. He gave me a quick nudge on the shoulder and left ahead of me, to pick up my trail once I had wandered off the quay, much as I had on the previous dummy runs. Just as I left the quay, I saw Yves in the distance. What was he up to? Surely not a chance encounter? He appeared to be wandering along the road without purpose, stopping occasionally to chat to a friend or look at a vendor's stall. At one point I lost sight of him. He came out of an alley farther down the road. To me it looked like he was checking for follow-ers. If he saw me, he didn't let on. I walked slowly in his direction but seeming to ignore him. Then, before I could react, two small urchins, fighting each other with much abandon, appeared from nowhere, barreled into me, and knocked me flying. Quickly disentangling themselves and apologizing profusely, they helped me up, shook my hand each in turn, and ran off, continuing their fight. A piece of paper was in my hand. It seemed to be from Camille. On it was the letter Y.

The only association I could think of was Yves. I looked up. Yves had moved off. He was slowly walking toward the entrance to the Rue de Pont, still happily taking in all around him—no different than before. In like manner I started to follow. I hoped he wouldn't revert to his hidden passages and back alleys, as it would look strange to have a bunch of seemingly separate groups of English sailors straggling behind. I was relieved to see him stay in the throng of people up the road toward the Church of St. Sauveur, at least what was left of it—the bell tower. We moved on up the road to approach the church, an odd multi-sided building. Yves slipped inside. I, after admiring the fabric of the building, followed a group of fellow worshippers in. I wandered around gazing in rapt attention at the simple design and furnishings of this Protestant church—where else would an Englishman wish to pay his respects?—before sitting to wait. It was peaceful. I found myself becoming sleepy. It was much warmer in the church, away from the biting wind. People moved about me, and I lost track of time. I must have fallen asleep for a few minutes because I was nudged from behind. Looking back I noticed Yves walking back toward the entrance and away. I looked down. A prayer book was on the seat next to me that had not been there before. I picked it up. A scrap of paper was inside the front cover.

On the paper was this message: *"I have been compromised. I need passage to Plymouth. I will board immediately prior to your departure. Destroy this note."*

Leaving my seat and holding the prayer book, I walked back up the aisle toward the entrance. As far as I could tell, none of the people in the church, whether seated, walking, or standing, appeared to have any interest in me. The piece of paper I had screwed up into a tiny ball in my other hand. I had to get rid of it as quickly as I could. A table near the entrance held an array of books and religious tracts. I put the prayer book on the table. Just beyond the table was a grate in the floor. I dropped the tiny ball into the grate as I walked over it. Coming out of the church, my head bowed in a devotional manner, I failed to see a lady carrying a basket until the last second. I looked up and dodged around her. The flower seller. We both seemed unduly flustered—like we had been caught doing something wrong. I quickly moved on, away from the church. Suddenly, a hand grabbed my shoulder and spun me round. Tred Gunt.

It was the first time he had touched me since that time long ago in Dorchester. I felt revulsion and, dropping on one knee, hit him as hard as I could in his privates. He gasped and let go, doubling over holding himself. Scrambling to my feet, I swung my arm back to hit him again. Someone caught it from behind and grabbed me in a huge bear hug. I couldn't move. I remembered that grip—the blond giant. Gunt straightened and lashed out, catching me on the side of the head. My legs buckled and I went limp—dazed, hurting. I felt hands reaching into my pockets and, after emptying them, I was dropped to the ground. I rolled away onto my feet. I grabbed the whistle on a chain round my neck and blew it as hard as I could. Gunt and the blond giant looked up and clutched at me. I ducked and ran. Bystanders had started to gather, curious but not wanting to participate. In the recent strife, such incidents were not uncommon. Where the hell were J.B. and the rest of the crew? I ran down Rue de Pont looking behind me. No pursuit. Puzzled, I slowed down and stopped. Yves appeared, beckoned to me, and ran back up the street. I wondered why we were running back into the thick of trouble, but I followed.

Coming back into the church square, I saw J.B. and Tiny holding a semi-conscious Gunt. The blond giant was on the ground with two other crewmen on top of him. People had gathered, watching the scene, talking and cheering as though they were watching a bear baiting. Two of the City Watch appeared. J.B., aided by voluble spectators, explained that the two had attacked a crewmate unprovoked, pointing at me as I appeared. I told them, to J.B.'s consternation, that Gunt was a drunken crew member. We would take him back to our boat. Regarding the other man, I said we didn't know him— he had probably joined in for the fun. City Watch seemed happy not to have anything further to do. The blond giant was let go. He shambled off—not the brightest star in the heavens. Gunt was "helped" back to *Rosie* by his former crewmates, a surreptitious knife pricking his ribs. J.B. was puzzled.

"Why did you do that?"

"Gunt is a traitor," I explained. "He has much to tell."

On our return, a crewman took Gunt below, securely tied him, and put him in the hold. I was called to the skipper's cabin. He had a bemused expression on his face.

"Stanfield. Once again you amaze me," he said. "Much as I hate the idea of Gunt back aboard, it was the right decision. You did well."

I told him Yves had made contact and what happened thereafter. He shook his head frequently like he couldn't believe it.

"Our spy will appear as we depart, will he?"

"So I believe."

"We will have a full passenger load. M. Giradeau and his family will also be joining us. Apparently, he is finding La Rochelle too dangerous. He is bringing a number of his retainers with him, worried they will be exposed to retribution if they stay behind. They will be coming aboard late tonight. We sail as soon as the harbor chain is raised in the morning. I've been informed that there are pirate ships about. A boat came in a short time ago saying they had given one the slip west of Ushant. The extra men on board might be useful. We shall see."

The rest of the day was spent loading Mr. Bushrode's cargo, mainly wine and brandy tuns, as well as fur pelts. The first two had wonderful aromas and the last, a terrible stink. I learned the beaver hats were being sold in London for as much as I was paid in a month. I hoped they got rid of the smell beforehand. I also got J.B. to have a seaman deliver a reward to the Pewter Platter for Camille and Yves.

I have now finished with my journal for the time being. I hope to continue writing when we get to Plymouth. Weather has been fair but cold. Winds from the south, expected to veer southwest, ideal for our trip to Plymouth. Pirates pose a continuing major concern, and we keep a vigilant watch.

CHAPTER 6

Journal entry—*15 to 18 November 1613*

We sailed at first light on 15 November. As we were slackening our lines ready for departure, a group of about ten seamen appeared. Their leader requested permission to come aboard, which was granted. The skipper told them to assemble on the lower deck, out of sight, while he took their leader below. A few moments later, I was called to the skipper's cabin. Now what?

"Ah, Stanfield. Do you recognize this man?" he asked once I'd arrived.

Startled, I looked hard at the man who turned to face me. He took his cap off. Mid-twenties, about 5 feet 8 inches tall, broad shouldered, short brown hair, clean-shaven, slim, thin-faced, blue-eyed. His nose had been broken, possibly more than once. He had a thin white horizontal scar that started by his right ear and disappeared into his eyebrow. Certainly there was something about him. He held his arm up as if it were in a sling. He put a finger over his upper lip. Still not sure. Then he spoke.

"Remember Agincourt."

Of course.

"Aye, sir, he is Sir Ferdinando's spy."

"Right. Now, what's your name?" the skipper asked, addressing the newcomer.

"David Tremaine, sir."

"Who are these men you brought with you?"

"They are English seamen, sir, they were recently taken by pirates but have been ransomed. I prefer, if you would trust me, to wait until I meet with Sir Ferdinando before discussing their circumstances any further."

"How competent are they?"

"Highly. Several gunners among them. All have many years offshore experience."

"And you. Were you a captive?"

"No, sir, I am former Navy, with rank of cox'n."

"How did you become one of Sir Ferdinando's spies?"

"I can't tell you, sir."

At that, the skipper nodded his acceptance. He said it was most oppor-tune as we now had a full complement, if not over-full. We were heading out to sea with the distinct possibility we would encounter a pirate vessel. Now we had more than enough crew, with guns and ammunition for all. I was dismissed, told to tell Mr. Jones that the captain requested his presence and that of Messrs. Glynn, Babbs, Lee, Couch, and Braddock, which I did. On the lower deck, the recently arrived seamen were making themselves known to *Rosie*'s crew. Shortly, thereafter, J.B. came down, introduced himself to the new men, and started assigning them to the two watches, warning them to stay below till we had left port. The details would be dealt with later. For now, we needed to leave. Starboard watch on duty, being the morning watch, six bells just sounded. Peg Jones, duty officer, now on the quarterdeck, quickly brought the crew back to their duties. We slipped between the two towers guarding La Rochelle's inner harbor heading out to sea. A cold southerly blew fifteen to twenty knots on a clear morning. *Rosie* felt keen to be off. The rest of the morning watch and the start of my forenoon watch thereafter was spent sorting out the duties of each crewman and making sure they knew the ropes. They all seemed keen and experienced. They were happy to be back aboard, heading home. I had not noticed M. Giradeau and Vivienne come aboard, nor the three retainers he brought with him. They had been given officers' accommodation and had stayed below. No doubt I would have a chance to see Vivienne at some point.

After clearing the outer harbor and rounding Ile de Ré, we headed northwest. The skipper called all hands to the main deck. Leaning over the quarterdeck rail, he explained what had been happening and what he was planning. He wel-comed the new crew members and Mr. Tremaine who, though a Navy cox'n, was to be a passenger aboard. The skipper's intention was to make all sail, heading for Plymouth. There had been warnings received that a pirate vessel was off Ushant. This meant first that we would be working our passage 'round Ush-ant to sail northeast along the French coast. With current weather, we should close Ushant in the afternoon watch tomorrow. Second, it meant we would be practicing more extensive gunnery than usual under Mr. Babbs. The crew had, on every trip to and from La Rochelle, gone through their gun drills. I had not participated as my duties on watch were elsewhere. Now, the off-watch crew were told to assemble on the lower deck. The skipper had Mr. Babbs and his gun captains work with the new crew.

Normally, cannons on merchant ships the size of the *Sweet Rose* are only used for deterrent purposes, primarily against pirates. The crew are not trained, nor are there enough to handle the guns in any type of serious engagement. Another reason is the lack of room to be able to handle recoil after a shot is fired. Each gun after initial loading is run out. Almost half the gun barrel is pushed through its gun port. The gun is lashed to deck and hull bolts to prevent recoil, causing real strain on decking and the hull. It also makes the process of clearing and reloading the gun quite difficult. The crew can't get to the mouth of the gun to do so.

The skipper's experience with pirates together with Peg Jones' experience in the Navy had, some time ago, persuaded Mr. Bushrode to invest in guns and ammunition that could be used with intent. He had recruited Mr. Babbs, a gunner most of his adult life. *Rosie*'s decking and hull had also been strengthened. As a result, the skipper always ensured that there were a sprinkling of trained gunners among his crew. He had Mr. Babbs work with the crews to develop a method whereby the guns were allowed to recoil after firing. That method allowed the guns to be cleared, re-loaded, and run out within the limited space available. Still, the limited space made a challenge. Only the aft minions and falcons had room enough to recoil. The for'ard minions were constrained by the lower structure of the capstan, the falcons in the forepeak, by the lower end of the bowsprit. By shortening the tackle on each of the guns to constrain the recoil, a process of trial and error, we were able to reload the guns, though considerable dexterity was needed.

With the warning that pirates were about, and the late but welcome addition of Mr. Tremaine's new crew members, the skipper redoubled his efforts to ensure the effectiveness of his gun crews. Throughout the day, both starboard and larboard watches were kept busy during their off-watch periods, continuing to do gun drills, alternating between the guns on starboard and larboard sides. Firing was kept to a minimum, but was simulated to ensure the handling of guns was practiced repeatedly. I worked with Obi, learning how to be an effective powder monkey. Each double-shot tray contained a pyramid of fourteen shot and a mixture of grape and canister. We had to replace all shot used from the armaments store in the hold. We had to refill the gunpowder lockers and ensure sufficient wadding. These supply needs meant regular trips to the hold while avoiding the gun crews and the recoiling guns. During the constant drilling, the fun and excitement soon disappeared. The noise, dirt, smell, sweat, and physical effort overwhelmed everyone. The crew's living quarters, alternating paillasses with tables and benches (all of which had been stowed away), became a kind of hell. Beggars belief what it would be like if we were engaged with the enemy and working for real. By nightfall, Mr. Babbs expressed himself moderately satisfied with progress. Gun drill ceased, and the lower deck returned to some semblance of calm. Those of *Rosie's* crew who chose to belly ache were quickly advised that *Rosie's* guns were mere toys compared to the eighteen, twenty-four, and thirty-pounders on a Navy ship. I couldn't imagine what the gun deck of a man-o'-war must be like when fully engaged with the enemy. In our practice, we hadn't had anyone actually firing at us. By Neptune's trident, it didn't bear thinking about.

I had forgotten about Gunt, but J.B. mentioned he had been down to check him out. The disgruntled prisoner was being fed and taken care of. I had no idea whether or not Gunt realized that he was known to be a sodomite. If he did, he would be more than disgruntled—he'd be terrified of impending doom.

Morning saw us several hours of sailing short of Ushant, with patchy fog closer in to shore. Wind still from the south, a fresh breeze blowing. Farther out, we could make out a thicker fog bank. After the exertions of yesterday, the skipper allowed the off-duty watch to rest up. I was on the morning watch. Seven bells were struck as Vivienne came on deck, leaving me thirty minutes of duty before my watch ended. Afterward, I had the opportunity to spend a little time with her, attended by her father and Peg, the watch officer. She had come topside onto the quarterdeck, looking pale and lovely. *Rosie* rode the waves well but the rolling movement caused some distress to those not used to it. Vivienne hoped the fresh air would ease her seasickness. The smells below deck—from the bilges and the bodies of the crew to the fur pelts—would have turned a stronger stomach than Vivienne's. In fact, her father didn't look much better. Anyway, she brightened a little when she saw me.

Seeing I was not allowed on the quarterdeck, now being off watch, she came down into the waist. We chatted a little. She had been made aware of the pirate danger. I expressed surprise that her father had thought to risk passage with the threat of pirates. She said they were always aware any voyage from La Rochelle held that threat. Her father believed that the internal unrest in La Rochelle and the potential for subjugation by the Catholics were greater threats than pirates. There was a significant Huguenot population in Plymouth, including members of the Giradeau extended family. They had chosen to move there, permanently. With that she looked sideways at me, seeking a reaction. My immediate response was a spasm of excitement, which she saw.

Smiling, she turned away, not noticing my secondary reaction—Aby. I could foresee conflict. What was a man to do? I was not going to worry or plan, with so many other events unfolding. Throughout the day, whenever on watch, I continued to assist the watch officer on the quarterdeck, which meant I was aware of Vivienne as she came and went but had no opportunity to talk to her. Off watch, I went below to eat and sleep.

The fog had increased as we moved farther out to sea to avoid islands and rocks off shore. Lookouts were doubled, soundings taken constantly. On watch, I was kept busy. By the end of my afternoon watch we were still some miles south of Ushant, and the fog had started to lift ahead of us and toward shore. Taking advantage of the increased visibility, the favorable wind and tide, the skipper took us into the Fromveur passage inside Ushant. We had a clear sail heading northeast, wind southerly, course east of Ushant. We continued on the same heading, hugging the French coastline to our starboard until nightfall. We came up two points, sailing out into the English Channel. As we moved offshore, fog returned. All watches were split, reduced to two hours on and four hours off, to ensure maximum alertness by on-duty watches and lookouts. The goal was to get as much rest as possible, pending engagement with pirates the next day.

Morning of the 17th we were in patchy fog, a strong breeze veering to the southwest, our heading now north. Watches returned to normal. The skipper had taken us on a course that had us well east and north of Ushant, hoping to avoid entanglement with the reported pirate vessel. I had the forenoon watch starting at 8:00 and was stationed on the quarterdeck with the watch officer, Mr. Glynn. I had sounded five bells, when the masthead lookout called down to the deck that he had sighted something. The skipper, now on deck, sent Mr. Glynn with a telescope up the ratlines to the main top. Mr. Glynn returned to say that there was an indistinct shape in the fog some five miles off our port bow—a ship, but what kind? He had told the lookout to keep his eyes peeled and sent another crewman up to act as messenger. Skipper advised me not to sound the bell any further until he ordered otherwise. Word was passed to reduce all noise on board. *Rosie* continued to make good progress on port tack steering full and by. The masthead messenger reported back to the quarterdeck. It was a ship, seemed similar in size to *Rosie*, on our approximate heading, tops'ls, t'gallant set but courses furled. We were rapidly gaining on her. She had not given any impression she had seen us. The fog thickened.

The skipper called all hands to the main deck. He said he was inclined to believe it was the pirate vessel we'd been warned about. No self-respecting merchantman would be sailing short in this weather. We would head up and attempt to slip by her on the weather side. If sighted, we would have the weather gauge, which would anyway be to our advantage. He called for action stations with larboard guns loaded and run out. They would be ready for use and would help balance the heel with that weight out to weather and would be out of the way of the starboard guns which were being readied for action, loaded with round shot. The initial excitement caused minor incidents and a few oaths, but the earlier training and drill practice quickly pulled the gun crews together. *Rosie* headed up and, with the wind abeam, sails were set. We moved through the water at speed with minimum fuss, pushing the chop aside with an easy, rolling motion. The fog remained thick but low on the water, and the sun appeared to the south as an indistinct globe. Occasional thinning of the fog above gave an impression of blue. It looked like the fog might burn off. On the quarterdeck, the skipper told Mr. Glynn that he believed he would be abreast of the other ship within an hour and, he hoped, a mile or more to windward. The excitement built in the crew. The passengers had been asked to go below, although Mr. Tremaine was welcomed on the quarterdeck. The sandglass ran out, and I turned it. In my distraction, I reached for the bell out of habit. Mr. Glynn knocked my hand away.

"No, you fool. No noise."

Mr. Tremaine winked at me.

Damn, I was meant to be a powder monkey but couldn't tear myself away from the action. Then, a strangled cry from the masthead. We had sailed into clear air. Looming off our port bow at some thousand yards was a mast with t'gallant spar just poking up from a bank of fog, flying a French flag. It had obviously seen us earlier, guessed our action, and turned to intercept us. There was an oath from Mr. Tremaine. He recognized her. The flag, he said, was a standard ploy to fool unsuspecting merchantmen. It was the pirate. But, still sailing short, it had not expected us that soon. We were gaining on it rapidly. Skipper ordered helm hard up and all sails braced, leach and tack lines hauled hard in and we were sailing jammed and due west back into fog. The wind had lessened, and the fog thickened.

Skipper said to Mr. Glynn that the pirate might not have seen us, as his lookout would probably have been in the main crow's nest, which hadn't cleared the fog. We needed to creep around him to weather but with no noise. The orders were passed by hand signal from the quarterdeck to the bosun to the bosun's mate, who whispered them to the crew. The masthead lookout had crew stationed on the ratlines to pass on messages. Now came the waiting. *Rosie* slipped through the water making three knots, the wind dropping to ten to fifteen knots from the south-southwest. The gun crews were tense from seeing nothing but fog through the gun ports, as their captains gestured for no movement and no chance of noise. I turned the hourglass at thirty minutes and remembered not to sound the bell. The fog above seemed lighter, the blue more evident as a pale wash, and the sun a hazy orb. Masthead in clear air reported the pirate's t'gallant had reappeared but was now abeam to starboard. It had not changed course but was still about a thousand yards off.

I tried to remember my geometry. Pirate heading northwest at maybe two knots. *Rosie* heading west at three knots. Seemed like we were sailing the base leg of an equilateral triangle. If we were a thousand yards off when we first sighted her, we would be a lot closer if she was now on the beam. It seemed the skipper was already well aware of the danger. He sent Mr. Glynn up the mast with his telescope to check. He came down fast. Yeah, we were close—too close. Would the fog bank that was enveloping the pirate hold? *Rosie* crept on for another half hour. I turned the glass again, eight bells unsounded—the end of my watch. I wasn't going anywhere, nor was Mr. Glynn. Masthead reported pirate off starboard quarter. Now definitely a good thousand yards off, falling farther back. Skipper checked the traverse board. We had been logging boat speed continuously. He had the information he needed to calculate relative positions of the two boats and the rate of separation.

"Not out of the woods yet," the skipper said. "We need at least three more hours on this course to clear the horizon. Mr. Glynn, change watch if you please. Mr. Jones, please take over."

Obi came onto the quarterdeck and took over my duties. I went down to the gun deck.

J.B. wanted to know what was happening. I told him, and he passed the information on to the gun captains. Though the stress of the situation was still intense, the information allowed for a few grins. Someone relaxed a little too much, tripped over a gun tackle, dropped his swab with a clatter, and was hit with whispered oaths. No orders had come that we could stand down, but I suggested to J.B. that we were now at least a mile off. He growled at me. Orders is orders. The ship's boy of a seaman had no business interfering. We continued whispering and tiptoeing for the next three hours. Then, the skipper ordered helm down, sails reset, main course weather side re-clewed up to its spar. We headed for Plymouth with wind now dead astern. I came on deck to see that visibility had increased to about four miles, the fog had largely dissipated, and the sun was bright above us. No sign of the pirate.

The sail back to Plymouth was without incident. I was able to spend a little time with Vivienne. She had taken on the role of nurse to two of M. Giradeau's retainers who, from a combination of over excitement and *mal de mer*, had become incapacitated. After hearing of her gentle ministrations, a number of the crew offered to go sick themselves. We made Plymouth midway through the afternoon watch on 18 November. The Giradeaus were quick to disembark.

I was intrigued to see what would happen to Gunt. A message was sent to the fort, and a short time later, two soldiers and an officer appeared by boat to take him ashore. I assumed I would be able to find out more later. Instead, I sought clarification on the underlying worry about pirates from one or two of Mr. Tremaine's men, who expressed real concern and horror, giving me a glimpse into the nature of the threat pirates held over their prey. I had not realized that the pirates, operating in the Atlantic and the western approaches to England—and Ireland for that matter—saw men and women as goods to barter. Mr. Potts at the Minerva hadn't mentioned that. They were exchanged as hostages for money or were transported to the north coast of Africa and sold as slaves. Their prey were not only small merchantmen and their crews, like the *Sweet Rose*, but coastal villages, where they would come ashore to take men and women captive. They were like the Vikings of old. There were remote villages in the southwest of England and Ireland that were in terror of pirate raids. Even more horrifying was that the pirates weren't Turks from the Barbary Coast, but Englishmen—sailors who'd turned against their country for profit. Captives being taken back to places like Tunis and Algiers suffered such conditions on board that many died on the way. Once on land, the surviving captives were sold in slave markets. Men normally went to the galleys, where they were chained to their oars, never to be released—sitting and sleeping in their own shit, dying of exhaustion, malnutrition, and thirst. Women were sold into harems or brutalized as servants. Any pirate ship that attacked *Rosie* was in for a shock. Merchant ships were not expected to fight back. Pirates wanted to damage neither ship nor crew, thus wasting assets to be bartered or sold. They shied away from aggressive engagement, preferring not to risk damage, death, or injury themselves in pursuit of profit. There were always easier pickings to go after, so they preferred to scare their prey into submission. An initial show of force would do—a gun fired into the rigging, followed by boarding, overwhelming the prey's crew with a much larger number of screaming, heavily armed pirates.

CHAPTER 7 ———

Letter to Will—*18 November 1613*

Will

I am sending this letter to you, via Silas, as I won't be back for a while. *Rosie* will be shipping out to Weymouth tomorrow. I have been asked to stay over to meet with Sir F. The skipper said he will arrange for one of his fellow skippers to give me passage to Weymouth but that won't be for at least a week, possibly longer. I hope to be back to enjoy the Christmas season with you all. My escapades are all in my journal. I have enclosed a letter to Aby and would be grateful if you could read it to her.

Isaac

Journal entry—*19 to 28 November 1613*

Rosie left Plymouth for Weymouth on 19 November, taking my journal with her. Obi said he would find Silas, if he was still there—he might have moved back to Dorchester already. Obi would arrange to have it delivered to Will by any means, if not Silas. It was my first assignment for the boy, which I hope he manages.

I am back staying at the Minerva. I have been given a special rate, as I was told by Alfred that I should consider the inn my home away from home. I have a tiny closet for a room of my own, up the back stairs under the eaves, cozy and quiet. A small skylight allows daylight to struggle in through the grime on the window. Sir F., on my inquiry, was otherwise engaged. I was told to stand by and wait—how long? No idea. So I went hunting for the Giradeaus. Vivienne was pleased to see me, as I was her. She still looked a little pale from the journey, which must have been terrifying and uncomfortable for her after the rich, pampered life she had led back home. The Giradeaus were staying with a cousin. M. Giradeau was out establishing connections and reorganizing his business affairs, which he now hoped to run from Plymouth. When I came calling, Vivienne showed me into a small sitting room and invited me to sit on a large double chair. She sat next to me, holding my hand, which she didn't let go from the moment I arrived. I suddenly started feeling ill-at-ease. I had, I insisted to myself, come visiting out of *courtesy*. I had not come courting. I looked at Vivienne. She turned her head and with the widest, roundest eyes gazed into mine. I felt there were messages being sent that I was incapable of understanding. Here was a beautiful, sophisticated young Frenchwoman trying to communicate in a language foreign to a young, inarticulate country swain more used to being beaten up—as an expression of love from Aby—than being seduced with looks. This was a *lady*. I cleared my throat, got up, and started pacing round the room.

"Are you comfortable here in Plymouth?" I asked.

"*Oui.*"

"Have you many friends here?"

"*Non.*"

"Does your father's cousin have children your age?

"*Oui, une fille qui a seize ans.*"

"That's good, do you like her?"

"*Trop tôt pour dire, mais elle semble belle.*"

"Seems beautiful?" I puzzled.

"*Non, je veux dire sympathique.*"

"How is your English? You must learn to speak it fluently."

"*Oui.* Yes. What is fluently?"

"You must learn to speak English *correctly*."

We both laughed. As we continued to talk, we both visibly relaxed. I asked about her father's servant, who'd met me on the night I came to her house. She said that he had been dismissed by her father. Shortly after that, Vivienne had been told to pack her valise with essentials, as they would be leaving La Rochelle for a time. She said she had cried a little but was glad to leave as she was feeling unsafe. My discomfort disappeared as Vivienne changed her demeanor toward me. It all happened too quickly for me to understand why, but I sensed that our relationship—or the expectation of the relationship—had suddenly shifted. We had become friends, comfortable with each other.

Later, I came to understand that I had not only not responded to her signals, I hadn't even recognized them. Her interest in me as a potential *amour* had lasted a few brief moments in that room. She offered me some refreshment, which I was happy to receive in the form of tea and some simple French pastries that she had made herself. We chatted for some time. I suggested she should only speak English, and that she was welcome to practice with me. We had a wide-ranging conversation that enabled us to increase her vocabulary and grammar. We both enjoyed it, a sweet lady and a friend. M. Giradeau returned and greeted me cordially. The comfortable atmosphere between Viv and me was evident. He thanked me for the warning about his servant. He had been over-trusting, and the warning had explained a number of strange happenings that had worn on his nerves. The three of us parted in friendly manner, M. Giradeau even suggesting I come to dine with them in the near future. I would be most obliged, I said.

I spent the evening in the barroom of the Minerva. Two of Mr. Tremaine's men were there. As I'd had little time to get to know them and their history on *Rosie*, I approached them. I was welcomed and invited to sit. They did not want to talk about David Tremaine, except to say they were in awe of him and his accomplishments, though they wouldn't tell me what those accomplishments were. They did say that as soon as *Rosie* arrived in Plymouth, he had been rowed to the quay and had made directly for the fort. The two men had sailed with the East India Company since the start of the company's shipping activities in 1600, and told wonderful tales of their adventures.

As the evening wore on with much ale consumed and food served, I asked them whether they could tell me how they came to be in La Rochelle that night. They were uncomfortable. They'd been given orders to say nothing, but their tongues were loosened by the ale, and I gathered that they had been on a ship sailing south off the northwest coast of Africa when they had been set upon by two pirate galleys. The pirates captured the East Indiamen, took the crew and sailed through the straits of Gibraltar into the Mediterranean, their ultimate destination being one of the Barbary ports, though the men didn't know which. On the way, they had stopped offshore from a port in southeast Spain. For some reason unspecified, nine of the captured crewmen were taken ashore. A ransom had been paid for them and that was that. They would say no more about it.

The next few days I spent wandering around Plymouth, getting to know the city and the surrounding countryside. Maddie was still stabled at the Minerva. I decided to return her to Fowey, hoping for a boat ride back from one of the fishermen or traders active along the coast. The weather was clear but cold, a biting wind coming from the southwest. I was well bundled up and enjoyed the trip. Maddie and I had become good friends. I would be sorry to say goodbye. We made the journey in daylight on the 24th, getting an early ferry to Cremyll to ride the coastal path I had taken previously. I stopped for a bite and a drink at the Finnygook before continuing on my way. Memories of Charlie came back to me as I passed the spot of his misbegotten episode, and I wondered what he was doing. I took another ferry at Looe and on to Polruan, boarded the ferry there, and arrived in the early evening at the Ship Inn in Fowey. In the stable, I settled Maddie and rubbed her nose sadly. She mouthed my coat, nodding. One final pat before leaving her as she tucked into her hay. Next morning, I inquired about the possibility of a boat trip back to Plymouth. After a fruitless search, I began to get a little worried. I had been given leave by Sir F.'s office to be away for two days but no longer. It seemed like I would have to ride back again. I went to the ostler in the stables and asked who owned Maddie.

"She belongs to the landlord. Why do you want to know?"

"Is she used much?"

"No, she is a bit young—a two-year-old, too frisky. The landlord bought her for his daughter, but that plan didn't take."

I went off to talk to the landlord. We came to agreement without too much bargaining and I became the proud owner of my first horse, including an old saddle and bridle. It left me tight for money, and I wasn't sure how I would square the purchase with my expense report to Sir F., but him being a knight I was sure he would think it entirely reasonable for an audacious young squire to have his own mount. We returned to Plymouth and I gave Maddie her head. The miles rolled by. Riding was a pleasure. There was a level of intensity, of bonding with my mount that I had not experienced before. With ownership came a sense of belonging, clearly. On the way back, I thought hard about riding back to Dorchester. It was unlikely there would be much more sailing this side of the New Year. My birthday was shortly thereafter. I would have to see. Back at the Minerva, Maddie comfortably stabled, I went to the barroom for some food and drink. I was confronted by Captain Turner.

"Where the hell have you been?"

"I went for a ride," I said. "I had notified and received approval from Sir Ferdinando's office."

"You didn't notify and receive approval from me."

"Was I meant to?"

"Don't give me that," he snapped. "You need me if you want to gain any advantage with Sir Ferdinando."

"Advantage?"

"You know what I mean. You, like everyone else, hang on his coattails waiting for an opportunity."

"Wait. All I want to do is get back to Dorchester for Christmas. It's you people who want me here, available at all times."

Captain Turner took a deep breath. I suggested he have a drink. On duty, he said. He had been waiting for me for most of the day. No one had told him I was gone, and Sir F. was not amused. No one had bothered to tell him either. Anyway, it was too late tonight. We would have to see him first thing tomorrow morning.

"What is happening?" I asked.

"He's planning another voyage to Northern Virginia. He's had information back that has restored his enthusiasm for exploration."

"What's that got to do with me?"

"I don't know," he admitted. "I assumed you had some kind of backdoor access. I apologize. You obviously know no more than me. We shall see tomorrow. Come to his offices at 07:00 hours. I will meet you there. Do not be late."

With that he stomped out, his face as red as his tunic.

What the hell was going on? I was an underage seaman of no particular skill apart from seeming to be in the right place at the right time.

Annie appeared. "You look out of sorts. Anything to do with that officer?"

"*That* officer?" I asked. "That was said with some feeling. What happened?"

"He was in a state all evening, wondering where you were, thinking you were off chasing girls. I asked him if he would like a drink, he refused. Anyway, he was rude. He took up space without generating any business."

I laughed. "Enough of him! I've hardly seen you. You know, looking at you, all the worries in the world disappear."

Blood! What was I *saying*? Just the relief of a lovely, interested friend with no axe to grind. No axe to grind? She might not have, but I wasn't doing too badly.

"Isaac Stanfield. Are you making me a proposition?"

Oh no, the axe was grinding.

"Annie, the last few months have taken a terrible toll. To be able to sit and talk to a real friend is like being cosseted in a . . . feather bed."

"Feather bed? Isaac Stanfield! What are you saying?"

Oh dear. A definite fire in her eyes. She leaned over the table and gazed at me, seemingly willing, tempting.

"Annie!" came a shout from Alfred, with a clip across her backside. The spell was broken. Annie scuttled off to the kitchen to her duty. Alfred laughed and asked me if I knew what the hell I was playing at. Annie was a tigress on wheels when roused.

"Aroused? Oh boy."

Tired from the day of riding, I went to my little eyrie and within minutes fell into a deep sleep.

Some time later, I was awoken by a soft body slipping under the blanket and nestling up to me. A warm breath in my ear whispered, "Some feather bed."

I was helpless. It was the most glorious, educational, and exhausting night of my life. Annie was insatiable—no, that's not fair. We were both intoxicated by the moment, the sheer joy of our mutual lust.

The guilt hit me when I woke up next morning, Annie gone.

At the appointed time, I presented myself at the required place and was met by Captain Turner, who told me to follow him. We once more found ourselves outside Sir Ferdinando's office, and were bidden to enter. Sir F. greeted me with some favor. Captain Turner moved to a corner of the room and sat down.

"Mr. Stanfield, sit. I expected to see you yesterday. I gather you were given leave to be absent. I hope you enjoyed your trip to Fowey."

I looked surprised. Had I been followed? Sir F. laughed at my discomfort. He told me that Captain Turner had made a few discreet inquiries when he had found me gone. Yes, I had told Alfred where I was going. I glanced at Captain Turner. If he knew where I had gone, why the commotion at the Minerva? I put it down to jealousy. He had admitted he thought I had somehow bypassed him to get to Sir F.

"I have a job for you. I don't know whether you are aware, but for some time now I have been looking after some native Indians on my brother's estate at Wraxall, near Bristol. I won't go into detail here. Suffice it to say, they were brought back from Northern Virginia several years ago. I am teaching them English and, when appropriate, they will be returned to their own country as interpreters and guides. I have another two ready to return with another expedition I'm mounting. I've had some difficulty establishing a close relationship with these two. They are suspicious of the men I've had work and live with them. My men aren't the brightest, predisposed as they are to seeing themselves superior. Considering your youth, you've shown extraordinary resourcefulness. You appear equally comfortable with people of all ages and stations—officers and men alike. I want you to join Sir Edward Gorges's household, befriend these people, and establish an honest relationship with them. Use your youth to beguile them. I want you to be an eager, interested young man. I need to know whether or not I can trust them."

I was stunned. I immediately thought of my dream of Christmas in Dorchester. But I was in no position to reject this extraordinary offer. I'd heard of these strange foreigners but had never seen them. Lurid stories, exaggerated in the telling, had been told by the seamen on *Rosie*.

"If you are willing, I would like you to start in January. I will be spending Christmas with my family. I do not want to mix family time with this activity. What do you think?"

"Aye, sir. Thank you. It would suit me fine. It means I can spend Christmas at home, too."

"Good. Before you go, I want you to spend some time here learning about the activities we have undertaken to explore and open up Northern Virginia—especially how we came to have our Indian guests, where they came from, and how we hope they can help us."

"Aye, sir."

"Captain Turner will brief you and give you access to any other information he deems pertinent."

"Thank you, sir."

"When do you plan to be back in Dorchester?"

"I was hoping to be there by Christmas week and stay until after my birthday, the day of Epiphany, sir."

"How appropriate. I am sure your parents thought you were one of the kings on your arrival."

I smiled. It was a remark often made.

"How are you planning to travel?"

"I thought I would ride, sir. I've just bought a horse, and I'd like to take her back to Dorchester. Better there, while I am on my travels."

"That plan could be opportune. My son, Robert, has need to travel to Exeter. He plans to leave on 10 December. He is joining the army in January. You might want to ride with him. You will want to get to know him as he will be at Wraxall for a short time when you are there, before he has to join his regiment. He is a little older than you, I believe. Born in '95."

"Aye, sir. I was born in '97."

"Goodness! You certainly belie your age. I am sure you will get on well with him. He is something of an adventurer like yourself."

"Is it possible you could get a message to Captain Brown of the *Sweet Rose* to advise him of your plans for me?"

"I will. I wouldn't dream of keeping a vital crew member from his Captain for longer than necessary. I have it in mind you'll be back on board the *Sweet Rose* by early spring."

With that, Sir F. dismissed me. Captain Turner suggested we meet in his office that afternoon, though I presumed the suggestion was an order. I left him for the time being.

It was raining as I walked through the Barbican, trying to collect my thoughts. Nothing like the cold and wet to focus my mind, for it churned. One thing I needed to do was to get my own word to the skipper, not just leave it to Sir F. I was still a member of his crew. I certainly did not want to be absent without his leave. He worked *with* Sir F., but didn't work *for* him. I returned to the warmth of the Minerva, having sorted those matters out in my mind. But being there brought back with urgency the question of what to do about Annie. Last night had to be a singular happening. Overwhelming but not to be repeated. I was concerned about Aby, and more to the point, what she would do to me if she found out. I found I did not feel too guilty, as there hadn't been much I could've done about my seduction by an irresistible Annie. At least I was able to convince myself of that—maybe. Annie was cleaning tables. She looked up when I came in and grinned. I sat her down, not knowing where to start.

"You're looking serious, my sweet."

"Annie, I am."

"Ooh! That sounds ominous."

"About last night."

"Ah, yes."

"Ah, no," I replied. "You took serious advantage of me."

"I know. It was clear you weren't going to do anything."

"Exactly. I am spoken for. I have a girl who is very important to me back home."

"Silly boy. I have no designs on you. I enjoy a tumble. I enjoyed the tumble with you, but that's all it was."

"So, I can continue to make the Minerva my home away from home without complications?" I asked, incredulous.

"Of course. We now know each other—biblically as well."

She laughed as I pulled a face.

"We'll be friends. We can tell each other secrets, just as we share a secret of our own," she said cheerfully. "Now, I must get back to work. Do you want something to eat?"

Thus began a good, close friendship. I saw with a start that two girls of my acquaintance were both happy to change what might have been possibly disastrous relationships, translating whatever was between us into a much more satisfying, permanent friendship. There was a definite moral here, a good lesson.

But back in the recesses of my mind there was a nagging worry. Something was not quite right. I couldn't—or wouldn't—explore it further.

In ten days, I was due to leave with Robert Gorges on our ride to Exeter and onward. I had much to do, but my activities were interrupted by a request for my attendance at a court proceeding at the fort. Tred Gunt had been brought to trial, closed to the public as the evidence included secret intelligence reports. He was accused of treason and sodomy. I had hoped the latter charge would not be necessary, considering treason was a capital offense. I appeared to be the main witness for the prosecution on both counts, and was asked by the prosecuting lawyer what my involvement with Mr. Gunt had been. They asked me to recount my first encounter with him, which I did.

Mr. Gunt, who was a sorry and tortured sight in the accused's dock, looked up, mouth open. He had no idea. He had not made any connection. They asked me what happened on the *Sweet Rose* leading to Mr. Gunt leaving the ship at La Rochelle. I told them. Gunt looked startled, then relapsed into misery. He looked to be in serious pain. I was asked about Johnny, and said he'd been returned to his mother in a mentally enfeebled state. Grievous bodily harm was added to Gunt's slate of charges.

I was asked about the circumstances leading up to Gunt's capture and return to the *Sweet Rose*. I told them. I was not asked any questions by the defense lawyer, which I found surprising. It seemed Gunt was not expected to offer much in the way of defense. I was released and told to wait outside the courtroom in case there were other questions. There were none. A little later, Sir F. came out and congratulated me on the manner in which I gave my evidence. He said the judges had retired to consider their verdict. There was no jury. A short while later, the court reconvened. Gunt had been convicted and sentenced to be hanged. No appeal. As he was taken from the dock, he mouthed obscenities at the judges and swore vengeance on the squid who had shopped him. I supposed he meant me. Thinking about Johnny, I had no sympathy and no concern about Gunt's threat. He would be dead in two days.

The following day, I began my lessons with Captain Turner. What I learned I wrote down in my journal.

CHAPTER 8

Journal entry—*28 November 1613*

I met with Captain Turner on 28 November to learn more about Sir F.'s interests in North America. The first thing he did was to take me to Sir F.'s study to show me a globe of the world. Turning the globe, his finger rested on a map of England, then traced a path across the Atlantic to a large land mass. I was transfixed, as I had never seen a globe up close before.

"Stanfield, pay attention. This is the coastline of North America. To keep things simple, North America, at least the coastal portion, is divided into three. The Spanish own the southern portion, the French own the northern portion—which they call New France—north of the St. Lawrence River and Acadia, south. England owns the middle portion."

"Owns, sir?"

"Yes. The Spanish, French, and English have taken possession of the land in the name of their sovereigns over the past hundred years or so. In the 1580s, Sir Walter Raleigh and Humphrey Gilbert explored the mid-Atlantic coastline of North America, claiming the territory in the name of Queen Elizabeth. This new land was named Virginia, in honor of the Virgin Queen, though nothing further was done until Charles became king. Some among his subjects wished to exploit this new land, to the advantage of the crown and, therefore, England, of course."

I asked if Sir F. was the driving force.

"Sir Ferdinando was very much involved but it was at the instigation of Lord Chief Justice Sir John Popham in 1606 that King Charles divided Virginia so it came under the control of two companies—the Northern and Southern Virginia companies. It is a tract of land one hundred miles wide along the Atlantic coast of North America, from the 34th to 45th latitude.

The Southern Company's land stretched up to approximately Cape Cod; the Northern Company's up to Acadia."

Captain Turner had me examine the globe and pointed out the lines of latitude.

"Sir Ferdinando's interests lie with the Northern Virginia Company and has supported or instigated a number of exploratory voyages to Northern Virginia," he continued.

Many of the questions I raised came from the remarks made in the conference I'd attended in early November, where numerous voyages had been mentioned, including Captain Challon's trip in 1605, when he'd been captured by the Spanish; Captain Weymouth's exploration of Maine in 1605; the Popham expedition's unsuccessful attempt at settling Sagadahoc in Northern Virginia in 1607 and 1608; and Harlow's exploration and survey in 1611.

Of serious concern to Sir F. had been the encroachment by the French into Northern Virginia. Two years ago, reports had come back that a French vessel had been warned by English West Country fishermen to remove itself from an island called Matinicus, close to Monhegan Island, which it did. Then, early this year, Captain Argall, on a fishing trip from Southern Virginia, discovered and destroyed an encampment that the French, sailing southwest from their base in Acadia, had begun building on Mount Desert. It seems that with no obvious English presence in the area, the French had taken the opportunity to attempt settlement. While Captain Argall's removal of the French threat was welcomed, apparently Sir F. saw the Argall voyage as a deliberate incursion by the Southern Virginia settlement into Northern Virginia. Thus, in spite of his previous failed attempt at Sagadahoc, Sir F. had added reasons to want to establish permanent presence in Northern Virginia before the acquisitive Southerners took over.

Sir F. had other worries in addition to the threat to English sovereignty. English fishermen spreading southward from Newfoundland had found that ideal fishing comes earlier in the year the farther south they sail, but to exploit the abundance they need to have fishing settlements on land to dry and salt the fish for the long return journey. The French and the Basque already have these settlements in New France. For Northern Virginian fishing to have success, English fishing settlements need to be established there. Regrettably, English fishermen seem incapable of or disinterested in living off the land. Nor do they deal with the natives, who might otherwise provide needed support as well as opportunities to trade. In fact, they have little contact, whereas French trappers and missionaries have established close, profitable working relations with the natives in New France and Acadia.

Captain Turner told me that a number of exploratory trips were being planned for next year. Captain John Smith, a name I had heard spoken of many times, was being sent from London in early 1614. He would lead a small fleet of ships. His second in command would be a Captain Thomas Hunt. Smith was keen to further survey the coast from Monhegan to Cape Cod and gather more detailed information about sites for future settlement. He wanted to bring back evidence of the opportunities for trade. Hunt was to fill his holds with fish, bartered goods, and possibly evidence of gold mined locally. Another captain with transatlantic experience, Nicholas Hobson, shared Sir F.'s belief that copper and gold mines existed on the island of Capawak. They agreed Hobson would sail to Northern Virginia. The Indians currently at Wraxall Court said they could lead Hobson to the mines.

The meeting ended with Captain Turner talking about the two Indians at Wraxall. These were the two I was to meet and try to get to know, Epenow and Assacomet. According to Captain Turner, they were very different people from any I might have come across previously. He said he would not cloud my judgment by making any personal observations about them. Suffice it to say, he indicated they were as different from himself as chalk from cheese. In his opinion, it would be difficult to develop any kind of close relationship with them.

Journal entry—*29 November to 9 December 1613*

Tred Gunt was due to be hanged at dawn on 4 December at Plymouth Fort in secret. When the soldiers went to his cell to take him to the scaffold, the cell was empty. The shape of a sleeping man on the ground was but a bundle of straw under the blanket. Gunt couldn't have gone far. He had been racked and was barely able to walk. It was probable that he had two accomplices at least. He'd have had to have been carried up from his dungeon. Captain Turner told me to make myself scarce until they had found him. I was considered valuable property, apparently, and clearly now at risk. Assuming they were holed up somewhere in Plymouth, I took Maddie and rode into the countryside. On my return, I was told that Gunt had gotten away. Apparently, three men had been seen boarding a French fishing boat in the outer harbor—one bent and disabled—in the early hours of 3 December. The boat had immediately sailed, and by the time the authorities were alerted it was daylight and the boat had gone. The men who helped Gunt must have found a way past the guards, unlocked the door to the dungeon cell he was in, carried him up the steps, through the guard room, and out of the fort. It didn't seem possible without someone on the inside being involved. My questions were met with shrugs or tight-lipped grunts. I assumed it was embarrassment all round. I wondered when I would meet up with this man again, feeling in my bones that we were somehow inextricably bound up in each other's futures.

Between meetings with Captain Turner and others, I spent pleasurable time with Vivienne and her father. We had a delicious meal together at which I met some of M. Giradeau's colleagues and their wives. I was much gratified to be included. It was clear I was considered a safe escort for Vivienne. Annie and I also spent time together. She showed me parts of Plymouth I had not known about and introduced me to some of her friends. Perhaps just as important, she advised me as to what new clothing to buy and where to find it. I had been given money by Sir F. to buy myself some suitable clothes for more gentrified living, and Annie advised a white shirt with full sleeves and ruff, black hose and shoes, a deep blue doublet, and a leather sleeveless jerkin. I didn't recognize myself when fully adorned. Plymouth was becoming another home for me as I gathered friends and acquaintances. I had developed a thorough familiarity with the town and surrounding countryside. In my spare time, I tried to find out what had happened to the naval cox'n David Tremaine, but nobody seemed to know anything about him. Captain Turner played dumb, and I wasn't going to approach Sir F. on the subject. Tremaine seemed to have disappeared completely.

I met Robert Gorges and found him to be a serious, active young man and a good horseman. He looked like a younger, clean-shaven version of his father. Slim and intelligent, he was at first reserved with me. He was the product of a privileged background and had received excellent schooling. Now he would join the army with the idea it would further broaden his mind. His father had made him work and learn to lead men, as well as to ride and become an excellent swordsman. I don't altogether know what he made of me, but he was able to ask perceptive questions that got to the essentials of whatever we spoke of. He didn't seem to know—or maybe he didn't like or trust—Epenow and Assacomet. Anyway, I got little out of him about them.

I write this entry on the eve of my journey back to Dorchester and Christmas with Aby.

CHAPTER 9

Journal entry— *10 to 15 December 1613*

One major benefit of close association with the Gorges family is their concern
for appearances. Maddie's saddle and riding tackle, which I had acquired from
her previous owner, were greatly worn. Having ridden bareback most of my
life, I wasn't particularly bothered. For me, the delight was to have a horse of
my own at all. But in the stables, Robert introduced me to the head groom,
Trevor Heeley, and at Robert's direction, he showed me into the tack room.
Peg upon peg of shining leather, brass, and steel greeted me, with the saddles
in their own room. I came away with as fine a set of bridles, reins, stirrups,
straps, and saddle with bags as I could ever have wished for. Robert dismissed
my profuse thanks with a wave. Surplus—past their usefulness. He seemed
happy to be rid of them. He was not particularly gracious, which I put down
to discomfort with my obvious pleasure and gratitude.

On the day we left, Robert and I headed out on the coach road to Exeter. It
was a clear day, cold, good for riding. Maddie positively pranced as we set off on
the forty-five-mile ride to Exeter. Robert's steed was equipped as if for a royal
procession. Magnificent—but perhaps a bit overdone. Maybe Robert likes his
creature comforts o'er much. The road rose as we approached Dartmoor, cresting
a hill the moors spread before us way off into the distance north and west of the
road we were taking. The air was so clean it sparkled, the rolling moorland in
rich hues of brown and gray, fading to shades of dusky blue and umber in the
distance. Specks of birds—raptors—wheeled and hovered, looking for prey. We
talked in a casual way, friendly without being too inquisitive about each other,
and shared companionable silences. We rested the horses by clattering streams,
letting them browse on long rein. On open grassy strips we gave the horses their
heads and had exhilarating canters with the occasional gallop. As time passed,

however, Robert became moody and withdrawn, and his reserve increased the nearer we got to Exeter. He told me that we would be parting our ways soon, as he had an appointment to keep. My inn was in the center of Exeter, a different direction from where he was headed, he said. I asked him what was wrong. He didn't answer for a while.

As we reached the crossroads he looked at me and shook my hand. In turning his horse's head away, he said, "I am to meet the family of a man I killed."

He rode off, leaving me in stunned silence with questions spinning. He looked back to see me, like a mounted statue, staring back at him, and raised an arm. I did likewise, and with that we went our separate ways. My way was to South Street and the White Hart, where I was to stay the night. The next day I had some sixty miles to ride. Clouds had come in overnight. It looked like snow. I was given instructions at the White Hart to follow the old Roman road, as far as I was able, which would take me, via Axminster, directly to Dorchester. The countryside was turning brown, and the meadows and ploughed fields were encroaching on the open land. Farmers were increasingly enclosing the land by hedging and ditching. Small farmers who'd previously used the open land were being forced off it, into penury. Certain parts of the Roman road could no longer be followed, where it had been enclosed or otherwise ploughed up.

I felt I was coming home. As I walked Maddie over the farmland, memories came back of me as a boy helping the ploughman with his team of oxen, ploughing the furrows to form "S"-shaped strips into furlongs, exploring the endless meadows of sheep, woodland filled with deer, and innumerable foxes and rabbits. Reaching Axminster and the Cross Keys in the village center, I had an early supper. I couldn't get Robert's situation out of my mind as I brooded over a final drink. With insufficient information, increasingly fanciful and wild explanations coursed through my head. I didn't sleep well in the crowded sleeping quarters with much snoring and farting from my bedfellows. I was away early. Maddie was pleased to be off. She had been well fed and bedded down in her own stall. They had their priorities right, horses over humans.

Snow had started overnight and continued lightly into the morning. Even wearing all my warm clothes I was cold. Our breath blew clouds of steam, and only a hard early ride on a wide, flat swath warmed us up. The snow was barely an inch deep. We needed to take more care. I didn't want Maddie turning a fetlock in a rabbit hole hidden by the snow. The Roman road had kept to the ridges of the Devon and Dorset landscape. The views under the scudding clouds were distant and welcoming. I was on familiar territory as we came up to Eggardon and the three west-facing rings of its defensive camp. How we had played and fought all over the hill, gangs of us, refighting the battles of our history—Romans against Britons, Normans against Saxons, Stephen against Matilda, the War of the Roses. Then there were the ghost stories told over a fire at night, with the wind howling through the trees that skirted the hill below us, every night sound suddenly unnatural. The headless horseman, the white-gowned mother carrying a child in her arms, the shapes of wild beasts—we thought we saw them all. I rode the remaining miles in the gathering gloom.

By the end, I was glad to be off the hill and into Dorchester. I passed through the west gate onto West Street to the Patriarch's house. I hoped my message had been forwarded by Obi. Mrs. White greeted me with a warm embrace. Maddie was taken round to the stables to be given suitable attention. She had served me well and was tired. I was ushered into the kitchen, in time for supper with Mrs. White and her boys. Reverend White was out but would be back later. The next few days passed in a whirl. P. was too busy to spend any time with me other than in passing. He was affable though, and promised to sit with me to find out what Sir F. was doing and answer any questions I had.

I spent much time with Aby, welcomed by her and her father—becoming, it seemed, a part of the family. Christmas is a heavy burner of candles. Old Man Baker's badly damaged chandler's shop was in much use, with the dark of winter upon us. A temporary roof and walls kept most of the snow out. The roaring fire kept us warm as I helped Aby with her candlemaking duties. We had been friends for so long that our close companionship remained largely unaffected by my new role as formal suitor. Aby's latent wry humor had me surprised, confused, delighted, and oftentimes crying with laughter.

Will was away with his father in London. I was told he would be back for Christmas. Charlie and his mother had settled in. He was working as a laborer for a builder. Mrs. Swain, arm healed, if a little bent, was back working as a washerwoman. She had a number of clients, including the Whites.

I rode Maddie down to Weymouth to make contact with Mr. Brown and the rest of *Rosie*'s crew. On the way, I stopped in Bincombe to check on Johnny Dawkins. The vicar was in his vestry. We sat in a pew and he told me how difficult it had been, especially for Mrs. Dawkins. Johnny had been very low, wanting to kill himself. Reverend Stoddard had eventually persuaded Johnny to confess his "sins," which, in retrospect, they both recognized was a turning point. Johnny had long carried the secret burden of what had happened to him, and it had burned into his very soul. I did not put much faith in confessions, but I saw the merit in unburdening. Reverend Stoddard had been helping Johnny and also Mrs. Dawkins. He believed that with time

Johnny would be able to work again. I told him that Gunt, the perpetrator, had been caught without blame being attached to Johnny. In fact, the sodomy was deemed an act of grievous bodily harm, and Johnny was considered an innocent victim. Mr. Stoddard thought that information would greatly relieve Johnny and help his recovery. I didn't tell him Gunt had escaped. He thought it best I didn't meet Johnny, as it would bring back a bleak period in his life. I understood, and before going on my way, I asked him to give Johnny my best wishes when he thought the time appropriate.

Silas was still at the King's Arms. I spent time with him, while leaving Maddie in his capable hands. He was due to return to Dorchester before Christmas to see his family and hoped to be working back there in the new year. He was keen to learn of my new life as a sailor. My stories opened a reservoir of memories for Silas. We had not talked together of his previous life other than the odd ribald story. Now I found myself listening to a man whom I had not really known. Silas had a deep fondness for the sailing life, in spite of—perhaps even *because* of—its hardships, and he sorely missed it. My involvement enabled him to re-live his experiences through me, and he had no one else who could fulfill that role. He'd never married, and his aged mother lived near Dorchester with Silas's younger brother, a farm laborer. In his eyes I had become an adopted son. As he'd grown older, the hardness in him had softened. I had been a little afraid of the man as my mentor. Now, I saw him as a kind and caring older friend. I need to make sure I kept in touch with him. I also wanted to help him settle into a working life that gave him some security and peace of mind.

Rosie had a skeleton crew under the command of Peg Jones. Mr. Brown was away for some part of the winter, and many of the crew likewise. Obi was aboard, a willing and enthusiastic apprentice sailor in training, but sometimes his crewmates despaired of him. I had a drink with the off-watch crew ashore at the King's Arms, then rode back to Dorchester.

The following morning, I met with P. in his study, a room filled with books. There must have been at least fifty. I had never seen that many in one place, even at the library at Mr. Cheeke's school. I brought him up to date, though I did not mention Gunt and his escape. P. was most interested in what Sir F. was doing with respect to Northern Virginia. He was aware Sir F. had sent numerous ships across the Atlantic—exploratory expeditions as well as attempts at settlement. He was interested in the Indians to whom Sir F. was teaching English. He was intrigued at the idea that I had been asked to befriend them.

P. was certain that Sir F. was missing a critical ingredient. He felt it would be difficult to recruit men to form a settlement—a *plantation,* he called it. Such a plantation would need a sense of community and purposeful commitment. Sir F.'s men were paid to be there, so they had no inherent loyalty or commitment. In P.'s view, a successful settlement needed, above all else, settlers with a powerful reason to leave their homes and life as they knew it to risk a perilous adventure into an unknown hostile place with their families. The reason would need to be compelling. In that context, P. mentioned the problems of the Separatists who had escaped persecution in England and fled to Leiden. He said he was most concerned about them.

I had heard some about the Separatist movement and asked why he was concerned. He leaned back in his chair, put his hands behind his head, and looked at the ceiling. I waited.

"Isaac, as you probably know, Reverend Cheeke and I have considerable sympathies for the Separatist group in Leiden, living as a community under the leadership of their pastor, Mr. Robinson."

"Sorry, sir. Before you go on, I don't understand. Why are they being persecuted?"

"Simply put, they see vestiges of popery in the hierarchy and ceremony of the Church of England, and rather than seek to reform, or purify from within, they decided to separate from the Church. The Church feels threatened by an increasing number of reformist clergy throughout the country. Coming down hard on Pastor Robinson, they hope to deter others."

"Have they deterred others?"

"No. There's a Separatist movement gathering momentum. The response by the authorities varies. Some bishops turn a blind eye, others prosecute with fanatical zeal. They worry that disaffected parish clergy will turn whole communities against the institution of the Church of England, and therefore against the authority of the king, which is why I am keeping a close eye on Leiden. Other groups led by their priest might find it intolerable to live in an atmosphere of potential and actual persecution. In which case, fleeing abroad to start a new life where they are free to practice their beliefs is clearly an option."

"Then the Leiden group having escaped can now worship as they like?"

"Well, in part. The Leiden group had motivation: They had been driven there from Nottinghamshire in 1607 by persecution and the desire to worship in their own way. They went as families and took all they had with them. The problem now is how to overcome the alien environment they've found themselves in. They have become part of a foreign, oppressive community of the Dutch. They want to remain English, but their children are becoming Dutch. They are trying to retain their own sense of community, but are totally dependent on the Dutch for work. Rural people, they are now confined to an urban life. They never owned land in England, and worked without hope of that level of status and independence. Even so, in England they'd worked and lived as Englishmen on the land they loved. In Leiden they have none of that, yet they can't return. The faith that sustains them is too strong to cede to the religious authorities in England."

P. said he follows news of the Southern Virginia settlement with much interest, but recognizes the inherent limitations of that settlement, devoid as it is of religious and community cohesion. He is therefore paying attention to what Sir Ferdinando is doing by attempting to send settlers to Northern Virginia, land of boundless resources. That land could be owned by communities that could immigrate and prosper without overarching civic and religious authority. They could build their own villages with their own church and elect their own leaders.

"Tell me, what do you think of Sir Ferdinando?" P. asked.

"Well, sir, he is very much a military man. A leader with specific objectives. He lives well, certainly a significant person in his business and social circles. I like and greatly respect him. He has an engaging personality. I admire him for all that he has taken on and pursues with little support from the state or the town."

"Have you met his family?"

I said I had not met Lady Ann, his wife, nor his elder son John, who lived in London. I did tell him about Robert and the reason he had ridden to Exeter.

P. nodded, said he had heard something, and that what he had heard had been behind the question he'd asked me. He said he didn't know much, but that what he did know didn't reflect well on Robert.

"The boy is certainly dutiful," he said. "His father has given him a difficult assignment, which it seems he is completing. His impending army career will build backbone, we hope."

P. returned to the subject of Sir F. and the settlement trips. He had heard that Sir F. was planning another major expedition. He asked me how I would react if the *Sweet Rose* were to be chartered by Sir Ferdinando to participate in that expedition to Northern Virginia.

I was stunned. The idea of going to Northern Virginia had never occurred to me.

"I don't know, sir."

I was overcome with excitement. Unbelievable! What an adventure.

"Well, as you know the *Sweet Rose* is half owned by Mr. Bushrode," he continued. "I am reliably informed that Mr. Bushrode is considering Sir Fer-dinando's invitation to participate on some basis. Your knowledge of this information is not to be divulged. Nor are you ever to admit your foreknowledge should this trip come to pass. Do you understand me?"

"I do, sir."

"The reason I am telling you is to allow you to prepare yourself. If it happens, you will probably be asked to volunteer. It's a dangerous journey," he warned. "I would like you to go. I need eyes and ears to give me an honest and intelligent appraisal of the situation and conditions over there."

I felt overwhelmed, but P. continued, oblivious to the effect his words were having. "I know you are young, but imagine yourself with wife, even children. I want you to think about the conditions under which you would be interested— no—*eager* to start a new life in Northern Virginia, together with a community of other families."

His words were almost too much for me to take in. I could not imagine taking such a voyage, gaining at some point a wife and family, doing the job of being P.'s eyes and ears, and leaving England—perhaps forever.

P. realized he had gone too far. "Isaac, I can see I have startled you. I just want you to consider the idea and imagine what it might be like. You would be going to a new land. People who have seen the place give accounts that it is beautiful but rugged, with more extreme weather than we have here. There is also a population of natives that might be hostile."

"Aye, sir," I said. "If you would allow me, I need to put my thoughts in order. May we discuss this again over the next few days?"

"Of course."

And we did. P. was concerned that he was placing me in a difficult position. It was clear that Sir F. had some new role in mind for me, although we did not know exactly what it was or even if it was still in play. It seems, however, that my days as a courier to La Rochelle were over. All I knew was that Sir F. wanted me to get to know his Indians on my return from Dorchester. P. said that I was a trusted and useful servant to Sir F., and that if I kept my wits about me I could continue to provide services to both men without any sub-stantial conflict. P. and Sir F. were pursuing similar goals but with potentially very different outcomes. Without dissembling I felt I could report back what I saw to both. They would use the information in whichever way they wanted. So, with these complexities settled somewhat in my mind, I determined to enjoy the rest of my time in Dorchester.

Letter to Isaac—*24 December 1613*

Dear Isaac,

I had planned to be back in Dorchester by now. My father needed to go up to London on business. He thought it would be a good experience for me to accompany him. We had planned to go to the Globe Theatre to see Mr. Shakespeare's latest play—*The Tempest*—which P. recommended. It is partly about Sir George Somers and his misadventures being shipwrecked in the Bermudas while sailing to Virginia in 1609. Unfortunately, unbeknownst to us, the Globe was burned down last June and hasn't yet been rebuilt. Still, we did see *The Tempest* at the Blackfriars Theatre. I didn't discern much of Sir George in the play. Apart from a shipwreck there wasn't a mention. I suppose the Bermudas provided a starting point. P. said he found the play an allegory about the current situation in which people sailing from England and shipwrecked could be likened to Pastor Robinson being "shipwrecked" in Leiden, with Prospero standing in for Robinson. Eventually, Prospero goes home, where the authorities accept his beliefs and welcome his return.

It seems we will be in London over Christmas and won't be returning till after Twelfth Night. I imagine you will have returned to your ship or Plymouth by then. In which case, I am most sorry to have missed you. I am hoping that you will have left more material for me to read. I am quite excited for the next installment. About all that you describe, I say better you than me. I know P. wants you to continue to keep him abreast of Sir F.'s activities.

Will

Journal entry—*16 December 1613 to 7 January 1614*

I will be riding back to Plymouth first light tomorrow. I need today to recover, having spent the Twelve Days in merriment. The latter part of last year has made me appreciate the family and the community spirit that is Christmas at home. Previously, though always exciting and something eagerly anticipated, I had a childlike acceptance as the Twelve Days unfolded. I enjoyed without understanding the significance and the long history. I'd always enjoyed the Christmas song "The Twelve Days of Christmas." What I hadn't realized, until P. explained it to me, was that the significance of each gift was thus: My true love is God, the partridge is Jesus, the turtle doves are the Old and New Testaments, the French hens are the Holy Trinity, the calling birds are the four Gospels, and so on. P. preferred that the complete cycle wasn't generally known as, he said, the song or carol was a Catholic-inspired code to remind people of the dogma of their faith. I asked P. why, then, did he—a staunch anti-Catholic—allow it to be sung.

"It's a pretty song," he replied. "The children love it and think it is about family. Why spoil it for them, when they don't know the hidden meaning? In fact, only the older Catholics in this parish have any understanding, and some of the gifts in the song are ones we Protestants appreciate, too."

P. wanted a Yule log for the huge hearth in his house. It had to have been aged to burn, but not too fast, as it had to last through the Twelve Days. On Christmas Eve, P's family with me, arm in arm with Aby—who was glowing, sparkling of eye, in constant, happy, even gleeful enjoyment—went off through the thickening snow to the woods with saw and sledge. We found a long-fallen tree from which we cut a four-foot-long log about twelve inches thick. We dragged it back, shouting and laughing. On the way home, Aby, unladylike, more like her old self, was riding the log, driving us beasts of burden forward and homeward with her encouragement.

We hung decorations around the family rooms and hall and arranged green foliage from holly and ivy in long garlands around doorways and windows and over the fireplace. Candles were set. Most important, for me anyway, was the Christmas kissing bough, a circle of woven willow branches festooned with mistletoe and sprigs of holly with their bright red berries. This wreath was hung in the main hall. Anyone entering the house would be met and greeted with a handshake, hug, or kiss—whichever was deemed appropriate. Aby, ever the leader, experimented, with me for her willing accomplice, in all forms of greeting. Mrs. White tutted with a gleam in her eye.

Having prepared for the Twelve Days of Christmas, the first day was Christmas Day itself. We spent the day in religious observance—P. held three separate services, each of which the family celebrated. The yule log was lit from the carefully stored remnants of the previous year's log. It was a quiet, contemplative day. People were at home or in church with their families. By now the snow was six inches deep, higher in drifts. The roads were shoveled clear in front of every house and, if piled too high, taken away by horse and cart.

The second day of Christmas was Boxing Day. The alms boxes in the churches were ceremoniously opened and, with added contributions from the community, the contents were distributed to the needy. There was carol singing prior to and throughout the Twelve Days, which I always enjoyed. We sang the well-loved words with great gusto, if not entirely in tune, Aby's sweet voice soaring above mine. We gathered in groups and visited neighbors in the evenings, singing outside their houses as the snowflakes covered us. They would bring out cups of hot punch and mince pies if we were lucky. Alms were offered which we collected and, at the end of the evening, put in the alms box in the church. We went wassailing, where the singing was more secular and the company more convivial than caroling. The evenings always seemed to end at one or more of the Dorchester area inns. The following mornings we were disciplined with headaches.

At the first dinner hosted by P. and Mrs. White, I wore my new clothes for the first time. Aby, escorted by her father, had been invited. When she arrived, I was waiting for her in the hallway. She stared at me, and then gave a long, slow curtsey, to her father's great amusement. I bowed deeply to them both, laughing. She removed her hooded cloak. Our love crackled around us as we embraced under the mistletoe. Her long, golden brown hair cascaded over her shoulders, no longer bunched under a cap. I felt as though I were seeing her for the first time. I marveled at her large brown eyes and perfect oval face, her slight blush, soft red lips, and her heart-stopping figure. Her blue-gray dress was open-necked, revealing her milky white, unblemished neck and shoulders.

The Whites were warm and hospitable, and that hospitality begat lavish hospitality in return. At that one time of the year, the community came together irrespective of anyone's station in life to share and celebrate the glow of Christmas. It seemed that bad blood had been temporarily leached from Dorchester's collective body.

With Epiphany, Christmas was over for another year. I wondered where I would be next Christmas. I wondered where *Aby and I* would be. We celebrated my birthday together away from crowds. She cooked me a lovely meal and we went for a long walk. Aby ensured we maintained our somewhat chaste relationship, but my departure and possible absence for some time drew us together. I was also mindful of my promise to P. I couldn't pass on to Aby the foreboding I felt about the length of time I might be away, but she sensed my concern. Luckily, Aby also had a delicious sense of the absurd. We were like children who delighted in each other's company, and then again, not like children. Aby deftly steered any unpleasant emotions and questions into safer waters. We left each other with the certain knowledge we were bound to each other for the rest of our lives. Absence, then, became merely an inconvenience, nothing more. We had our entire lives together to look forward to.

CHAPTER 10 ———

Journal entry—*8 to 14 January 1614*

In Plymouth, 10 January, I returned to the Minerva and left word with Sir
F.'s office that I was back. Next morning, Captain Turner came by the inn and
escorted me to see Sir F. It was a quick meeting. After an exchange of pleasantries, he told me to make my way to Wraxall Court. I was to introduce myself to
Mr. Wellings, Sir Edward's household steward, who would be expecting me. I
was to follow his directions in all things, as I had been assigned, on a temporary
basis, to the Wraxall household under his authority. Mr. Wellings had served
in the army under Sir F. and was his sergeant at the siege of Rouen. Sir F. had
introduced him to Sir Edward, who employed Mr. Wellings first to manage his
stables, and then to be his steward for the past ten years.

Sir F. gave me a sealed packet containing my instructions, addressed to Mr.
Wellings. There was a note requesting that I account for the money previously
provided and informing me that I should consider the amount to have been my
wages paid in advance, covering the months of December and January. Assuming I could prove I was managing my accounts satisfactorily, I could expect
further payment in February and March. Sir F. said that he hoped my assignment would've been successfully completed by then. I was dismissed with the
promise that the skipper would be kept informed of my whereabouts and timetable. I left feeling I was now very much a minion in the Gorges household. As
I'd spent most of the money advanced on my clothes and Maddie, I had just
about enough left to get me to Wraxall.

After getting detailed directions to Wraxall from Captain Turner, I was back
on the road with Maddie by ten a.m. It was a cold, clear day, with the snow
sparkling in the sun under the bluest of skies. I had much on my mind, particularly Robert Gorges and his penitential journey. P. had told me the name of

the man Robert had killed in a quarrel, Alex Hamon, and that the incident had happened a year ago. Robert had been pardoned in court in March of 1613. The killing had been deemed accidental. It was a difficult visit Robert had undertaken or, more likely, had been ordered to undertake by his father. I admired Robert for doing it.

First stop for me was Exeter and a room at the White Hart. It was early evening; the winter weather had caused people to gather early to enjoy warmth, good food, drink, and conversation. I found a nook near the fire. I settled down and fell half asleep over a pot of ale. When I awoke about an hour later, the room had filled with much conversing. At a table close by there was a group of men. I overheard a reference to the anniversary of a death in a local family. One of the men said that his master was still grieving. The grieving had been made worse by a recent incident. "What was that?" his companion asked. I came wide awake.

"You won't believe it, but the man who killed the master's son was due to visit the family before Christmas as a gesture of contrition. It was expected and the gesture appreciated."

"And?"

"The bastard never showed up! The family waited for two days and gave up expecting the visit."

"Did they try and find out what happened?"

"No, the mistress was heartbroken, and the master let it drop."

The following morning, I made an early start on the main road to Taunton, noting it had become colder overnight. Low clouds hung overhead. I had been told by Sir F. to go to the Vivary Arms, as he knew the owners. I was to mention his name and would be looked after. It was a brisk ride, especially as I was distracted, leaving Maddie to make the pace. I was troubled about what I had heard the night before. I was expecting to meet Robert at Wraxall the following day. I had no idea how to deal with this information. It seemed too much of a coincidence not to be Robert they'd been talking about.

Reaching the outskirts of Taunton in the early afternoon, I rode into Wilton to the Vivary Arms. The stables were full, but room was made for Maddie. The name of Sir Ferdinando Gorges opened welcoming doors for me, and I was treated well, despite what appeared to be a full house. After a good night's sleep and a hearty meal, I was ready to continue our journey. I tried to feel less worried. It might have been a coincidence, surely?

This time Maddie struggled with her footing. The wind had picked up and sleet was mixing with the snow on the ground. As we approached

Bridgewater, I decided to stop there for the night. I looked for shelter as we made our way to the river and the quay. I was advised to go down Fore Street to the Cornhill and the Crown Inn, which had stables. After seeing to Maddie, I went to the bar to warm up. The sight of a crippled man reminded me of the last time I saw Gunt. I wondered who'd rescued him and why. Clearly, someone thought Gunt valuable enough to risk much to save him. Was it the information he possessed that had to be protected? Perhaps he was altogether more politically sinister than I had imagined. That speculation set me thinking back on my last trip to La Rochelle, and the Navy cox'n turned spy, David Tremaine. What had he been doing? Clearly a brave man. Talk about opposites—Gunt and Tremaine.

Then there was tomorrow and Sir F.'s directive to think about. I wondered how I might accomplish what Sir F. required of me. What was the situation at Wraxall Court? I wondered what Sir Edward was like. The Indians had been there on and off for years, seemingly dividing their time between Sir F.'s London and Plymouth homes in addition to Wraxall. Robert Gorges seemed to have been indifferent toward them when we rode together to Exeter. I wondered what Mr. Wellings, the steward, thought of them. More to the point, what did they think of their captors, and of England? Still musing, I went to check on Maddie. I gave her a final rubdown and saw she had been fed and watered. Then with relief I went to bed, wanting to make an early start for Wraxall in the morning.

The next morning brought no snow but cold. Road rutted, the sludge of yesterday had frozen overnight. I kept Maddie off the road as far as possible. We completed the thirty-mile ride by late lunch, finding Wraxall Court without trouble. It was an impressive house on high ground with long views over the valley. I rode up the long drive and around to the stables. A groom showed me the kitchen entrance, which led into a large room with a center table. Several people were seated there, eating lunch. A rosy-cheeked, cheerful, round cook oversaw a few serving maids. Mr. Wellings was a forbidding presence at the head of the table. He waited for me to make my way to him. I felt as if I were back on duty.

"Stanfield, sir. Reporting for duty." I almost saluted.

"You are late," he said. "Expected you yesterday, damn it."

"Aye, sir."

"Have you eaten?"

"Aye, sir," I lied.

I did not want to sit down at the tail end of the meal and be interrogated by Mr. Wellings in front of the others. I glanced 'round the table and saw six in all, including two dark-skinned men wearing working men's jerkins, like the others. The taller one was watching me; the other had his head down.

"Good. Mr. Robert Gorges is in the study. He asked to see you as soon as you arrived."

"Aye, sir." I handed him the instructions from Sir F.

He gestured toward a maid to show me the way. I followed her along a dark corridor toward the front of the house. After a knock, I was admitted into the study with a brusque "enter." Robert was slouched on a large leather armchair. He seemed disheveled and not entirely sober. He looked up and did not offer me a chair.

"So, you've come at last," he said. "You are here to befriend the savages, I gather. Good luck. They are surly, stubborn, uncommunicative, and idle. No idea why my father has lavished the time on them. I tried to get to know them, but it was like talking to a brick wall."

I was prepared to continue the relationship that had developed on our ride together, and greeted him in a friendly manner. I was rebuffed. It seemed I was now a member of the household staff, meaning there would be no social intercourse. I asked how his trip to Exeter went.

"None of your damned business."

I looked at him. He appeared uncomfortable and stared out the window.

"Will that be all, sir?" I asked.

He nodded, and I left to find my way back to the kitchen. I was shown the way to Mr. Wellings' office, invited in, and told to sit. Mr. Wellings was reading the instructions I had brought from Sir F. Eventually, he put down the document and for a while just looked at me. I looked back. He had a well-used face—battered even. He had certainly been in the wars. Grizzled hair that was balding, sunken eyes of black under heavy eyebrows, a broken nose, trimmed moustache, and short beard.

"Sir Ferdinando speaks well of you."

Another long pause.

"It seems you've been busy."

"Aye, sir."

"Damn it. That's all you've said to me since you got here. Tell me who you are."

I told him, briefly. He asked pertinent questions and was a good listener. I began to see the man Sir F. and Sir Edward clearly trusted.

"You *haven't* eaten, have you?"

With that he rang a small bell on his desk and a maid came.

"Bring bread and cheese and a pot of ale for my friend here."

It seemed I had passed some test. Sir F.'s evident endorsement had been important, but Mr. Wellings wanted to make up his own mind. While I ate, he explained that Wraxall Court was the Gorges seat owned by Sir F.'s brother, Sir Edward Gorges, who allowed Sir F. to use it as a second home. Sir Edward and family were in London. He described the workings of the household, the domestics, stable staff—grooms and coachmen—estate workers, gardeners, and the like, until he came to the Indians. Apparently, numerous Indians had been quartered at Wraxall over the years. While Sir Ferdinando had them in Plymouth occasionally, there wasn't the same accommodation. For political reasons, he had them stay at his home in Clerkenwell, a village outside London. Two of them were now quartered at Wraxall, as I knew.

"Their names are Epenow and Assacomet," Mr. Wellings continued. "At least that is our understanding of the pronunciation. Epenow appears to be a leader, possibly some kind of chieftain. I have watched him closely. He would make a fine soldier; a man to follow in battle. He is distrustful of us all here. He acts like a prisoner on parole—which, of course he is—civil but distant. He has learned English but does not use it. A difficult man to understand. Sir Ferdinando has had some success in talking with him. I feel it is because Epenow sees Sir Ferdinando as a man of equal rank. Sir Ferdinando always treats him with courtesy, which he clearly appreciates. Mind you, it hasn't improved communication between them to any great extent. Mr. Robert Gorges has tried, but unfortunately that attempt has been a disaster. His appointment to Sir Ferdinando's old regiment will teach him much about men and how to deal with them—that is the hope, anyway."

I was surprised that Mr. Wellings would speak critically of his master's nephew. He saw my look and laughed a little bitterly. He had watched the junior Gorges grow from birth. Robert had much of his father in him, but had not experienced life outside the shelter of the Gorges household. I mentioned that I had ridden with Robert to Exeter before Christmas and that during the journey he had seemed friendly and engaged for the most part. I told Mr. Wellings I was aware of the reason for Robert's journey. He shook his head. It seemed the whole incident had been a serious embarrassment to the family. Sir Edward had needed to be persuaded to allow his nephew to return to Wraxall. In fact, Robert was here to keep him out of mischief until he joined his regiment. Sir Ferdinando had ordered him to make the visit to Exeter as an education in the consequences of one's actions, to help him understand the necessity of standing in other people's shoes and thinking beyond his own self-interest, something he'd have to learn in the army. Mr. Wellings said the trip to Exeter had affected

Robert badly, as he returned a morose man. He wouldn't talk about the meeting with the family of the dead man other than to say it had been difficult. In fact, Mr. Wellings said that he was surprised Robert had made the trip. It showed a depth of character that hadn't been apparent. I said nothing, but I wondered if Robert's morose attitude came rather from guilt.

Returning to the subject of the Indians, Mr. Wellings said that with respect to Epenow, it would be important for me to project that I had sufficient social status in order for him to even consider recognizing my existence. He told me by way of explanation that the other Indian, Assacomet, appeared to be of lower rank to Epenow, and was treated as such by his better. When the two Indians had first met, they'd had difficulty understanding each other. It seemed Assacomet was first taken in an inter-tribal skirmish and shortly afterward captured by Captain Weymouth in 1605 and brought to England. Having been sent back as a guide with Captain Challons in 1606, Assacomet was captured again, this time by the Spanish, and carried to Spain to be sold as a slave. He was severely injured during that capture. Through the efforts of Sir F., Assacomet was freed and returned to Plymouth. I can understand his reserve.

"I must apologize for the way I greeted you at lunch," Mr. Wellings said. "I saw a young lad, late and unapologetic. I had no idea of your importance to Sir Ferdinando, and I cannot abide poor timekeeping. Unfortunately, as a result Epenow will by now have established your social rank as being inferior to him. We must see what we can do to change his mind."

He told me that Sir Ferdinando and Lady Ann would be down tomorrow, Saturday, traveling by coach. They would be taking their son with them to London on Monday, where his regiment was being mustered. Perhaps Robert's moody reserve, which I'd put down to guilt, was more due to foreboding about his upcoming new life as a soldier. At least his father had bought him an officer's rank and privileges. Mr. Wellings suggested I take the rest of the day to find my way around the house and grounds. He would rectify any misunderstanding about my position with the staff. They would be pleased to assist as necessary. As for the Indians, it would probably be best to avoid them and wait for Sir Ferdinando. We should discuss the situation with him and have him advise accordingly.

I returned to the kitchen. The meal over, the men had left. I recognized the importance of a good relationship with the kitchen staff, both to ensure I was suitably well nourished and to keep me abreast of household gossip. I made myself known to the cook, Mary Applethwaite, born and raised in Yorkshire. She'd trained in the kitchens of the Earl of Lincoln, and was now happily ensconced as the queen bee of the Wraxall kitchens. A friendly, motherly woman with an ample bosom encased in a starched white apron, Mary wore a white bonnet covering a mass of gray, curly hair and a smudge of flour on her nose. I gave her a brief summary of my life, including how I had been orphaned, how I was betrothed, in a way, to my childhood sweetheart, and how we were now separated by circumstances. By the end of my account, Mrs. Applethwaite and I were friends for life. A maid showed me to my room, which was to have been in the men servants' quarters in the stable block, but Mr. Wellings had been quick to rearrange matters to establish my social status at a higher level. I was provided with a small bedroom at the end of a distant corridor in the guest wing. There I found a bed, cupboard, and sideboard with a bowl, pitcher, chamber pot, and towel. I could sit at a small separate table before a window and look down three stories to the spacious lawns at the side of the house. My few possessions were in my saddlebags, which had been brought up.

I went to the stable block. Mr. Wellings was crossing the yard as I appeared. It had been swept clean of snow and looked tidy. Grooms were about, as was Epenow, but in the background, clearly not a part of the staff. Mr. Wellings gave me a salute and greeted me with some civility, addressing me as Mr. Stanfield. After a few quick words with him I entered. A groom was seated, polishing tackle. He rose respectfully as I approached. Out of the corner of my eye, I saw Epenow watching. Ignoring him, I went to check on Maddie—who'd been brushed, fed, and watered—before leaving to spend the rest of the daylight exploring my new home. The property was extensive with parkland, with a substantial walled kitchen garden and pleasant walkways along hedge and tree-lined paths. Returning tired and hungry, I was advised by Mrs. Applethwaite that dinner would be served in the secondary dining room at seven p.m. for Mr. Robert Gorges and myself. That could be awkward, I thought. I retired to my room to dress in my finery.

At dinner, Robert was in better form. He'd had a conversation with Mr. Wellings. He acknowledged that my assignment as set by his father was a difficult one, and agreed that my social standing should appear somewhat more elevated than was actually the case. Robert would do his part and was prepared in the short time before leaving Wraxall to maintain cordial relations with me. He wasn't excited about my new clothes, and felt my wardrobe needed to be improved. What I was wearing was more appropriate for daily use than for a gentleman. He would arrange with his valet to find some suitable clothes he no longer wore and have them delivered to my room. I was grateful and said so. The subject of Exeter was not raised. We spent the evening talking about sailing, of which he knew next to nothing, and soldiering, about which I knew a little through Silas's friends, from a foot soldier's viewpoint. Robert had no knowledge of the type of man he was going to meet and command in the army. I advised him that these were not men with many graces, to say the least. The difference between new recruits that I had heard about and the men who had lasted a year of training and discipline was extraordinary. Further, it was my understanding that the better the officer, the more disciplined and reliable the men he commanded. Robert nodded but did not look confident.

He talked about his father's career—rising to the rank of lieutenant colonel, knighted by the earl of Essex at the siege of Rouen, wounded several times, and much respected as a professional soldier. He mentioned how his father's loyalty to Essex had almost cost Sir F. his head. I had heard, obviously, of Essex's treason, but was not aware that Sir F. had been implicated. Robert didn't want to explain. Sir F. was obviously in favor and governor of Plymouth Fort, so the issues were now history, if not forgotten—we could move on. I was intrigued to learn more.

Mr. Wellings served us himself and was happy to join the discussion. He was quick to describe Sir F.'s life as a soldier. He'd caught the tail end of my observations about the type of soldier Robert would be dealing with, and provided a much more detailed picture of the rabble that arrived, pressed or out of prisons, and what strong leadership was able to turn them into. On the continent, the British soldier was considered to be the best fighting man of all. It was a hard-earned reputation. We had a convivial evening and parted company in good fellowship.

Letter to Will—*14 January 1614*

Dear Will,

I am currently resident at Wraxall Court, the family seat of the Gorges family. Along with this letter, I am sending you my latest journal entry together with a letter for Aby. I do wish she could learn to read it for herself and to write back to me. The journal will provide you with my news to date.

I hope you enjoyed London. I am intrigued by Mr. Shakespeare. I wonder if there is a copy of any of his plays here. I will check with Mr. Wellings. There is a regular courier traveling between Wraxall and Plymouth. I will send this packet by that courier, so that it can be taken to Dorchester the normal way.

Isaac

Journal entry—*15 to 22 January 1614*

I have now been working for a week to build rapport with Epenow and Assacomet. It seems there is jealousy between the two of them—at least as far as Epenow is concerned. If attention is paid to Assacomet, Epenow reacts angrily. Such interaction as I've had with Assacomet has needed to be out of sight of Epenow, who clearly feels he is the more important person.

Sir Ferdinando and Lady Ann arrived with much bustle on Saturday, 15 January. I was aware they were due, but not knowing the time of their arrival, I went for a brisk ride to exercise Maddie and my mind. I was in the clothes Annie had helped me buy, which, thanks to Robert's generous donations from his own wardrobe, were now my day clothes. I was returning up the drive when I heard the clatter of the Gorges' coach approaching behind me. I pulled Maddie up and doffed my hat as they drove past. The coach stopped a little ahead of me, and Sir F.'s head appeared at the window. I rode up and wished him good day.

"Stanfield," he said. "Glory be, you look different! Didn't recognize you. Follow me and we'll talk further."

At the front door, Sir F. alighted and reached for the arm of Lady Ann, who with considerable grace descended and smiled at her husband. A groom took Maddie, and I waited, hat in hand.

"Stanfield. Come. Meet Lady Ann."

I was introduced, holding and bowing over the hand outstretched. Lady Ann said a few words before proceeding to the house, where a bevy of servants awaited her at the door—including Mr. Wellings. Sir F. advised that he would like me to join him in the study in one hour, then followed his wife into the house. Servants carrying boxes from the coach trailed him like ducklings. An hour later, fetched by Mr. Wellings from the kitchen, we joined Sir F. in the study. He said that he'd had initial chats with his son and Mr. Wellings each about me. Apparently, the information he received from both was satisfactory. He approved the donation of clothes to me, finer than I'd ever worn before. He agreed that I needed to be seen as having sufficient standing in the household in order to establish some level of communication with Epenow. He was attracted to the leadership qualities in Epenow, but wasn't sure about the worth of Assacomet. He would reserve judgment.

We discussed how best to build my relationship with Epenow. The conversation was mostly between Sir F. and Mr. Wellings. I mostly listened, only speaking when asked to. Sir F. chided me for it.

"First thing, you have to stop being diffident," he said. "You should contribute your thoughts to conversations such as these without being bidden. In the Indians' presence, Mr. Wellings will defer to you and call you 'Mr. Stanfield.' Mr. Wellings will assign a valet to you for the duration of your stay here. You already have a horse, and a groom will be told to make her more presentable."

I raised my eyebrows but saw the sense and didn't say anything. Sir F. studied my face, smiling.

"Your horse—Maddie, is it?—will enjoy the attention and results. I presume you can hunt. I will let it be known locally that you are an honored guest, a close friend of my son, Robert, at Wraxall Court. With that you will likely receive social invitations. Be careful—there are many country ladies with daughters they want to see wedded. As you look and act considerably older than you are, and Robert was born in October '95, it makes sense to give you two more years. Happy nineteenth birthday."

He smiled again at the look on my face.

"Epenow has become intrigued with horses, and spends much time near the stables," Sir F. told me. "He had come to understand that horses were a part of city life—a life he abhorred. As yet he hasn't ridden, but he's clearly intrigued and has taken to following riders on foot, which has roused no small amount of concern in the neighborhood. People don't like being tracked—especially by a well-built foreigner who can keep up with a hard-ridden horse. It seems his speed of foot and stamina are extraordinary."

Given that information, a plan was hatched whereby I would offer to teach Epenow to ride, using that exercise to get to know him. Mr. Wellings would make arrangements with Trevor Heeley to ensure that I was perceived to have full responsibility for organizing and handling the exercise. It also made sense for me to cease engaging with Assacomet, at least until a more appropriate time, whenever that might be. Sir Edward would be apprised of the situation, as would Sir F.'s elder son, John, who lived in London. They both would probably be at Wraxall Court at some point while I was there.

It seemed to me to be a rather elaborate scheme with doubtful outcome, just to get a better idea of Epenow's character and trustworthiness. I voiced these misgivings, mindful of Sir F. 's admonishment of my diffidence earlier. He replied it was vitally important to continue to find and prepare trustworthy, knowledgeable guides to help us navigate "the uncharted waters of the local Indian communities in Northern Virginia," as he put it.

I didn't see any of the Gorgeses again that weekend. I made it my business to stay well clear, understanding that they would soon lose Robert to the army. The three of them left early on Monday morning. I stood at the door with the household until Mr. Wellings whispered of my new status and I stepped back into the house to bid them farewell. Robert remarked that his clothes looked nearly as fine on me as they did on him. We laughed, shook hands, and he was gone after his parents. I returned to the stables, but there was no sign of Epenow. Everyone was respectful—overly much to my mind, as if they were playing a game.

I rode Maddie down the drive and cut through the parkland surrounding the house into the woods beyond. From there, I traversed the open fields toward the coast, some four miles distant. Snow was crisp under hoof. I saw a flock of dunlin shimmer past, heading away from the water. I stopped and turned in the saddle as they flew over me. From the corner of my eye I saw movement—slight but definite—at the edge of the woods from whence I'd come. The birds circled and flew back toward the water. I continued to follow their direction with my head, keeping an eye on that spot of movement. Nothing. I continued toward the coast.

I was daydreaming and not minding my course, riding Maddie alongside a deep ditch, slick with ice and full of water, when a rabbit suddenly started out from under her hooves. Maddie shied, bucked, and threw me off. I hit my head on a rock before sliding down the bank and into the ditch, stunned and underwater. Next thing I knew, I was being hauled out feet-first, spluttering the muddy water from my mouth and throat. It was Epenow beside me, sitting on his haunches looking at me as I finished hacking and sat up. I looked at him, and we stared at each other a long while, though it could only have been a minute. How the hell did he manage to get so close, so quickly? If he hadn't, I would have been in serious difficulty. I nodded to him, considerably obligated and grateful. With that, he rose and quite literally disappeared into the countryside.

I was wet and cold and my head was sore. I rode back to the house at a brisk canter, hugging Maddie for warmth. Once in the stable yard, I slipped off Maddie, gave her to the attendant groom, and turned to enter the house. I saw Epenow watching me. I raised a hand to him as I passed and went looking for a change of clothes and a fire. How on earth did he get back that fast? Mr. Wellings met me in the kitchen and raised an eyebrow at my appearance. He introduced me to my new valet, Mark Appleton, and suggested he accompany me to my room to help me sort myself out.

Later, dried, warmed, and re-clothed, I returned to the stables to seek out Epenow. His duties were variable, which meant he was mostly left to his own devices. As he wasn't a permanent member of the household, he spent much of his time in London. Currently, he was in the tack room, running his fingers over the leather and metalwork. I went up to him, holding out my hand. He turned, and there we stood, as if trying to out-stare each other. Then, slowly, he took my hand and *squeezed*—a strong man.

"Thank you for rescuing me," I said and smiled.

Epenow gave the slightest nod and let go of my hand.

"You like horses?"

He nodded.

"Have you spent any time with a horse, grooming him, mucking out?"

He shook his head.

"Would you like to?"

I had his attention then. Slowly, he looked 'round the tack room—through the windows, into the stables, at the horses in their stalls.

He said, quite simply, "Yes, I would."

I got the sense that his English was a lot better than he let on.

"Come on, then."

I led him first to Maddie's stall. Maddie stuck her head over the half-door, looking for the carrot I had in my hand. I gave it to Epenow.

"Go ahead. Feed her."

He did, tentatively touching her brow. Maddie tossed her head, and Epenow backed off, then tried again. As I watched the two of them, I recognized kindred spirits coming together in the most remarkable way. Time for Epenow to be provided with a horse of his own. I didn't want him stealing Maddie away from me. Trevor was watching the proceedings from afar. I called him over. I suggested that Epenow be given a horse to use while at Wraxall Court. Trevor called over a groom, and I told Epenow to go with him. The two of them went to a stall at the end of the stable block, where a mature and steady chestnut gelding called Corbin had residence. I left Epenow in the stable block and went to find Mr. Wellings in his office. I gave him an update, including an account of what now, in retrospect, seemed to have been my fortuitous fall into an icy ditch. I asked Mr. Wellings why Epenow hadn't had any opportunity to handle horses before. It seemed he had expressed no interest, and Sir F. had only recently started sending Epenow to Wraxall, anyway. Most of the time he'd been in England was spent in London or Clerkenwell. There, horses were regarded as part of the transport scene, not animals with unique personalities.

The following day, I went to the stables early. Epenow was in the stall with Corbin. He had been given some lessons in grooming and mucking out already. Everything clean and tidy, the two of them fast friends.

"Time you learned to ride."

"Yes."

Corbin already had a halter on him, connected to two lines fixed to either side of the stall to hold him steady for grooming purposes. The groom went to fetch a riding bridle with bit and reins, plus a saddle, girth strap, and stirrups. I also asked for a lunging rein. Corbin was saddled up and led to a mounting block. I showed Epenow how to use it. With me holding the bridle, I explained how to mount. I will always remember the joy of my first time on a horse—no saddle then, or reins. The inscrutable Epenow was beginning to border on the scrutable.

"Feel the horse through your legs," I said. "Control comes through the reins and from your legs and feet."

I attached the lunging rein to Corbin's bridle and led him out to the center of the stable yard.

"You have control," I said. "Gather the reins in your hands with a light hold, but keep Corbin's head up. Now, kick gently. Walk forward and steer Corbin by pulling gently on the left rein."

Epenow was a natural rider with a close affinity for Corbin. Even Trevor was appreciative. After a few minutes, I detached the lunging rein and let the two of them walk 'round the yard, changing direction, stopping and starting for about an hour. I told Epenow to ride over to the mounting block and dismount.

"How do you feel?" I asked.

"Sore. Muscles I haven't used," he told me. "My bum aches, but I feel good. When do we go again?"

I told him that his body needed to get used to riding and that was best done in easy stages. We would have another go later in the morning, and again in the afternoon, which we did. After that, I told him he could continue to build knowledge and understanding whenever he wanted, as long as he wasn't a nuisance. Trevor would advise him accordingly. Over the next few days, it quickly became apparent that Epenow wanted to move out of the yard and develop his riding skills in the open country. On a clear, cloudless morning, we rode out of the stables and down the drive. I explained the different gaits of a horse, focusing on trotting and cantering. Epenow was quick to attune his body to Corbin's motion. He became one with his horse. It was a pleasure to see such aptitude. It gave Epenow a sense of freedom, a peace he had obviously and demonstrably missed until then. The plan was unfolding successfully. As I write this entry in my journal, it being 22 January, Epenow has been riding every day with me out in the open fields and woods around Wraxall Court. We have established an easy rapport with each other. I haven't plied him with questions. Instead, we've talked mostly about riding. He speaks English well when he wants to, which seems to be only when he is alone with me. Over the next weeks I want to find out more about him and his home country, but I need to proceed slowly.

I have managed to spend some time with Assacomet, out of sight of Epenow, which is easier now that Epenow lives in the stable when he is not riding. Assacomet's English is not good, and he is not a warrior. He does not give the impression of being a leader in the mold of Epenow. Still, there is an evident depth to him that makes me wonder. His homeland, or at least where he was captured, is near the Island of Monhegan and the St. George's River, whereas Epenow comes from an island called Capawack farther south, beyond Cape Cod. They speak different languages, being from different tribes. Assacomet is an Abenaki, and Epenow a Wampanoag. According to Assacomet, Epenow was captured by Captain Harlow in 1611. I need a better understanding of the flow of Indians back to England and the uses to which they are put, in both England and Northern Virginia. I will talk to Mr. Wellings. I will also ask Sir F. if he has the time and is available.

So I complete another entry. While Aby is a background thought in my daily round, it is at these moments late in the evening, writing my journal, that she becomes an almost tangible presence. Although I am writing this account for Will's safekeeping, she is in my thoughts as I write about my adventures. I wonder what she might be doing this moment, what her thoughts are. I miss her dreadfully.

CHAPTER 11

Journal entry—*23 January to 13 February 1614*

I have settled very well into the life of a country squire. Sir F. and Lady Ann returned from London but went directly to Plymouth, where I was asked to attend him and report progress. I have just returned from Plymouth now, but will record the events since my last journal entry.

For the most part, my days were spent either with Epenow or Assacomet. Epenow has become an accomplished rider in just a few weeks. He has taken to riding Corbin without saddle and stirrups. He says it gives him a much better feel and understanding with the horse, and I must agree with him. As we spent the days wandering on horseback through the countryside, I realized Epenow was constantly alert. I watched and became intrigued. I began to ask questions about what he was doing. The only way I can explain what he told me is that he was using all his senses to be a part of the natural world around him. He saw, he heard, he smelt, he felt. He interpreted all the signs. He put everything in the right order. The movement, no, the very *lives* of the animals, rabbits, foxes, deer, and birds. He had extraordinary eyesight, and was able to separate smells into a hundred variants. As he moved through the woods and fields, he seemed to leave only minimal evidence of his passing without effort. Being a country boy, I was able to track animals and detect their behavior, but I was a total novice compared to Epenow. I watched and I learned, gaining much, but of little consequence compared to Epenow's prowess. His skills came, I believe, from his belief that he was both part of and partner with nature. He was entrusted to care for it, to pass it on undamaged.

"Does that include people?" I asked Epenow.

"People are a problem," he replied.

I was able to ask more personal questions. It seemed his calm demeanor concealed the angry man beneath. He had been tricked, captured, and held prisoner in a foul, stinking ship's hold for weeks. He survived because he had friends who'd been captured with him. When they reached London, they were paraded, poked, and prodded, his dignity and privacy shredded. People paid money to view him. They seemed pleased that this *savage*, as they called him, was able to speak a few words of English. They admired his wit, because he could greet them in their own tongue, saying "Welcome, welcome." He was an exotic performing animal.

Eventually, the Indians were separated and Sir Ferdinando assumed responsibility for him. At which point life became bearable. It was explained to him the purpose of his capture. What had stuck in his mind and remained a constant sore was the arrogance of the English sailor, Harlow, who'd captured him. If Epenow had been invited to go to England to represent his people, to learn their language and their ways in order to return as guide and interpreter, he might have accepted the offer. Sir F. seemed an honest man, unlike Captain Harlow. In spite of the clear benefits to both the English and the Indians in the strategy Epenow laid out, he didn't trust the English. There had been too many Indians captured, not only by the English, but by the Spanish, too. Now there was complete distrust on the part of all his people. Any captain inviting Indians aboard their ship, in line with Sir F.'s strategy, would be ignored, ridiculed, or attacked, resulting in probable loss of life and even deeper enmity.

He didn't talk about his life back home, though he longed to get back. He didn't want to dwell on the life lost to him. I said I thought the whole idea was for him to go back with another ship. Yes, he said. He understood the English wanted him to lead them to the gold and copper mines they had heard about. I expressed surprise, hoping he would be more forthcoming, but he didn't elaborate. We ended that conversation with him telling me he would lead them anywhere they wanted if it meant he could go home. At other times, we played hubbub, a game he introduced me to. We couldn't play it at Wraxall Court, as it is a gambling game—strictly forbidden in that God-fearing house. Hubbub is a noisy game. Indians take it seriously, even playing family against family or tribe against tribe through a representative player. Every roll of the dice is accompanied by shouts of "hub!" "hub!" They are serious gamblers, too. Epenow, given the opportunity, would have gambled everything he had to win, even things that didn't belong to him, like Corbin. I enjoyed the game. Great fun, but I was most unhappy at Epenow's unhealthy attitudes when playing gambling games. It seemed out-of-character. When we played, it was for fun rather than money.

I asked him about fighting. Stories abounded from explorers that different

Indian tribes were more or less warlike. How do young Indians train to be warriors? If one tribe is dominant, would they not overcome all the other tribes, resulting in one nation only? Complicated questions, he said. Tribes in his homeland were, for the most part, each fixed in their own locality. They grew, hunted, and cared for the land they called home. There wasn't the sense of ownership that seemed to drive the English. Tribes didn't fight over land that didn't belong to them. Young warriors wanted to prove themselves as being brave, and it is much braver, and harder, some would say, to defeat warriors from another tribe without killing them. Sometimes, a tribe felt a wrong had been committed by another tribe, which was not resolved peacefully. It still had to be resolved. There were various levels of non-peaceful resolution which could escalate into a major attack, the result of which could be a few deaths, but more likely the captured warriors would be enslaved and the women taken as wives to strengthen the breeding stock. He said new chiefs needing to make a mark could cause unrest, and that some tribes were inherently hostile, so neighboring tribes would make treaties with each other for protection. They needed to have warriors capable of defending themselves. More disquieting was the influence of the foreign traders. Greed was changing the attitude of the Indian toward ownership. What they had to sell, they wanted to protect.

We talked about his feelings toward England and the English coming to his country. He said his country was huge and beautiful, with unlimited resources. People lived well, looked after their land and each other. It was a perfect existence. Then he came to England and saw more people in an hour than he'd seen in his whole life. If England was more like London than the countryside where we were, then he was terrified of that teeming mass of humanity flowing like a huge wave over his land. England is powerful and wealthy, yet it has terrible poverty, the like of which he could never have imagined. Why is England unable to feed its own people? He sees Wraxall Court and other huge residences owned by single families. He sees palaces in London, and people dressed and living in incredible luxury. All of it surrounded by people with nothing. Nothing but the stench and diseases of their lives. Even in Clerkenwell, miles outside London, the smell of London was gagging. The specter of death from malnutrition or disease sat on every shoulder. It was a sobering judgment.

Epenow was very strong and fit. We wrestled occasionally, once he had come to trust me. Indian wrestling tends to favor using different parts of the body for different forms, such as arm wrestling and leg wrestling. Even body wrestling was done standing chest-to-chest, attempting to push one's opponent back using only the chest. I was whipped every time, although I learned technique and timing from Epenow, rather than brute strength. I showed him our form of wrestling, and despite his strength I was able to pin him fairly easily. He was quick to learn and agile. He was surprised that I was clearly stronger than he'd realized. He became more respectful, more thoughtful, and, as a result, he was the victor as often as not.

Early on we went hunting for game. Epenow had his bow. A shorter bow than we use, but accurate to 100 yards. We were able to provide Mary in the kitchens with a steady flow of rabbit and pigeon. I warned Epenow off the deer—they were protected. Sir Edward would have us in chains if we shot any on his land, and, not knowing the extent of his land, we decided not to shoot any. Epenow was quick. He could release two arrows—even three—to my one. He was keen to retrieve every arrow. He rarely missed, but when he did, he at least regained the arrow. I did not introduce Epenow to the crossbow or fowling piece. I had a sense that what his mind didn't know, it wouldn't be able to ponder.

I was summoned to Plymouth to report to Sir F.

"You seem most impressed with Epenow," he said.

"I am, very much so."

"Should we send him back?"

"Yes. He is desperate to get back. The promise of a return will commit him to anything required of him."

"Do you trust him?"

"I do, sir," I told him honestly. "But I have a very different relationship with him than probably any other Englishman he might meet. I think you will have difficulty holding on to him. If he wants to desert, it will be difficult stopping him unless you kill him."

"We won't go that far. He has the potential to be helpful to us in Northern Virginia, but not in England. You have done well. You should know that we intend to send him in the next month or two. Captain Hobson will command the expedition. You can advise Epenow accordingly."

"And Assacomet, sir?"

"We have plans for him to go, too. We will talk about him another time."

"A very different man, sir," I said.

"You should know that I plan to send another boat to Northern Virginia in secret, probably early next year, to provide me with a detailed understanding of exactly what is going on there. There is clear evidence of English settlements, if any besides Monhegan can be even called that, in Pemaquid and islands along the coast to Sagadahoc. I am in discussions with Mr. Bushrode and your

Captain Brown to charter the *Sweet Rose*. It will be a difficult and possibly dangerous voyage."

He was flicking through pages on his desk as he was speaking. He stopped and looked at me. My stomach gave a lurch.

"I believe you would be an important, if not vital, member of the crew."

"I would be happy to go, sir."

"Good. You will be spending time in Assacomet's homeland. Go back to Wraxall and find out from him all you can about the area and the Indians there."

With that I was dismissed and returned to Wraxall. P.'s sources had been spot-on.

Journal entry—*14 to 27 February 1614*

While continuing to spend pleasurable time with Epenow riding most days, I focused on Assacomet. Over the past weeks I had been present with him, rather than actively engaged. He was polite but distant. He commented on the peace that enveloped Wraxall Court and how it was different from London and Plymouth, where he'd spent much of his time. He was vague about what kept him engaged. He had been taken from his tribe eight years ago. He'd had extraordinary adventures, but Assacomet did not want to talk about his earlier life. He had become attached to the team of gardeners whose primary responsibility was the large walled kitchen garden at Wraxall Court. Being winter, seedlings were grown and nurtured in the glass houses, and most days Assacomet could be found there. He'd established a good relationship with one or two of his fellow gardeners, their conversations centering on plants and plant life. His command of conversational English did not seem to improve notably, however. As March approached, heavy spade-work was required, which he threw himself into. I had heard that Indian men spent their time being warriors and hunters. Crop growing was the responsibility of the women. Presumably, Assacomet adapted to local customs. Perhaps he still considered himself a slave without status, from his original capture by Indians. With time pressing, I now started to push him more to tell me about his homeland. He was unresponsive. I had to accept that, despite my success befriending Epenow, I was unlikely to break through Assacomet's reserve.

For all this time, I had been largely unaware of the outside community. Apart from occasionally meeting neighbors on horseback, I had kept to myself. One evening, with nothing else to do, I decided to walk down to the local inn. The barroom was packed as I entered, and noisy. As I approached the bar, the noise lessened and there was silence. I had been focusing my attention on my wallet, but once I noticed the silence I looked up and found I was the center of attention. Surprised, I looked around. No animosity as far as I could tell. It seemed I was a major curiosity that needed inspecting. Making my way to the bar, I was greeted by the barmaid.

"Evening, Mr. Stanfield. What can I get for you?"

"Do I know you?"

"No, sir, but we know you. At least, we know you are from Wraxall Court."

The conversations I had interrupted on my entry resumed, and soon the tavern was as noisy, or even more so, than before. As I paid for my ale, I was tapped on the shoulder and Mark, my valet, invited me to join him with some of his colleagues at a corner table some distance from the bar. As we walked over, I passed a few total strangers, who each looked me in the eye and smiled, making some gesture of respect. Room was made for me at the table. Mark introduced me to the others. They seemed to be servants from estates in the local area.

I remarked at the manner in which I was greeted when I first entered the inn.

"Well, sir," one of them replied. "There is little that goes on in this part of the county that isn't known about, commented on, and protected by the local population."

"Protected?" I asked.

"Yes, sir. The gentry belong to the people. What goes on among the gentry is of abiding interest. It adds to the texture of the community, like family, but it stays in the family. You and the Indians are an amazement to us. Well, *you* aren't, but what you're doing is. We are proud that such things are happening here. We talk about it and build whole adventures around what we see. Your arrival tonight was startling—like a hero stepping out of an adventure story into real life."

It was an enjoyable evening. Mark and I returned to Wraxall Court together. He passed on to me one bit of startling news: Assacomet was seeing a girl from the village. Though they were being discreet, a few people had expressed some disquiet.

A couple of days later I was riding Maddie along a bridle path through the local woods when I heard raised voices ahead. I slowed, walking Maddie quietly to the edge of a clearing. Three men had Assacomet surrounded, threatening him. At that moment, two of the men grabbed Assacomet while the third swung a wooden club against the side of his head. I rammed my heels into Maddie, and we launched ourselves into the clearing. At a cry of warning from one of the men, all three jumped back from the prone Indian. One man grabbed Maddie's bridle, hauled her head 'round and down. The others grabbed at me, half out of my saddle, and pulled me off. I was on my feet and at them. My only weapon my dirk. The man with the club swung at me, heavily. Bad if it connected but good if he missed, as he would be off balance. I ducked, he missed, and I stabbed him in his right shoulder. He cursed, dropped the club, and backed off. The other two had become entangled with Maddie but had cleared her away and were advancing on me.

"What are you doing?" I yelled. "You are risking death for the damage you do."

They paused, confused. I made a feint to my left and swung right, slashing a coat and drawing blood from the second man. They were wavering. I stepped forward toward the third man, dirk high. His eyes and hands lifted toward the dirk and I kicked him hard in his privates. He went down with a groan, clutching himself.

"Sit," I ordered. "No, together."

They sat on the ground, groaning and disconsolate. I went over to Assacomet. He was bloody and dazed but coming out of it. Back to the forlorn group.

"What the hell are you playing at?" I asked them again.

"It's that savage. He is seeing my sister," said the man whose shoulder I punctured.

"So? Does your sister mind having that gentleman seeing her?" I demanded. "Probably not. What concerns do you have?"

"He's a foreigner. He has strange ways. He might be bewitching her."

"What would your sister do if she knew you and two of your friends attacked her friend?"

Assacomet got to his feet, wiped the blood from his eyes, and walked over.

"What do you say?" I asked him.

He looked down at the brother. He worked the English he wanted to say 'round his tongue. Slowly and haltingly, he shamed the men in his broken English.

"She is gentle and kind," he said. "She sees in me a lonely man far away from his home. She comforts me with sweet words. We do not touch. We walk together. Because of what you have done, I can no longer enjoy that friendship. You must tell her that I will not see her again." With that, he walked away.

I looked at them and shook my head.

"You are stupid, bloody idiots."

I mounted Maddie and continued on back to Wraxall. The next day, Assacomet came to me and thanked me for rescuing him from a nasty situation. He had a black eye, a cut, and a large bruise on the left side of his face. It had been cleaned. No lasting harm done, it seemed. We shook hands and went about our separate business.

Later that day, I sought Assacomet out in the kitchen garden. He was sitting in the pale afternoon sun, on a bench with room beside him for me to join him. We watched a robin fly to the handle of a spade stuck in the ground where Assacomet had been digging. It looked at us and cocked its head as if expecting us to dig his worms for him.

"You call this friend of mine a robin. He is with me every day I am here. Where I come from, we have a bird with a similar red breast. He is larger, more like what you call a thrush."

He started talking about the birds, the similarities and differences to those from his home. It was not easy to follow him, but his voice was filled with emotion—the voice of a sad man, friendless and missing his home. Even the animals, birds, trees, and countryside were different, all there to enjoy but also to remind him of what he missed.

One thing bothered me about the attack on him. "How is it that you allowed three men to ambush you?" I asked. "I have watched how you walk, how aware you are of your surroundings. They wouldn't have heard you before you were aware of them."

He glanced at me, saying nothing. I thought for a while.

"You wouldn't necessarily have heard them if you were distracted."

Another pause.

"It can't have been that your thoughts distracted you, you are too much aware. You must have had someone with you. Your lady friend, then. What happened?"

He nodded.

"I was walking with her when we were stopped by four men. Two of them were her brothers. One of the brothers took her and forced her to leave with him. The rest you saw."

We sat in silence. After a few minutes he started telling me about his homeland. I wished he had a broader command of English vocabulary, but his quiet, controlled passion helped me understand. He also drew a map with a stick on the ground. His favorite location is on the island we call Monhegan. It guards the entrance to the river that is his home, which we call St. George's. Monhegan is a circular island with high cliffs, especially on the seaward side, with wonderful views out to sea. To the west there is a small island nestled close in, creating a channel that makes for a sheltered harbor. Winds from the south can cause waves to roll through that channel. It's not as protected as it would appear.

On the north side is a sheltered bay. The island is heavily wooded but there are paths made by generations of Indians who visit for its beauty and isolation. They might camp there, but there is no permanent presence. It seems that the English settlement on the island happened after Assacomet was captured, because he was unaware of any English presence there.

He told me more about his homeland. Due north of Monhegan are two islands at the entrance to St. George's River. Traveling up the river, it opens out into wide, fertile land with large sheltered bays on either side. Many Indians live along the shores of the river. To the north are two mountains, good landmarks visible from afar. There are other islands to the east and the west. To the northeast is the land and water of the Penobscot, dotted with many islands. They are beautiful, but under constant threat from a warlike tribe called the Tarrantines from land to the east, Acadia, where the French have settlements. A wide bay lies to the northwest, again with many islands. Muscongus is the name of the place, bounded to the west by a peninsula, where his tribe, the Pemaquid, live. This area continues west a number of islands, stretching to the Sagadahoc several leagues away. On a good day, it is possible to see a long way in every direction. But there is often thick fog, which might last for days. Then, Monhegan seems isolated. With the use of his hands, Assacomet described a landscape and coast that seemed beyond compare. My heart turned over, thinking of the secret voyage to this magical-sounding place. His longing for home was evident in his descriptions. I was nearly moved to tears. But he would soon be returning, and I told him of the plan for him to return with Captain Hobson. He was silent a long time. Eventually, I stole away.

I sought out Mr. Wellings to talk. He said that Assacomet had been brought back to England by Captain Weymouth with four other Indians from the Monhegan area. Three of the five were brought down to Plymouth and given to Sir F., including Assacomet. The other two stayed in London. Sir F. had been quick to understand the importance of learning about the country and the people directly from the mouths of local Indians. He saw the necessity of local guides who spoke English and who could interact, even intercede, with the local people on future voyages of exploration and settlement. He was much taken with his three Indians. I asked Mr. Wellings what happened to them. True to his word, Sir F. had made use of and returned the Indians to their homeland, apart from Assacomet, and one who'd died.

"Having caused significant unrest by their capture, the situation must have been eased by their return, no?" I asked.

Mr. Wellings shook his head. "Remember, it was assumed by their people that those five had been killed by their captors. There was deep anger and distrust etched into their collective perception of the English. In addition, unfortunately, Harlow's ham-fisted capture of Epenow and four others did nothing to ease the situation."

"What happened to Epenow's companions?"

"I have no idea. It is possible Sir F. knows."

I felt that I had gone as far as I could to meet Sir F.'s objectives for me to get to know and learn from Epenow and Assacomet. I was anxious to get back to my normal life. I sent a note to Sir F. requesting a meeting, and received word that Sir F. and Lady Ann would be coming to Wraxall on Friday, 25 February. I should await their arrival. As this date was in a few days, I began preparations for my departure in expectation that I'd no longer be needed. Part of those preparations involved spending as much time as possible with Epenow and Assacomet, separately. I liked them, and I didn't know if or when I would see them again, only that if I did it would likely be back in their homeland. I wanted to make sure we had established a bond of friendship. Having friends in the right places seemed like a good strategy.

On the Gorgeses' return to Wraxall Court, I was summoned to a meeting with Sir F. We exchanged pleasantries. He asked how I had enjoyed being a member of the gentry. I said very much, and that I had escaped the social spider's web that I understood was being spun even now. I asked him how Robert was finding the army. Sir F. grimaced and said that it was too soon to tell, but that his regiment was being posted overseas. He would probably be in live action before long. "Can't temper steel without fire," he said, though he confided that Robert's mother was worried.

"You have done well, according to Mr. Wellings," Sir F. continued. "You have settled well. The staff here like you, and you seem to have established good relations with our two Indians. Tell me how you got on since I last saw you."

I told him everything.

"Assacomet needs to return home," he responded. "You told him of the Hobson voyage. He should be pleased. I see little personal value in using him, but you have astutely established a relationship with him that should stand you and us in good stead on the trip you will be going on. We will get Hobson to drop him off in time to re-engage with his people before you go over there. No point in him waiting to travel over with you. It will be a shock for him and his people meeting for the first time after eight years. Now, about you. I imagine you are looking forward to returning to normal life. Do you have any special plans?"

"Two, sir. I would like to go back to Dorchester for a few days. Then, I am keen to rejoin the *Sweet Rose*."

"That seems reasonable. The *Sweet Rose* has had a busy winter," he told me. "Apart from coastal trading to satisfy Mr. Bushrode's commercial interests, she has been on a number of trips for me. You will remember at a conference late last year in my Plymouth office that we had discussed the problem of piracy. In fact, you came across one on a voyage back from La Rochelle, I recall. The pirates are becoming a scourge, threatening our safety and England's commercial interests in the region for which I am responsible. I need information about them. We need to counter their actions. We need to intercept the trafficking of their English captives into slavery."

I tried a shot in the dark. A stupid one, perhaps. "Is that where Mr. Tremaine is involved, sir?"

Sir F. looked at me long and hard.

"Sorry, sir," I said hastily. "I didn't mean to blurt that out, but Mr. Tremaine has been in my thoughts. He has an extraordinary way about him that attracts people to him. My dealings with him clearly identified him as one of your spies. His appearance with freed English sailors was strange. It set me to thinking, trying to put two and two together."

Sir F. grimaced. "I am in somewhat of a quandary. I would like to believe that your active engagement with Tremaine and your deductive powers are a unique combination. I need to ponder further. Go to Dorchester; leave here on Monday. The *Sweet Rose* is due to return to Weymouth the first week in March. Join her then. She will be picking up merchandise and coming on to Plymouth before heading out. I will talk to you further then. Meantime, clear your belongings. We will find a traveling chest for you to use. We will deliver what you don't take with you to the Minerva. Make your farewells and enjoy Dorchester. You've done well. See Mr. Wellings about settling your financial affairs before you go as, from Monday, you are back on the payroll of the *Sweet Rose*."

I thanked Sir F., telling him these last six weeks had been an extraordinary experience I had greatly benefited from. He agreed. We shook hands and I left him. My last two days at Wraxall went by quickly. I had stuffed my saddlebags and the travel chest was filled. Mr. Wellings was kindness itself. He'd been concerned I was not sufficiently armed. A dirk was a toy in his mind, albeit a useful toy. He had talked to Sir F., and between them had produced a sword and scabbard, which Mr. Wellings presented to me as a farewell present from Wraxall. I was overwhelmed. It was a fine rapier, but with a slightly broader blade that had an edge to it, heavier than a typical dueling sword. A military rather than civilian weapon. Mr. Wellings was quick to distract me by taking me outside to the stable yard, where he proceeded to exercise my sword play with some practice bouts, much to the amusement of the stable hands, including Epenow. Mr. Wellings was a competent swordsman of the old school. My new sword was a fine one. Once I became more accustomed to its balance and feel I began to enjoy myself. It was soon evident that Mr. Wellings had his limitations. I made sure I neither disgraced myself nor embarrassed him.

We returned to his office. He looked at me. "Thank you," he said. "You are a fine swordsman. Our gift to you is in good hands. It was my favorite sword when I was in the army."

He told me not to bother with the paperwork that I had been expected to provide to account for my expenses while at Wraxall. I had spent little, apart from the clothes I had bought with Annie's help. I had as much money as I felt it wise to carry with me. He gave me a small wallet, heavy with coins. Given, he said with the gratitude of Sir F.

I spent time alone with each of my two Indian friends. They were eager to be off back home. It was clear we parted as friends, with the hope we would meet again in their homeland. Each would be happy to act as my guide whenever that might be.

So it is Sunday evening and I have now completed my journal entry. My chest is packed, locked, and strapped, the money wallet hidden in the recesses. It will accompany the Gorgeses on their return to Plymouth next week. The key I hung on a leather thong round my neck. Tomorrow I am off to Dorchester. My arrival will be a surprise visit, as I have not had an opportunity to advise them of my return. I am very much looking forward to being there and being with Aby again. Apart from the two notes I've sent her, I have not been a good letter writer.

CHAPTER 12

Journal entry—*28 February to 4 March 1614*

I left Wraxall at the crack of dawn and rode cross-country to pick up the Bath–Yeovil Road. Then, I had a forty-mile ride to the Angel at Yeovil, and from there the last stretch was an easy twenty miles to Dorchester. Maddie and I were eager to be off. We were going home.

On this cloudy, cold day, the snow was largely gone and the ground firm. We made good progress. Mrs. Applethwaite had kindly packed me food for the trip, which she parceled up together with a stopped flagon of ale. Our journey took us through the Mendips. As we climbed, the air cleared and we could see for miles. We stopped occasionally to catch our breath at the top of a rise before descending into wooded valleys. Streams and brooks chattered in greeting as they met and parted again, playing rolling tag down the valley. It was a day full of eager anticipation. I was going home to Aby.

A tiny cloud appeared over my mental landscape: Aby didn't know I was coming. What if she was away? I hadn't let P. and Mrs. White know either. If I could not stay with them, I could always find lodging, probably at the Sun, Lower Burton. As I rode, I thought about Aby and our future. We were committed to each other—young in age but mature in mind, body, and spirit. As matters had developed, I had a number of trips in my future this year. It seemed my base would be Plymouth, but I wouldn't be there enough to justify Aby moving down there in advance of our wedding. We needed to plan for next year, or to at least recognize that 1614 would not see us together much. She would be best living at home in Dorchester. Was I being too casual about planning to be away on so many long overseas trips? I wondered how Aby might react when I told her.

I thought about my last meeting with Sir F. It was clear my blurted-out question—I still blush to think of it—had hit the mark. With more intrigue swirling, I supposed there was some information not meant for young Stanfield's ears. We rode through Midsomer Norton and on to Shepton Mallet. Finding little traffic on the road, we continued onward still. When I stopped to eat, I left Maddie to crop at the grass verge and drink from a swift-flowing stream. We rode into Yeovil at about four p.m. and found the Angel on the junction of High St. and Hendford St. It was a tavern with substantial stables. Maddie was well taken care of, and I was given a room befitting my apparent station. How clothes *do* determine one's social status. I had an early meal and went to bed, planning to depart for Dorchester at sunrise.

Leaving Yeovil the next morning, Maddie cast a shoe. We returned on foot to the Angel, where I was told the blacksmith was due that morning. Maddie returned to her stable, and I sat to write up my journal. We left Yeovil again at about midday, having had lunch. Much as yesterday, we continued to make good progress. I felt I was into home territory as we moved through Dorset, reaching Dorchester in the late afternoon. I rode directly to the rectory. Mrs. White greeted me warmly, but she admonished me for not letting her know of my intended arrival. The rectory was full and Mr. White was out. I said not to worry, I was sure there would be room at the Sun. I asked her to let Reverend White know I was in town for a few days and that I would be by to see him in the morning. We hugged and parted. As we did so, she said she thought I looked too grand for her Isaac. I laughed.

I rode directly to the Sun and found my host, Mr. Jeremiah Gosling, behind the bar. He said there was room. I stabled Maddie there, walked back down to the West gate, and approached the Baker's house. I found it as Will had described in his letter—largely rebuilt and looking as good as new. Butterflies now in my stomach, I walked to the corner of the house, where I heard Aby's sweet voice. Looking into the yard, I saw Aby in Will's arms—*oh no*! Stunned, I ducked back out of sight. I couldn't breathe. I couldn't make sense of it. I turned and stumbled away. At that moment, Mr. Baker appeared, shouting at me. It made no sense until I realized he must not have recognized me in the dusk. Presumably he thought I was up to no good. Will and Aby came to investigate the cause of Mr. Baker's displeasure, but after a hasty glance in their direction I hurried away unrecognized. I returned to the Sun and sat in front of a large pot of ale with my mind churning. It was like a dream—or a nightmare. I felt a nudge, and Charlie Swain sat down next to me.

"Hello, Isaac, you back from your adventures?"

I muttered some response.

"I am in the building trade now," he said proudly. "In fact, I have been working on rebuilding the Baker house. Now there's a coincidence. Aren't you and Mr. Baker's daughter going together?'

I said nothing. Nothing to say.

"Are you all right? You look like death. I followed you from the Baker house. I had just finished tidying up when I saw you. Didn't know it was you in all your finery, but as I was coming here and you obviously were, too, I followed. I was a little concerned, as you seemed sick. You weren't walking steadily."

Charlie's cheerful babble was too much.

"Charlie, I have had a long ride from Bristol and am tired. I would love to talk to you, but not tonight."

"I understand, Isaac," Charlie said. "I'm off now back home for supper. My mum and me live in a cottage a short step from here. Sleep well. See you tomorrow."

I finished my ale and went to bed, unable to eat. I lay on my back looking at the ceiling. What was I going to do? I couldn't stay in Dorchester now. I couldn't look at Will or Aby, let alone *speak* to either of them. There was only one thing: I would leave first thing for Weymouth. I wasn't sure when the *Sweet Rose* was due. I would find out and either go with her to Plymouth or ride there. With that plan settled, I went to sleep—a troubled sleep. Next morning I was on the road after dropping into the rectory, leaving a message that I was called away suddenly. I left my latest journal entries for Will. I did so out of habit, but it made sense. He had all the others.

I had time to spare. Once clear of Dorchester, I decided to drop in on Reverend Stoddard at Bincombe and check on Johnny. Mr. Stoddard was on his way back from the church when I rode up and re-introduced myself. He seemed, as others had been, startled by my apparent transformation. He said that Johnny was getting on very well and asked if I would like to see him. We entered the kitchen where Johnny was seated at a table chopping vegetables, chatting with his mother. He rose, grinned, and came to shake my hand. We spent a happy hour together, a salve to my tortured soul. Johnny wanted to know what I had been doing, and I told him some of my recent adventures. He said that he had found peace with the help of Reverend Stoddard and that he was contemplating a religious life. It would be a tough road, as his education was greatly lacking, but Reverend Stoddard had plans. I was invited to stay for lunch. In the early afternoon, after bidding everyone farewell and promising to stay in touch, I continued on my journey.

When I arrived in Weymouth, it was clear after checking various sources that *Rosie* would not be back for several days, if not a week. I checked for Silas at the King's Arms, but he had returned to Dorchester. With nothing to keep me, I turned Maddie's head toward Plymouth. We set off on the long, sorry, unbearably lonely journey away from my home and the two people who were, in one way or another, my life. I couldn't in my heart blame them. Two lovely people had found each other—without the baggage between them of long trips and separations such as I carried.

We made for Bridport along the coastal route. A cutting easterly wind on the exposed headlands was at our backs, which was good. It was not a day for travel, so we had the bridle ways to ourselves. The twenty miles to the Bell on South Street went by quickly. My mood was dour and Maddie set the pace. I came out of myself as we approached Bridport, realizing that I had been pushing Maddie too hard and she needed rest. I decided to stay over for a day to recover. After working on Maddie in the Bell's stables, I found a corner and thought through all that had happened over the previous forty-eight hours. Deep down I couldn't accept that with so much put into the melting pot of Aby's and my relationship, a single spill could empty it all. For the next several months, possibly even the rest of the year, I would be otherwise occupied. Unfortunately, in conflict between head and heart, the heart was winning out. By the time we set off for Exeter, I had resolved nothing. I was cold, tired, and miserable. Maddie, sensing my mood, kept to herself. At our occasional stops she would nuzzle me before starting to crop the winter grass. We arrived at the White Hart by late afternoon.

The following morning, 3 March, we set off for Plymouth in sleeting rain, which eased off as we approached the edge of Dartmoor. I was deep in my despair, letting Maddie walk us through a wood, when two horsemen crossed my path and halted. The first was a tall, cloaked man, hatted and still. His companion was a smaller, nervous man who raised a pistol and told me to drop my saddlebags. I was still in a befuddled state, my mind elsewhere. I let Maddie continue to approach the two horsemen. The pistol went off with an enormous bang and cloud of smoke. My hat was snatched from my head and I felt a sharp sting over my left ear. When Maddie shied and bucked, I was too stunned to keep from falling off, though I kept hold of the reins.

The man who shot at me jumped off his horse and advanced with a second pistol. I got to my feet, my back to the man. As he reached me, I let go of Maddie, swiveled—sword drawn—and lunged. The man shielded himself with his right arm. The blade pierced the muscle of his upper arm through to the shoulder. He dropped his pistol, howled, and staggered away. I swung to face his partner, who was still sat on his horse, hands on the pommel of his saddle, calmly watching the proceedings. He sighed, gracefully dismounted, flung off his cloak, and advanced, swishing his drawn sword in front of him. Something in me broke—from my loss, my mood, my fury at being shot at, his arrogance. I suddenly felt a cold, focused commitment to destroy the man. I met him and attacked in fast cut-and-parry, pushing forward and working faster than I had ever done before. I was totally focused on the man, his body language, and his sword. Caught unprepared, he backed off. He was a fine swordsman, but had assumed I would be easy prey. I would prove not to be.

My anger drove me forward. I had hatred for the man. He embodied all the hurt I had suffered. The duel, for that was what it was, went on and on. His eyes began to show worry. This encounter was becoming for him not a typical robbery. Thus engrossed, neither of us was aware, at first, of a body of horsemen who began gathering at the edge of the clearing. They were watching the contest, and I was startled when I became dimly aware of their movement. Then came a sharp command from the group to "put up your swords." I jumped back and looked 'round. My concentration had been so focused that it took a moment for me to realize what was happening. We were surrounded by mounted horsemen, swords drawn. The leader, a gray-haired, distinguished-looking gentleman with a beard, looked down at us. My opponent now seemed less tense, almost indifferent.

"Well, well, well!" said the leader. "Jack Melrose and Slocum Smudge. Caught at last, and by a young lad—half your age!"

We both reacted. Why did he call me a young lad? What was going on? My opponent sheathed his sword, approached me with his hand out, and congratulated me. Surprised and not wishing to seem churlish, I took his hand. I did not sheath my sword, though, instead transferring it to my left hand, ready for any surprise. My opponent had deep-sunk gray eyes that were flat and merciless. His face was thin and clean-shaven. Lithe and slim, he was taller than me by several inches.

"All right, enough of that," the leader said. "Mr. Melrose, your sword, if you please."

Mr. Melrose was taken in hand by two of the horsemen, who had by now dismounted. Two others had hoisted Smudge to his feet.

"Bind them, put them back on their horses, ready to proceed. I have some words to say to our young friend here."

"If I'm not mistaken, you must be Isaac Stanfield."

Shocked, I stammered that it was so.

"Your reputation goes before you," he said by way of explanation. "What I saw today can only enhance it. You did well."

"Thank you, sir."

"Courtney, we must be going. Exeter awaits. Please give Mr. Stanfield a note confirming his capture of the notorious highwaymen Melrose and Smudge, for which there is a significant reward posted. Get Mr. Stanfield to sign the note. Then make another note to the same effect for my signature. Mr. Stanfield can carry it with him to Plymouth, from whence we've come and, presumably, whither he goes."

Such matters quickly attended to, me still not knowing who the gentleman was—his signature indecipherable—the party of horsemen moved off down the path toward Exeter. As Jack Melrose passed, he said: "Your anger and passion won the day. You must do more to learn technique. You can become a fine swordsman. Good luck to you."

I was speechless. Collecting my hat, I mounted Maddie and watched them till they were out of sight. There went as cool a man as I have ever met, nonchalantly going to his public hanging. And who was the fine old gentleman? How did he recognize me and know my name? With these questions much in my mind, we proceeded on to Plymouth and the Minerva. Somehow, Sir F. was tied into this incident, I felt sure. He would have to tell me. It was only as we entered Plymouth that I got to thinking about the reward.

The Minerva greeted us as family. Maddie was welcomed and fussed over to her satisfaction. I walked through the door from the stables and bumped into Annie, who squeaked her delight. She gave me a kiss and a huge hug. I told her I needed to go to my room and draw breath, but I would love to spend some time with her later. With that promise, I went upstairs with my loaded saddlebags. My chest had arrived from Wraxall. It was at the foot of the bed, locked and strapped. Having tried to sort my things out, I was suddenly overcome with thoughts of Aby. I flung myself onto my bed and sobbed myself to sleep.

When I awoke it was much later, and dark. I'd been woken by a soft body lying beside me, with my head nestled into her bosom. I tensed. Annie stroked my hair and face and whispered gentle soothing noises.

"You have been crying," she said. "And your ear, it is bloody. What happened? You weren't due back for days."

So I told her about Aby and Will. Annie put her arms round me and said, "silly boy." It was all too much for me. I fell again into a deep, dreamless sleep. When I woke up, a bright clear day was breaking and Annie was gone. She had cleaned my wound, bless her, and also the skylight of the little room. Still fully clothed and feeling most uncomfortable, I went down to the stables to relieve myself and wash up in a water trough. When I went back upstairs to change, Annie was in my room, having heard my movements.

"Annie. I need your practical help. With the clothes you helped me buy and the clothes I have been given at Wraxall Court, I am overwhelmed with belongings. I haven't an idea how to deal with it all. Another thing, I am accumulating more money than I can spend. I need to keep the excess somewhere safe."

"Isaac, my sweet, as to the money, you might want to buy a strong, lockable box which we can keep in a secure place. For the rest, go downstairs and have breakfast while I sort everything out up here."

I opened the chest. She started running her fingers over the clothes. She was excited and complimentary. I pulled out my wallet. I had counted the money earlier—twenty crowns. I had never had to save or set aside money before; I'd never had enough. Together with the money I had on me, it was becoming bulky and worrisome. I wasn't sure a strongbox was a good idea. With my travels coming up, it would be better to give it to someone who would give me access to it and account for what I used.

Then there was the reward. I asked Annie if she had seen any posters offering rewards for captured highwaymen. She had. In fact, there were some downstairs. The rewards varied depending on the notoriety of the highwayman, but she remembered seeing the figure twenty-five gold sovereigns. She asked why and I made up some story about seeing what I thought was a trussed-up highwayman being led away and wondered about it. She looked at me, and I thought she hadn't believed a word.

"Mr. Isaac Stanfield, what have you been doing?" she asked.

I grinned.

"Twenty-five gold sovereigns, you say. Who would have thought it?"

"Well, are you going to tell me?" she pressed.

So I did. She sat on the bed shaking her head. We agreed that at the speed I was gaining wealth, I might need to come up with a better plan than a strongbox. She checked my burn from the pistol shot. It had seeped a little blood but nothing more. She was not happy about the hole in my hat, but she was a practical girl. Nothing very bad had happened in the end, so there was no point in moaning. I left Annie to it and went downstairs. Alfred slapped me on the shoulder in greeting and told me Annie had informed him of my arrival. Gave me a big wink and an even larger breakfast. He'd been instructed to let Sir F. know when I had returned, although as Annie had said, I had not been expected this soon. A messenger was already on the way to the Fort.

By ten a.m. I was sitting in front of Sir F.'s desk, where he sat gazing back at me.

"You really do surprise me. I received a note early this morning from a cousin of mine telling me you had captured the infamous Melrose and his partner. When he came upon you he thought you were Robert. You were wearing his clothes. That didn't work, however, because he knew Robert was away in the army. He had been to see me on his way through to Exeter and London. I talked about you, and he drew a likely inference."

That had been one hell of a guess, I thought.

"And now, he says you are owed the reward. It comes to fifty sovereigns for the two of them."

I was staggered. What was I going to do with that amount of money?

"Isaac, if I might be so bold to call you that, you need a business manager," Sir F. said. "Someone with broad interests and connections. They hold accounts for the merchants they do business with. Through their commercial network, a client of theirs can draw against the financial resources they hold on the client's behalf. Money can be drawn in London, say, on an account the manager holds for the client in Plymouth. It can even work overseas. I know managers who have offices in La Rochelle, the Hague, and London. You are given a token with a maximum, single drawing amount that you present to the manager or his representative. You receive the amount requested and sign a receipt. You have a small ledger book into which the amount drawn is entered. And there you go. There is a bit more to it than that, but that's the essence."

It seemed perfect. Sir F. promised to make the necessary arrangements. I gave him the signed note that his cousin had given me, which he needed to ensure the reward was paid. I thanked him, and we moved to other business. He asked why I had arrived in Plymouth that far ahead of schedule. I said my plans had changed in Dorchester, and I had decided to come straight back. He looked at me with a thoughtful expression on his face. I was clearly uncomfortable under his scrutiny.

"Whatever happened, I hope it works out for you."

"Thank you, sir."

"As it happens, it was opportune."

He went on to explain that he had been startled by my perceptive question regarding Mr. Tremaine at our last meeting. He had needed time to ponder the implications. Not wishing to denigrate me in any way, he was worried that if I had reached that conclusion, who else might? A meeting had been planned later in the week to discuss the piracy situation and steps to be taken. He had decided that he would allow me to attend as an unobtrusive observer. A chair would be found for me in a corner. The skipper, who was currently heading for

Plymouth, was expected to attend. I was stunned. I thought *Rosie* was going to Weymouth. Just as well I came straight down to Plymouth. With that, I was dismissed. I would be informed as soon as the meeting time had been determined.

Journal entry—*5 to 8 March 1614*

I took to spending time over the next few days on the Hoe, watching out for signs of *Rosie*. I must have missed her, as I was in the Minerva's taproom one evening when the door opened. JB and a couple of *Rosie's* crew came in. They greeted me with affection, and though they didn't talk much about where they had been, they did allow as they'd had a busy winter. They were interested in my doings, which I summarized for them. The evening went well. I felt much better being with my shipmates. Annie kept us supplied with drink and food. She was clearly happy that I was having a good time.

Next morning, Tuesday, 8 March, I received a message from the Fort. I was required to attend a meeting there at two o'clock that afternoon. I went down to Sutton Pool. *Rosie* was alongside. I was able to go aboard and report to the duty officer, Peg Jones, who welcomed me back. We discussed the resumption of my duties and which watch I would be on. I told him that I was still under Sir Ferdinando's authority, but I expected to be released from my charge sometime that afternoon. Meantime, I should transfer my kit to *Rosie*. On *Rosie*, crew sleeping arrangements had changed. Skipper had gone Navy. Paillasses had been replaced by hammocks, for all sorts of good reasons. I was assigned my own chest, inherited from an able seaman who was no longer a crewman. The ship's boy Obi greeted me warmly, glad at the reunion. It seemed a long time since I had seen him, and I suppose it had been three months now. Happily, he seemed more confident and settled, moving with more assurance. He had lost that alarming sense of impending disaster with every step taken. Obi showed me the lower deck where my chest was located and my hammock would be slung and stowed during the day. He had me test one out. I found it difficult getting into and out of it, taking a definite knack, but I soon got the hang of it. It was good to be back.

By two p.m. I was in my corner chair trying to be inconspicuous. The room was filled with perhaps twenty men—military, sea captains, and merchants. Skipper arrived with Peg. They both looked surprised to see me but nodded in passing. Sir F. entered. We all rose to our feet, but he quickly motioned us to sit. He proceeded to talk about the pirate situation, explaining that the problem had been a concern for almost as long as he had been in charge at the Fort. On several occasions, notably in 1605 and 1611, he had requested assistance from London. Nothing substantial came of these requests, apart from King James offering amnesty to pirates, which had met some success. Now the problem had become worse, and it was likely to continue to worsen. With King James ending sanctioned privateering and attempting to make peace with Spain, any semblance of patriotism had given away to commercial greed among many English, Irish, and continental sailors. Navies were being run down, which meant more sailors were out of work and fair game for piracy. Disaffected sailors were offering their skills and services to the Barbary pirates. With a reduction in the number of active naval vessels, the merchant fleets were that much less protected.

Furthermore, he continued, the number of Christian slaves taken and sold to the Turks had seen enormous increase, as well as the numbers kept by the rulers of Tripoli, Tunis, Algiers, Rabat, and other city-states along the North African coast. It beggared belief how many poor souls were in captivity, but estimates ranged from tens to hundreds of thousands. Most of these people were captured by raids on the villages and towns of Italy, Malta, and Spain. A large permanent pirate fleet used the Sicily Isles as a base. The coastal communities between here and Penzance, as well as the south coast of Ireland, were all threatened.

I had heard some of this alarming news already, but the way he presented what was happening made me more fully aware of the dire conditions. For the most part, England had the shore defenses needed to keep the pirates at bay—certainly in the area for which Sir F. bore responsibility. He was worried at the number of merchant vessels being taken, the home ports of which he felt were under his protection. I sensed this obligation was one he had taken on to fill a void left by other responsible officers of the Crown. While he could do little to protect the ships, Sir F. felt he needed to do what he could to try and rescue the sailors. Certain locations in Spain had become centers for negotiating hostage release. A Catholic order of monks had made their calling the redemption of Christian slaves from pirates and their Turkish overlords. People in both public and private realms were donating money to pay ransoms. With the Barbary pirates, opportunities had therefore come into being for the lucrative ransom and exchange of Christian slaves for captured pirates. Sir F. had found a network of informers provided the pirates with details about shipping movements, cargoes, and the potential ransom value of passengers and crew. He had a plan to have his spies build contacts in Spain to find out more and develop a better process for finding and returning English sailors.

I presumed he had in mind a follow-on from the sailors returning with Mr. Tremaine from La Rochelle.

Sir F. opened up the meeting for questions and discussion. It became clear that local business leaders were well represented, as well as representatives from towns along the coast. They were vocal in their concerns, with many anecdotes in support of the need for action. Naval representatives at the meeting talked about raids on pirate lairs and, with government commitment of adequate resources, greater coordination and with greater intensity. Shipping owners and their captains discussed how tactics might evolve to avoid pirates; the need for increased information gathering and distribution among them; and the costs and limitations of coastal merchant vessels to arm themselves adequately.

Sir F. brought the discussions to a close by saying he had already initiated his plan to infiltrate the network of pirate informers. He was not at liberty to disclose the details of the plan, as it contained some highly confidential information, but more voyages were planned to begin immediately, weather permitting. That meant *Rosie*. Presumably, we would be sailing south. After further effort, Sir F. hoped to be able to report back some specific accomplishments and demonstrable gains in this ongoing piracy war. The attendees to the meeting, Sir F. said, all had bitter and continuing experiences with this scourge. His office would continue to be a clearinghouse for all information gained. Everyone needed to gather from their own sources information that might pertain and pass it through to his office. As everyone left, I scanned the room looking for Mr. Tremaine but, to my surprise and disappointment, he had not attended. I wondered where he could be. Perhaps he was at that very moment rescuing other sailors.

I had already shipped my seagoing kit back to *Rosie*. I had left much on board, foul weather gear and the like, when I last left her. I bid farewell to Maddie and Annie, who promised to keep my fine wardrobe safe. A hug for Annie and some tears of gratitude and friendship. I returned to *Rosie*.

Letter to Isaac—2 March 1614

Dear Isaac,

I am sending this letter with Charlie, who is riding like the wind to catch you before you disappear. Please, please come back. There is nothing but brotherly and sisterly affection between Aby and me—all because of you. We both miss you dreadfully. We share that emptiness together. Charlie came into the Baker yard this morning. He told us he had seen you and that you had been to the yard. Clearly, you saw us and drew a mistaken conclusion. Aby was saying how much she missed you and how miserable she was, and I was giving her a hug. Nothing more.

Aby was distraught. She became very angry—at herself, me, the circumstances, even her poor father. Mr. Baker asked for my help. I checked with the Sun and the rectory, but you had gone. Oh damn, damn, damn. Please come back.

Yours ever,
Will

Letter to Isaac—*3 March 1614*

Dear Isaac,

Where are you? Charlie came back, having hunted all over Weymouth for you. He left my previous letter for you at the King's Arms, to be delivered in your absence to the *Sweet Rose* on its return. I have to assume you are either in hiding and licking your wounds or are riding back to Plymouth. I have read the latest journal entries you left with the Whites yesterday. Extraordinary reading. I have an idea of your plans and movements.

I have spent much time with Aby, but she is inconsolable, constantly blaming herself. I have asked P. to spend time with her, which he has promised to do. I told her it was a terrible mischance, no one to blame, and as soon as we can get to you to explain, everything will be all right again. I said that your love for each other was stronger than this mishap. It's not herself she weeps for, she says. It's Isaac. What must he be going through? Seeing her in the arms of someone else. Not just someone else—his best friend. What must he be going through? She keeps repeating it.

I very much doubt you have gone to ground. Not the sort of thing you would do. I have Charlie finding out when *Rosie* is due in. I will ride down to Weymouth and deliver this letter to be handed on to you as soon as *Rosie* gets to Plymouth. Probably a surer way of getting this note to you than by overland courier. Please, please write and tell us you have received my letters, that you understand, and all is now right again. Please, at your earliest opportunity, come back to Dorchester.

Will

Letter to Isaac—*10 March 1614*

Dear Isaac,

Aby and I are beside ourselves with concern. Latest from Charlie, who has been in Weymouth every day since you left, is that *Rosie* never made it to Weymouth but has instead gone straight to Plymouth. I am sending this letter by courier, but I feel I need to do more. I will probably ride down to Plymouth myself. You will not have read my earlier, frantic letters. I must repeat: What you saw was me comforting Aby. She was overcome by your absence. When I went to the Baker house to check on her, she was crying. As you know, Aby doesn't cry. I was shocked. A dreadful misunderstanding. Aby is now worried she will never see you again. I keep telling her that as soon as we have made contact everything will be fine. She's a strong girl. She loves you and wants you back.

Will

Letter to Isaac—*13 March 1614*

Dear Isaac,

I am staying tonight at the Minerva. I arrived a few hours ago. I met Annie. I said I knew her from your description. She knew who I was immediately, and said you had sailed off with the *Sweet Rose* on the ninth. Damn. I keep missing you. We spent some time talking about you. She asked after Aby. She said you had told her what had happened. Women's intuition led her to think there had been a misunderstanding. How right she is! I went to the fort on the off-chance I could get to see Sir Ferdinando. He wasn't available, but Captain Turner gave me some time. I briefly summarized the reason I was in Plymouth. Captain Turner expressed sympathy. The *Sweet Rose* wouldn't be back for at least a week and possibly longer. He said he would let Sir F. know of my visit, and we parted.

I can do no more. The letters are piling up, awaiting your return. Charlie retrieved my first. I enclose that, as well as my second, with this one. There is another, which I sent to you by the courier service. I do need you to understand the depth of our feelings, but especially Aby's. Annie understands the situation. It seems that even Sir F. might. All we can do is await your return.

Will

CHAPTER 13 ————

Journal entry—*9 to 21 March 1614*

We left on the morning tide 9 March. Larboard watch under Peg. I had been moved from the quarterdeck as I was now a full-fledged seaman. On watch, all was organized mayhem and clear away. In the twenty-four hours *Rosie* was alongside, cargo had been hoisted ashore, and—Mr. Bushrode will be pleased—replaced with bundles of long-haired worsted and semi-worsted in large sacks, apparently much sought after in Spain. We loaded a lot of ballast, a tiring, dirty job, working in the depth of the hold. We still rode high in the water, which made *Rosie* frisky as we moved south-southwest into open water. It was a bright, cold day, steady strong breeze from the east. Wind on larboard quarter, all sails set. *Rosie* was happy. I had lost my sea legs; the next twenty-four hours were going to be rough. I received no sympathy from my watch mates as I made regular visits to the head gratings. Mr. Brown called us all to the main deck. He looked down as I looked round. In my sickness, I hadn't paid much attention, but we had a full complement with many new faces, the same officers. A number of strangers who seemed apart from the rest of us. I imagined they were something to do with Sir F.

The Skipper told us we would be heading down the Bay of Biscay to Bilbao, a distance of some 450 miles. That fact caused a murmur. The French and Spanish privateers are still inclined to take English ships on the slimmest of pretexts. King James' attempts at making peace did not reduce the ill will with those nations, especially among the seamen. One thing going for us is that Bilbao is a Basque town. Fishing and, increasingly, whaling are important with English West Country fishermen interacting with Basques in Newfoundland and along the American coastline. Basque fishing boats are regular visitors to English West Country ports. What's more, Basque privateers out of Bilbao see their opposite numbers out of

La Rochelle as their primary enemy and vice versa. While it might appear strange for us to be venturing into Spanish waters, Bilbao, the Basque capital of Biscay, provides the English with relatively safe access to Spain. The politics of Bilbao are not too dissimilar to that of La Rochelle, broken into political factions with the merchants representing wealth and the farmers in the surrounding countryside in fairly constant argument. It is a busy trading city with a large population of native Basque, proud and independent, as well as citizens from every other country. We will not be staying long. We are to exchange cargo and some passengers. The skipper said he did not wish to be forced to stay because of any crew member getting into trouble ashore, so shore leave would be curtailed. He said he wants *Rosie* to be back home by Easter, 20 March.

He further explained that we were on a mission that promised benefit to Spain and England. We were establishing a joint effort to contain the pirates, as well as to expand the repatriation process for Christian sailors to their home countries. Spain's primary concern was Catholics, while England's was Protestants. Means to accomplish anything would come from cooperation. The *Sweet Rose* had a responsibility to transport men to and from Spain, as required. We'd be sharing this responsibility with other vessels. The farther we ventured into the Bay of Biscay, the more likely we would become involved in hostile action. Safety would increase as we approached Bilbao. We would have to be vigilant and prepared. Once 'round Ushant, we would post double lookouts. Mr. Babbs would be exercising the guns regularly. New crew members were being assigned to gun crew duty, based on their past experience.

"You will notice that we have a full crew. In fact, in expectation of trouble, we have increased our complement by ten, with the appointment of a Master-at-arms, former marine sergeant Mr. Owen Llewelyn."

At which point a gray-haired, bow-legged, barrel-chested Welshman stepped forward. He had command of a squad of men that he had brought with him. We were fast becoming a man o' war.

We were off Ushant in twenty-four hours, and as we sailed into the Bay of Biscay, our heading changed to south-southeast in fine sailing weather, wind abeam. The bay was being kind to us, renowned as it was for atrocious weather. Three days later, after much exercising of the guns, having sighted numerous sails, none of which showed any inclination to approach us, we were closing on Bilbao. The skipper preferred to make landfall in daylight. We reduced sail in the late evening some fifty miles off. Next morning, we were alongside in the inner harbor by four bells of the forenoon watch, 14 March. All hands were active in offloading cargo and cleaning ship. I was called to the skipper's cabin.

"Stanfield, we are here to pick up your friend Tremaine. Sir Ferdinando has informed me that there is a bar close to Santiago Church where messages can be picked up and left. You will see the spire from the quay. You shouldn't miss it. The bar is in the Plaza de Santiago, to the right of the church on the ground floor of a building with two shields, Castile and Basque. I am not sure of the movements of Mr. Tremaine, but we are to await his arrival. I want you to leave a message, nothing in writing, with a barmaid called Roseanna Garcia. The message is: 'Cuckoo.'"

"'Cuckoo'?" I repeated.

"Don't play games with me, Stanfield," he said. "Just follow orders."

"Sorry, sir. Might there be a message waiting for us?"

"No idea. You will have to use your initiative. I am having Mr. Llewelyn, with two of his men, cover your back. They will be suitably armed. You, I want to look small, inconspicuous. You should appear to be unaware of Mr. Llewelyn. There should be no association, unless needed."

Mr. Llewelyn with his team were waiting for me. Dressed as I was as a simple seaman, they were somewhat contemptuous. I played meek and went ashore. I paid no further attention to them but was pleased to be back on dry land. The spire of the church was a good landmark. With the crowded streets, I casually worked my way through the throngs, a meaningless stroll in a direction that slowly brought me into the plaza. With the day getting on for midday, I was just one in the crowd. Finding the bar, I entered with a number of other seamen. The room was long and narrow with a bar counter on one side; tables toward the rear. Two barmaids were working, and I waited to be served. The customers seemed like regulars. They joked with the barmaids, who flirted back. At one point, someone called "Roseanna!" and one of the barmaids responded. I gathered that I should buy a drink with tapas here, which would be delivered to the table, so that was what I did.

I caught Roseanna's eye and asked for a glass of Rioja. I pointed at a dish on display on the counter and paid with coins received from the skipper. I went to a table to wait. A short time later, she deposited a plate in front of me. As she turned to go, I spilt my wine. She quickly caught the glass and bent to wipe the wine off the table. I whispered "Cuckoo." The glass was still half full. Roseanna disappeared, seemingly not having heard. I ate my tapas. A short time later, another plate of tapas was put in front of me. As I moved the plate toward me, I saw a sliver of paper underneath, which I removed. I drank and ate for a few more minutes, then left. Across the other side of the plaza I opened the paper. Everything went blank.

Sometime later, I woke up with a splitting headache and blood down the back of my head. I appeared to be in a small room with no windows—pitch black with straw on the floor. I slowly worked my way to my feet and felt around. The room seemed to be a storage room, with boxes, barrels, and the smell of food. The door by the feel of it was solid, immovable. I found space against a wall, sat down to nurse my head and awaited developments. So much for Mr. Llewelyn and his crew. I must have fallen asleep. I was woken with the opening of the door. Light flooded in. Two men grabbed me, hauled me to my feet, and marched me down a long corridor into a room. There was a man with a crutch looking out the window, his back to me. Crippled as he was, he turned slowly to face me. I staggered back—Gunt! He was barely recognizable, thin—even emaciated—with deep pain etched into his face. He glared at me, the hatred palpable. He moved slowly toward me. Groggy as I was, I felt the danger. The two men holding me shifted uneasily. A step and he lunged forward with his crutch aimed for my privates. Off balance, he missed, but the end of his crutch hit my hip, knocking me sideways. He then struck down on my exposed neck using his crutch as a club with both hands. Luckily, without the support of his crutch, he staggered and the mortal blow to my neck landed on my shoulder, half parried by my raised arm. It felt like my shoulder blade had been broken. I was forced to my knees. The pain was mind-numbing. I was defenseless, in serious trouble.

"Get out," he screamed at the two guards. They left.

"Now, you little worm. I am going to kill you, slowly. You're the reason for the miserable life I have. The constant pain. I'm crippled for life. What did I ever do to you?"

He bent over me, huddled at his feet. "Answer me," he screamed. I was in no position to answer, my teeth gritted in pain. He raised his crutch again to strike when I heard the door open. Someone blocked the crutch, hurling it to one side. Gunt fell heavily beside me. His face was inches from mine, with the look of a madman. I looked up—and saw Tremaine.

"That surprised you, you bastard," said Gunt. "You think he's come to save you." He spat the words out, slowly climbing to his feet. "How do you think I escaped hanging? Who do you think saved me?"

"Shut up, Gunt. You've done enough damage," Tremaine said. "Destroying a barterable property makes no sense."

I was lost. Tremaine one of *them*. My supposed friend was now my enemy—a traitor. I couldn't get my head 'round it. I was helped to my feet, standing, left arm now useless, cradled by my right, looking at Tremaine. Pain, shock, horror writ large on my face. Tremaine grimaced.

"Stanfield needs some attention. Gunt, you're a miserable sod, bully, and coward."

Gunt's only reply to Tremaine's insults was obscenities.

With that, Tremaine led me, limping, from the room, down to a kitchen with water and linen. I wanted nothing to do with him and shrank from his touch. He was gentle but insistent. He cut away my shirt, gently probing my shoulder. I winced but said nothing. No way was I going to talk to this traitor.

"Seems like a heavy bruise but nothing broken," he said.

My left forearm was scraped, bleeding, and bruised from parrying the crutch. He cleaned it. The hip was bruised but otherwise useable. The back of my head was still bloody. He cleaned that, too.

"Sit," he instructed.

I sat.

"Look at me."

More difficult, but I did. I had to concentrate to hear him, so low was his whisper.

"No matter what you've seen, heard, or might see, *trust me*."

I looked at him, stupefied. He went to the door and shouted something in Spanish. My two guards came running. Tremaine gave them further instructions in Spanish. Showing me some care and attention, they took me to an upstairs bedroom, locking the door as they left. I was able to sink onto the bed and sleep, waking some hours later. It was dark, but a candle had been lit, and a tray left with bread, cheese, water, and a glass of brandy. I took a mouthful, letting the liquor slowly seep down my throat. Good medicine, much needed, as I was thirsty and famished. I emptied the tray and glass and lay back down. I tried to reason with what I had heard. Gunt here, rescued from Plymouth Fort by Tremaine, who was working with Gunt, though apparently with no love lost. How had I been identified and picked up? Had Gunt recognized me and arranged my capture? If he had, where and when? In the harbor, he saw *Rosie* arrive? Followed me. No, he could not move easily. He had someone follow me? The bar. No longer a safe place to leave messages? Perhaps Roseanna had been got at? There seemed to be no valid reason to take me, other than because of Gunt's hatred. Back to Tremaine. Was he a double agent? I wanted to believe him. I realized I was in no position to do anything else.

I went back to sleep, and when I woke again, it was daylight. My empty tray had been refilled, my filled chamber pot emptied. Another day went by. My aches and pains eased, but I was stiff. I tried to stay loose, working hip, arm, and shoulder. My head still felt dazed, but at least I had an opportunity to sleep and recover. I was able to think of Aby. My feelings came back to a deep certainty that our love was stronger than the present hurt and confusion. A piece of me wanted to wallow in despondency, to convince the rest of me that what I had seen I had judged rightly.

Against that, I became more certain that I had chosen one of several other possible interpretations, all of which were, actually, more likely. I remembered Annie's remark in bed—"Silly boy." She clearly thought I had jumped the wrong way. My headache eased. I was able to walk round the room, moving my arm a little, with my mental state over Aby eased. At that point, my self-absorption changed to one of concern. What was I thinking? A momentary guilty feeling with the image of Annie and me nestled in bed. Understandable given the circumstances, but how much more compromising if Aby had walked in on *that* than what I had seen between Aby and Will? Charlie would have told them that I had been there and seen them. Drawing a wrong conclusion, I had fled. Could I have been that selfish as to leave this mess unresolved? Aby must be distraught, thinking I had left her. My mind had difficulty grasping it all. So, now my mood darkened again. I became frantic to get out of this imprisonment, to get back to *Rosie*, England, and Aby.

On the fourth day of my incarceration, an unsigned note was slipped under the door. I was being ransomed with other English sailors. I thought it best to tear up the note and eat it. Sometime later, I was blindfolded, led from my room, down stairs, out into fresh air, and into an alleyway. As I rounded a corner, the blindfold was whipped from my eyes. By the time I reacted and turned, people were looking at me oddly, with no indication of who had led me there. I was close to the harbor. Without more ado, I went searching for *Rosie*. She was still quayside, looking like she was being readied for departure, with crew in the rigging, others at the mooring lines. I hailed her, and Peg saw me and gestured me aboard. He told me to await the skipper in his cabin. I watched from the stern gallery as we eased away from the quay, making our way down the harbor, onward out to sea. Two bells sounded—afternoon watch. It was 18 March, Good Friday.

I heard footsteps. The skipper entered, followed by Tremaine. I opened my mouth.

"Be quiet, sit down, and listen. Mr. Tremaine has some explaining to do."

Tremaine looked at me long and hard, while the skipper filled three glasses with brandy—medicinal, he said.

"I have to apologize to you, Isaac," began Tremaine. "I hadn't understood the extent of your past involvement with Gunt. Nor, as a result, his overwhelming hatred. His informer had seen the *Sweet Rose* arrive. On finding out you were aboard, he had you followed. You were being held in a pirate safe house. One of the pirates guarding you came to warn me that Gunt was out of control, beating you to a pulp. I got to you just in time, I think. I didn't know it was you who'd been captured until I came into the room. It was one hell of a shock."

I nodded, taking a sip of the brandy.

"Luckily, my work there is done," Mr. Tremaine continued. "Gunt was in league with the pirates' spy network. In fact, he was *part* of it, as was discovered when he was put to the rack. It had its roots in La Rochelle and Bilbao. Realizing that a dead Gunt wouldn't be able to expose this network, Sir Ferdinando arranged for Gunt to escape with my help. My involvement convinced him that I was on his side. He led me back to La Rochelle, then Bilbao. It is a porous network. We know how it works. We have placed spies to keep us informed of their activities, as well as to pass on false information. We could have destroyed it, but another would have sprung up. Better the devil you know, especially if you can manipulate it.

"Finally, we were able to build an escape route for captured English sailors who were being offered for ransom or exchange in Malaga. Funding flows to a Catholic monastic order who negotiate for the release of sailors there. They have been persuaded that even Protestant souls should be saved. The freed sailors are escorted by land or sea, depending on circumstances, to Barcelona, and from there across Northern Spain to Bilbao. Merchant ships, such as the *Sweet Rose*, make regular trips, bringing back any sailors who have used the escape route. In fact, there are five on board now."

"And Gunt?" I asked.

"Ah, Mr. Gunt became suspicious. It was important that the pirates did not suspect me. Otherwise, the spies we infiltrated would have been compromised. I've had him quarantined. He is thoroughly disliked; it was easy to do. Then, with help from my people, I was able to dope and smuggle him out in a large basket. I let it be known that he had escaped with the help of some English friends. He was understood to be going to La Rochelle. I said I was leaving in pursuit. His erstwhile colleagues were well pleased and didn't think to question it. They won't worry about my absence. He is on the *Sweet Rose* now, confined in the hold."

With the final sip of brandy, I began to lose track. Tremaine and the skipper exchanged glances. The glass was taken from my hand just before I let it fall and remembered nothing more. I was moved to a hammock in the focsle and put under Dusty's protection. Three days later, after having been isolated even from Obi, I was rested, restored, and eager to get back to work. I returned to watch duty. Something must have been said, as the crew were friendly but didn't ask questions, apart from Obi, who badgered me for information at every opportunity until I had to say enough.

"Obi, be patient. Now's not the time. One day, perhaps when we are back ashore."

I bumped into Mr. Llewelyn, who apologized to me with some embarrassment. He said they had missed me leaving the bar, spotting me only when I was halfway over the plaza. By the time they reached that corner, I had disappeared. He got a right bollocking from the skipper. His future had been in serious jeopardy until I turned up, bloodied but unbowed. I grinned, saying it was partially my fault. I had forgotten I had minders; they had done such a good job of their unobtrusive tracking. We shook hands and parted on friendly terms. Mr. Babbs and his gunnery practice had become a daily ritual. On my return, I resumed my powder monkey duty, being deemed useful but not too arduous. I was being treated with gentle hands without knowing why, but I wasn't too bothered. The weather was clear, wind from the southwest, a loom gale (between strong breeze and gale). We were steering north going large (wind over the quarter). *Rosie* moved well.

I was fascinated by navigation and while on watch, well out of sight of land, Mr. Jones used the cross-staff on clear days to obtain the sun's altitude in degrees, or angle above the horizon. With good timekeeping, the altitude obtained could be read off a table to obtain the ship's latitude. Knowledge of a ship's latitude on a chart gave the ship's position on a line north to south. We were heading just about due north. The cross-staff, therefore, enabled us to keep a good approximation of our course. This was cross-checked with the readings from the traverse board, added to the chart at the end of every watch. Peg allowed me to use it. I quickly got the hang of it, once I got used to the motion of the boat. That evening, off watch, I caught up with my journal.

Journal entry—*22 March 1614*

We cleared Ushant on the last leg home. I was on watch duty, with the double lookout about to be changed, when a cry came from the masthead: "Sail off larboard bow." Peg sent J.B. up the ratlines with a telescope. He came back puzzled. Its heading is much the same as ours, but sailing under tops'ls only, and we are making ground on it quickly. Other sightings on our journey up the Bay of Biscay had been dismissed without too much concern, but this one seemed odd. The skipper was called. He had been in his cabin with Mr. Tremaine, and they both came onto the quarterdeck.

"David, take a look yourself."

Tremaine, with telescope, quickly climbed to the main top and studied the vessel, then returned to the deck. It had presumably seen us although there was no obvious sign of that. It flew the French flag and seemed in no hurry. Tremaine thought it was the same pirate ship we had avoided last year. The skipper told Peg to call all hands to action stations. Mr. Babbs was sent for and told we would be continuing on the same heading. He was to prepare the starboard guns for action. Load and run out. They would not be seen. After the starboard guns are run out, load the larboard guns, he said, but leave their gun hatches closed. It was his intention to run up close to leeward of the pirate and at the last minute cut across her stern. As we turned, he should run out the Larboard guns to get them out of the way. As each starboard gun found a target, it should fire ball from both the minions and falcons. Aim to fire into the stern to sweep the lower deck and to attempt to disable the rudder. Reload with grape in the minions to bring down rigging and canister in the falcons to aim at the crew, especially on their quarter deck. Once we had passed under the stern, we would ease sails and run down the windward side. Fast reload time was essential. Something much practiced. Mr. Llewelyn was called and told to have his men ready with muskets and spares loaded, crew assigned to reload as required. They should remain out of sight until the last moment. As we braced up, they were to be ready in two squads, split between the focsle and our quarterdeck to pick targets, especially on the pirates' quarterdeck.

I was sent below to join Obi. We were powder monkeys. All powder, wadding boxes, grape, canister, and ball trays had been filled. We were ready to add more as the guns were loaded. Training had achieved good teamwork with fast, efficient action. We suppressed our excitement that all the training was going to be put to the test. I sneaked a look topside. The crew on deck had been told to appear unconcerned. The pirate was still maintaining its heading. Everything seemed peaceful. The pirate was now less than a half mile off our larboard bow, we were closing quickly. I ducked down below to relay the news. Not long now.

Two hundred yards short, the pirate's gun hatches burst open, their guns were run out. With an order, our helm was brought up, sails braced, hardened, lines reset, and *Rosie* crossed behind the pirate before they had a chance to fire. They saw the danger and began to head up—too late. Frantic activity on the pirate ship. Tops'ls, sprits'l, courses set and braced—all of it too slow. Each of *Rosie*'s guns found their target and fired. At that range, the round shot hammered into the stern. One minion ball struck the top of the rudder at the tiller tenon joint, breaking it off, and with it the tiller. The pirate ship immediately started to swing back to starboard as the rudder hung free. The other balls smashed through the stern windows and the inner partitions, into the lower deck. Screams signaled carnage. Sailing out beyond the ship, *Rosie* eased braces, turned downwind, and reset. At one hundred yards, her guns, now loaded with canister and grapeshot, fired again. More carnage as the grape tore through lines and sails, the canisters mowed down the pirate crew who had been readied on deck, expecting to board a terrified and compliant prey. Llewelyn's men fired at will until out of effective range. Blood poured through the scuppers down the sides of the pirate ship. Belatedly, one pirate gun fired. The ball struck *Rosie*'s starboard quarter; she sailed away, the pirate ship unwilling or unable to follow.

Below deck, the ball had penetrated the hull into the gunroom, hit the side of the starboard falcon's barrel, ricocheting off, upended the falcon, throwing it into its crew. Obi and I were at the aft end of the lower deck. We ran back and entered the gunroom, the upturned gun carriage was hard up against the door. We scrambled into the chaos, followed by more crewmen. Cries of agony came from under the upended carriage, which was righted and moved off the men. Three crewmen had been crushed. One was dead and the other two had broken legs. The two injured men were eased out. Space cleared on the larboard side. Dusty arrived and took charge. The wounds were cleaned, legs straightened to howls of pain, and splinted. We would be back in Plymouth within twenty-four hours. Possible complications would have to wait until then. There didn't appear to be any internal wounds. Both men were standing away from the gun when it was toppled. The dead man had been hit by the ricocheting cannonball full in the chest, smashing every bone. He'd been killed instantly. The ship's carpenter set to with assistants to plug the hole in the hull and begin repairing the gun carriage sufficiently to house the barrel, now cracked and useless. The lower deck was scrubbed and brought back to proper order.

An hour after the pirate ship disappeared over the horizon, another sail was sighted by the masthead lookout. It rapidly approached and was quickly identified as a Navy man o' war out of Plymouth. As it approached, the skipper had a signal flown requesting a meeting. *Rosie* was brought up into wind, tacked through the wind onto starboard tack with foretop, sprits'l backed, main top, main, and fore courses furled. *Rosie* continued barely making steerage way, waiting for the man o' war to ease sails and come up to windward. The skipper called across to the naval captain that he had just come out of an engagement with a pirate, leaving the pirate discomforted, probably ripe for picking should the Navy be interested. He would be grateful for a consideration with respect to any prize money. The Navy captain, who knew the skipper, laughed. The skipper told the captain the last known bearing of the pirate, after which the captain trimmed sails and set off to claim an easy prize and deal with a renegade English crew. *Rosie* reset all sails, braces eased to gain speed, tacked back onto port and her former heading. The skipper called the crew together to congratulate them on their first active and highly successful engagement with the enemy. They cheered him in turn. After which he led the sad duty of the burial at sea of the dead crewman.

CHAPTER 14

Journal entry—*23 to 24 March 1614*

We were back in Sutton Pool late afternoon, quayside, with Gunt once more removed to the Fort. Tremaine slipped away with his rescued sailors. He said he looked forward to spending time with me. We had a lot of catching up to do. I agreed and we shook hands on it. Llewelyn and his men returned to the fort, from whence they had been sent by Sir F. We were expected to remain in Plymouth for two days, then sail to Weymouth with the cargo we had aboard for Mr. Bushrode. I was tired with the battering I had had and the excitement of the engagement with the pirates. I requested leave to have my wounds taken care of. Permission granted, I returned to the Minerva. Annie was there.

"Merciful heaven," she called out to me. "What have they done to you?"

I hadn't looked at myself since Bilbao. As none of the crew had said anything, I hadn't thought of my appearance, battered though I felt. I had a black eye, and bloodstains on my shirt; I was limping and favoring my arm. The sleeve had been cut to expose the scrape and shoulder so they could be cleaned. Dusty had concerned himself with cleaning my wounds but not with how I looked, other than a rough stitch to close the shirt. As he and most of the other seamen tended to wear the same clothes until they were unwearable, a tatter here or there and a few bloodstains counted for nothing in his view.

Once in Annie's care, she whisked me into the kitchen scullery and stripped the shirt off my back. I yelped with pain. She pulled my britches down, exclaiming at the massive bruise on my hip. Nothing to be done with that one, apart from a liberal application of some clear liquid that smelt funny and stung. After that, I was allowed to pull my britches up again. With great efficiency she started swabbing me down, cleaning up the blood. Alfred came in, whistled in shock, and left hurriedly. Annie put some nasty-smelling paste on my arm and head and bandaged my arm. She told me to sit still, not to move, then disappeared, returning a few minutes later from my room with a change of clothes, my other set of seaman's garb. She helped me dress, led me to a corner of the taproom, and sat me down. Again, she told me to wait. A large tankard of ale appeared, followed by a large dish of stew with hunks of fresh bread. As I tucked in, I thanked her. She sat down across the table from me.

"Isaac Stanfield, you have been a silly boy."

"You told me that before."

"I did. When you told me about Aby and Will, I couldn't believe you immediately jumped to the worst possible conclusion. Well, I was right. Shortly after you sailed away, Will came down here."

"Will? Here?"

"He was in a state. He told me what had happened. He was frantic to get to you to explain. It seems Aby is a very unhappy girl."

With that she placed a package of letters in front of me and left me to read them. My heart sank. I had been a bloody fool, causing huge, continuing suffering to the two most important people in my life. I had to get back to them, and was ready to leap onto Maddie and be off. I calmed down. *Rosie* would be in Weymouth in a few days. I sent a note by courier to let them know I was back, that I understood the situation, and sent them both my abject apologies. I explained I was due in Weymouth around 26 March, and I told them when they could expect me in Dorchester. That way they could relax a little anticipating my arrival. I returned to *Rosie* in a contemplative mood. Most of the crew had been given shore leave. I needed the peace, the sounds of *Rosie* at rest—the slapping of the halyards, the hum of the wind through the rigging, the lapping of the water, the creaking of the hull as *Rosie* talked to herself, the constant mewling and screaming of the seagulls. I slept well.

Next morning, I was advised by the skipper that my presence was required at the fort. I accompanied him and Peg Jones. Captain Turner waylaid me just before we entered Sir F.'s office. He told me he'd had a meeting with a Mr. William Whiteway, who was attempting to get in touch with me. I thanked him, embarrassed. I said I had received letters from my friend Will, and I had already replied. I said that we were due to depart for Weymouth tomorrow. Thereafter, I planned to see Will in Dorchester. Captain Turner nodded, his mission accomplished.

On entering Sir F.'s office, he greeted us, telling us to sit. He looked at me and said my presence was required back in Dorchester, presumably by way of the *Sweet Rose* to Weymouth. The skipper looked at me. I nodded, unhappy, red in the face.

"Thank you, sir. I have been fully informed. A return visit to Dorchester is my intention, subject to being given leave to do so."

Sir F. looked at the skipper, who hadn't a clue what was going on.

"I will have a conversation with Mr. Stanfield on our return to the *Sweet Rose*, sir."

With that, to my heartfelt relief, the meeting moved to other matters. Sir F. said that he'd had a full briefing from Mr. Tremaine about the Bilbao voyage and the encounter with the pirate ship. He congratulated the skipper on his success. There would be prize money, indeed. The Navy had taken the ship, put the crew in irons, and had a prize crew sail the boat back where it was now in the naval dockyard.

"The primary reason for this meeting," he continued, "is to discuss the trip to Northern Virginia by the *Sweet Rose*. I have invited Mr. Stanfield to the meeting because he has an important role to play. As has been discussed, the reason for this trip is to find out the extent of English settlements between the Penobscot and Cape Cod. Captain Smith is about to leave from London, under the patronage of merchants who have been led to believe gold and copper mines are to be found. He has been tasked with carrying out a detailed survey of the coastline in those parts. He is taking several vessels with him, and is expected to return with strong evidence of the commercial viability of trade with the Indians."

Sir F. explained that Captain Smith's voyage was not being made at Sir F.'s request, nor was it to his immediate benefit or control.

"Instead, I have Captain Hobson leaving in June," Sir F. said. "He has two Indians accompanying him who have been my guests for several years here in England. They speak English and, of course, are keen to return to their homeland. Mr. Stanfield, perhaps you can provide us with your assessment."

"Yes, sir. I spent January and February with them. I believe I have established their trust and friendship and have a pretty good idea of their strengths and weaknesses, as well as their homelands, one coming from the Monhegan area, the other Capawack, an island near Cape Cod."

Sir F. picked up the thread. "Mr. Stanfield advises me that they are likely to escape once in home waters. I will tell Captain Hobson to attempt to keep them confined as long as possible, as their presence on board is to advise him about local navigation, provide introductions to their tribes, and be interpreters. It is vital we develop a strong trading relationship with the Indians. The French are encroaching into our territory, and have established good relations with the locals. We stand to lose major commercial advantage if we don't build our own contacts and through them build settlements."

The skipper asked about the expected timing for *Rosie*'s trip.

"I need to ensure that the Smith and Hobson expeditions are completed and that I receive reports back of their accomplishments before sending you off," Sir F. responded. "It will be too close to the end of the year for you to leave and return this year. You should plan to leave in early 1615. I have every expectation that by the time you get to Northern Virginia, the two Indians, Epenow and Assacomet, will be long back with their people. It seems to me, we stand a better chance of engagement if they are back, settled with their people, and do not see us as a threat. I expect Stanfield to make first contact with them. I don't require you to enter into any trading activity unless it is a byproduct of your interactions. Keep in mind, though, we need to have a permanent presence there as soon as possible to encourage trade and to ensure there is no encroachment by the French from the north or by our Southern Virginia fellow countrymen from the south."

Peg Jones said he had heard from fishermen that there were settlements there already.

Sir F. smiled wryly. "I believe there are a number of settlements in formation. The Popham attempt in 1607-1608, which ended ignominiously, resulted in a few of the colonists staying, possibly in the Pemaquid area. Fishermen have established settlements as supply centers, to allow them to dry their fish prior to shipping the catches back to their markets on this side of the Atlantic. I need to know whether any of these settlements could form the basis for substantial, permanent colonies."

Sir F. asked if we had any further questions. I had none. The skipper and Peg had been across the Atlantic several times to the fishing grounds off Newfoundland. They were comfortable with the northern route, which they discussed with Sir F. He agreed, and said he'd told Captain Challons as much, but his advice had been ignored, resulting in the ill-fated outcome of that expedition. He ended the meeting by suggesting that we read Richard Hakluyt's published works, especially the 1600 edition of his "Principal Navigations," third volume, which he had a copy of in his study. It describes the many voyages made by English explorers to America. In addition, and more relevant, we should read John Brereton's account of Gosnold's trip in 1602 and James Rosier's account of the Weymouth trip in 1605. Sir F. had been told that there was an excellent description of the Northern Virginia coastline with a chart, produced by Samuel de Champlain, from his voyage under the direction of Sieur de Monts of 1605, which overlapped Weymouth's, published last year in France. Sir F. said that he understood that we were due to go to Honfleur later this year. He suggested I see if I could get a copy when there. Looking at me, he said that when I had a free afternoon, I might want to write out a copy of the Brereton and Rosier accounts to keep and study. They were precious to him. He didn't want them leaving his possession. It would be a good educational exercise for me, having recently left school. I grimaced, and there was a general chuckle at my discomfiture.

As I sat and listened, I was astonished at the investment in time, capital, and effort expended by Sir F. over ten years in Northern Virginia. It seemed, for the most part, he was the only one who saw the strategic importance of these English possessions, beyond short-term commercial gain. I was further amazed at his persistence, fortitude, and commitment.

We returned to *Rosie*. Back in his cabin the skipper eyed me thoughtfully.

"It seems we need to do a better job of looking after you. You seem to attract danger or perhaps danger attracts you."

"The former, I'd like to think, sir."

"Tell me, what was Sir Ferdinando getting at about you and Dorchester?"

"I am in a close relationship, sir. I made to visit her in Dorchester before our Bilbao trip. Due to a terrible misunderstanding, I left without talking to her, in the belief our relationship had ended. She became aware I had been to Dorchester and why I'd left. She thought the same by my behavior. Sir Ferdinando was made aware while we were at sea. He was kind to show his interest."

The skipper looked at me a long time without saying anything, then sighed.

"A long time ago, I was to be married. We had a stupid row. I left on a fishing boat for Newfoundland. On my return, some six months later, she was no longer living in our local village, having left to stay with a cousin in the north of England. I was told her heart had broken. There was no response to any of my repeated attempts to contact her and I have lived every day since mourning the loss."

I grimaced, slowly shaking my head at the sad tale.

"So, young Stanfield. We will get you to Weymouth by Saturday, 26 March, weather permitting. You have leave to return to Dorchester on our arrival. You will have six days. Our next scheduled sailing is on or about 1 April."

"Thank you, sir."

"And don't screw it up like I did," he added.

I left him with his sad memories. Beneath that gruff exterior, he had a tender soul.

I was permitted to go ashore. I sought out Captain Turner and requested access to Sir F.'s study to undertake the assignment I had been given. It took most of the day. I returned to the Minerva, found Annie, and told her what had happened. Under other circumstances, I thought, but I put that thought away. Annie was a beautiful, warm-hearted, loyal friend. Keep it right there. I went to my room, collected my finer clothes for my Dorchester visit, packed them in my saddlebags, and found Mr. Alfred Potts. I settled my account with him, asking him to make sure Maddie was suitably exercised and looked after. Annie came by and overheard. She told me not to worry, she would consider Maddie to be hers as long as I was away. I couldn't ask for anything more. At the same time, she presented me with a new hat. A cavalier with a feather in the band, no less. She said she was keeping my old hat as a keepsake. The cavalier had been left ages since by a non-returning traveler. She had added the feather, a pheasant's. It fitted perfectly.

I went back to the taproom and saw David Tremaine. We sat and had an ale or two. He asked me about my life. I found myself confiding in him. He had heard about how I ran away to sea. It seemed another lifetime ago. We were both surprised it had only happened last August. He told me a little about his past life but was more comfortable telling stories of strange, funny, wonderful incidents along the way. I asked him what the skipper had meant about prize money from the capture of the pirate ship. He laughed.

"What would be likely to happen is that the boat will be sold with all its appurtenances, or if not sold, valued by a prize court. The pirates would have prices on their heads that would be added, any ill-gotten gains found on board—captured cargo, jewelry, gold, whatever would be valued—and that amount added to the total. A portion would be retained in the king's name, the Navy man o' war would receive half of the balance, and *Rosie* would receive the other half, depending on the generosity of the prize court. Let us say that *Rosie*, which means the skipper, as co-owner, is awarded around £1,000, the probable disbursement would be about a third to the skipper, a third to the officers, and a third to the crew. Not sure how many crew there were on board that would be counted, but let's say, for ease of arithmetic, thirty, including Mr. Llewelyn's men. You, Isaac, would stand to receive about £10. This is an educated guess, and there are all sorts of provisos here. You might end up with nothing. Don't hold your breath."

Still, I thought to myself, more possible accumulating assets, all to the good. As we parted company, he informed me that Gunt had been hanged the night before, privately in the fort, his body removed to be buried in an unmarked grave, elsewhere. Poor wretched, twisted man. I could not think of him with much compassion, but I did find a little pity for the miserable man, now dead. I returned to *Rosie* with my saddlebags, added to my journal and, watch-keeping aside, slept till morning.

Journal entry—*25 to 26 March 1614*

We left Plymouth, start of afternoon watch, 25 March. Weather held, loom gale from the southwest. Once round St. Nicholas Island we had a fast sail on starboard tack all the way to Weymouth and were quayside as three bells of the forenoon watch sounded, 26 March. Skipper released me from further duties with a handshake and a whispered "good luck."

I changed into my finery, and wearing my new cavalier hat and carrying my saddlebags I went to the King's Arms stables and found Silas.

"Silas, what the hell are you doing here?" I asked. "I thought you had moved back to Dorchester."

"And a good day to you too, sir. Christ, it's Isaac! I didn't recognize you. You just caught me. I was back talking to Adam on an errand and will be riding back to Dorchester in a few minutes."

"Excellent. I will ride with you, but I need a horse."

Adam found me one, called Whistler, at a generous rate, which he tacked up. I promised it back by 1 April, and we were off. It was good to catch up. We were that distracted, it took two hours to get to Dorchester. For the most part Silas plied me with questions about my adventures, and as he listened, he kept whistling—that only happened when he was seriously impressed. As we rode up South Street, he stopped. We sat looking at each other. He sniffed. With a tear in his eye, he leaned across, grasping my arm.

"Isaac. I remember you as a little tyke, always in trouble, full of lip. I thought you had potential. I was happy to act as a replacement for your father, God rest his soul."

I was slightly startled at the depth of emotion in this normally taciturn man.

"I'm proud of you, my boy. I am proud of what you have become. I am proud of the little I have done to set you on the path you are now on. God bless you."

I kneed Whistler close, reached over, and hugged him.

"Now go to your Aby. I have work to do."

He turned and left me. I smiled looking after him, my wonderful teacher and friend.

Journal entry—*27 March 1614*

Up South Street, I turned left on West Street and rode into Baker's yard. Hearing the clatter of hooves, Aby looked out the kitchen door. Puzzled, she moved out into the yard.

"Can I help you, sir?"

I took off my hat.

"Aby."

"Isaac," she whispered.

I was unaware of dismounting. She sobbed, stomach-heaving sobs, as she held both my hands and looked up at me, tears streaming. Then she fell into my arms.

"I'm sorry, so, so sorry," I whispered.

We just stood clinging to each other. Not another word was spoken. There was no need. We slowly eased our almost desperate binding and looked into each other's eyes—windows deep, deep into our souls. Our minds engaged, our hands rested lightly on each other's shoulders. I gently brushed a soft wisp of hair away from her eyes, then the tears. There were deep remnants of pain and sadness in them, which slowly blossomed into wide-eyed wonder.

"My father is away till tomorrow," she whispered.

Moving indoors, Aby led me by the hand to her bedroom.

A long time later, we came back to earth. Dressed, we sat holding hands, silent at the kitchen table, knowing that once we started the talking, we had much ground to cover until we each knew everything that had happened and been felt by the other since we saw each other last.

After we had talked a long while, I ventured, "What about Will?"

"Oh Isaac, my love, I forgot. We got your letter and assumed you would probably come here, but somehow thought it would be the twenty-seventh. He said to let him know when I thought it safe for him to see you."

She laughed as I mouthed the word "safe?"

"I will go and see him tomorrow morning, my sweet. I'm not moving from your side till then."

Aby started making supper while I tended to Whistler. Mr. Baker was due back on the morrow mid-morning. He was on a journey buying stock. I would need to be out of there before then. Rather than seek a bed with the Whites, I wanted freedom of movement at least for the first few days. I needed to be with Aby, but I had to come to terms with her father, when he was back and watchful, on what was allowable.

As I thought about it, I said to Aby, "I think it better if I removed Whistler tonight. The evidence of his presence overnight might take some explaining."

Hand in hand, leading a patient Whistler, we walked over to Lower Burton. I booked a room for myself at the Sun for that night. They gave me a room next to the stables and provided a stall for Whistler. Aby and I walked back arm in arm, with frequent stops, too happy, mesmerized by each other, to talk much beyond little expressions of love and intimacy. Back at the house, Aby continued her cooking. As she worked, I told her everything that had happened and admitted to the plans for more sea voyages, including one to Northern Virginia which needed talking through to calm her concerns. Much later, we went to bed, but first with water heated on the kitchen range, we undressed and bathed each other. Then, she explored every bump, bruise and scrape, wanting to know the reasons for each. She cleaned and, as necessary, rebandaged every blemish, kissing each, including some places where there weren't any. In bed, we continued to delight in the touch and feel of each other's bodies, the areas that lulled, soothed, and excited us, which brought us to a climax. Then, wrapped together, we slept.

We were up by seven o'clock and removed all signs of my presence. We agreed that I would return about lunchtime to visit with Mr. Baker. We kissed goodbye, and I went back to the Sun to establish residence and then on to the Whiteway's house to find Will. He and I both expressed huge regret—me for my foolishly jumping to wrong conclusions and he for creating a confusing tableau as he tried to comfort Aby. He was quick to ask if I had seen Aby and when did I get in. I gave him a brief account of my return to Aby and that I had promised to return to her at lunchtime. Slightly embarrassed, he expressed his pleasure that we had made up and everything was wonderful again between us. I gave him the journal entries I had completed since the last batch I had sent him, up to 24 March. He wanted to dive straight in but said he would wait until I had gone before doing so. My changed appearance needed immediate explanation, however. I had left Dorchester at Christmas looking like a cross between a sailor and a farm laborer. Now I'd arrived with my fancy cloak, hose, and cavalier looking like a popinjay. What accounted for this transformation? I gave him a short version of an answer, just the highlights. I did drop the fact that the cavalier was a gift to replace my previous hat, which had a hole in it from being shot off my head.

"Tell me, tell me," he urged.

"No, Will, it's all in the journal," I said. "By the way, have you ever heard of anyone called Jack Melrose?"

"The highwayman, of course. He and a henchman are the scourge of Devon and Somerset. Their reputation is one of merciless cruelty. They have killed many. There is a huge price on their heads. Why?"

"Aaah."

"Does that have anything to do with your hat?"

"Will, be patient. It's in the journal."

Will sighed, fingering the pages, torn between them and me. He asked where I was going next, though in truth I think he really meant *when*. With a friendly wave, I told him that I was leaving right then and there for the rectory to see P., and off I went, immensely relieved Will and I were back again in easy relations as we had been.

I met P. as he was leaving to go to Holy Trinity Church. Mrs. White and the boys were with him. Obviously, Mrs. White had warned P. that I had changed, as he didn't bat an eyelid. He invited me to join his family, which I was pleased to do. While P. went to the vestry to prepare for the service, I walked down the south aisle with the White family to the side aisle pew near the front. Heads turned; many of the faces I knew. Puzzled looks changed to startled expressions as I caught many an eye and grinned. There was a definite interest from the congregation. After the service, I was able to disengage from my old friends with the promise I would see them during the week. I snatched a few words with P., who told me to meet him at the rectory at nine o'clock Monday morning.

I returned to the Bakers' house, seeing as I approached that Mr. Baker had returned. A large cart and horse were backed into the yard. Aby was there to greet me. Mr. Baker came out of the house, stopped, and looked at us with our arms around each other.

"Thank goodness, you've come back! Aby has been miserable. We've had a perpetual thunderstorm, aye and with lightning, for the last month it seems."

With that he came over to shake my hand. He stepped back, looking at me.

"You've grown. Up and out. How's that possible in just the last few months since we last saw you?"

He came closer and studied my face.

"You have matured. Your eyes are older. You have been experiencing life. It makes you look calmer, steadier. The boy has gone," he said.

He looked at Aby, nestled up against me, holding my arm in both her hands. His eyes narrowed for a moment, then he nodded to himself. "You look like your mother." He paused, looking down for a moment, his eyes on something we couldn't see. "She looked at me the way you are looking at Isaac now the morning after we first lay together."

Aby started against my side. I put my arm round her, saying nothing but gazing at him, frozen. There was a long silence. Mr. Baker was deep in thought.

"We loved each other. She was your age, Aby. I wasn't much older. Once we had taken that step, we knew we would marry and soon. Coupling is for married people."

Another long silence. Aby was trembling. I couldn't believe what I was hearing. Mr. Baker reached forward. He took our hands, one in each of his, and looked long into our eyes.

"This is a silly question, but do you really love each other?" he asked.

I had to clear my throat to get the strangled "yes" out. Aby just nodded furiously, tears in her eyes.

"God bless you both."

Holding our hands, he brought them together, lifted them to his lips, and kissed them. He turned and walked, head bowed, back into the house. Aby buried her head into my shoulder, her arms wrapped around me, still shaking. She lifted her head and we kissed.

"Aby, I'm confused. I haven't even proposed to you yet. I haven't asked for your father's blessing, but hasn't he just given it?"

Aby smiled, kissed me again. She left me, going after her father. As she entered the house, she turned, saying quietly, "I need a moment with him."

After she had gone, one word reverberated in my mind: marriage. The idea had been floating in the recesses of my mind, coming to the forefront occasionally, but I had not thought it through. Now, it came crashing in, obliterating every other thought. I would be away. I was leaving for Northern Virginia in twelve months, and I would be gone for several more months before then. I was due back on *Rosie* in a few days. Doubts about the enormity of it all began to surface. We needed to talk, as well as to P. Was there an age issue? I was seventeen for Heaven's sake, Aby sixteen. Surely we were too young.

With these thoughts whirling round my head, Aby came back out. As she'd suspected, she had found her father in some state in the kitchen. With her arms round him, he had, through his tears, told her how vividly our happiness had reminded him of her mother and the too-short time they had together. With Aby's birth came her passing—a continuation, but a new and different life. He told Aby that the happiness she had now was God's most beautiful gift. It must be cherished. It was, in a way, a handing on of the happiness he had once shared and was guarding, waiting for the right moment to pass on to Aby. Overcome, ignoring the doubts, I went down on my knees in front of her, holding her hands in mine.

"Aby, my darling, darling friend and lover, will you marry me?"

She lifted my head, and a joyous peal of laughter rang 'round the yard. Five pigeons startled and clattered away.

"Yes, yes, yes! A thousand times yes!"

I buried my head in her lap, with her arms pressed around me.

"Now, we need to talk. We are to be married. My father has given his blessing, but the news is all too sudden for him. He is dependent on me for care and companionship, to run his home, help him with his business. He wants me to have everything I wish for. He sees how happy I am, but he can't help feeling a huge loss. He is also worried about your ability to support a wife. So, let's not be hasty. My father needs the time to plan his future without me and be convinced you can look after me."

Brought back down to earth with a huge sense of relief on my part, we joined Mr. Baker in the kitchen, sat 'round the table, and began to unravel the consequences of what had just happened. The discussion continued, branching down many alleyways, over lunch. Finally, it was agreed that nothing further could be done or planned until tomorrow, when I was to see P., my legal guardian. That being settled, Mr. Baker said he had to sort out his new supplies. The poor cart horse was still in its traces, half asleep, weight on three legs. While Aby sorted out the kitchen, Mr. Baker and I went out, with me carrying as ordered until the cart was empty and the supplies stowed. He hopped on the cart, driving away to return horse and cart from whence they came. I returned to the kitchen. Aby's speed of recovery to her former irreverent self was remarkable. In little time, she was retelling the whole, unfortunate episode, stretching the facts till we were both laughing at our stupidity. But we did agree that I should return to the Sun, coming back tomorrow after my meeting with P. Aby said she thought it better if I left her to spend the evening with her father. He would be much less inhibited if I wasn't there. They would be attending evening service at Holy Trinity. On Mr. Baker's return to the kitchen, I told him I had errands to run and I would see them tomorrow. I hugged Aby, shook Mr. Baker's hand, and left them.

My mind was full of Aby. I wanted nothing to interfere with the wondrous images that flooded my thoughts, but I couldn't dispel the doubts. I walked back to the Sun. The coming spring was bringing all its scents and frantic animal life, afternoon sunlight picking up the many shades of fresh green in the trees. I went to the stables, got Whistler, and took him for a long ride out along the Exeter Road, off into the countryside. Where the bridleway allowed it, and where the going was reasonably firm, we cantered for miles while I attempted to put my thoughts of Aby and our future into some kind of perspective. Married or not, wouldn't Aby need to stay with her father in Dorchester? Why would we marry if she and her father had to remain dependent on and a part of each other's life while I was away? Should she not continue that close relationship with her father for the next year? It will be soon enough that they'll be parted.

Was I unconsciously looking for reasons to delay or even deny the marriage? I tried to ignore the thought as I turned for home. Then another thought struck me: No matter how long or short the engagement period might be, I needed to buy an engagement ring. I would ask P. about that tomorrow.

Next morning, I made my way to the rectory and was shown into P.'s study. He greeted me with great warmth and bade me sit across from his desk where he'd been working on some papers. He stopped what he was doing, leaned back, and looked at me over his spectacles. I became a little uncomfortable as the silence continued.

"Isaac, it seems we have much to talk about."

"Yes, sir, we do."

"I want to hear about your adventures, and to find out what Sir Ferdinando is doing, but there is something more immediate to discuss. I think you were aware that Will asked me to talk with Abigail Baker."

I nodded, wondering what was coming.

"I did," he said. "Between you, you appeared to have drawn some incorrect conclusions that have caused much unhappiness to Abigail, most certainly, but knowing you as I do, to you too."

"Yes, but—"

He held up his hand.

"Abigail and her father were at evening service last night. They asked to see me afterward, and I was happy to do so. I have to say, I hardly recognized the radiant young lady. Abigail told me that you two had made up and everything between you was clear and in accord. I said I found that news most welcome. Abigail's father said he understood I was to meet with you today. I said that was the case. He told me, somewhat to my surprise, that you and Abigail wish to be married. He had given his unconditional blessing, and told me that you wished to talk to me, as your legal guardian. They desired to make sure, ahead of our meeting, that I understood the depth of their feeling."

I looked up at P., who was gazing at me with a benign smile on his face.

"I have watched you both from infants. I baptized you both in Holy Trinity's font. I have seen how you have developed as friends and have become close. I realized how close when I saw you, inseparable, last Christmas—the joy you had in each other's company. I suffered with you both over your misunderstanding. When I saw Abigail last night we talked about you. Her love was almost incandescent. I looked at her father, and his face confirmed my suspicions that you and Abigail must know each other, biblically speaking."

I blushed a deep red and did not deny it.

"Fornication out of wedlock is a sin. Yet for perhaps a third of all the couples I marry, the bride is already pregnant. There are the other poor wretches who, becoming pregnant, are deserted by the men whose seed they carry. Abigail insisted that night had been an overwhelming, unstoppable happening. It had not happened before and would not happen again until you were married. Is that so?"

Again, I nodded, not remembering any discussion of *that* particular commitment.

"You love each other and you have placed this burden on yourselves. It's admirable from a moral standpoint but questionable as to your ability to sustain it."

He got up and started to pace.

"Isaac, the normal marrying age for a man and a woman is in their mid-twenties. Society frowns on a couple getting married before the husband has the income and assets to take care of her. The bride's father will offer a dowry, but should not be expected to shoulder the costs of looking after his married daughter, let alone an impecunious son-in-law."

My heart sank. Mid-twenties—a delay, yes, but the time he spoke of was ten years away. It would be impossible.

"But sir, what is the legal marriageable age?"

"Fourteen for the man, twelve for the woman with parental consent. I am your legal guardian, and the union would be with my consent."

I was confused and felt the whole conversation spinning away from my understanding and control. The conflict must have shown on my face.

"Isaac, Isaac, my dear boy. You are like a son to me. I am concerned for your happiness, above all. I have already told you how I have watched you both grow up. Needless to say, you have become many years more mature than the seventeen-year-old body you inhabit. Likewise, Abigail has been the mistress of the Baker household for as long as I can remember. Now talk to me about your situation."

I wasn't sure what he meant by situation, but his words steadied my thoughts. I said it was my understanding that the *Sweet Rose* would be based in Weymouth. Aby and I would be together frequently, either in Dorchester or Weymouth. I also said that, for me, there would be long trips overseas, including a voyage to Northern Virginia in 1615. Therefore, I felt that it would be best if Aby remained living at home, looking after her father while I was away. If it was inconvenient for me, once married, to live under Mr. Baker's roof, I could rent a property of my own. He asked me how I expected to afford that expense. The wages of a seaman were known to be not munificent. I told him about the reward for capturing Jack Melrose. His eyebrows shot up.

I said there was a possibility of further prize money from the pirate ship we captured. I said this with a laugh, because P. could hardly contain himself.

"You have captured a notorious highwayman and been in a victorious battle with a pirate ship?" he asked. "Ye whales and fishes! I *must* know about these bold actions."

I told him that as a result of these and other events, I would have more than enough resources to find a place for Aby and me, if necessary.

"Enough, Isaac," he said with some emotion. "I must tell you in a clear fashion that I am most happy to give you my consent. I am happy to marry you both. But you say you will be away for long periods, including a planned voyage to Northern Virginia. I would suggest you wait to marry until after that trip—to be newly married only for you to disappear into unknown dangers would be most stressful for your wife. We must think of Mr. Baker, too. He has given his blessing, but Aby was insistent he be given time to plan his future without her."

I felt an enormous, if somewhat conflicted, sense of relief—pleased for P.'s approval and for the delay that would give me time, I hoped, to allay my doubts. Then asked him about buying an engagement ring. He said that he had something that he had kept these last seven years, and now was a good time to give it to me. He went back to his desk. From a drawer he brought me a small leather pouch with a drawstring.

"Open it."

I upended it, and jewelry cascaded into my hands: two rings, a bracelet, a pendant on a chain, and another necklace. I looked up, dazed.

"These pieces belonged to your mother. Before she died, she asked me to take care of them until you married. I was to give them to you to pass on to your wife. One of those rings was her engagement ring. She was buried wearing her wedding ring, as was your father. Now, you wait here while I tell Mrs. White that everything has gone as planned. She will be most glad to hear."

He left the room. I felt quite exhausted. We were to be married, though thankfully not immediately. I hoped the interim would give me time to reconcile my thoughts. My fingers traced each piece of jewelry. I was overwhelmed, envisaging a mother long gone. I needed the right time to give these to Aby. I put them away. When P. came back into the room, I asked whether we might postpone further conversation. I wanted to go back to tell Aby and her father of his consent. He laughed.

"No need, dear boy. I told them both last night that you had my consent. I said to Aby that she might like to come here at about ten o'clock this morning.

She's been in the kitchen talking to Mrs. White for the last half hour. All right, Abigail, you may come in."

Aby bounced in with the sweet greeting, "Hello, my husband-to-be."

I grinned, feeling slightly embarrassed and a little guilty as P. beamed at us. We discussed our plans, unformed as they were at this point. Two matters had to be dealt with prior to our marriage: Mr. Baker's future and my trip to Northern Virginia next year. The former would take time to evolve. The latter depended on Sir F. We had no control over either matter. All agreed that we should enjoy our engagement and use the unsettled time to build our mutual commitment, interdependence, and love. I glanced at Aby, and she was gnawing her lip. She looked at me and smiled. P., oblivious, settled back into his chair and demanded a full account of my activities.

We spent time discussing Sir Ferdinando's intentions in Northern Virginia. P. thought Sir F. was on to something, looking for existing fishing settlements. He was aware that fishing boats would double up on crew to provide shore support or exchange those shore-based crew with replacements. He expressed concern that these groups of men would be isolated from the word of God and its steadying influence on what might otherwise be unbridled licentiousness. He was fascinated by the time I'd spent with the two Indians. That was one part of Sir F.'s plans P. thoroughly approved of, though he was doubtful about the rest—unrealistic in his opinion. He was convinced whole communities needed to be persuaded to form plantations, as he called them, and be given the means to become self-sufficient. There would need to be compelling reasons for them to go. Investors would have to think long-term and to the intangible returns on their investments. That would be difficult, but necessary for there to be any chance of success. We ended the conversation with P. saying that, when I was over there, I ought to keep in mind his concerns and, where there were any existing settlements, how they might be expanded into the type of plantation he'd described.

Looking at Aby, he said, "Isaac, as I mentioned to you before, I imagine you and Aby transplanting over there. Consider, what would you require as a minimum to convince you that you could not only survive, but thrive?"

Aby looked at him open-mouthed. She couldn't believe what she had just heard. It had never entered her mind that moving to the New World might be an option. I hastened to calm her. P. apologized and said he only meant it as a hypothetical exercise in evaluating what the problems and possibilities might be.

We were entertained to lunch and left with much affection shown by all. I walked a very thoughtful Aby back to her home. Mr. Baker was hard at work restoring the damage from last year's fire. He had rebuilt the pit and had a cauldron prepared. He sat down with us in the kitchen. I thanked him for the conversation he'd had with P. the night before. It had made everything much easier for me. He smiled. Aby confirmed for him that we had no immediate plans to get married since I would be traveling and working. More importantly, we needed time to discuss and plan how the marriage would affect Mr. Baker's life, a point he appreciated.

After a good visit, I left them and went to the school to find Will and my other school friends and tell them my news. I walked down South Street, past the shell of the old school building. Work had progressed, but it seemed as though it would be a long time before it was rebuilt. I hung about outside the temporary school building until the afternoon classes were over. At the sounding of a bell, a mob poured out. Some students had been in church and had seen and recognized me in my finery, some had not. Will and I, along with a group of particular friends, disentangled ourselves from the rest. There were perhaps ten of my closest friends there, boys I'd grown up with from babyhood almost. Chattering like starlings, we moved up South Street to our favorite gathering spot, the graveyard behind All Souls. Will must have provided some commentary on my deeds, as the questions came thick and fast. They wanted to share what one of their own was doing, one who had escaped the bonds of adolescence and the scholastic cloister. They most wanted to know about my meetings with Jack Melrose and the pirate ship. Poor Will, seeing I was surrounded, waited in the background until he and I could have our own time together.

When they had been satiated with the tales of derring-do, the conversation came around to Aby. She'd been with me, a part of their company, throughout Christmas. She was a friend to them, and they weren't stupid. They'd seen her become distraught and withdrawn recently. Will, bless him, had kept his mouth shut, but her visible unhappiness still caused speculation. I told them I'd wanted to find and talk with them today to reassure them that Aby and I were not only fine, we were betrothed. They greeted this news with great excitement, if not wonder. They still saw me as a seventeen-year-old masquerading as a man, and Aby they saw as one of the gang. What was this marriage plan, then? I felt a subtle shift in the mood. I had always been considered something of a black sheep, as I'd had no parents from the age of ten, and tended to get into as many scrapes as the rest of my friends put together. They'd been slightly bemused about my long relationship with Silas, my preference for the stables over the more genteel home life they all came from. Still, they were happy to follow and enjoy me for who I was, someone who took them to places and into situations they might not otherwise have experienced. Now, I had moved on. I was older, more worldly, and independent. I had a new life. To cap it all, I was to be married—to Aby of all people. Marriage was something that, in their families, usually happened to brothers and sisters ten years older—virtual strangers to them. The afternoon was getting on, and they started moving off in ones and twos, wishing me and Aby well. As they walked away, I sensed the separation. I was someone they used to know. Sad, but inevitable. I, too, sensed my own transformation from the schoolboy I was. Their interests were no longer mine.

Soon only Will and I were left. He, too, was moved by the separation. We were too close for our relationship to falter, but he saw the change in our friends and recognized that he'd become a bridge between them and me. It started to rain, and we hurried back to his house and sat in his father's study. I said I would be pleased to have him as my best man. He said he would be honored. I told him the date couldn't be set yet and explained the reasons, keeping my own concerns to myself. Then, we got to my journal. Will had me relive everything as he kept the pages in front of him, extracting every last jot and tittle.

I returned to Aby and her father. The one thing I most needed was a mutually agreed upon understanding of the living arrangements. That issue was quickly resolved. Aby would live at home. Of course, I would be welcome to visit at the Baker home whenever I was back in Dorchester, but in the interests of decorum, I should find separate accommodation for myself until we were married. The next two days I spent mostly with Aby. We talked about everything from our childhoods onward. We explored the subject of our lives separately, our plans together, and what the future might hold. I gave her my mother's jewels, first taking her left hand and placing the engagement ring on the fourth finger. The ring was a little loose, but to me it was a magical link tying us together. I told her what P. had told me. She wrapped her arms 'round me and wept. I had distant memories of my parents, and Aby's response touched some heretofore untapped reservoir in me. Gently, she asked me to tell her what I remembered about them.

"Isaac, my sweet, in all the years I've known you, as someone I played with and had wild adventures with, I have never asked you about your family," she said.

I told her what I remembered.

"We had a large farm in Piddletrenthide," I began. "I was the only child who survived. Three sisters were born after me: two died at childbirth and the third, six years younger than me, died with my parents during the plague epidemic that hit parts of Dorset in 1607. My mother had curly brown hair, a button nose, and the happiest green eyes. In memory I can see her now, fleetingly. Her name was Judith, and she was just twenty-nine when she died. My father was from Cornwall. His name was Roderick, he had a full beard, and was built like a barrel. He was immensely strong and had been a champion wrestler. We used to wrestle together. He was a good father. He was thirty-two when he died, a successful, respected member of the community. They are buried with my sisters in All Saints Churchyard in Piddletrenthide. I have never been back."

Aby asked how P. came to be my guardian. I said that I had been attending the Free School for a year before my parents died. P. had known my parents for a long time and had baptized me. It was through him I started at the school. I boarded with P. during the week, returning home at the weekend. When my parents were dying, P. promised them he'd look after me. He has done just that ever since.

Aby and I examined the pieces of my mother's jewelry together. We felt a mixture of joy and sadness, both of us touched that my mother's dying wish had been fulfilled. Aby said she would arrange to have the engagement ring fitted properly while I was away.

We had breakfast together the following morning, before I returned to Weymouth. With fond farewells, we parted. I hoped to be back in a few weeks.

─── CHAPTER 15 ───

Journal entry—*2 April to 1 May 1614*

We made fast passage to Honfleur. M. Giradeau was no longer comfortable with the politics in La Rochelle and the escalating Catholic pressure on the Huguenot city-state. As a result, his commercial engagement with France had moved to Honfleur and Rouen. Honfleur was a pretty port and harbor at the mouth of the Seine, guarding the approaches to Rouen upriver. A channel heading southeast led to the inner harbor, where we docked. We were delivering woolens and a consignment of weapons, pikes, swords, and firearms. We were to bring back salt, wine, brandy, and honey. We would be seeking to establish a relationship with pelt merchants, specifically those trading in North American beaver, as an alternative source to Giradeau's former suppliers. The skipper told me more about Honfleur. It was the port from which Samuel Champlain had departed to build French settlements in New France, the country to the north of England's possessions in Northern Virginia. He, with others, had created a "*Compagnie du Canada.*" It was his intent to establish a trade monopoly to deny the Rochelais access to trade in New France, which they called Canada.

I had made it my business to find a published account and maps that Champlain had produced on his trips into Northern Virginia waters. Once off watch, I headed into the town. The harbor was noisy and exciting, surrounded by warehouses, tightly packed houses, bars, and shops with crowds of sailors from many countries. The weather being fine, I wandered away from the harbor's immediate vicinity and came to a square with small alleyways leading from it. In one, I found a chandler's shop with nautical items in the window. I entered and a tiny man with spectacles perched on the end of his nose appeared from behind a counter and greeted me in French. When I replied, he responded in English. We introduced ourselves. His name was Josef Medec. He asked what he could do for me, and I told him I was looking for accounts written by or for M. Samuel Champlain of his voyages to North America.

"Why? For what purpose?" M. Medec asked.

I explained I was a student of exploration and hoped, one day, to make my own voyage there. I had read the accounts of English voyages, but I had heard that Samuel Champlain had made a much more detailed and insightful account of his voyages. The man looked at me for a while before going to a shelf. He pulled down a book, telling me it had been recently published—*Les voyages des Sieur de Champlain . . .*

With the book came two maps of the coastline. He said this copy was his own, not available for sale. My disappointment showed, and he hastened to tell me that the book was published by Jean Berjon, Paris, in 1613 and it was likely available in Rouen. He asked if I intended to travel there. I said I didn't, that I was on an English vessel leaving in two days. He asked whether I'd be returning. I said yes, that the vessel I was on would be making regular trips to Honfleur. M. Medec indicated that if I would leave him a consideration, he'd be prepared to order a copy for me. I offered him a crown, which he accepted. He took my name and that of the *Sweet Rose*, as well as the skipper's name. He wrote out an order for me, showing I had paid him a crown as an initial payment. After our transaction, we talked about North America. He said he knew sailors who had been on the long voyage with Champlain from 1604 to '07. Perhaps next time I was in Honfleur, he might introduce me to some or other of them. They frequented a bar nearby. M. Medec told me he was the proprietor of the chandlery—a proud Breton, he said. We parted friends, with a mutual *"à bientôt."*

I returned to *Rosie* and informed the skipper of my shopping expedition. He expected we'd be back in Honfleur within two months. He'd been following leads given him by M. Giradeau to establish relations with a new business agent who could procure pelts and other North American goods for export to England. He'd had some success, but it required the presence of M. Giradeau before any contract could be signed. This fact meant that our next trip would include him, which meant we'd need to go to Plymouth to pick him up. Even without the North American merchandise, *Rosie* left for England with holds full. The wind changed with us off Le Havre, on the north shore of the Seine, downstream from Honfleur. We put into port to wait out the adverse conditions. After a week of steady westerlies with driving rain, the wind backed to southerly. We made for Weymouth but were becalmed off the Isle of Wight for another two days. We had no wind, only heavy rain. Strong tidal currents required us to anchor close inshore, off the south coast of the Isle. We eventually made Weymouth on 1 May. The delays meant we had a quick turnaround. The cargo was offloaded, and a light cargo for Plymouth was loaded in. We were away within twenty-four hours. I had only time to send a quick note to Aby, worded so Will could read it to her, along with my latest journal entry, which I sent with Adam.

Journal entry—*2 to 25 May 1614*

As soon as we made Plymouth, I reported to Sir F., who was pleased with my shopping expedition. Mr. Brown met with M. Giradeau. The outcome was that M. Giradeau accompanied us on our next trip to Honfleur. To my surprise, he had persuaded the skipper to allow Vivienne to come, too. Another full cargo and we were off to Honfleur by 8 May. Winds were changeable but mostly from the south. Leaving the Isle of Wight well astern, at about three bells in the morning watch, we were hit by a sudden squall. We broached before we were able to shorten sail, and as *Rosie* headed up into wind, the starboard bow buried itself in a large rogue wave. I was on watch on the main deck. Obi had visited the head and was immediately swept overboard. I heard his cry. "Man overboard, larboard side!" I shouted, and ran to the rail with a line. I saw Obi floundering as *Rosie*, nose clear of the wave, paid off and started picking up speed. Hands were called to douse sails, the helm brought up, but Obi was slipping out of reach. I grabbed a second line, freed by a seaman, stripped, took hold of the lines, and went over the side.

When I hit the water—so cold—Obi was splashing some ten yards off, appearing and disappearing in the waves, fast receding in the darkness. I tied the first line around me, hitched the second to it, and swam like a devil toward him. I hoped the lines were long enough and that the seaman aboard had them under control. As I approached Obi, his splashing stopped and he went down. I dived, grabbing his clothing and pulling him back up to the surface. The darkness, noise, cold, and waves made it difficult to focus on staying afloat, let alone seeing to Obi.

I tied the second line 'round him, pulling the knot up to his chest, and put him on his back, his head on my chest. I yanked three sharp pulls on my line and felt the tension take up on both. We were being pulled slowly toward *Rosie* on our backs. I looked over my shoulder to see *Rosie* had gone head to wind, sails flapping but drifting away. I turned back to Obi. He was unconscious. I put my arms around him and squeezed his stomach several times, my fists between his ribs. He retched seawater and groaned. I told Obi he was safe now, that he would be all right, and that all was well. He was hauled up the side first and I followed. When the cold and tension hit me, I collapsed in a sodden, naked heap. We were both carried to the warmth of Dusty's lair, from there to two hammocks in the focsle. As sleep overwhelmed me, I felt *Rosie* back on course, butting through the waves, as if nothing had happened.

As daylight dawned, I was up and back to retrieve my clothes. I had forgotten Vivienne was aboard. As I left the focsle, climbing down to the main deck, I was aware she had joined Peg and others at the quarterdeck rail looking down at me. She appeared totally unfazed. Her father appeared beside her at the rail, and as he pulled her away, she waved and blew me a kiss. I was called to the skipper's cabin. He sat me down and was silent. There wasn't much to say. He just sat there looking at me, shaking his head. Eventually, he said that M. Giradeau had witnessed my escapade and would like a moment to speak to me. He asked if I felt up to it now. I grimaced at the thought of Gallic overstatement, but nodded my assent. He grinned and called for a crewman to request M. Giradeau's presence.

M. Giradeau came in, with an effusive, gentlemanly manner. He kissed me on both cheeks, exclaiming how brave I was. What an honor it was to have me count him as a friend. I thanked him. He said Vivienne sent me her best felicitations, and no doubt would wish to tell me directly at some point. I was dismissed by the skipper, probably to save himself further embarrassment. I went back on deck, had a few back slaps from the crew, and went to see Obi, who was still fast asleep. Dusty said he'd be fine, though he'd swallowed a lot of sea water. I told him I had got him to retch while we were being towed back. Dusty said it probably saved Obi's life. Years ago, I had fallen in a river and had been fished out by Silas, who had done the same to me. I wouldn't have thought that I remembered his actions, but thankfully they came back to me when I needed them. What I'd done was without thinking.

Back to Honfleur, and, when permitted, I went to see M. Medec—this time accompanied by Vivienne. She had given me a hug after the Obi incident and told me her father couldn't stop talking about it, saying what a fine young man I was and, without any subtlety, went on about what a fine husband I'd make. Vivienne knew about Aby and advised her father that I was promised to another. It didn't seem to slow him down. I think M. Giradeau comes from a culture of arranged marriages.

M. Medec greeted me warmly, saying that the book I wanted had arrived. It was wrapped, and I was presented with a bill for the amount. Vivienne took it from me—"Papa insists." From her purse she paid M. Medec his sum, and we returned to *Rosie*. M. Giradeau and the skipper were ashore on business, and would not return for several hours. Offloading continued, followed by loading and stowing new cargo. Before my watch started, Vivienne and I unwrapped the parcel from M. Medec. It contained all the Champlain voyages, but most importantly, it included the account and maps of his journeys along the coast of Northern Virginia. Now the problem was to translate it all into English. Vivienne said that her father had someone based in Plymouth who was paid to translate documents to and from French. On his return to *Rosie*, M. Giradeau accepted my thanks and said he would be pleased to have the account translated. He was happy that his business transactions in Honfleur had proceeded well. He'd reached agreement with a business agent, an arrangement which promised considerable flow of North American produce through Honfleur and Dieppe to England.

Obi, now fully recovered, had become devoted. I'd saved his life, and he felt the life he'd been given back should be dedicated, in some way, to my service. This sense of obligation would be difficult to satisfy, as he was a ship's boy and I just a seaman, sharing the same watch as a coastal merchantman. I assured him that he owed no debt to me. Maybe it would be his turn to save my life next. I urged him that our best course was to continue as before.

Weather again played tricks on us and we were delayed, finally putting into Weymouth, 20 May, as the winds strengthened from the west. Our destination was Plymouth. The skipper said the weather looked like it would worsen. He did not expect to leave harbor for several days. He gave me leave to go ashore, saying I should be back within three days.

Whistler was available, and Adam was pleased to hire him out to me for three days. He told me to give his regards to Silas if I saw him. I was in Dorchester, approaching the Bakers within two hours. I found Aby at home; her father was out making deliveries. We enveloped each other. Conversation came later. We were sitting at the kitchen table when Mr. Baker returned. In the seven weeks I had been away, much had been accomplished. Her father had decided to retire from his business. He'd hoped to pass it on to his daughter and son-in-law, but, clearly, that plan wasn't to be. His sister, Aby's aunt Hilda, lived in Devizes. She was a recent widow and infirm. She wanted her brother to come to live with her and look after her, and he was content to do so. They had taken inventory of their possessions, determined what should go to Aby, what her father wanted to keep, and what should be sold or discarded. He had someone interested in buying the business, but that transaction might not take place till late in the year. So, for three days we settled into a kind of half-married life. Nights we spent apart. I had my bedroom at the Whiteses'. But during the day, we walked, talked, and worked. Mr. Baker reminisced about his wife, Aby's mum, and marriage in general. He talked about the learning process that only came from living with someone—"farts and all," as he indelicately put it. We both understood, deep down, that married life would be a balancing act. Misunderstandings would occur when what was said was not what was intended. We'd already experienced a most terrible misunderstanding. But life was good, and time apart was forgotten as soon as we were together. We were young and carefree. Tomorrow would take care of itself.

The days flew, and in no time I was galloping Whistler back to Weymouth to meet the skipper's deadline. I was greeted by Vivienne and her father, both on the quarterdeck as I came aboard, lines about to be cast off. All these greetings were more than offset by a growl from Peg.

"You're late," he said. "You are on watch. Get to work."

We had a break in the weather. Wind had abated and backed to the south. We beat our way out of Weymouth and 'round Portland Bill, a good reaching run west with the wind on the beam. We were alongside in Sutton Pool by second dog watch on 25 May. By the time I came off watch, a message had been delivered requesting my presence at Sir F.'s office. The Giradeaus had disembarked on our arrival, taking the Champlain account to arrange for its translation. Sir F. was with the skipper when I was shown in.

"Come in, Isaac. Sit down," he said. "I gather you have found the Champlain account and maps, paid for by M. Giradeau—with translation, to boot. Seems like your latest escapade brought its own reward. Well done, by the way. Mr. Brown and I have been talking about how we could reduce the life-threatening risks that you are forever taking. We decided it came with the territory. If we want you for the many attributes you have, we have to accept the other with good grace. Isn't that right, Isaiah?"

The skipper grunted, not graciously.

"The reason I asked you to come to this meeting is to set you to doing some serious reading and writing," Sir F. continued. "You will be accompanying Mr. Brown and the *Sweet Rose* to Northern Virginia in early 1615, in about eight or nine months, depending on weather and final planning. As you know, we have the accounts of the 1602 Gosnold voyage, and *Rosie*'s account of the Weymouth expedition in 1605, which you copied last March. Now, thanks to your efforts, we have the account of Champlain's voyages in 1605 and 1606. There is the Popham settlement story of 1607 as well, narrated by Mr. Davies. In addition to those published accounts, I have notes and maps of Challons' voyage and Pring's return voyage, both in 1606, as well as Harlow's voyage in 1611. Finally, we have two voyages currently underway—Captain Smith's and Captain Hobson's. I am hopeful that by the end of this year we will have full accounts of both.

I looked puzzled. Was I to copy all the other accounts? If so, it would be a major effort. Sir F. saw my look.

"I need you to study every one of the voyages I have listed and prepare a detailed report covering navigation, description of the coastline, weather, and Indian relations—their lifestyle, culture, food, and anything else you might discover. I understand that Mr. Brown needs your services through the summer, but start the process whenever you have the opportunity. By September, I want you here in Plymouth for a couple of months working on that report. It might keep you out of trouble, ahead of your Northern Virginia adventure."

I returned to *Rosie* and have found a corner to complete my journal entry.

CHAPTER 16

Journal entry—*26 May to 31 July 1614*

I wanted to surprise Aby on her seventeenth birthday, 3 June, to no avail. I was dependent on *Rosie's* movements, and she was kept busy with numerous trips along the south coast and across to France. We made a trip 'round to Bristol and a rough sail down to Cork. I wrote a couple of letters to Aby, and was surprised and overjoyed to receive a short one in return. She said Will had been working hard teaching her to read and write. He had read my early letters to her, and also used them to help teach her. Her learning was a secret she had kept from me when I was with her last. Her writing was incredibly neat, legible. She was obviously excited to be writing to me, but not yet ready to write much.

As requested by Sir F., I had begun studying the accounts of voyages he had in his study, next to his office in Plymouth. I was left to my own devices and enjoyed being able to spend my time focused on the research and the writing.

Tomorrow, 1 August, *Rosie* is returning to her home port. Her bottom needs scraping with other serious maintenance and repairs required to hull, mechanicals, and spars before setting off for North America. The crew is being released, once *Rosie* is hauled out. The work is expected to take three months. They will be on half pay and looking for part-time work. Obi wants to come back to Dorchester with me but I convinced him otherwise, persuading him to go home.

Journal entry—*1 to 12 August 1614*

I was required back in Plymouth by 15 August. I rode to Dorchester on Whistler, stopping to check on Johnny, who was on a trip to Oxford. His plans to enter a religious life have remained a steady commitment. Then to Dorchester and Aby. She proudly showed me her engagement ring, now fitting perfectly. We rode—with her sitting sideways behind, arms around me—to Eggardon Hill, to the summit looking out over Dorset toward Devon and the coast. Aby announced that everything was organized and planned at home. The business would be sold, the transaction completed by early December. Her father wanted to be in Devizes by Christmas. This news meant, Aby said pointedly, we needed to think more seriously about when we were to be married. My doubts and conflicts, long suppressed, bubbled to the surface. The voice in my ear questioned whether I wanted to get married at all.

"Aby, my love, I still don't know for sure when *Rosie* leaves or even if I will be part of the crew," I said.

"Isaac Stanfield. You told me, and I was impressed, how important your role will be with the Indians."

I stopped myself. "No, Aby," I said. "I'm not being honest with you or myself. The trip is planned for the spring of next year. I will be a member of the crew."

I felt trapped by my own indecision. My face must have revealed my thoughts. Aby leaned over and cupped my face in her hand.

"Isaac, what is troubling you?"

I smiled ruefully, and tried to put my thoughts in order. How honest could I be?

"Aby, the more I've thought about it, the more it frightens me."

"You mean the voyage? Surely not. It sounds like a grand adventure."

I shook my head.

"Isaac, my sweet, every time you sail away, I worry about *Rosie* sinking or you not surviving one of your regular adventures. I will be no more worried this next time, or the time thereafter."

"Aby!" I blurted out. "It's the marriage."

She moved off and looked away, far away. I was miserable, out of my depth. I thought I knew what I thought but didn't know how to word it.

"Aby, I love you," I said. "Marriage is like a huge mountain. I don't know how to climb it. Help me."

A long moment. Aby seemed to pull herself together, straighten her back. She came back to me.

"I'm sorry, Isaac. I was swept up in the whole idea of marriage. I've been housekeeper and caretaker to my father for so long, marriage is not a strange and fearsome beast to me. It is something I've wanted more than anything—to be married to you, the person I love, to care for you, have your children, and grow old together. I didn't think of it from your perspective—young, free, and full of the excitement for adventures yet to come."

"Aby, I want more than anything to be your husband. I want you as my partner and companion forever. I want to love you, sleep with you, close the whole world off, and share our own space together."

Aby smiled. "That's what I want, too. Perhaps we should ban the word *marriage*. It seems to be getting in the way."

I realized I could go no further with my doubts, and pushed them to the back of my mind.

"Yes, dearest Aby. We will ask P. to allow us to live together as man and wife."

Aby laughed, and we settled down together in a dip on top of Eggardon Hill, out of the wind. Much later, we agreed on a Christmas joining together. Then, Aby felt we could move to Plymouth. She would find a home and build her life while I was in North America. Aby had thought it through. I tried to see nothing but advantages for us both. We declared that that was exactly what we wanted more than anything in the world. I was carried along by Aby's joyful enthusiasm. We agreed I would meet with P. to ensure he was happy with our plans and to set the actual wedding day. Mr. Baker was already aware of Aby's thinking and approved. I had to warn Aby I would be busy for the next three months, in Plymouth, with only the occasional visit to Dorchester. Not only was I doing written research for the Northern Virginia trip, I had to meet with Captains Smith and Hobson, who were due in Plymouth shortly from their own exploratory trips. Aby said those commitments would fit well with hers, as the detailed work of closing the business and dealing with their possessions would take time. An early December wedding was perfect. I met with P. and told him that Aby and I wanted to be married sooner and explained why. After some serious discussion, he said early December would be fine and suggested the first Saturday, which would be 3 December.

I returned to the Bakers to find the two of them in the kitchen. I told them what P. had agreed. For me, it was overwhelming, as the marriage had changed from an event in the distant future to one organized with a date and the church set to announce it. Something private between us was becoming a reality, official and public. Aby, with barely suppressed excitement, repeated, "The banns are going to be read. The wedding will take place on 3 December." Mr. Baker leaned back, put his hands behind his head, and looked up at the ceiling.

"I would like to organize an event. After the wedding at Holy Trinity, there should follow a celebration, a wedding feast. Isaac—this gathering is something that Aby and I can do. I will make arrangements with Reverend

White. As your guardian, I am sure he will want to be involved. We need to find a venue for the wedding feast.

"I imagine Will Whiteway will be your best man," he said with a wicked gleam. "Remember, if you don't show up, he will be required to stand as groom in your place."

Given the cause of Aby's and my earlier upset, I thought the remark could have been better left unsaid. Aby looked at me. I could see she felt the same way. Mr. Baker, looking at the ceiling, appeared unconcerned. Then he looked at me.

"It's funny. When you first returned to Dorchester, and Aby did her best to kill you, she told me that you were to be her husband."

I was stunned, Aby dismayed. I laughed it off, forcing myself to focus on what we had agreed. The following morning, I made an early start from Dorchester. The sun was out, clear and low on the horizon. Whistler and I made good progress. We were back in the stables at the King's Arms by eight o'clock. I went in search of a ride back to Plymouth. *Rosie* was still dockside. By ten o'clock, four bells in the forenoon watch, I was back aboard and called to the Skipper's cabin. I told him of our marriage plans. He congratulated me somewhat brusquely. He told me he had arranged a ride for me on the *Maid of Avon*. She was about to leave, and I had better hurry. He wished me a pleasant rest of the summer and expected me back in Weymouth around the beginning of November.

I am writing this on board the *Maid of Avon*. She is bound for Bristol but will drop me off in Plymouth. The master is a friend of the skipper.

CHAPTER 17

Journal entry—*13 August to 1 November 1614*

Back in Plymouth on 15 August, I set to with a vengeance. I cleared a large table in Sir F.'s study, collating what I'd already put together, and continuing the detailed study and capture of the relevant data from the accounts before me. My intention was to write a complete report, combining the information from all sources. I returned to the Minerva each evening worn out. I was getting to know the regulars reasonably well. I think Annie had been stirring the pot a little, as they would ask what further adventures I'd had. They were a combination of townspeople, sailors—both merchant marine and Navy, with the occasional soldier or marine—and even the ever-changing impressment squads that continued to use the Minerva as a shore base of operations. I was a known quantity and in no danger. It was a good, changing, and mixed crowd.

Captain John Smith came to town, sailing in from his voyage across the Atlantic. I was called to Sir F.'s office to meet him. He was a small man, with a wild beard and dark shining eyes. He looked like a zealot, propagating a new nonconformist religion—perhaps he was. He was full of stories of New England, as he called Northern Virginia. Sir F. said he approved of the new name, suggesting we use it from now on. Smith had produced an account of his exploration. Sir F. had one of his clerks writing a clear copy, which was added to my assignment. I'd heard the stories of this extraordinary man. The energy that emanated from him was startling. Restless, he paced about the room, expounding on the incredible opportunities awaiting England in their possessions in New England. But the energy exploded in the most overwhelming anger when he talked about the treasonous, traitorous, and traducing behavior of one of his subordinates, Captain Hunt. It seemed he was captain of one of the vessels making the trip to New England under the overall command of Captain Smith. He had been left by

Captain Smith to collect a hold full of merchandise from the Indians whom they had been dealing with before returning to England. The merchandise would more than pay back the investors. Meanwhile, Captain Smith planned to continue to explore the coastline and make his separate way back to England. On his return, Smith had found that Hunt had proceeded to capture some twenty-four hapless Indians, not to bring them back to England to teach them English or train them to be guides and interpreters, but to sell as slaves to the Barbary pirates. Mr. Hunt had gone missing after that exploit. Such an action was beyond reprehensibility, after the efforts of many to improve relations between the Indians and the English explorers. Captain Smith would be available to answer any questions I might have once I'd read his account. He said I should be discreet with the information, as he hoped to publish his account in a book soon.

A short while later, I met Captain Hobson. His journey had been a total failure. He had lost his two Indians. In spite of the warnings I had given, Epenow had escaped. Much worse, Hunt's actions had made it impossible for Hobson to establish friendly relations with anyone. Captain Smith had left the coastal Indian tribes, for the most part, settled, friendly, and prepared to barter. Hobson was induced to leave Assacomet behind as a gesture of good faith, but with Epenow gone and Hunt stirring up the local tribes—especially in the Monhegan and Capawak regions where he'd taken the Indians captive—it had become too dangerous for Hobson to continue. He returned to England, resulting in great loss to the investors, mainly to Sir F. It would make it that much more difficult to find others, as Captain Smith was already finding.

I was given the chance to catch a ride on a merchant vessel to Weymouth in early October, which I rejected. My work for Sir F. had given my doubts time to return. I'd tried to ignore Mr. Baker's parting words, but in spite of attempts to laugh it off, I felt increasingly that I had somehow been maneuvered into the marriage. I wasn't ready to confront Aby.

I bumped into Mr. Bushrode, who told me about *Rosie's* refit. She was still hauled up on a slipway, but she now had a shiny, clean bottom and fresh planking, rails, and spars. Caulking was proceeding, and some new sails were being made. The whipstaff was being replaced with a wheel, which was a large, ambitious change. There would be a secondary wheel in the steerage room, but the main wheel would be on the quarterdeck with its own binnacle.

Finally, late in October, I completed my research and delivered the work I had done to Captain Turner, in Sir F.'s absence. I returned by sea, once more, to Weymouth. I met with the skipper in his cabin on 1 November.

"We leave on Wednesday morning's tide for Dieppe," he told me. "From there we go to Gravesend, back via Portsmouth to Weymouth. Depending on weather, that should take no more than two weeks. I can spare you for a few days, probably around 28 November. But to allow for delays, you might want to let your people in Dorchester know you will be there by the thirtieth, at the latest. This is going to be something of a proving run for the *Sweet Rose*. The new steering mechanism needs to be put through its paces. I'm not at all sure about these newfangled inventions. Might be all right for the Navy, but they have skilled mechanicals on board in case anything goes wrong. Sir Ferdinando wants us to start our New England run at the beginning of March from Plymouth. Heavy weather then. We can't have the steering fail."

I left notes with Adam at the King's Arms to pass on via Silas to P. and Aby.

Journal entry—*2 to 30 November 1614*

The next two weeks went quickly. Dieppe had a large Huguenot population, and we were there for Vivienne's father, in partnership with Mr. Bushrode. Commerce included trade with the east—spices, much sought after in England. Dieppe was a major fishing port, with fleets in constant voyages to Canada and Newfoundland. The beaver and other pelts they brought back were a commodity of major interest to us. From Dieppe, we sailed across the English Channel to the Thames, where the exotic scents of spices from the hold mixed with the stink of untreated fur pelts. The amount of shipping in the Channel was incredible. East Indiamen like huge floating castles, Navy triple-deckers, and merchant vessels of all shapes and sizes from every country meant we had double lookouts the whole way. Once we approached the Thames estuary, precise navigation became a necessity, with the traffic, sandbars, and tidal flow a constant menace. Eventually, we made our way up the Thames to Gravesend. The mightiest river in the world was dirty, crowded, and smelly. The town was aptly named, sordid and disease-ridden. We were forced to wait, once loaded up, due to contrary winds. Eventually, we managed to work our way downriver with the ebbing tide. Out of the estuary, moving offshore, we were able to breathe clean air and make a clear passage to Weymouth by 25 November. As the skipper feared, the new steering system proved unreliable. *Rosie* was laid up again to have her old whipstaff steering put back. The boatyard wouldn't start the work till after Christmas.

The skipper was going to allow me to leave a few days prior to the wedding. I remained on duty until the thirtieth, clearing cargo and performing boat maintenance. I had sent a message that I was back. Will brought Aby down to

Weymouth for a surprise visit on the twenty-eighth. I asked the skipper if they might be permitted to come aboard. He said he would enjoy meeting Miss Abigail. I went to fetch her in *Rosie's* boat. Our reunion was only observed by Will, who looked discreetly at other things. I was unable to mention my concerns. I was just happy to be with Aby again. Hands were eager to help her aboard, Will making his own way. The skipper whisked her away to his cabin, telling me I should escort my other guest around *Rosie*. Startled, I did so. Will was spellbound, and I was distracted. Eventually back topside, Aby was on the quarterdeck, seemingly much at home, the old Aby much to the fore in animated conversation with the skipper. She was introduced to a number of the officers who'd somehow made their way there. Seeing me, the skipper invited us to join them. Aby, with shining eyes, turned and told me that Mr. Brown had presented us with our first wedding present—a beautiful polished leather box containing a ship's decanter and two small, stemmed glasses. After I expressed my gratitude, graciously acknowledged, it was suggested that Miss Abigail should be escorted safely back to dry land, which I did, with Will in tow. I was silent while Aby chatted to Will. The skipper's present was a reminder of the inevitability of the marriage, now a few days away. Despite Aby's evident joy, my mind was becoming numb with a sense of impending doom. On shore, Aby, apparently oblivious, asked me if I had the wedding ring. I hadn't. Aby said we should go, immediately, to a local jeweler. We did, and with Aby's gentle direction, I ordered and paid for a simple gold band with an inscription on the inside—Aby 3 Dec 14. It would be available to pick up in two days. Aby, in leaving, put her arms 'round me and whispered, "Be strong, my love."

I was given leave on 30 November with the admonition to rejoin *Rosie* in Plymouth by 1 March 1615. Once ashore, I picked up the ring, found Whistler available, and with Adam's blessing rode off to Dorchester, the skipper's wedding present carefully wrapped and strapped to my saddlebag. My mood somber, I tried to rationalize my feelings—my love for Aby and the sense of the weight of the edifice being constructed around me. My first stop was the rectory. P. ushered me into his study and told me what had been arranged. Everything was set for Saturday. Service at Holy Trinity at two p.m. A large room was made available at the Shire Hall for the wedding feast. Mr. Gosling had promised that the Sun was preparing a special wedding night bedroom. P. smiled when he spoke of this room and asked, innocently, what our plans were post-wedding. Where would we be living, and would there be room for children?

I blanched—another brick in the edifice.

"My goodness, I don't think we are ready for children," I said. "Anyway, Mr.

Brown has given me till the end of February. I am then to rejoin the *Sweet Rose* in Plymouth. I haven't told Aby yet, but I plan to ride with her down to Plymouth to visit some of my old haunts on the way. Once I rejoin *Rosie*, Aby will return to Dorchester by coach. I will arrange for someone to accompany her back, probably Will."

P. settled back and gazed at me.

"Isaac, you seem distracted. Are you thinking of the wedding?"

I shook my head, looking down at my hands in my lap.

"What's wrong? Having second thoughts?"

I looked up, startled.

P. smiled.

"Most of the young men I meet just before they are married are scared witless. They feel they are being led defenseless to the slaughter by their bride."

I acknowledged that was part of it. P. told me to just give in to the process. The arrangements, the ceremony, and the aftermath were all set. Just enjoy each moment and banish all worries. All would be well. We parted. I wanted to go to Aby. I rode to her house, but, finding no one at home, I returned to the Sun. There, I was greeted effusively by Jeremiah and shown to my room. I left my bags and the present, and have now completed the journal entries for Will.

Letter to Will—*30 November 1614*

Dear Will,

This brief letter is to let you know I have arrived. My latest journal entries accompany this note. I am off for a long ride to clear my head and be ready for the next few days.

Isaac

Part 2

CHAPTER 18

Journal entry—*10 to 17 March 1615*

We are at sea, heading west, having passed Fastnet Rock a few days ago. The skipper said the intended course should be on a latitude of approximately forty-four degrees, but we're currently north of that. *Rosie* is moving as well as can be expected in heavy swell with contrary, changeable winds, and it's cold. My understanding is we are heading for Monhegan, about six weeks away.

I came from a meeting with the skipper, confused. He asked me to keep a journal, which seemed an odd request, saying it might help me with my memory. My memory? He said he had been concerned about me since I rejoined *Rosie* immediately prior to our departure from Plymouth. When I came aboard, he asked me where I had been. I didn't answer, not knowing what he was talking about. He said he'd put it down to me not wanting to talk about it, so, thankful to have me aboard, he had left me to it. At today's meeting, he started asking me some serious questions. Did I know what date it was? I said I've not being keeping track. Did I know why I was on the *Sweet Rose*? I am a member of the crew. Did I know where we are going? Northern Virginia, I guessed, as we are heading west out into the Atlantic. Where was the last time I saw Sir Ferdinando Gorges? At Wraxall Court. When? I can't remember. Who were the Indians I met there? Epenow and Assacomet. Where are they now? I don't know. How's Abigail? Abigail? I think she is fine. When did I last see her? I can't remember. When I rejoined the *Sweet Rose*, I had an old bandage wrapped round my head. Do I remember why? Did I? I felt my head. No bandage, but a large healed scar over my right ear—still slightly painful to touch. Dusty had been caring for me, the skipper told me. No, I have no memory of that. What is the last thing I remember, prior to rejoining the *Sweet Rose*? I don't remember rejoining the *Sweet Rose*. I didn't know I had left. How am I feeling now? Fine, but his questions were confusing me. He apologized. Dismissing me, he repeated that I was to keep a journal of my daily activity, especially my thoughts.

Sometime later, J.B. told me he needed my assistance on the lower deck. He started asking me questions. Did I know how the pumps worked? The construction of the capstan? I started answering, then stopped and looked at him.

"Why are you asking these unnecessary questions?"

He didn't answer. He took me up to the focsle deck and asked me what all the lines and halyards were for. Puzzled, I told him. I knew every inch of *Rosie*, and J.B. *knew* I knew, since he had taught me. He grinned, obviously relieved about something. He reminded me larboard watch was thirty minutes from being called. I said I knew. He left me and I saw several crewmen watching. As I caught their eyes, they looked embarrassed and turned to continue what they were doing. I was beginning to feel something strange was happening to me. My mind seemed clear, but something was wrong. I went to see Dusty in his cook house.

"Dusty. What the hell is going on? People are reacting strangely to me."

He was making bread, his arms enfloured to the elbows.

"How much do you remember of the last two weeks?"

"To be honest, it's all been a bit of a blur."

"Do you remember us leaving Plymouth?"

I thought about it. I admitted having memories of many departures but couldn't identify when or in which order they had happened.

"Isaac. Before you came aboard, we thought we had lost you. We were casting off from quayside when you appeared. We took you aboard. You looked distracted, dirty, like you had been sleeping rough. The skipper told me to take care of you and not to ask questions. Today, for the first time in two weeks, you appear to have returned to your normal self, but, there is a gap in your memory. According to the skipper, he had a meeting with you back in late November. Do you remember?"

I remembered many meetings with the skipper.

"Was there anything special about that particular meeting?" I asked.

"It was in Weymouth. You were about to go back to Dorchester?"

"No, I don't recall."

"Then you don't know why you were going back to Dorchester?"

"Not specially."

He grimaced and looked at me for a long time, wondering what to say. It was as if he had a huge weight on his shoulders.

"Isaac. The skipper told me not to push you. Today is 10 March. It has been over three months from the time you left *Rosie* in Weymouth to when you turned up in Plymouth. We have been ten days into our current passage, and you have no memory of this period, even the last ten days. Do you remember even going back to Dorchester at Christmas?"

"Not really. I remember Wraxall Court."

"When was that?"

"I can't remember."

By now I was becoming agitated. Dusty saw it. He immediately backed off and apologized, saying that the memory loss was easily explained. I'd taken a bad knock to the head at some point. When he removed the bandage, the wound had largely healed and whatever caused it looked to have been some time ago. Not to worry, as the body heals itself, so does the brain. My memory will come back, I just needed to be patient.

Larboard watch was called. I went to my duties. Peg, officer of the watch, called me to the quarterdeck and told me I was to have watch-keeping duties. He looked at the ship's boy next to him.

"Burch, you are being reassigned, report to the bosun," he said.

Burch? I looked hard at him, and he began to look uncomfortable. I nodded, and he left, a worried frown on his face. Peg had seen the exchange.

"What was that about?"

"Don't I know Burch?" I asked.

"That's Obi Burch."

"Ah, Obi."

I had no problems with watch duty: turning the glass, ringing the bell, recording log speed, marking up the traverse board, and taking sun sights with the cross staff. At the end of the watch, Peg was pleased. I seemed to have come through a test.

"How are you feeling?"

"Good, sir."

I went below to find Obi, who was still looking worried. He said I had acted as if I didn't know him. I calmed him down, saying it seemed I'd taken a bad knock to the head, which had temporarily affected my memory, but it was coming back. Obi looked relieved. The crew seemed to welcome me as if I had been away on a long trip. I told them I had a slight memory loss. They were happy to remind me of their names. As the days went by, I found I was back to normal as far as *Rosie*, my duties, and the crew were concerned, but I obviously had a serious memory problem with some odd exceptions going back some time. I continued to worry about what had happened to me. I had lost part of my life. Dusty had been given Stanfield recovery duties. I spent some time every day with him as he probed what I remembered. It seemed I was pretty much up to date with my adventures in La Rochelle. I couldn't remember Bilbao, but Dusty said that had been a relatively recent voyage. Regarding Dorchester, I remember the fire. Asked whether I had friends there, I said there was a girl friend called Aby and, of course, my best friend Will. He asked me to describe them, but I was not able. It seemed I hadn't seen them for such a long time their faces were indistinct. The worry continued, a background weight on my mind that wouldn't go away.

Journal entry—*18 March to 25 April 1615*

I was confused about our passage from Plymouth taking us past Fastnet Rock, and I asked Peg about it on one of our night watches. Apparently, the skipper had got wind of pirate activity off the Scilly Isles, so he plotted a course tight round the Lizard, off Cornwall, northwest toward the Irish south coast. The weather conditions had become clement. We made good time, and saw no pirates, passing Mizen Head off the southwest tip of Ireland, well north of our intended course—it being about forty-four and a half degrees of latitude. From there we worked our way west, dropping slowly down to forty-four degrees. The voyage across was largely uneventful, except for the interest when we saw other vessels, mostly fishermen. Whales were in abundance as we approached land, by our reckoning some hundred miles off.

When my mind wasn't occupied with my duties, I spent much time exploring the fringes of my memory. It had become like a fog bank I couldn't penetrate. I thought of Will. When I wrote the journal, he came to mind. There appeared to be some connection. The more I thought about him, the more I wrote. At times, my writing seemed to be unguided, with the words not making much sense. I thought about Aby. There was something missing. I had warm feelings about her. I remember when the fire started at her father's shop, but I couldn't see her face. I needed some kind of key to what had gone before. It seemed important. I felt that skipper knew pieces of my lost life he was keeping from me and wondered why that was. I talked to Dusty about it, but he shrugged it off. If what I thought was true, the skipper would have his reasons. The most important thing with memory loss was not to try to force anything. All will be well, just be patient, Dusty told me, but it was not easy. At one point, the skipper showed me some documents he said I had written, though I had no memory of doing so. They comprised a detailed description of past voyages made to New England. New England? I was told it was the name now given to Northern Virginia.

Just after three bells, morning watch 25 April, masthead lookout called, "Land ho!" One point off the starboard bow. It was two more hours before we saw the land from the deck, an island, Mattinicus, by which time the lookout had sighted the blunt shape of Monhegan farther away, just off our starboard bow. The weather was calm but cold, with a gentle breeze from the south. In a clear, light blue sky, we saw wisps of high cloud. Feeling much excitement, the crew, both watches, enjoyed the slow approach of land after seven weeks at sea. The water turned a deeper blue, with waves rippling the surface and occasional gusts creating isolated darker patterns. Small birds skimmed over the water, dodging the waves. A crewman said they were petrels, seagulls following in our wake, screaming over food scraps that Dusty had thrown overboard. Then, closer to land, white birds with a yellow head and long beak plunged vertically into the sea, exploding out of the water with a fish in their mouths: gannets. We were accompanied by many porpoises who played in our wake and alongside before disappearing. Farther off, we saw and heard whales heading south, long sleek shapes slipping effortlessly through the water before submerging to reappear a few minutes later farther along their chosen track. It was another four hours before we were close to Monhegan.

Cliffs rose perhaps 150 feet straight out of the water, crowned with thick forest. Sails hard braced on Larboard tack, we sailed around the southern end of the island sounding as we went, passing by a rocky ledge with water breaking over it about a mile east of the southern tip. Depth varied fifteen to twenty-five fathoms as we rounded, easing our courses, furled tops'ls and sprits'l. Now heading northwest at about two knots, we passed the entrance to a harbor bearing north. As we got closer, we saw it was formed by a smaller island and seemed to open up at the far end, too deep to moor off. With winds from the south, the harbor was a little too exposed, and we continued round to the west. We found a mooring in about eleven fathoms some 300 yards off the shoreline, with rocks awash, equidistant to the north.

The skipper was concerned about the security of our anchored position, but the afternoon continued fair. The on-duty watch proceeded to their duties in cleaning and making *Rosie* shipshape. The off-watch crew, including me, cleared and lowered the longboat, then rowed south, with Peg in command, round the small island into the harbor. Cliffs on either side, we were able to beach on a small strip of exposed mud on Monhegan itself. Across from that landing area, on top of a cliff of the small island, there appeared to be a wooden cross. That would need investigation. The ground rose sharply from the harbor, and a path led up the hill disappearing into trees. Peg, with two sailors, armed with muskets, walked up the path. They were gone for about five minutes. They returned, reporting that there was at least one trail that continued south. There was a clearing with evidence of fishermen's or other explorers' presence, not long ago. It was possible that the encampment was extensive, but Peg wanted time to explore. We needed to check the rest of Monhegan's coastline from the boat. Skipper wanted a secure anchorage.

We rowed back down the harbor, turned north inshore of *Rosie*. We continued northeast, sounding for water depth as we went. We checked the northern end of the harbor. A rock blocked the harbor from the north, but there was a good anchorage beyond it in some twelve fathoms with a rocky islet protecting it from the north, but open to westerlies. We approached a large rock ledge at the northern end of Monhegan with a passageway we could row through between the ledge and the island. The rocky shoreline and a large, partially submerged rock made the passageway tight, too tight for *Rosie*, but through that we were quickly into deep water, an anchorage well-protected from all winds, bar northerly to easterly. We continued to row round the island, about two miles long on a NE/SW axis, about three-quarters of a mile wide. There was no obvious anchorage to the east or south. We returned to *Rosie*. Peg reported to the skipper. Shortly after, we were back in the longboat towing *Rosie* closer into the shoreline, due north of the little island. We could see the southern exit of Monhegan's harbor, but we were protected from winds that might funnel through.

I was summoned to the skipper's cabin. Peg was there. They'd been entering what we had discovered on a chart.

"Stanfield, come in. Look at this," the skipper said. "We've sketched out the salient features identified on this afternoon's row. Any comments?"

I studied it. Peg had noted the soundings. He had taken bearings. I said it looked complete to me.

"Any memories of studying past voyages to Monhegan?"

I thought frantically. Something nagged at the back of my mind. I felt I'd been here before or somehow I knew Monhegan. I shook my head.

"What did your Indians tell you about Monhegan?"

I thought for a moment. That was it. Assacomet had told me about it.

"Assacomet said that they consider Monhegan a special place. While they don't have a permanent encampment here, they visit frequently. It seems small groups come here to be at peace, to enjoy its beauty."

"There is evidence of fishermen, presumably English or French, living here."

"Aye, sir. We would need to explore that, how recent, any signs of contact with the Indians or Indian activity of any sort. We need to see how extensive their presence has been. In fact, it would be worthwhile exploring the whole island."

I must have sounded eager. I had remembered something! Peg smiled.

The skipper looked at me. "According to Sir Ferdinando, we—you—are to see if you can contact, presumably, Assacomet. How do you propose to do that?"

I was feeling more confident now.

"I doubt our arrival has gone unnoticed, sir. If they don't come to us, we could go to them. We could row up the St. George's River. The river that Rosier described is the river that Assacomet told me about."

The skipper looked sharply at me.

"You remember Rosier?"

"Aye, sir. He related Weymouth's voyage in 1605."

"How did you know about Rosier's account?"

I felt the fog creeping in. Stammering that I didn't know, I started getting agitated.

Peg and the skipper glanced at each other.

"Don't worry. It'll come back to you," the skipper said. "That's enough for now. We'll have you on the island tomorrow. Now be off with you."

I went up to the focsle deck to lean over the rail, feeling sick, looking at the shoreline a few hundred yards off. How did I know about Rosier? When did I? I remember the account but can't remember the circumstances. I went over in my mind what Assacomet had told me back at Wraxall Court. Why do I remember that account clearly but so much else is fog-bound? I went below, to the solace of writing in the journal.

Journal entry—*26 April to 15 June 1615*

I am in Damariscove, due to ship back to England on a fishing boat tomorrow. But I must start at the beginning.

After arriving at Monhegan, we spent two days exploring the island. We saw ample evidence of past presence of sailors, with their belongings and supplies presumably stored for future use. It was apparent that Monhegan was being used as some kind of base or destination point. We checked out the wooden cross, which looked like it had been there for some time. I seem to remember Rosier saying something about it, but I couldn't recall the details. It certainly seemed that Monhegan was being used by fishermen. We could see an attempt to build racks to dry fish as well as to store gear, but these efforts hadn't seemed to have come to much. Possibly, the fishermen had been frightened off by Indians. The fish drying racks didn't seem to be located in a particularly convenient place, requiring too much effort to haul the fish up to the racks. Some trees had been cleared but there was no obvious extensive flat rock close to the water's edge. There had been a garden plot cleared and planted, not long previously. Various vegetables had grown but gone to seed. Peg said that he understood from the skipper that Captain John Smith had sailed over a few months before us. He had intended to aim for Monhegan. Perhaps this plot was his.

Why did I feel I knew that already? Wherever the ground was open, grass grew in abundance. There were tracks through the trees, evidence of Indian feasts, piles of shell, and fire pits on the cliffs looking south over the Atlantic. The island was as Assacomet had described—beautiful and peaceful, surrounded by ocean views, teeming with bird life, rabbit, and deer. While we were exploring, others of the crew were restocking *Rosie*. Water casks were cleaned, to be refilled from a sweet spring on the island. Wild berry bushes grew in abundance, promising fruit in the months ahead, as well as game for fresh meat. As for fish, no skill was required. Throw a line with hook, and a huge cod would strike immediately. The waters around Monhegan teemed with fish. According to those who had fished Newfoundland, the size and the amount were beyond anything they had previously experienced, all there for the taking and much earlier in the year.

On the third evening, with the skipper's blessing and no sign of Indians, I indulged the need to exchange the squalor of the lower deck for the sights, sounds, and—above all—sweet smells of land, deciding to camp ashore with three crew, armed and prepared for any trouble. We had a small campfire for cooking. It was a clear night, and although no moon, the starlight was extraordinary. I slipped away from our camp to relieve myself, after which I walked through the trees to look north toward the dark strip of land five or six miles away. There was a stillness that I gradually became aware of, no animal sounds, then a slight whisper of a branch moving and no wind. I turned, puzzled, wanting a simple explanation. I heard a slight noise, then felt an intense pain in my left shoulder. I was pinned to a tree by an arrow.

Next thing I knew, I was in a canoe with Indians traveling fast by the sound of the water rushing past. Time was a blur. I remember waking up, lying in some kind of hut on animal skins with a fearsome headache. I was hot and sweating, my shoulder inflamed. Fever, I thought. I slept and woke in daylight, the sun high, feeling terrible. Someone, behind me, was bathing my shoulder and head.

I couldn't move. I slept again, having nightmares. Things were running through my head that made no sense. I saw Aby, tears streaming down her face, huddled in a corner, and Will on horseback galloping through the countryside shouting my name. I saw P. dancing with Sir Ferdinando. There were faces I knew but couldn't remember, cheering on the dancing couple, whose faces were red, sweating, angry. In more lucid moments, a cool wet cloth wiped the sweat from my face. Voices spoke in a strange language. I had no idea of the time of day or days of the week. I seemed to be suspended, timeless. At some point, I regained my senses. It was night, raining and blowing a gale, followed by thunder and lightning. With the lightning flashes I caught glimpses of the inside of the hut. There seemed to be someone else asleep in the room. I tried moving but was hopelessly weak, so I gave up. My shoulder and head were bandaged, but neither seemed uncomfortable. How long had I been there? I had no idea. I tried to make sense of my dreams, but unable to, I didn't dwell on them. I had a clear picture of Aby. Why was she crying? Will? Why was I dreaming of them? The fog bank was in my head. I couldn't penetrate it. I went back to sleep.

Sometime later I awoke. Looking around, I was alone. I was able to move my right arm. My left shoulder was sore. My left arm was strapped to my chest, and I was naked under the bedding. I'd been bathed; my wounds were healing, no longer bandaged. I tried sitting up, but was too weak. A young woman came in smiling when she saw I was awake. I was startled. She didn't appear to be wearing much. She came over, knelt down beside me, and with an arm 'round me lifted me up, placing something behind my back so I could lean. I was disconcerted as my covering slipped down, and there we both were as good as naked, her only modesty a short skirt around her middle. She laughed, seeing my discomfiture. She said something that I didn't understand. Taking a cloth, she mimed washing me all over. I blushed. She laughed again and handed me a cup, beckoning me to drink. It was a broth, which tasted good. I was hungry. She gave me a kind of pot with a long neck, empty, and pointed at my now-covered privates, waggling the pot. I was confused. With a sigh of impatience, before I could react, she stripped the covering off me, grabbed my tassel, and stuffed it into the pot. I was shocked. She started giggling and couldn't stop. The tears were running down her face. I grinned, started laughing too. I had a good pee and handed her back the pot.

We both calmed down. She examined my wounds. The shoulder was swollen but did not look infected. There was a neat closed wound, another presumably where the arrow had gone through me, without hitting bone. She took the strapping off, gently moved my left arm, which was sore and stiff but mobile, just. Again, to my surprise, pleasant, I have to say, she put my hand on her chest, above her firm, young breasts, and started massaging my shoulder with some ointment. As she did, my hand moved down over a breast. She looked at me, smiled, and moved her breast gently in my hand, which I took to be an invitation. Too much excitement. My hand dropped. I went to sleep soothed by the gentle massage.

Next time I woke, I had another visitor—Assacomet. We greeted each other as old friends. He asked whether I was being looked after well. I said yes, and asked who the girl was.

"Her name is Malian. She's the daughter of a local sagamore. She has adopted you. She considers you good husband material."

At least, I think that's what he said. I asked how long I had been there. He said a month.

"Oh no, the *Sweet Rose*. Is she still there? They must be frantic?"

Assacomet smiled sadly. *Rosie* had gone. In their rowing boat they had hunted for me for a week. They tried to catch the attention of Indians, but no one would go near them. They eventually sailed away, heading down the coast. I asked why I'd been attacked. He told me that a few months previously, relations with the English had been good. Captives had returned from England when it had been assumed they were dead, but an English captain had abducted a great many people and sailed away with them. This had caused much anger, which had quickly spread to other tribes along the coast. As a result, the English were hated. The attack on me was an example, carried out by young braves as a rite of passage. I was lucky to have been brought to where Assacomet was. He'd recognized me, gone to the sagamore, and told him I'd saved his life, that he was my brother.

Instead of torturing me to death, Malian had brought me back to life. I was very grateful. He said that there was a war going on. The Micmacs, a fierce, warlike tribe to the northeast, were fighting the Wabanakis, of which the local tribe was a part. This meant that young warriors were anxious to prove their bravery. He mentioned that the English had an opportunity to help the Wabanaki. Indians feared the guns and large ships of the English. They'd have welcomed an alliance, but not now. He said that he would shortly be leaving here. He was not of this tribe, having been captured by the tribe many years ago. He'd become a servant. His subsequent capture by the English and return a short time ago resulted in the tribe giving him his freedom. He was moving south. He would have another name, if ever we met. I asked him what that was.

"You English have problems with my name—Assacomet or Sassacomoit.

These names were given me by the tribe that captured me. They have freed me. As a mark of respect they have given me another name. I am now called Samoset."

"What does the name mean?"

"He who walks far."

I laughed. He had certainly traveled a long way. We said goodbye and he left, parting as friends. We were each beholden to the other. I felt certain our paths would cross again. Over the next two weeks, Malian had me walking and continued to massage my shoulder. I was a little worried about how possessive she was. When I walked about the village, some of the young braves glared at me. The mature warriors ignored me. But the women smiled, acknowledging my greetings. As I got stronger, Malian started making me work harder. Outside, I was made to walk faster, then run, following her. She was nimble. Then, one evening in my hut, Malian indicated that we should wrestle. She made me lie down on my back and she lay down beside me, with her head at my feet. I recognized we were to leg wrestle. I lifted my leg, the one next to her. She did likewise. She was wearing a covering that wrapped between her legs, but I was uncomfortable. It was all very intimate. We wrestled. At first, she won every time, but my legs gained strength.

We did this nightly, and also occasionally arm wrestled. One evening, I won at leg wrestling. She toppled over on top of me. She lay there, pressing against me. She felt me responding. Before I knew it, my breeches were down, she'd unclothed herself, and I was straddled. I was totally and effectively seduced. Afterward, she hugged me, and I was left like a beached whale. A daily visit had been Malian's custom, but she did not see me the next day. I'd spent the day thinking about what had happened. Although exciting, it was, in retrospect, worrying. I was hearing Assacomet's—now Samoset's—words about husband material. My mind had been seduced. I had to find the *Sweet Rose*. If she had gone, I needed to find a way to get back to England. Late that evening, I was taking a walk in the woods close to the village, when I was attacked again. Blows rained down on my arms, back and shoulders. I tried to protect myself, but they came from everywhere. I recognized three of the hostile young braves. Beaten to the ground and barely conscious, I was dragged to the shore and put in a canoe, which set off traveling swiftly through the water. When I came to, I was lying on a ledge late at night by a harbor. I tried sitting up but the pain everywhere was intense. I lay back. My left arm was useless, right ear torn, blood and bruises elsewhere. I was naked with a leather thong tied round my tassel, which I removed. The end had turned purple. The message was clear enough. I could have been castrated or worse. It seemed Samoset was still protecting me.

Next thing I knew, two fishermen were looking at me from a boat.

"What happened to you?" one asked.

"Jealous boyfriend," I said.

They laughed.

"Can you move?"

"No."

"Stay there. We will bring help."

I wasn't going anywhere and went back to sleep, curled up, cold. I woke to the noise of a group of men walking over the rocks toward me, carrying a stretcher. They covered me with a blanket and carried me along the shoreline to a collection of huts. I was put on a rough bed. One of them, who seemed to know what he was doing, examined me. With a basin of water, he cleaned me up. Shoulder badly bruised, as was my body front and back. Wasn't that an arrow wound? He said I was a mess. I felt like one. It seemed he wasn't a believer in bandages. Good sea air was the best healer, he said, but did strap my left arm up again. He gave me a dirty shirt and breeches to wear, several sizes too large. Another man came in, who seemed to be the leader.

"What's your name?"

I told him. He said that some six weeks ago the vessel the *Sweet Rose* had anchored in the harbor here. The skipper said he'd lost an important member of his crew, probably taken by Indians, not known whether dead or alive. He told them my name. They'd searched but couldn't get anywhere near any Indians. The man explained to the skipper that Captain Hunt, a short time previously, had kidnapped a party of Indians, causing fury among the tribes. It had made life for any Englishman that much more precarious, and he said he prayed to God to rot Hunt's soul. Anyway, if I should turn up, I was to be told that, given the circumstances, the *Sweet Rose* was returning to Plymouth and that the skipper would be obliged if I could be returned to England. The man asked my caregiver how mobile I was.

"Give him a few days."

Apparently, there was a fishing boat heading back to Bristol that week. Hammock space would be found for me.

"Where am I?"

"Damaril's Island, otherwise known as Damariscove."

The following day I was able to hobble outside, supported and guided by a friendly fisherman. I wandered around as best I could. It was a long island lying along a north-south axis. The island had a large, well-protected natural harbor, extending up the middle, entered from the south. English fishermen had taken it over as a base of operations. There were many fishing racks assembled and in use. Monhegan was about fifteen miles east and could be seen on the horizon. I had not come far. Damariscove lay a few miles south of a large bay, with an island guarding its entrance. Looking west, my guide informed me, was Saga-dahoc, the site of the Popham settlement. I asked about Pemaquid. He pointed out the headland to me about midway to Monhegan. I asked whether there was a fishing settlement there, too. I was told that it was thought that one or two men from the Popham settlement had stayed behind and made their way there. They had probably gone native, becoming tribal members. But relations being what they are right now with the Indians, it wasn't known what the current situation was. I asked what the date was. 15 June. My guide told me the vessel for Bristol was leaving on the morrow and I should meet the captain. I limped my way slowly up harbor to a landing stage and was introduced to Walter Morris, captain of the vessel *Mary Evans*, who looked at me wondering what he had taken on. By now I was feeling ragged. He suggested I accompany him aboard, where he would find me a suitable spot. I thanked the man who had cared for me. He wished me luck, and I went aboard. Captain Morris gave me a closed berth, a bunk bed in a canvas-walled closet. He said by the look of me, I should bed down immediately.

After thanking him, I asked him for something to write on and with. I had a duty to record what had happened, before I forgot. He obliged me. I collapsed and slept. Later on, I woke, scared. I was sweating. I barely knew where I was, what had happened to me. I had an overwhelming urge to account for my journey and started writing by daylight, at night by candle. As I did so I felt calmer. As I wrote, remembering everything that had happened over the past few months, I enjoyed the retelling. But as I started reaching back further, the fog descended once more. A vision of Aby haunted me, and a sense of guilt over my seduction by Malian. The two faces started circling each other. My head started to whirl. The journal complete, I slept.

CHAPTER 19

Journal entry—*16 June to 30 July 1615*

I awoke to the noise, smell, and movement of a ship at sea, having missed the departure. I was unwell. The fever had returned and I slept, barely remembering the journey back, which took a little over a month. The crew cared for me as best they could, but by the time we docked in Bristol, I was in a bad way. The fever had subsided, but it had left me too weak to do much of anything. I was not entirely right in my mind—constant nonsensical nightmares, similar to those I'd suffered before. The captain had no obligation or responsibility for me now that we were in Bristol, but he came to see me and asked what he could do to help. After some moments to gather my wits, I asked whether it was possible to hire transport—a horse and cart—to transport me to Wraxall Court. I was certain payment would be made on my arrival. The captain was surprised.

"How the hell do you know Wraxall Court?"

I gave him the name of the steward, Mr. Wellings. He went away, and I slept. I was dimly aware of being offloaded, placed in a wagon on a bed of straw with a covering. I went back to sleep. Next thing I knew, I was in bed at Wraxall Court, with Mary, the cook, and my faithful valet, Mark, looking down at me with anxious faces. I felt clean, warm, comfortable, bandaged, and secure. I smiled up at them.

"Hello. I am so happy to see you both."

They both smiled back. Mary gave me a hug, fighting back tears. I asked her how long I had been there. "Three days, hovering between life and death," she said. The doctor had been to see me every day. He had, today, pronounced me clear of the fever, but needing sleep and plenty of wholesome food. Consequently, Mark fed me whenever I was awake, which wasn't often, but within twenty-four hours I was able to sit up. Mr. Wellings came in and greeted me warmly. He sat, looking at me. Then he said a funny thing.

"Do you know who I am?"

I said of course, why? He settled back in his chair and proceeded to tell me about a letter he had received from Sir Ferdinando. When I appeared like some ghost, Mr. Wellings immediately sent a note to Sir F. to say I'd turned up. It had taken a few days for the note to get to him, but he had written back immediately saying he was coming to Wraxall and would be arriving tomorrow. He said that he'd met with Mr. Brown of the *Sweet Rose*, recently returned from New England, who told him that I'd been taken by Indians and possibly killed. Mr. Brown had recounted my strange appearance in Plymouth as they were leaving for New England. He said that it was clear I had suffered a serious blow to the head with significant memory loss. I had no knowledge of what had happened, nor did I have much knowledge of my life in Dorchester. The one memory I did have was of Wraxall Court. His letter said Mr. Brown had been informed of my reappearance and I was to be looked after with the best possible care as I awaited his arrival. Mr. Wellings gave me a packet with a note from a Captain Morris. It was the journal entry I'd written that last night in Damariscove. I asked if my transport from Bristol had been paid for. He said Captain Morris did business with Sir Edward, and there was nothing to pay. I made a mental note to thank Captain Morris in person at some point. Next morning, I desperately needed exercise. With Mark's help I stumbled 'round my room, down the corridor, downstairs, and out into a balmy end of June morning. The exercise made me feel better, but it was tiring. After a rest, Mark escorted me to the kitchen, where Mary gave me a huge meal and I was joined by a beaming Mr. Wellings. I was then settled in the study in a comfortable wing-backed chair, wrapped in a blanket, and allowed to nap until Sir F. arrived. I woke with him gazing at me.

"My dear young Isaac. What the hell have you been up to?"

I laughed. "Wars, sir."

He had me recount everything that had happened on my trip to New England. I covered the salient facts briefly.

"Amazing, simply amazing."

He stopped, then rose to start pacing.

"Mr. Brown tells me you have no memory of how you came to be in Plymouth at the moment the *Sweet Rose* was about to leave for New England."

"Yes, sir."

"You have no memory of being in Dorchester or any recent memory of Dorchester."

"Apparently not, sir."

"Do you remember Abigail Baker?"

I pondered, wondering how to respond. I told him what I'd told Mr. Brown. I also said in a fever during my stay at an Indian village I had strange, bad dreams about her. I asked him why he was concerned. He was biting his lip, thinking deeply. He didn't say anything for a long time.

"Until the *Sweet Rose* turned up in Plymouth a month ago, I thought you were dead, as did your friends in Dorchester. Having told me you were alive, Mr. Brown said that he had lost you to Indians and feared that you were likely dead, again. I then received a note from Wellings saying you had turned up at Wraxall a few days ago."

Another long pause.

"Mr. Brown dropped you off in Weymouth on 30 November for you to return to Dorchester. He had arranged for you to rejoin the *Sweet Rose* in Plymouth by 1 March. I now know what happened to you since then. We don't know what happened to you from December to the end of February. I understand that you got to Dorchester. Mr. Will Whiteway told me that he found a journal entry you'd written on the evening of the thirtieth, with a note to him that you were going for a ride. Do you have any idea why you were given leave by Mr. Brown to go to Dorchester?"

I listened to all this with increasing concern. With his last question, the fog descended and enveloped me. I felt a lump growing in my throat. I couldn't contain it; I started sobbing and buried my face in my hands, moaning incoherent words.

"Damn. Oh, Isaac, I am sorry. I forgot what all this must be doing to you."

He went over to a sideboard and poured two large glasses of brandy, came back, and sat next to me with a calming arm over my shoulder.

"When was the last time you let go like that? Best possible thing to happen. Clears the mind, possibly even the soul."

He was right. I had felt a release. I took a sip of the brandy, swallowing slowly, then dried my tears with a handkerchief Sir F. gave me.

"Isaac, we need to resolve a serious matter that still exists in Dorchester. When I received Wellings' note of your return, I sent a note to Will Whiteway, suggesting he come to Wraxall. After you disappeared last November he'd come to Plymouth. He said he had hunted for any trace of you for weeks. He told me everything he knew from the time you left the *Sweet Rose* until your disappearance. There had been no trace, except the horse you had been riding, which, according to the ostlers at the Sun, had returned there several days later, without you, with blood on the saddle."

I felt a sense of horror. I remembered my nightmares. How would I have reacted if I thought my best friend had died, mysteriously and without trace, only to be told he had turned up seven months later having lost his memory? How did Aby feature in this? My thoughts were interrupted by Sir F.

"I expect Will to be here within a few days. My questions have been enough for you."

He refilled my glass and left me to sleep. I was exhausted. I spent the rest of the day either sleeping or having Mark exercise me along the corridors and stairs, building my strength. Next morning, Mark had me up early, washed and dressed. I was to have breakfast in the main dining room with Sir F. He wished me a good morning. He was sitting at the head of a long table. He invited me to sit next to him where a table setting had been prepared for me. As soon as I arrived, Mr. Wellings came in and proceeded to serve us both. When finished, Sir F. leaned back saying he needed to talk to me—he felt a full stomach was needed. He said he had been pondering all yesterday after our meeting. He was worried how much he should tell me of what he knew about the missing months in my life. He had concluded that, with the imminent arrival of Will from Dorchester, we needed to talk. As a result, it would help me remember—that was the hope. He said he would ask questions. I was to think about them before answering, and I was to take my time.

"You remember staying at Wraxall?"

"Yes, sir."

"You were looking forward to going back to Dorchester from here. Why?"

I thought. I seemed to remember an excitement. Could it have been to see Will, or Aby, possibly?

"Not sure, sir."

"My understanding is that you and Aby had become close at Christmas. Do you remember any part of that time?"

"Mistletoe."

"What about it? You kissed someone under it."

"Aby?"

"Are you asking me? I wasn't there. Close your eyes and imagine where it was, who was there."

I did. The mistletoe was hanging in the hall of the rectory. The Whites had parties and Aby was always there. The fog was beginning to lift.

"Let's go back to your trip to Dorchester from here after Christmas. Were you going to see Aby?"

"Yes, I think so."

"What happened when you got there?"

I tried to remember the journey. I was riding . . .

"Maddie. I had forgotten, my horse Maddie. I rode to Dorchester on her then rode her back to Plymouth. I'm confused. Where is she now?"

"She remains stabled at the Minerva Inn. Do you remember the Minerva?"

"Yes—Annie."

"It is thanks to Annie that you still have Maddie and your possessions. She always refused to accept that you were dead, adamant that you told her to look after your belongings, including Maddie, until your return. This is good. Your memory is coming back."

I savored the flood of memories about Annie, the Minerva, and Maddie, insinuating themselves through my mind.

"Back to Dorchester. You remember riding there. You were in Dorchester for a much shorter time than you planned. What happened?"

"I rode to Dorchester to see Aby. I went to her father's house. I found her and Will embracing."

Then it came to me. Suddenly, the fog lifted.

"Yes, yes, yes!" I shouted, leaping to my feet. "Thank you. Oh, thank you. I remember. I love her."

My mind raced through the events leading up to my last journey back to Dorchester. The love, the night, the proposal, the marriage plan, then . . .

"Oh no!" I sank to my knees in horror.

"What?"

"We were due to be married on 3 December. I went to her house on 30 November straight from Weymouth. She and her father weren't there, so I went for a ride. I was in a state, terrified of the impending marriage. Something happened. I remember falling or being pulled off the horse—everything went black. I can't remember what happened until I found myself in Plymouth. That was the beginning of March."

"Let's leave that last part of your hidden journey till later. You remember you were going to get married."

"Will and Aby were close," I said. "I had already mistakenly thought they'd fallen for each other. Will was to be my best man, and if the groom fails to show, the best man is required to marry the abandoned bride. If they thought me dead all this time, they will have married. I found Aby, and in an instant I have lost her again."

I was distraught.

"Easy, Isaac. That is a gross supposition. You did not abandon Aby at the altar. It was four days beforehand. I know for a fact Will spent weeks searching for you. You will be seeing him soon. You will find all is well."

I wouldn't be consoled. I'd abandoned Aby and vanished. Nothing from 30 November until a note from Sir F. at the end of June. Seven months! For all she knew I could have run away or was dead. I thanked Sir F. and asked to be excused. With much concern he put his arm 'round my shoulder.

"Have faith," he said. "Your love for each other is strong."

I went to my room. I collapsed on my bed, trying to imagine the anguish I had caused Aby. I remembered my nightmares when I had the fever in the Indian village, of Aby sobbing her heart out, huddled in the corner of her kitchen, and Will riding like a wild man through the countryside, shouting my name. The mind is a funny thing. Deep down, it knew what was going on. After a while, I realized Sir F. was right. I needed to look forward with eager anticipation, not dreading the outcome. I walked downstairs, out into the cold morning air and slowly down the long driveway to the gateposts at the end. I walked out onto the road. I noticed a coach pulled by four horses coming up the road toward me. I stood back from the road into the driveway, expecting it to pass, but it stopped. The coach driver called down to me. "Is this Wraxall Court?"

I nodded. He turned the horses into the driveway. As it passed by me, I looked in and saw Will's face leaning forward, talking to someone opposite him.

"Driver, stop!"

At the sound of my voice, Will's head appeared. The coach stopped some ten yards on.

"Isaac. Thanks be to God."

The door opened. He jumped down, lifted Aby to the ground, and stepped away. Aby, with a hooded cloak wrapped 'round her, stood looking at me. I walked toward her. All I could see were her round eyes grown large. I reached her, took her hands in mine, and pressed them to my chest, drawing her close. Then, we put our arms around each other, hanging on for dear life. I could feel her trembling like a captured bird. Her lips parted as if she was moaning from deep, deep within her, but not a sound. I bent down and gently kissed her. Her eyes closed and opened again as I drew my head back. We were in another world. I was distracted by a discreet cough from the driver. Still not saying a word, but clinging to each other, we entered the coach, followed by Will, and proceeded up the drive.

I looked at Will. He was pale and tense, saying they hadn't slept since leaving Dorchester two days ago. Horses changed every twenty miles or so. Driver changed less frequently. Arranged by P. at what cost? Aby was leaning against me, clutching my arm in both her hands, totally exhausted, eyes now closed, shaking. We arrived at the front door. Sir F. was there to greet us, with Mr. Wellings. He took one look at Aby and told Mr. Wellings to fetch Mary, immediately. I helped Aby down, but she was in a state of collapse. Mary, with two maids, ran to her, helped her into the house, and disappeared. Sir F. turned to Will. He shook his hand.

"Hello again. Welcome to Wraxall Court. You made extraordinary time."

"Good day, sir. As soon as your note arrived, Aby was like one demented and insisted on an immediate departure, frantic with the need to organize the fastest trip possible. Luckily, Reverend White has innumerable contacts of the right sort. We were able to be on our way within a few hours. Aby has been in a state of total shock from the moment we set off. Unable to say or do anything, willing the coach to go faster, anxious at every stop. I'm afraid she is completely spent."

"You look pretty much done in yourself. Mr. Wellings, I suggest you organize a bedroom for Mr. Whiteway here with a tray of refreshments. Mr. Whiteway, we will meet again this evening. I am assuming you are done with your transport for today. I will deal with that. Sleep well."

Will thanked him. He followed Mr. Wellings away. Sir F. told the coach driver to move his coach to the stables, where he and they would be taken care of, and to await further instructions for the homeward journey. Sir F. turned to me with a raised eyebrow. I had been tensed up, almost rigid since their arrival, consumed by Aby—her presence and her condition. My fault, to blame or not, that she had obviously suffered much and for long. But she was here, and we were together again. I couldn't fail to notice she wore no wedding ring, but she was wearing our engagement ring. I nodded in response, smiling ruefully.

"You were right, sir. I should have realized her love, her faith."

"She is in good hands. Now, I want to talk about your experiences in New England in more detail. I am leaving tomorrow to return to Plymouth. Before I go, I want to salvage as much as possible from your voyage. Come to the study."

Sir F. gave me some fatherly and generous advice as we walked.

"You need to stay here until both of you are rested. It's for you to decide with Will his course of action, but you and Aby need time alone together. Take Aby to Plymouth, if you like, either on your way back to Dorchester, or later. It will also give us a chance to talk further. You might even think about whether, when you are married, you might want to move down there. I have need of someone of your caliber. I have questions to ask."

We returned to our chairs in the study. Before the questions, Sir F. said he had things to tell me. He understood from Mr. Brown that I had no memory of the report I had written for him, nor of my meeting with Captain Smith or Captain Hobson. He said that Captain Smith had given me an account which was in the report I had written. However, there was more which Sir F. then proceeded to tell me.

"Captain John Smith's voyage with three ships had left London in March 1614, making for Monhegan. He hadn't taken an Indian from England with him, but he met one, by name Tisquantum, in the Monhegan area who was preparing to travel south and was happy to accompany Smith as he continued his exploratory progress down the coast toward Cape Cod, close to Tisquantum's home, where Smith left him. The unfortunate Tisquantum was included among the hapless Indians that Hunt captured. Hobson, who followed after Smith, found that Hunt's actions had so inflamed the local population that he was unable to achieve anything. Incidentally, you were right, Epenow escaped at the first opportunity. Hobson returned Assacomet to his people, or at least from whence he was captured by Weymouth. To your considerable advantage, it would seem."

I agreed.

"Yes, sir. Hunt really caused huge, lasting damage to our interests. It will take a great deal of time and effort to regain any sort of trust with the Indians. Weymouth's capture of the original five was mitigated by their return. But, Hunt's actions set back that awakening trust greatly. From what Assacomet, now Samoset, told me, they have a good system of communication over long distances, even though there doesn't seem to be much love lost between the different tribes. Hunt's action was known quickly throughout the region. One approach might have been to make defensive alliances with key tribes. Samoset told me that they fear our guns. He said they would have preferred to have our backing in disagreements with their more aggressive neighbors, but not now."

Sir F. asked me for more details on what I had discovered.

"Monhegan is already being used on an occasional basis by English sailors. It is easily defended and would be an ideal permanent offshore base for a small settlement. Like a hilltop castle, it would need to be kept supplied if there were a significant presence, but a small group would have enough food and water with game, fish, and wild berries in abundance, and the ground appears fertile for growing vegetables. The place is thickly wooded as well. English fishermen have used it, but they have a much better location for their needs at Damariscove, with a good harbor and a large flat rocky landscape close to the water to rack their fish. There already appears to be a fishing settlement developing there."

"What about the mainland?" Sir F. asked.

"Unfortunately, I was barely aware of my canoe trips from Monhegan and to Damariscove. I have the impression that, with their light canoes, they can quickly travel long distances. Leaving Monhegan, the young braves who snared me were, obviously, wanting to get out of there as fast as possible. I had the sensation of great speed through the water, much, much faster than one of our oared boats. When I was able to walk around, the village I was in was or certainly looked permanent. The huts were well-built; some were substantial, with fields about, heavily cultivated. There was plenty of game food. It seemed an idyllic lifestyle.

"I don't know where I'd been, but from Rosier's description of the St. George's River and the countryside he saw, it seemed the village was on or near that river. I never went to Pemaquid, but one of the fishermen on Damariscove said there was a rumor one or two of the Popham settlers who went there in 1608. There is an Indian village there and, if the rumor is true, the settlers might or might not have survived. That would need further investigation. Explorers say it is a rocky peninsula or neck, a promontory sticking out from the coastline, marking the western boundary of a large bay, I think called Muscongus. I, on the other hand, was on low-lying cultivated land by a river that I think must have been the St. George's River. The land stretched as far as I could see, with gentle rise and fall. It reminded me of England."

Sir F. interrupted my musings.

"Thank you. Mr. Hobson was unsuccessful, but Mr. Brown did sail down the coast. You confirmed his findings about Damariscove. He put into a bay to the west of Pemaquid. He was looking, in part, for you, but as far as he went, he found no obvious places to land. He didn't want to become trapped by contrary winds or aggressive Indian war parties. Just as well, given the information you got from Samoset, about the war between the tribes. From Damariscove, Mr. Brown sailed across the mouth of one major river, which he felt needed to be explored, to Sagadahoc, the site of the Popham plantation, which was well protected behind an offshore island, Seguin. As that location had been well documented, he sailed on, passing another enormous, island-filled bay. The coastline started turning southward, at which point he headed for home. Hobson's report was encouraging with respect to the opportunities for settlement, subject to resolving the issue of Indian hostility."

I asked him what had happened to Captain Smith.

Sir F. sighed. "He persuaded Plymouth citizens to support a further voyage to New England in 1615 with two ships. His plan was to establish a settlement of seventeen men, with himself as its leader in the Pemaquid area. Tahanedo, a Captain Weymouth captive Captain Pring returned in 1606, was the local Sachem. Captain Smith had met and become friendly with him on his earlier voyage in 1614."

I was confused. "Why, sir, if Smith was going to New England, did you feel it necessary to send *Rosie*, as well?"

"I couldn't rely on Smith," he explained. "I had no idea if and when he'd return, and his objectives were very different from mine. Anyway, his two vessels left a few days after the departure of the *Sweet Rose* in March 1615, heading for New England. Unfortunately, Captain Smith's vessel proved to be unseaworthy and had to return to Plymouth, while Captain Dermer in the second continued on to New England. Captain Smith found another vessel and sailed from Plymouth once more in late June of 1615, expecting to rendezvous with the *Sweet Rose* and Captain Dermer at Monhegan. That rendezvous did not take place. Captain Dermer arrived in Monhegan after Mr. Brown had left in search of you and waited a month for Captain Smith, his leader in the planned settlement. When he didn't show up, Captain Dermer returned to Plymouth, arriving a few days ago. No one seems to know where Captain Smith is, currently. As I said, Captain Smith is not reliable."

I chanced a remark that came by way of P.

"I wonder what would've happened if the Popham settlement had consisted of a community of families with children, all the necessary artisan skill sets, an existing social order, and a minister. They would have gone to New England for reasons of economic improvement, religious persecution, or both. If they had disposed of their possessions in England in order to make a new life overseas, taking their worldly wealth, together with family and friends, there would be nothing for them to long for back here. That would be especially true if they were given the opportunity to own their own land."

Sir F. thought about that, looking into the fire. "You might well be right. Unfortunately, I don't have that kind of influence. I can raise money; I can employ people; I can induce people through the promise of commercial gain, as has Captain Smith in his latest exploit. I wouldn't know where to begin to create a settlement by transplanting an existing village from England to New England. I suspect you have been talking to others about this. Your thoughts are profound."

I admitted that P. had been gracious enough to expound his theories to me. Sir F. smiled and nodded. He thought as much. Perhaps he needed to spend some time in conversation with the redoubtable Reverend John White.

"Invite me to your wedding," he said out of the blue. "It would be a good opportunity to have that conversation."

I was stunned. I stammered that I, we, would be honored by his presence. He said he might bring Lady Ann with him—she liked weddings. Sir F. excused himself after suggesting that I needed rest, perhaps as much, if not more, than Aby. He suggested that Aby would recover quickly, especially if her man was in need of her. I stood and shook his hand, unable to speak eloquently of the gratitude I felt for all he had done to help me back to full function, and for his generous hospitality. He bowed and left me. I went to see Aby. She was fast asleep. I stood looking down. Her sweet face was clear, unmarked by the anguish she had suffered. I knelt and kissed her forehead and returned to my room to complete my journal entries, before Sir F., Will, and I were to have an evening meal together.

Journal entry—*31 July to 13 August 1615*

The next morning, Monday, 31 July, Sir F. left. With him went Will to arrange for my belongings to be sent from the Minerva to Wraxall and to ride Maddie back to Dorchester. I gave him a letter for Annie and the journal entries I had. Missing were those I had written on *Rosie* at the skipper's suggestion. We wondered where they are.

Mr. Wellings said that the household had been given firm instructions to ensure that Aby and I were restored to the rudest of health, which they were content to do. Aby had already won the hearts of the household. It seemed that Sir F. was right yet again. With Aby and me back together, my body started shutting down. The stress I had been under, the battering my poor body had suffered, had been kept at bay by sheer willpower. I struggled to get out of bed and dressed with difficulty but managed to get downstairs. I was in the kitchen having breakfast, Aby still abed, when I gently slid from the bench I was on to lie shivering on the floor. Mary exclaimed and called for Mr. Wellings. He and Mark took me back to my bedroom, undressed me, put me to bed, curtains closed, darkness. I slept. Many hours later, there was a knock on the door. Mark came in and opened the curtains. It was late afternoon. I lay looking at him, still half asleep. I was told that there was someone here to see me.

Aby came in carrying a tray with food and drink. Mark was uncomfortable, but it seemed he was to be the guardian of the house's virtue. It certainly worked, because Aby and I were formal. Although we were together, we needed each other, to talk, to touch. Much had happened, much needed to be explained, and I needed the care, the attention that Aby as wife could provide but Aby the betrothed should not. It was frustrating and both sensed that building pressure inside us. But she was here, and that's what mattered. We both laughed and hugged, with Mark becoming more uncomfortable. For Mark's sake we behaved ourselves. She sat by my bed and wanted a detailed account of all that ailed me. She said pointedly to poor Mark, "If I am to help Isaac's recovery, I need to know what medicinal supplies are needed."

I went through everything. My right hand explored the various injuries on my ear and head, pointing them out to her. If it had started as a game, Aby soon became deadly serious and concerned. I said I was possibly suffering from a continuation of the fever I caught when I was stuck with an arrow. I dropped my bedcovers to show my barely functional left arm, the wounded shoulder and the scars and bruises from the beating I took still evident. It had ceased to be a game for me, too, and keeping up the pretense had exhausted me. Aby looked at Mark.

"Isaac is more ill and injured than I realized. Please come with me to Mr. Wellings in order that we can discuss the best ways to help him and do all that can be done."

She gave me a quick kiss, re-closed the curtains, and swept from the room, dragging Mark behind her. I went back to sleep, semi-delirious but happy that my lady was now in charge. Aby became my sole nurse, much to Mark's relief. Gradually I recovered sufficiently to converse, and we talked for hours. I told Aby everything that happened that I could remember. I found out what my disappearance had done and how Aby had barely survived the ensuing months. We were not disturbed. Aby bathed me, top to bottom. She applied suitable ointments to my wounds, rubbed other ointments on my bruises, and helped me exercise my arm. The main worries were the fever and the need for me to gain weight and strength. The fever persisted for several days, but finally broke, and I began to feel more like myself again.

CHAPTER 20

With the return of health, I was anxious to be up and active. Aby and I talked about the immediate future. After what we had been through, the excitement of renewing our wedding plans was a special gift, with my fears now gone. Aby told me about the horrors of her Christmas. What had been planned as a joyous occasion of wedding and Christmas celebration was transformed into a fearful, bleak time. Will had been away looking for me, hunting for any clues about my disappearance. Mr. Baker and P. had done all they could. Mr. Baker had even postponed the sale of his business and his move to Devizes. But Aby had withdrawn into a deep depression. Silas had used his extensive network of contacts to no avail. He reported back that it seemed the earth had swallowed me whole. He said he would keep looking. No one was going to take his Isaac away from him. Aby said she was comforted by his confidence that I would be found. We talked about my missing months—December, January, and February—wondering what might have happened.

Now, she needed to get back to Dorchester. The morning of Tuesday, 8 August, we bade our grateful farewells. The whole household was there to see us off as we departed in style, by coach. The return trip was made at a much more sedate pace than their breakneck speed down to Wraxall, for which I was thankful. Aby was the perfect nurse, and the balmy summer weather was ideal. We stayed at the George in Norton St. Philip, the Hart in Wincanton, and the George in Sherborne, arriving back in Dorchester in the late afternoon of Friday, 11 August.

We went directly to the Baker house, to be met by Mr. Baker, who was delighted to see us. I slipped away to find Will. Aby was grateful to spend time alone with her father, as there was much for them to talk about. Will was not to be found, so I left a message. I found Maddie, and rode her over to the Sun to be stabled and to find a room for me, after which I walked to the rectory. The greeting I received was overwhelming, so joyful were they with my return. They pressed me to stay in my old room. I sent a note to Mr. Gosling at the Sun that I would be delayed a day or two, and asked that he keep Maddie safe. Later that evening, after family supper, I had a long chat with P., bringing him up to date. He listened in silence, shaking his head at the misadventures. At the end, he bowed his head and gave thanks to God for my deliverance. We talked of the marriage. The banns had been read previously. They probably should be reread given the intervening time, but he thought that step could be dispensed with. We agreed on Saturday, 19 August, for the ceremony. He said he would announce it at Matins on Sunday. I told him about Sir F. and Lady Ann, and P. said he would send them a note, immediately, inviting them to attend the wedding and stay the night at the rectory. I hoped there was enough time. He also mentioned that Mr. Bushrode had been by to see him and had been pleased to hear of my return from the dead, as he put it. He also mentioned that the *Sweet Rose* was in Weymouth for a few days, should I be interested.

Next morning, after a heavy sleep, I was up early to be back to Aby. Mr. Baker joined us as we discussed plans, and we were all pleased with the date set, the nineteenth. That day we immersed ourselves in the events of the community over the past seven months. I was desperate to catch up on all that I had missed. On Sunday, after a happy breakfast, the three of us, dressed in our finery, walked to Holy Trinity. Mrs. White had us sit in her south aisle pew, although Mr. Baker felt more comfortable joining the men in the center pews. There was much interest in my return.

At the end of his sermon, which he had appropriately made on the theme of the prodigal son, P. asked the congregation to give thanks for my safe return. He gave a summary of what had happened, as far as any of us knew, to cause the cancellation of our wedding back in December. He said the marriage was now to take place next Saturday the nineteenth at two p.m., with a reception following in the Shire Hall. He asked Aby and me both to rise, and the congregation clapped and voiced their approval. At the end of the service, it took a long time for us to extract ourselves. We walked back to the Bakers' house with well-wishers all the way. It was wonderful and heartwarming.

After lunch, Aby and I went for a long walk. While we had talked on our journey from Wraxall, we had not dwelt in any detail on our post-marriage plans. Now, we needed to. I said that Sir F. had suggested that he would like to see me working for him out of Plymouth. Alternatively, I presumed I could have my old job back on the *Sweet Rose*, which would be out of Weymouth. Aby was intrigued about Plymouth and I said I would need to talk further with Sir

F. If he came to the wedding, I could talk to him then. Until we were married, I would stay at the Sun. Once married, we would live in the Baker house. I arranged with Mr. Gosling that our wedding night would be in the best room. Apart from anything else, we wanted to enjoy our first few weeks as man and wife at home in Dorchester.

I talked to Aby about her reading and writing. She reminded me that she and Will had been working hard on her education, but the lessons had stopped when I had disappeared. I remembered the surprise and joy when I received that first letter from her. She admitted that without Will's help she wouldn't have been able to do anything, but he persuaded her to continue the lessons. She said she had thrown herself into it as a distraction and knowing that was what I would have wanted her to do. Shyly, she asked if I would like to test her skills. We began immediately. Mr. Baker had a chalkboard in his shop. Aby opened the family Bible, read a passage, and then transcribed it onto the chalkboard. As Aby wrote, I watched her face. Her frown of concentration was a picture—a little wrinkle appearing between her eyebrows, her mouth silently saying each word. She'd been a quick learner. I was most impressed.

After Aby cooked us supper, I returned to the Sun and completed my journal entry. A knock on the door to my bedroom. I was told a man was in the bar looking for me. I descended to be greeted with a bear hug. It was Silas.

"Isaac, am I glad to see you. I have been to places and talked to people you wouldn't believe, searching for signs of you. Now tell me what happened."

It was a long evening, with much ale drunk. Eventually Silas was content that his Isaac had yet another series of adventures and had proved as indestructible as he had always known. He would attend our wedding.

Journal entry—*14 to 20 August 1615*

It was Monday, 14 August, a warm day with a gentle southerly breeze. A day for riding. But on waking a thought struck me. My wedding ring. My saddlebags, Whistler, I had forgotten. After dropping in on the Baker household to exchange affectionate greetings, I went in search of Will.

"Will, what happened when Whistler came back to the Sun without me? Were my saddlebags still attached?"

"Oh dear, I am sorry, Isaac, I forgot. I retrieved them from the Sun, together with the clothes you had in your room and the journal entry you were writing. They are back home. I didn't want to give them to Aby. With you unaccounted for, it would have been an extra, unnecessary burden for her."

"Good, thank you. Please bring them to the Sun, and if I'm not there, have them put in my room."

With that errand accomplished, I went back to the Bakers, to build the fire under the cauldron and to assist with the production of the candles needed for the summer religious observances. The business served the needs of three churches and countless houses. I could not see myself settling down to such a mundane existence, but over the next several days, that is what I did. However, one day I made my excuses to Mr. Baker and rode to Weymouth to find *Rosie*. Sadly, she had sailed that morning and would not be back for several weeks. I wrote a letter to the skipper, apologizing for not having contacted him sooner, regretting he would be unable to attend our wedding and telling him of my possible employment by Sir F.

My belongings that Will had promised to return were on my bed at the Sun. I had forgotten most of the saddlebags were empty. I'd removed their contents to my room before going on that fateful ride. But everything was there on the bed. Except my wedding ring. I sat thinking. When I returned to *Rosie* on 1 March, I had been wearing rough clothes, not mine. When I left the Sun on 30 November for the ride, I was still in my relative finery. I had had a money wallet and the ring in my pocket. Now both were gone. I had to buy another ring.

The loss of the ring set me to thinking about that ride. I must have been waylaid. If it had been a highwayman, Whistler would not have escaped. I wouldn't have been knocked unconscious. At least, I would have been aware of the situation before passing out. It might have been one or more footpads. Same problem. They would not have let Whistler go—valuable property, especially the tack. I might have fallen off Whistler, accidentally. Whistler may have shied or bucked, when I was daydreaming, and in falling, I may have hit my head on a stone. No, that theory doesn't work. There was blood on the saddle, presumably my blood. That evidence means I was in the saddle when my head hit something, hard. Unconscious, I must have folded over, my bloody head smearing itself on the saddle as I fell to the ground. I would have to have been traveling fast to cause the damage to my head. Whistler would have continued to canter after I fell off until of his own accord he would stop, graze, wait, and after a while (several hours, I would expect, and getting dark) with me nowhere in sight, would begin the process of finding his way home. Apparently, it took him a while. Strange no one saw him. Where was I going? It must have been very remote. Then what happened? I was found in Plymouth three months later, after having seemingly dropped off the end of the earth.

I went hunting for a jeweler. The fire had destroyed West Street shops, so I had some searching to do. Eventually, tucked away off South Street, I found a pawn shop. I went in and asked if the owner, Mr. Tatler, had any gold rings for sale. I was shown a tray of rings, all simple gold bands. There were two that fitted my finger, one perfectly. I mentioned that it was sad that people found it necessary to pawn their wedding rings. The proprietor said occasionally, as in the case of the ring I had in my hand, someone would come in to sell an item that the person had supposedly found, which, he said, was always suspicious, but no way of knowing the real circumstances.

I looked more closely at the ring. There, inscribed on the inside, was "Aby 3 Dec 14." Shocked, I asked when he had acquired the ring. Several months ago, back in April maybe. Did he remember who had sold it to him? He thought for a while. The seller was vaguely familiar to him, a struggling, down-on-his-luck farmer who lived somewhere north of town. He was a man who was seen on market days occasionally, but the proprietor didn't know his name. Why did I want to know? My ring, I said—stolen last November. He told me if he saw the man again, he'd find out more about him and let me know. I bought the ring for the price he paid and told him how to contact me. Aby was over-joyed at the recovery and spent the rest of the week in eager anticipation as we waited to be married.

The wedding went in a blur. The church was full. P. officiated with solem-nity, emanating joy and love all through the service. Aby, given to me by her father, looked totally, achingly beautiful, even veiled. She walked up the aisle on her father's arm, dressed simply in a long burgundy red robe. In no time, it seemed, we were married. We kissed and walked down the aisle, waving to the laughing and cheering congregation. As we neared the door, I saw Sir F. standing by the font at the back of the church, smiling at us as we approached. I nudged Aby. She looked up, saw him, and immediately went to him, dragging me with her. She gave him a huge hug. He grinned at me over Aby's shoulder and kissed her. Extricating himself, he shook my hand. We were swept away by the mass of the congregation following down the aisle after us. The wed-ding reception was a noisy, happy feast. Tables groaned with food and drink. It seemed as if the whole town was there, and the noise level increased with the drink consumed. Space was cleared for dancing, and the pipe and fiddle band played in the corner to everyone's enjoyment.

The time came for speeches. Guests sat or leaned on the walls, laughing and cheering at everything said. Many people spoke, some of whom perhaps shouldn't have, given their state of inebriation. Will spoke quietly and movingly.

P. gave a sweet homily, spoiling the religious context by entering into some humorous, slightly risqué stories involving me. I have to say that I don't remember them, the way they were told. Much laughter ensued. Silas was called to speak by P. Now Silas is not a public speaker and was acting shy. Aby, bless her, went to him and dragged him by the arm out into the center of the throng, cleared a place for him, and said, "Come on, Silas, tell us some of the scrapes your Isaac got into."

A foaming tankard was thrust into his hand. He took a large draught and began to speak, hesitantly at first. As his audience started to respond to his descriptions, he became more confident and louder. The laughter swelled to match the increasingly wild exaggerations.

I whispered to my beloved, "Now see what you have started. We'll be here all night."

But he did end to cheers from the assembly. He raised his twice-emptied tankard to us both, and we saluted him. Then Sir F. stood. Everyone stopped talking and was most respectful. He talked quietly to a silent hall. He described how, most recently, Aby and I had come into his life and made such a difference to it, speaking simply and with feeling. We were quite overcome. He ended by recounting some of my exploits, adding his own decorative descriptions, which made them seem even funnier if more improbable. But, at the end, he brought me down to size by saying how much more I still had to learn, and he had hopes that all would end well. Cheers and applause resulted. Aby gave him a big hug. At some point later in the evening, I noticed P. and Sir F. had their heads together sitting in a quieter corner. Sir F. had accepted P.'s invitation and was staying at the rectory.

Later, we returned to the Sun. P. and Sir F. had long since departed. I would have loved to have been a fly on the wall to the late-night conversations they were bound to have had in P.'s study. A number of friends came with us in varying stages of befuddlement. We settled in the snug bar to wait them out, trying to hide our increasing impatience with our young friends, single and merry—unaware. I caught Will's eye with a look that should have spoken volumes but didn't. Aby was calmness personified, only a slight quiver, her arm through mine, smoldering beneath her serene exterior to indicate her hidden passions. Will eventually ushered them away. We went to our room. Awaiting us was a large four-poster bed with curtains.

I will draw those curtains over that night. We were both ravenously hungry for each other, at last freed from any constraints, all our previous lovemaking having taught us what prolonged pleasure we could give and share. Eventually, supremely happy, totally spent, we slept wrapped around each other. The first night of the rest of our lives together. The next day, we were left alone apart from the occasional discreet knock announcing delivery of another laden tray. Hidden in our bed, we allowed them entry to clear away and set another meal on the table, cozily set in the window bay. We loved; we talked; we ate; we drank; we loved again, and slept. We didn't leave the room till late in the afternoon.

Sir F. had left me a note at the Sun wishing us health and happiness in fulsome terms. He apologized that Lady Ann had been unable to come to the wedding. Having received notice too late and with the pressure of work, he could do no more than "gallop through the night" to arrive in time. He repeated his invitation for us both to come down to Plymouth, saying he had a proposition to make to me. He painted Plymouth and the surrounding countryside in glowing colors, finishing the note saying he hoped to see us back there soon. Aby and I agreed that we should go to Plymouth in about ten days. We moved back to the Baker home, and Maddie was transferred to stables by the West Gate.

Journal entry—*20 to 30 August 1615*

Once we became used to being under the same roof as Aby's father, we settled quickly into marital life. During the day I helped Mr. Baker. I had large wicker baskets harnessed onto Maddie's back, behind the saddle, and I went all over the town and surrounding countryside delivering bundles of candles and taking orders for more. Nights in our room, we continued our intimate, exploratory way. We loved the freedom of being together, shedding our clothes, reveling in each other's mind and body. The time we had was a joyous period in our new life together. The pain of the past year withdrew into dark corners of our minds. To Will, Aby became a beloved sister, and we saw him often. Aby's reading and writing skills were a continual satisfaction to her and a source of great pride to me. She was willing, eager to demonstrate her proficiency, by now, thanks to Will, very competent. As a game, we even practiced in bed together. I would circle a nipple with my finger—"Ooooo," she said. Quite right. We made up letter associations by my drawing them on parts of her body with suitable responses both intimate and memorable: the tip of my finger drawing a line up from the side of her right breast around down between and back up round her other breast to her left side—"Mmmmm." Daytime sitting at the kitchen table with quill in hand, telling her to write out the letters, Mr. Baker was perplexed that each brought a giggle from his daughter. He looked at me, and I shrugged.

We rode Maddie together, Aby on pillion. As a young girl, Aby had learned to ride straddle. In boy's breeches she felt free and loved it and was a natural, but as a woman such freedom was not allowed. We found stables away from the town, where we could hire a horse for Aby. She took a bag of boy's clothes to change into discreetly so she could continue to ride straddle. The horse, a dappled mare about thirteen hands, was called Tess. The riding became a daily activity. Aby enjoyed it, so much so that I bought Tess for her. We also talked about Sir F.'s offer. We agreed that her father's imminent departure to Devizes reduced the pull of Dorchester as the place for us to live. I had already written to Sir F. to request an opportunity for us both to come down to Plymouth to meet with him. A week later, I received a note telling us to come the week of 4 September. We planned to be away for about two weeks, having decided to ride down. Traveling shorter distances in the middle of the day, it would take us four days to get down to Plymouth. We would travel as brothers, to avoid scandalous comment about Aby and her riding. We planned to leave on Friday, 1 September. Mr. B.'s business was being sold, after much delay, 4 September.

CHAPTER 21

Journal entry—*31 August to 15 September 1615*

We arrived in Plymouth on Monday, 4 September, in the early evening and made our way to the Minerva. We received a huge, warm welcome from Annie and were given a room more in keeping with our status as a married couple. Aby pleaded tiredness, genuinely needing sleep but also realizing that Annie and I had much to catch up on. Annie sat me down in a corner, and made me cover the whole missing seven months. She told me how frantic she had been. Sir F. had kept her informed when he heard I had turned up. Annie said she knew, absolutely knew in her heart, that I would reappear after some extraordinary adventures.

A message was delivered to Sir F.'s office that Mr. and Mrs. Stanfield had arrived awaiting Sir F.'s pleasure. A note came back to request our company at nine o'clock on Wednesday morning. Tuesday I spent introducing Aby to Plymouth. The next day, Sir F. rose to greet us as we were shown into his office by Captain Turner, who had, himself, greeted me with a smile, a firm handshake, and a heavy pat on the back and been charming to Aby. Sir F. kissed Aby's hand and shook my hand and led us to two comfortable chairs, while he sat in a third. At his inquiry, we talked about our marriage and our new married life together. He seemed pleased for us both. Settled and comfortable, he turned the conversation to our future. He asked about our ties to Dorchester. Aby explained about her father. I said there was not much to keep us there, apart from our friends. He asked about my interest in rejoining the *Sweet Rose*. I said I looked back on the eighteen months I spent as a member of the crew as the most formative of my life.

We spoke about voyages across the Atlantic. He gave us more information about Captain Smith's latest voyage earlier in the year. He told us how

Captain Smith had returned to Plymouth because his vessel had lost her masts. Smith, setting out once more in the second vessel, was captured by pirates under strange circumstances. He had gone aboard the pirate for some reason. His crew abandoned him and sailed back to Plymouth. Sir F. didn't know where Captain Smith was, but he seemed to be indestructible. No doubt he would turn up with more extraordinary tales to tell. Getting to the point of the meeting, he said he wanted me to be a member of his staff in Plymouth. The duties would be many and varied: being a courier, gathering information, identifying issues that need resolution, working to help resolve those issues, preparing reports on incidents, and participating in meetings or conferences to defend those reports. From his view, I had the talents to go places unobserved, meet people, and gain their confidence. I could defend myself, was bright, intelligent, and observant. Aby squeezed my arm, looking at me proudly. I was excited. I couldn't imagine having a better job or working for a better person. But I was worried. Sir F. saw my concern and asked what was wrong.

"It's *Rosie*, sir. Despite my absence I feel I'm still a member of her crew."

Sir F. nodded.

"Don't worry. I have informed Mr. Brown of my intentions and he told me to give you his blessings. However, he told me to tell you he looks forward to meeting with you to hear a full accounting of your adventures."

Sir F. went on that they would find proper accommodation for us both. Also, Lady Ann was looking for aid in her household with respect to helping her organize and manage her many social and civic duties. Aby's name had been mentioned, subject to our deciding to move to Plymouth. Aby squeezed my arm again, saying that she would welcome a chance to meet with Lady Ann. Sir F. suggested we take time to talk it over before coming back to him, perhaps tomorrow, with our decision. We both thanked him profusely and said we would. He told us that there was a small house available, Four Pins Lane, off New Street near the Barbican, which we might want to look at and gave us precise directions with the key. We went straight there.

Pins Lane is entered through an archway with a substantial dwelling running the length of the lane on one side. There is a terrace of a few small dwellings on the other, one of them number four, each with stone steps that lead up to a covered doorway. We entered a large kitchen and living area, with a fireplace and cooking range, the chimney taking heat to the bedroom, upstairs. Sparsely furnished but cozy. At the street level, a large storage room underneath the kitchen. We returned to Sir F.'s office the following morning and left a message for him that we thought the house on Pins Lane was suitable. A note from

Lady Ann was waiting for Aby to suggest she make her way to 32 New Street, the Gorgeses' Plymouth home, to attend her. I accompanied Aby there, close to Pins Lane, to an imposing house. We were invited in. While I was given a seat in the hall, a servant disappeared up the staircase with Aby in tow. Sometime later, Aby came down, accompanied by Lady Ann herself.

"Sir Ferdinando has been following your career with great interest and continuing amazement. Now, I have had the pleasure of meeting Abigail. I have discussed with her the position that I need to have filled and told Abigail that I would be pleased to offer her that position, subject to your plans, Mr. Stanfield. Abigail and I have agreed that we will await your further conversation with Sir Ferdinando before proceeding any further. Good day to you both."

With that dismissal, said gently with a friendly smile, she turned and went back up the stairs. A servant let us out. Wordless, we walked down to the Hoe to sit overlooking the sound. Aby pressed to my side, holding my arm with both her hands, bursting to tell me all. As soon as we had found an isolated perch on a rock, Aby told me that she found Lady Ann a joy, gracious and friendly. The position needed to be filled as soon as possible because the previous incumbent had not been satisfactory and was no longer employed. The job required Aby to manage Lady Ann's appointments both social and civic and to see to her travel arrangements, if separate from her husband's. It meant that she would have to accompany Lady Ann on her travels from time to time. We talked about how our life as a newly married couple might be changed by becoming part of the entourage of two active people. We would be very busy. Although occasionally separated, we would be part of the same extended family. It seemed like a perfect opportunity for us both. With that settled, I left a message for Sir F. that I would be grateful for an opportunity to meet with him at his convenience and returned to the Minerva.

By nine o'clock on Saturday morning, 9 September, I was seated in Sir F.'s office. I told him that we would be honored to be considered for both positions. Sir F. jumped to his feet and offered me his hand, which I shook vigorously. I said we would be most pleased to take the accommodation he had suggested in Pins Lane. He replied that the property belonged to the Fort, and the rental would be deducted from my wages, which would be, after those deductions, three crowns per week. That amount sounds generous, he said, but the position required my availability at all times and my ability to travel anywhere, at a moment's notice. I recognized that, having Aby in a somewhat similar position with Lady Ann, meant we would each have our adventures with times apart, but neither would be left moping at the hearthside. We discussed the activities needed to have us move down to Plymouth to take up our positions. With Aby's father leaving, there would be furniture and belongings to move from the Baker house. I would need to accompany Aby back to Dorchester, make my farewells, and return to Plymouth. Aby would return with filled wagon sometime later. I would be gone ten days. That suited Sir F.

"I expect to see you eight o'clock on Wednesday morning, 20 September."

I returned to the Minerva to tell Aby, who asked me to accompany her to 32 New Street to meet with Lady Ann. Lady Ann confirmed Aby's appointment and suggested it would be thought on kindly if Aby could be back here at the latest by 16 October. As to remuneration, the Pins Lane house would be considered an annex of 32 New Street. All housekeeping, including our essential food requirements, would be covered. In addition, Aby would receive seven shillings a week.

Monday morning, early, we slipped away from the Minerva, heading for Exeter, with Aby's male attire hidden under a cloak. Stars were out, dawn smearing the horizon. We had clear, excellent going under hoof. Maddie and Tess were keen to stretch out. As the sun came up, we loosened the reins and made quick progress. By Thursday morning, 14 September, we were at the Baker home. I soon met with P. and advised him of our plans. He was sorry to see us leave his parish, but he was keen for me to continue to keep him abreast of Sir F.'s activities. Mr. Baker came back from Devizes on Friday. He had already sold the business and, with the house emptied of the Bakers' possessions, he would be able to complete the full purchase quickly. I spent time with Will. He said he recognized the inevitability of our move. While greatly saddened, he said that he too would be leaving Dorchester for a while. His father wanted him to spend time in France to build commercial interests and contacts. He told me his ambition was to write a history of the world. We agreed to continue to write to each other. I promised to continue sending him my journal entries. We would use P. as a postbox.

Journal entry—*16 to 21 September 1615*

Saturday morning, I dropped off my latest journal entry at Will's house. After a quick breakfast and a long, fond farewell embrace with my wife, I was on my way to my new career in Plymouth. Overnight, the rain had come in with a vengeance. An easterly wind drove the rain at my back, the wet cutting through my heavy oiled cloak. We, Maddie and I, looked for low-lying roads and sought the shelter of woods, which meant we worked our way slowly west. We proceeded through the Winterborne River villages, St. Martin, Steepleton, Abbas, on to Littlebredy, following the River Bride past Litton Chaney to Bridport. It was, in fact, a lovely ride, if a wet one. After a bite to eat and a hot drink at a tavern, I pushed onward. I wanted to make as much headway as possible, fearing the weather would get worse. After Bridport, we headed north, with the wind still cutting from the east, the rain easing a little, away from the uplands on the coast, through Dottery. We skirted Marshwood Vale to the north making for the villages of Marshwood and Hawkchurch, on to the River Axe, where we rode downstream-side to Axminster. With Maddie going well, we made another brief stop in Axminster. In the late afternoon we made for Honiton to The Angel Inn. I had a bed to myself. I woke to the promise of a brighter day. We left just after dawn, skies overcast but warmer, with a light wind which had shifted southerly. We rode the Fosse way to Exeter then on the main road to Plymouth through Chudleigh and Ashburton, stopping for lunch at Buckfastleigh. We were welcomed back at the Minerva at dusk on Sunday evening. Monday and Tuesday I spent exploring and cleaning our new home in Pins Lane. At the end of each day, I returned to the Minerva.

As requested, I presented myself at Sir F.'s office at eight a.m. on Wednesday, 20 September. Sir F. told me that prize money had been awarded for the pirate vessel we had damaged in March, last year, allocated out of the pirate prize court. It had taken rather longer than usual, which is normally a long time anyway. The pirate was carrying captured cargo which added to the prize value. There'd been legal argument as to the ownership and the country of origin. In the end, it turned out that the value had been substantial. Of the balance due to the *Sweet Rose*, Sir F. said that the amount to me came to twelve pounds, thirteen shillings, and four pence. He'd taken the liberty of crediting my account with the business manager he had established to handle my highwayman award. I thanked him most sincerely, pleased to have my affairs in good order.

He had received a report that Hunt's captive Indians had been offloaded in Malaga. Hunt had hoped to make a substantial financial gain, but it seemed the Spanish intermediaries had prevented him from selling them. The local religious order had seen them as exploited heathens who should be converted to Christianity. Therefore, Hunt had failed in his objective. Now Sir F. was looking for ways to get his hands on him. Sir F. said that Captain John Smith had turned up with another improbable adventure to recount. He told Sir F. that his guide Tisquantum, one of the captives in Malaga, was much valued, and something needed to be done to rescue him.

Sir F. provided more detailed information about Captain Smith's successful 1614 trip to New England with Tisquantum. Smith found that Tisquantum was a visitor to Monhegan, coming from the Patuxet tribe farther south. More importantly, he had traveled and knew the land, the people between Monhegan and Cape Cod, and already had some rudimentary English from contacts with fishermen. He was fascinated with the English and saw us as some kind of demi-gods with incredible wealth, enormous ships, and instruments of war that could kill many people at long distance. Captain Smith told him that he planned to sail to Cape Cod. He needed a guide, Tisquantum agreed. As a result, Captain Smith sailed with him. Tisquantum became a loyal and useful companion. Before leaving Cape Cod to explore farther along the coast, an area Tisquantum did not know, Captain Smith left him with his people, feeling he had gained England a great ally, which could only bode well for the future. Then Hunt ruined the whole thing.

Sir F. felt that we should do everything in our power to correct the situation. We needed to find him, to rescue as many of the captives as we were able to, and bring them back to England to be returned to their people. We had to reduce the anger and hatred they had for the English. We already had a secret escape route for pirate captives and should attempt to use that same route to rescue Tisquantum. Whatever we did had to be done in complete secrecy. The escape route was known only to David Tremaine and, to a certain extent, by me. Sir F. wasn't certain where Tremaine was, but his base was Bilbao. Tremaine was the key. I had been able to reach him before, no thanks to Gunt. It was dangerous but Gunt was no longer a factor. Tremaine was presumably still involved with the pirates. I was known to them as a friend of Tremaine's, while a complete stranger attempting to reach Tremaine would be viewed with great suspicion. I pleaded with Sir F. to let me go, saying this was just the sort of mission he had employed me to carry out. Eventually, he agreed. My job was to sail to Bilbao, find Tremaine, and organize Tisquantum's escape.

There was a vessel belonging to a London merchant that had put into Plymouth for supplies and cargo and was about to sail for Bilbao. Sir F. would request passage for me. I was stunned at the speed of events. In the space of a few minutes, it seemed we had moved from me clearing our new home on Pins Lane to being sent back to Bilbao. I received a message that evening that the *Good Fortune*, currently quayside in Sutton Pool, would be sailing Friday, 22 September, with the afternoon tide. I was expected aboard by midday.

Journal entry—*22 September to 10 October 1615*

I dressed as a passenger rather than a sailor, with sword, dirk, and a bag of other necessities. I made my way to the *Good Fortune*. She was of similar displacement to the *Sweet Rose*. The passage down was straightforward. The captain and crew had sailed far and long together and were very competent. Four days later, the afternoon of 26 September, we were in Bilbao. The *Good Fortune* was expected to remain for three days and then sail to Gravesend. I went ashore, disguised as a nondescript, unremarkable sailor, seemingly without purpose, and made for the bar to see Roseanna, my only point of contact. I hoped the password was the same. I would have to think again if it wasn't. Roseanna was there. Once more I was able to whisper "cuckoo" to her. Again, a plate of tapas was delivered with a note. Outside, I read the note—a street address. I rolled the note into a ball, swallowed it with my wine and tapas, and left, memories of Gunt fresh in my mind. No one seemed to have the slightest interest in me. I went hunting for the address, which was a door in a wall on an empty street. There was a bell rope which I pulled and the door opened a crack. I saw no one and nothing was said.

"Tremaine?" I asked tentatively.

The door closed, a chain was pulled, and the door reopened, making a black hole through which I entered. I followed a candlelight up stairs and around corners to a side-door which likewise opened. The light stopped beyond, and the candle gestured me to enter. When I did, I was locked in. There was a barred window which looked out over an empty courtyard. In the room was a table, two chairs, a sideboard, and a crucifix on the wall. It looked like a monastic cell but with no bed. The sunlight faded. There was noise of a key turning and a knock on the door. I opened it, and on the floor outside I could just make out a tray of food and drink which I picked up. The passage was in darkness and I saw no one. I carried the tray into the room. The door was shut and locked behind me. There was a candle with matches on the tray, which I lit, and a note with a piece of charcoal.

"Who are you?" the note read.

I wrote "*Rosie*," ate my food, drank the wine, put the tray by the door, and knocked. The door opened and the tray was removed by a pair of arms that seemed disembodied in the shadows. The door closed and locked. I had to assume that something would happen soon. I must've been there for four or five hours before there was another knock. I opened the door. A candle beckoned me to follow. It was like walking in a maze, a rabbit warren, with a sense of door-lined corridors leading off in different directions. Eventually, we went up another set of stairs, and the candle stopped outside a door. I opened it and entered. The door closed behind me. I was in a beautifully appointed room, with bookshelves, deep leather seats, a desk, lamps lit, and a fire blazing in a large open hearth. A man seated at the desk with his back to me looked out of the window.

I started toward him, when a voice behind me said: "Hello, Isaac."

I nodded my head with studied nonchalance. "David," I replied.

The man at the desk turned and, seeing that David and I knew each other, got up and left the room.

"Come in, tell me why you are here."

We sat with a large glass of brandy each. David apologized for the way I'd been kept in the dark, but there was an absolute need for secrecy. The delay had been because he'd not been present. He had to be fetched, and had been disinclined to until my *Rosie* note had been passed on to him. Then, he needed to see who it was before revealing himself. If he hadn't recognized me, the man behind the desk would've attempted to find out more, and if he'd been dissatisfied with my answers, I would have been removed. I wondered what he meant by that. I told him that Sir F. had sent me, and explained my mission. He sat and thought awhile.

"This mission will take some time. Probably a month or more. It is a little complicated as I have had two roles here. One was to establish the hostage escape route, which is now working, and I have separated from that. The other is to keep a watch on the pirates and their spy network. The pirates receiving the ransom are happy to maintain the hostage escape route, but there are competing groups of renegade pirates that try to recapture those freed sailors. The escape network has a mechanism that ensures that the freed sailors are protected by the pirates that received the ransom. They do not want to risk losing ransom money if the sailors are deemed to be still at risk of recapture by the renegades."

"What about the Indians?" I asked.

"We need to find out if Tisquantum is one of them and, if so, persuade him to use the escape route. The route itself takes a while to traverse. A boat would need to be found to take him back to England. There is nothing more you can do. You should return from whence you came. I will take care of it from here on. I can send word through the network, I hope. Only if necessary will I get directly involved. Tell Sir Ferdinando that he will receive word when Tisquantum has been rescued."

He asked when the *Good Fortune* was due to sail. I told him. He said we should spend the evening having a good meal, and he wanted me to tell him everything that had happened to me since we last met 18 months ago. Over the meal I told him all, leaving nothing out. He listened in silence.

At the end of my narration he nodded, refilled our glasses. "You did well," he said simply.

He rang a bell, wished me a good journey back, and said he looked forward to us getting together again. I was shown to a comfortable bedroom and slept well. Early the following morning, I was directed to the door in the wall I'd first entered. I returned to the *Good Fortune*, and we sailed the same day. In Gravesend, I was fortunate to find a passage on a coastal vessel that would be making its way down the south coast as far as Weymouth.

Three days later I was in Weymouth. Adam had a number of horses available to hire between the King's Arms and Dorchester to be left in Dorchester for someone to hire for the return journey. I rode to Dorchester, surprising Aby and her father and making a happy reunion with them. They had almost completed the clearing of their house. A wagon stood in the yard, piled with the items Aby was bringing to Plymouth. It was an easy decision for me to travel with Aby on the wagon. Charlie was to be the driver, and the trip would take about five days. Mr. Baker had a quiet word with me before leaving. He'd left all his possessions to Aby in his will, except for the dowry he had promised to provide. He handed me a note in the amount of £150 that his correspondent agent would honor in Plymouth. I was staggered at his generosity. He said he felt more peace over that transaction than any other in his life. He loved us both and blessed me for making his Aby so happy. Next morning, with our bed the last item to be stowed on the wagon, we climbed aboard. Charlie cracked his whip over the two horses and off we set. Weather settled, and the road was clear. We had an entertaining trip down. We managed about twenty-five miles per day. We had the company of other travelers most of the time. We were not troubled by rogues on the way. We stayed at inns I hadn't visited before, for the most part. We talked, laughed, and enjoyed the scenery. We made a snug place where one of us could take a nap. Charlie and I took it in turns to drive the horses. We were warm. We were happy.

We arrived in Plymouth on 10 October. I organized some casual assistance to help Charlie and Aby offload the wagon while I went to report to Sir F. Mr. John Slaney, a wealthy London merchant and patron of Captain Smith, had agreed to finance the effort to find and rescue Tisquantum. Sir F. suggested that while we awaited news from David Tremaine, I might like to update my report on New England exploration in the light of Smith's experiences. I agreed, and returned to Pins Lane. The unloaded cart had been taken away, and Charlie was anxious to get back to Dorchester. Aby undertook to find a furniture dealer in the morning to add some essentials, such as a bed for two. Aby's bed was small. We hadn't thought much about its size before, seeing as how we spent our nights entwined. But we came to realize that we would probably do well by trading in the old bed for a bigger one.

Journal entry—*11 October to 9 November 1615*

Every morning at half past eight o'clock, Sir F. met with key staff to discuss the day's events and matters of general interest and to hear reports from the staff on their activities. Tasks were allocated. At that first meeting on 11 October, I met the other members of his staff. They had various assignments or departments for which they were responsible—such as Plymouth Fort, liaison with Plymouth mayor's office, liaison with local Navy command, liaison with county militia and local military, piracy intelligence gathering and dissemination, and liaison with the government in London. My department was New England. My first task was to put together a map of the New England coastline, to include the salient points of interest from the various accounts we had received on paper or by word of mouth.

Aby settled into Lady Ann's household. Her predecessor had left a mess of poorly written letters waiting to be redone, incomplete schedules of activities planned for Lady Ann, and missing or misfiled documents. By asking the right questions, Aby obtained the answers to settle simmering disputes. She located the errant documents, sometimes in the possession of people who'd overlooked or purposely withheld them, and established a more logically organized central repository. Aby kept her lady's appointment diary and established ways to keep everyone aware of Lady Ann's movements and needs. Aby's reading and writing abilities were a significant improvement over those of her predecessor. Needless to say, Lady Ann was most pleased.

At our new home on Pins Lane, the furniture Aby ordered arrived, and we settled into our new life with great contentment. We threw ourselves into our new working lives. Back home in the evenings, after supper, we shared our experiences of the day, seeing the humor and excitement of it all.

On 20 October, Sir F. and Lady Ann left Plymouth to travel to their Clerkenwell residence. They required us both to accompany them. The journey up was by coach. Sir F. rode inside with the ladies. I rode with two of my colleagues on top. One of those colleagues was David Thomson, a one-time apprentice to Sir F. He was there in support of his wife, still grieving over the loss of their first child, Ann, who had been named for Lady Ann. They had been invited on the trip by Lady Ann, to help in the healing. Amyse had married David when she was fifteen in 1613. Through the pain of their recent loss, David threw himself into his work. I spent time with him and, though he was a private person, he slowly told me about his life. He had been born in Clerkenwell in 1587, of Scottish parents. His father died in 1603. Lady Ann knew his mother and had offered her employment in the Gorges household in Plymouth. David accompanied his mother and eventually became apprenticed to Sir F., living in the servants' quarters. For a time, he was given the responsibility of looking after the Indians that Sir F. had taken on, after their capture. To David, they seemed exotic. The little he learned excited him to go to their homeland. In 1606, he left Sir F.'s employ and went to work for Dr. Richard Vines, as an apothecary's apprentice. When Sir F. helped organize the Popham expedition to Sagadahoc in 1607, David volunteered to accompany the voyage, which meant he already had experience of living through a winter in New England. I was fascinated to learn about his experiences.

On 25 October, we arrived at the Clerkenwell residence, a few miles north of London. It was a fine house among other fine houses in a protected enclave. Not far away were much poorer neighborhoods, with streets that were noisy, smelly, and crowded, some with bars and brothels. Neither Aby nor I were accustomed to the crowds and squalor of the big city. Coming from a relatively open Plymouth, it was a frightening experience dealing with aggressive, rude Londoners. It was as Epenow had told me. For the Gorges family and their entourage, it was necessary to travel to London in a closed coach, or in company with other horsemen, well-armed. Lady Ann, Aby, and the others in their group were always well escorted on their trips into London. On one such trip, Lady Ann bought Aby a new wardrobe, more in keeping with her new station as a sort of lady in waiting. Aby showed me her new finery, her dresses with bright colors and low-cut bodices, some which I felt were too revealing, along with her new chemises, petticoats, lace, and ribbons. She even wore a cloth roll at her hips, aptly named a bum-roll, to further accentuate the curves of her waist and hips, and a feathered coif or two interlaced with her hair. It was all incredibly grand. My Aby was moving up in the world.

CHAPTER 23

Sir F. wanted me to accompany him to a meeting with Mr. John Slaney. A message had come from Spain. One of Slaney's vessels had brought a note back from Malaga confirming what we heard from Captain Smith, but it was not known if Tisquantum was among Indians held there and there was still no message from David Tremaine. The same vessel, currently docked at Deptford, was being loaded for shipment back to Malaga. Would it be of value to send someone on that trip to find Tisquantum, bringing him, as well as the other rescued Indians, back to London? Sir F. thought it worthwhile and without so much as a word to me, he volunteered my services. It was agreed that I would join the vessel in Deptford the next day. The name of the vessel was the *Mary Evans*, and the master was my old acquaintance Captain Morris.

I spent the evening with Aby. My leaving was somewhat less painful to her because she was busy with Lady Ann, but still she knew that my adventures abroad tended to result in my returning in damaged condition, and she wanted to know exactly what I was planning to do. When I brushed aside the possible dangers, Aby became quite upset.

"In being that dismissive, you are treating my real concerns in the same way. Don't do that. I am your *wife*. I worry about you. Think of me before you leap feet-first into danger."

Of course, she was right. It wasn't just my life. Our fates and consequences were shared. I apologized and promised to be careful. I don't think she was entirely satisfied. On this, our last night together for some time, a little cloud remained. Aby would be traveling too. Lady Ann was visiting relations at their country seat in Essex. They would be away for two weeks before returning to Plymouth.

Next morning, I made my way to the river and took a boat down the Thames to Deptford. I met up with Captain Morris, who initially did not recognize me. I had filled out considerably and was dressed in my better wardrobe, befitting the courier of Sir F. I wore a sword and my favorite cavalier hat, not the outfit of a sailor. I reminded him of the bedraggled rat that he had picked up at Damariscove, earlier in the year. He shook his head at the memory and said he thought I wouldn't survive the crossing from America. He had been all set to bury me at sea. I thanked him with all my heart for getting me to Wraxall Court. He smiled and said he had many dealings with Mr. Wellings and Sir Edward and that it was good to have them beholden to him, but that, joking aside, it had been a small enough service and he was happy to do it. Mr. Slaney had sent him a note advising him to expect my arrival and explaining my need to travel to Malaga, so Captain Morris welcomed me aboard as a privileged passenger. Ebbing tide down the Thames, winds light but strengthening from the east, which gave us a fair run south and west toward Ushant. I had not experienced the passage skirting the Bay of Biscay before. I had always sailed south into the Bay along the coastline, either to La Rochelle or latterly to Bilbao. This time we were heading southwest, large rolling seas, wind on larboard quarter sailing full, tops'ls, courses set pulling hard. We had good sailing weather heading to Coruna and then down the west coast of Portugal, south round Cape St. Vincent, east toward Cadiz, on to Gibraltar. Wind filled in southerly as we headed farther south, then east. Days became warmer with blue skies. Seas were kindly. Many sails appeared on the horizon, but none that threatened.

I spent time with Captain Morris and his officers on the quarterdeck. His first mate, Enoch Bates, was delegated to provide for any needs I might have. I felt I had special dispensation. I didn't inform them of my life as a seaman, and tried hard not to show more than a passing interest in the handling and navigation of the vessel. I slipped up once or twice, asking a question or making an observation, unguarded, which no landlubber would've asked. Nothing was said, but I had the sense that they surmised more than they were letting on, but were prepared to play my game. After all, I thought, I was a man of mystery. I realized at one point that they, certainly the officers, must have memories of finding the bedraggled and abandoned crewman at Damariscove, so described by the skipper of the *Sweet Rose*. Who was I fooling? In fact, later in the voyage, Enoch Bates let slip that they'd been advised that it would be tactful to keep quiet about my first time onboard. He was a cheerful soul, and we spent much time in conversation. He was a natural philosopher, which was initially surprising as he had a gruff demeanor, with a full beard and twinkling eyes under a heavy brow. Straits of Gibraltar is a busy stretch of water, which meant we transited it in daylight and headed northeast to Malaga. Good sailing took us just over thirteen days, arriving late evening on 9 November.

Journal entry—*10 to 13 November 1615*

Captain Morris was due to depart Malaga on 14 November. He said he could stretch it by two days, if necessary, to accommodate me, but no longer. He advised me that the information he had on the Indian captives came from his contact in the harbor master's office, who in turn had heard it from his priest at the Santuario de la Victoria. I went ashore to proceed to the Santuario de la Victoria, one of several Catholic churches in Malaga. I had hopes of finding the priest or any priest who could advise me how to find the Catholic order that rescued the Indians. Entering the church, I wandered around looking for someone to talk to. Eventually, I was shown to a room, rather like a vestry, where a priest was working. He spoke a little English, better than my no Spanish. I explained my mission.

"Ah! You want the Order of Mercedarians, the Order of the Blessed Virgin Mary of Mercy. You must go to the Iglesia de Santiago Apóstol."

He gave me the directions. I thanked him and continued on my journey. At the Iglesia, I was introduced to a friar from the Order of Mercedarians. I explained my mission. He told me only five or six Indians were being looked after at a sanctuary outside Malaga. He said his name was Brother Danel, and he was due to travel there the following day. He asked if I would care to join him, to which I said I would be pleased.

The next day, we traveled by donkey. After a short, uncomfortable ride, I preferred to walk. Brother Danel said his order required a vow of silence except in the most extenuating of circumstances, and my mission certainly counted as such. He'd only recently progressed from being a novitiate. He had been a seaman, captured by Barbary pirates and rescued and ransomed by the Order of Mercedarians. In gratitude, he had joined the order. He was a Basque, where he had been known as Danny Ramos. His English, which was good, had come from his time on English fishing vessels. He was decidedly secular in manner, with lively anecdotes. He continued to ride his donkey as, he said with a laugh, its discomfort was a continuing form of penance. Arriving at the sanctuary which was, in fact, a monastery, my companion lapsed into silence. He beckoned me to follow him. We went first to the stables to leave our donkeys, then to a receiving office where he introduced me to a more taciturn friar, who spoke some English. I explained my mission. He showed some surprise. One of my countrymen had arrived that morning with a similar request. The friar asked me to surrender my sword for the duration I was in the monastery, then led me from the office down a long corridor into a large room. At a large table sat six Indians and a familiar figure.

"Hello, David."

David Tremaine started and looked around.

"Isaac, what on earth are you doing here?"

I explained. Sir F., not knowing where David was, had seized the opportunity and sent me down to find out if Tisquantum had been rescued. If so, I was to bring him back to England.

David explained that he'd only just arrived, having had difficulties getting here. He was in the process of trying to communicate with the Indians, who were all sitting stony faced watching us. It was clear that he was not having much success. An atmosphere of deep suspicion hung in the room. I turned and looked each of them in the eye, much as I had learned to do with Epenow and Samoset. I sat quietly looking at them as a group.

"Tisquantum? Captain Smith sends his good wishes," I said.

One of the Indians perked up. "You with Hunt?" he asked.

"No, Hunt is my enemy," I said. "He is a bad man for what he did to you and your people. Captain Smith is searching for him to punish him."

"That is good. Smith is a good man. I am Tisquantum."

I approached him and shook hands. I told him that Captain Smith had spent much time with me in England talking about the journey he had made with him, exploring the coastline of his homeland. I relayed how much Captain Smith enjoyed working with him and how helpful he was to Captain Smith, who was sorry that having returned Tisquantum to his home, the evil man Hunt had captured him with many of his people.

"Not all my people. Many Abenaki. They have been sold by Hunt. My people are here with me."

He gestured to the other five Indians. I wondered how he had managed to keep his band together and persuade the Catholic friars to rescue them rather than the Abenakis. I asked him. He replied that he was the only one able to speak to them.

"What do you want to do, now you are free?"

"I want to see Captain Smith again. He told me much about his country, England. I want to go there, first. The others want to go home."

David Tremaine, watching all this from the back of the room, said that we needed to talk and that the Indians should return to their own quarters while we worked out the next steps. Tisquantum was looking at me. It seemed I was the only one he trusted. I told him we needed time to organize their departure from Spain and promised to return tomorrow. David went to the door. He called for the friar, who returned and with Tisquantum's help persuaded the Indians to leave the room. David turned to me.

"You handled that well. I was getting nowhere. They have been treated badly. The friars are looking after them. Problem is they see them as souls to be saved. I'm not sure what the friars think of my appearing from nowhere wanting, presumably, to take them away. They don't know who I am. For all they know, I might be a pirate wanting to recapture them."

I hadn't thought of that. How would we persuade them?

"Another thing. The reason I was late in finding the Indians is that I've been identified as a spy, a threat to the pirates and their spy network. I was caught in Bilbao, but managed to escape before I was eliminated. I was followed. To complicate matters further, the people running the hostage escape route balked at dealing with the Indians. No matter how I tried to persuade them, they weren't interested."

I interrupted him. "I don't understand. Who are the people running the escape route? I thought they were pirates."

"It is complicated," he said. "The pirates spy network worked to identify opportunities for plunder, rape, and pillage. An entirely different group worked to ensure ransomed sailors made it home, otherwise there would have been no point in them being ransomed. The Mercedarians handled the ransom process and fed the freed hostages into the escape route."

"But didn't the pirates talk to each other? If you are now known as a spy, wouldn't the people handing the escape route be advised of that?"

"No, the people running the escape route were not pirates but were paid by them to ensure it worked successfully. Anyway, I had to get involved. Problem was, I had not had direct contact with the Mercedarians, only contacts on the escape route, so they didn't know who I was. I went to Barcelona, the location of their headquarters, hoping to lose those following me. I was given what I thought were the necessary introductions to the local Order here and was able to catch a local coastal trader. When I landed, I saw one of my pursuers. I hoped that they didn't see me, but it seems they knew I was coming to Malaga. Apart from that, my introductions from Barcelona didn't quell local suspicion."

The threat to David was a real concern. We needed to get him away as soon as possible.

"The vessel I came on, the *Mary Evans*, will be leaving Malaga for London in four days. We have that time to persuade the friars to let the Indians leave with us, get them on board, and smuggle you on board, as well."

We discussed our options. It seemed to me that if we paid the friars what they'd paid in ransom for the Indians and asked them to deliver them to the *Mary Evans*, we'd kill two birds with one stone. It would allow us to take them with us and, as important, have them take care of their delivery to the *Mary Evans*. David's fluent Spanish meant he would have to do the persuading. We were an hour's walk from Malaga. It would be better for David to persuade the friars now, rather than in the evening, then disguise himself in a friar's habit, return with me on borrowed donkeys to the *Mary Evans*, and stay hidden on board until we departed. David was less than happy about skulking aboard while I did the work, but he saw the logic. With him involved, not only would he be the target, but he would make it that much more difficult to rescue the Indians. I would also be in greater danger. David called for the friar.

I was shown to Tisquantum's cell, one of many along a narrow corridor, with a curtain for a door, a hard bed, small table, chair, and high, narrow window. Tisquantum lay on the bed. I motioned for him to stay there and sat on the chair. I told him our plan. Once we got to England, we would arrange for his people to be shipped back to their homeland. He, if he wished to, could stay in England for as long as he wanted and would be able to meet with his friend Captain Smith. Tisquantum was happy with the plan. I told him the friars needed to be convinced they should give him and the others to us for safekeeping. I explained the friars suspected we were pirates aiming to recapture the Indians to sell them into slavery. We wanted Tisquantum to persuade the other Indians that we were their friends intent on rescuing them and returning them home. Tisquantum said he would talk to the friars. I returned to the room where I had met the Indians to wait for David Tremaine.

After an hour or so, he returned with the friar. He said it had been difficult. They were suspicious of our intentions. I said that Tisquantum would tell them we were his friends, intent on returning them home. David relayed that on to the friar. They left together, again. A little later, they came back, David now much happier. Tisquantum had persuaded them. They planned to deliver the Indians to the *Mary Evans* on the evening of 13 November. They'd come in a covered wagon, delivering last-minute cargo for shipment. The friar told me the price for that delivery. Mr. Slaney had provided me with funds, in the safe-keeping of Captain Morris, to be used to obtain the Indian captives' release. The funds were more than enough. Payment would be made on delivery.

David was lent a habit and, as dusk fell, having picked up our weapons, we departed with our donkeys for Malaga. We had no trouble on the road to Malaga. David's pursuers seemed to have lost track of him at that point. The situation changed as we approached the harbor. We were leading our donkeys down a busy street, when someone leading another donkey appeared from a side street. His donkey lunged at the donkey David led. I hadn't thought. Our donkeys were jennies. The lunging donkey a rampant jack. Chaos ensued. When settled, David had dropped his habit, and his coarse oaths filled the evening air. We moved on. David, clearly not a friar, picked up the habit but didn't bother re-girding himself.

We continued walking down a busy street leading the two donkeys, followed by an increasing number of bystanders attracted by the donkey incident, both donkeys still slightly skittish from their encounter. I was on the left near the wall that extended down the street with alleyways at regular intervals on both sides. Four seamen overtook us, all on David's right side, where there was room. As we passed an alley on my left, the seamen pushed David violently into the alley, collecting me on the way. The donkeys, on their leads, were dragged after us. The seamen seemed not to have noticed the donkeys or, if they did, they didn't consider the consequences of their concerted action. The seamen crowded after us, placing themselves between us and our donkeys. We yanked the reins. The donkeys, now frightened, reared up, banging into the backs of the seamen, pushing past them, and knocking them all off balance. We released the reins and hit their hindquarters. The donkeys swung around looking to escape, the way now blocked by the four seamen still sorting themselves out. We struck the donkeys again, yelling at them. The seamen, having gained their feet, were knocked off balance again by the frantic donkeys. With reins free and whipping through the air, the seamen became entangled, tripping and falling over themselves.

The crowd at the entrance to the alleyway let the donkeys escape and cheered, even shouting "olé!" The four seamen were thoroughly distracted, which allowed us to draw our swords, me with some difficulty as mine was under my habit. David had a cutlass. We confronted the four seamen. They had probably assumed I was a peaceable friar, and now I was armed, dangerous, and looking for action in a public place.

I leapt at the first of them, slashing at his head. He raised his right arm to protect himself, holding a wicked-looking long knife. My sword bit into his upper arm. Blood flowed; he dropped his knife and backed off cursing and holding his arm. David was dealing with the second and third by sweeping his cutlass back and forth in front of them. The whistle of the blade in the dim light was more threatening than the sight, and much more worrying. Their long knives were not long enough. If they had thought they would be dealing with David alone, my presence had more than evened the odds. The fourth seaman had no real chance, though he tried. He used a cloak in his left hand to try to tangle my sword, while lunging at me with a knife thrust that started round his knees aiming for my stomach. I ducked aside, grabbed his knife arm with my left hand, and pinned him back against the wall, sword point at his throat, a thin stream of blood trickling down his neck. Another round of olés.

David was in difficulties. One of the seamen had worked his way behind him, and he was now attempting to fend off lethal attacks from front and back. He struck at one. The cutlass sank into the seaman's hip and stuck. To avoid the attack of the man behind him, he had to leave his cutlass embedded and dodge the intended blow. His cutlass now covered by the fallen body, he was defenseless. I had kicked my seaman in his privates, and as he doubled over, I reversed my sword and struck him on the side of his head with the pommel. I turned on the last seaman still standing. He'd had enough. Dropped to his knees, knife discarded, he surrendered. That drew more cheers from the watching crowd. We left, David retrieving his cutlass and the habit he had dropped, wiping the blood off on the shirt of his victim, who was moaning and clutching his hip, blood seeping through his fingers. We pushed our way through the crowd. The donkeys had gone. We slipped away, quickly losing ourselves in the busy, darkening streets. By a roundabout route we made for the harbor and boarded the *Mary Evans*. I reported to Captain Morris, introduced David to him, and advised him of all that had happened.

Captain Morris showed his grasp of matters with a gruff but humorous summation. "I am to harbor a dangerous fugitive on board for the next three days, while presumably protecting him from further pirate incursions. I am to await the arrival of six Indians, pay for them, and ship them back to London. And, pray tell me, what further escapades have you got planned, over the next three days, to keep us amused?"

I said that I thought it best to lie low myself. Unfortunately, I had promised Tisquantum that I would go back to him tomorrow. If I didn't, their distrust would be sure to return. I would leave first thing, dressed as a seaman. I had been in a habit. They were after David. I doubted anyone would recognize me, and it was evening and getting dark when we fought them. As for David, there were many English vessels in the harbor, and it would be difficult for them to find which boat he was on, if he kept his head down. If they were as incompetent as the first lot, I was sure we wouldn't have much trouble. But we did not want the authorities to get involved.

Early next morning, I slipped away dressed as a young seaman, with the emphasis on youth. I looked young, entirely innocent. I carried David's friar's habit in a bundle, both to return it and in case I needed a disguise. I made good progress. It was clear and cool. The monastery was in the foothills above Malaga. When I arrived I was not recognized at first, but Brother Danel helped and I was shown to the reception room where I had met the Indians and told to wait. Tisquantum came in and was puzzled for a moment. Where was his new friend Isaac? I explained to his evident relief, and he confirmed that the friars would be moving them by wagon in two days' time, to arrive at the harbor at dusk. He was pleased I had come. It allayed the fear of a trick.

I was given a meal. The taciturn friar, to my surprise, suggested that if I felt sufficiently threatened to want to disguise myself, brother Danel should accompany me back to Malaga. We had been attacked, and as we had come from the monastery, they felt in some way responsible. Incidentally, the populace had recognized the donkeys as belonging to the Order and returned them. I was happy to accept their offer. As I still had David's habit, it was suggested I wear that. The friar provided two more donkeys. For the disguise to be effective, I was to ride one of them.

Brother Danel and I set off on the ride back. My bum became very sore, very quickly. The back of the donkey is hard and knobby, and its gait is most uncomfortable. We rode slowly down toward Malaga. We passed through an olive grove, pausing to admire the view through the trees, looking over the town toward the sea, when, without warning, two large nets were thrown over us and we were dragged from our donkeys. The netting was removed and we were tied, our cowls stripped off our heads. Danel's tonsure saved him. He was let go, put back on his donkey, and escorted back the way he came. Two Spaniards, I assumed, stood over and interrogated me in Spanish. I just shook my head. One of them grabbed me by the scruff of my habit and yanked me to my feet, then bound my hands and feet and put into the back of a cart. One Spaniard was guarding me, the other up front. Pulled by a large mule, we worked our way into the hills away from the track we had been on. After what seemed like an hour's bone-jarring travel, we came to a small house, stone-walled, a roof with many tiles missing. A man came out. After a brief flurry of words from my captors, he helped me down from the cart. In English, he asked me my name. I told him. Why was I dressed like a friar? I had delivered some merchandise to the monastery. I was cold, they lent me the habit for warmth. That story produced a smile. Where was I going? Back to my boat. I had completed my errand. Why was I accompanied by the other friar? The donkey I was riding and the habit belonged to the monastery. He was there to take them back. Another smile.

"The two of you were talking too much, in English. Not the actions of friars sworn to silence. Not a good disguise."

I smiled ruefully.

"Where is Tremaine?"

"Tremaine?"

Without warning, one of them hit me hard, back-handed, across my face. A ring on his finger cut my lip. Blood flowed.

"Where is Tremaine?"

"I don't know what you're talking about."

Another hard blow, which knocked me off my feet. I was kicked in the stomach.

"Where is Tremaine?"

I just shook my head. They beat me senseless. Threw water over me.

"Where is Tremaine?"

Hopeless. So repetitive. I think they realized it too. I passed out again. I was dimly aware of being in the cart. At some point I was thrown out. I lay dazed, hurting, wondering what was going to happen next. I must have lost consciousness again. I awoke alone and tried sitting up. Not good. I had blood all over my face, my ribs hurt badly. My right arm was numb, useless. From where I lay, I looked round. I was back on the track, near the spot where we were attacked. I dragged myself to the nearest olive tree and gently hoisted myself to a sitting position with my back resting against the trunk. The sun was high. It seemed it was about midday. Maybe a couple of hours since the attack. I was close to Malaga and needed to get moving. I tried standing. Not good. Maybe rest a little. I tried again and managed to get to my feet. Good. Holding my right arm against my ribs with my left arm, I started down the track. Count steps. Rest when I reached one hundred. After the third stop, my head started working.

Why did they leave me? Probably because they figured I either didn't know anything or I wasn't going to tell. What would I have done in their shoes? I would've dumped me back on the track in order to follow me. I would somehow make my way back to my boat and, therefore, Tremaine. I was making for Malaga. It wouldn't be until we got to the harbor that my direction would provide anything meaningful to them. I continued, slowly, to make progress, heading for the Iglesia de Santiago Apóstol. As I moved into Malaga, people became more numerous, but no one was inclined to help. Eventually, I made it to the steps of the iglesia. They were too much. I collapsed on the bottom step in a miserable bundle. If they hadn't taken my habit, I could've at least wrapped myself up in it, pretending to be on a pilgrimage of the penitent.

"Isaac. It is you?"

I squinted up from the sandals to the robed figure leaning over me.

"Hello, brother Danel. I've been looking for you."

"In the name of Jesus, what have they done to you? Come let me get you inside."

I was lifted, half carried inside the church to a cool, dark room with a couch. Danel found help. A nun. They washed my face. They cut away my shirt to checked my ribs and arm. My ribs were badly bruised but not broken, right shoulder likewise. They washed and bandaged me, strapped my ribs, put my right arm in a sling. In treating my head, they couldn't do much more than wash away the blood that continued to seep from several points. Nose sore, probably broken. My lips were badly swollen. I had difficulty speaking. As best I could, I told Danel what happened. I was worried I was being followed. He told me that as soon as his escort had left him, he'd doubled back, but I had gone, who knows where. He came to the iglesia on the off-chance I'd managed to talk myself out of trouble and come here. He knew from the directions I'd given for the delivery of the Indians where the *Mary Evans* was. After thinking it through, he realized it was more likely that I would have gone to the *Mary Evans*. If I hadn't, he would need to alert the crew of my plight. He talked to the captain and Mr. Tremaine. He was told to return to the Iglesia and let them know if I turned up. Mr. Tremaine seemed to think that I would not have come directly back to the boat, for fear of being followed. Now we needed to get word back to the *Mary Evans*, where I was, and the mess I was in. Meantime, I should get some sleep.

I was awakened by a light shining in my eyes and a muttered exclamation. David leaned over me and said that they were going to move me in the early hours of the morning. David had organized a protective ring. All were armed crewmen under the command of Enoch Bates from the *Mary Evans*. They had gathered at the Iglesia, in isolated ones and twos, through the afternoon. With no one around, any watchers would be noticed and dealt with. Danel had organized with his Order for a number of friars to leave the Iglesia in pairs at regular intervals going in different directions. Danel would escort me as far as the Santuario de la Victoria. Each pair would be watched. Anyone following would be taken. I was helped to my feet, and we moved into the apse where people were standing around. It was late.

We executed David's plan. I was given another habit, then Danel and I left, the third pair of friars, and proceeded, very leisurely perforce, to the Santuario. I thought that many people moving aimlessly away from the iglesia at night would be obvious, but David said it was to confuse—better still, to expose the enemy without giving away our eventual destination. I was too muddled-headed to think further and just did as I was told. Underneath my cowl and habit, I was bandaged, bruised, and strapped. My legs worked, but not much else. At the Santuario, we waited. Sometime later, David appeared. His plan had flushed three pursuers, each of whom had been dealt with, but there might be others. Danel and I once more set off, as one of a number of pairs of friars, and we made for the harbor. The quay was clear, and we boarded the *Mary Evans*. By this time, I was dead on my feet. I thanked Danel, stumbled to my berth, and knew no more till late the following morning when David brought me some food and drink. He said the night operation had been a great success. All friars had returned to their normal duties, all crewmen had returned to the *Mary Evans*, the pirate pursuers had been dealt with, and no pirate any the wiser about where David Tremaine was. David and I talked more. He was most sorry that I had been put through the beating on his behalf. As far as I was concerned, once the aches had gone, it was another escapade to enjoy, in retrospect.

He looked at me oddly. "You could easily have been killed. I'm not sure it's wise for you to be dismissive of the dangers you seem to find yourself in."

I told him, with a tone of slight asperity, that I was aware of the dangers. I thought through how each danger could be mitigated. I wouldn't run from them. Once dealt with, I didn't dwell on what might have been. Later that day, we received a note from the Mercedarian order that the wagon would be arriving at dusk. Captain Morris had the *Mary Evans* ready for departure, with freight loaded, holds full. The wagon arrived and pulled up on the quay next to the *Mary Evans*. Six muffled shapes slipped out the back, boarded, and were escorted below. Next morning, we were at sea, heading south southeast with wind from the southwest.

Journal entry—*14 November to 5 December 1615*

Leaving the shelter of Malaga, the wind increased, seas choppy. Our Indians quickly succumbed to seasickness. As soon as Tisquantum was of a mind to, I spent time with him to get to know him. I told him more of my experiences with Assacomet, now Samoset, and Epenow at Wraxall Court, as well as my trip to Monhegan. He responded with a brief description of the time spent with Captain Smith. Once passed Coruna and heading for Ushant, we hit a major storm that came out of the Bay of Biscay. Luckily we were on the outer edges of it, and winds from the southeast meant we could run before it. The Indians were at first terrified by the noise, the strength of the wind, the violent motion of the *Mary Evans,* and the sea water cascading over the decks into every corner of the vessel. But, as the days wore on, and we were clearly riding the storm well, they came to enjoy it. Back at Deptford on 28 November, Mr. Slaney took care of the Indians. Tisquantum and I parted company with a firm handshake, wishing each other well. He thanked me once more for helping in his journey back home and improving his English.

Captain Morris was keen to return to Bristol. I was more than anxious to return to Aby in Plymouth, wondering how she had settled in with Lady Ann. I had been too long away and was wanting to be with her. Captain Morris said he would drop me and David off at Plymouth on the way. With *Mary Evans'* holds emptied and refilled, we were off on Thursday, 30 November. We were back in Plymouth by 4 December, late afternoon.

CHAPTER 24

We reported to Sir F.'s office but were advised by Captain Turner that we should return on Wednesday, 6 December, at nine a.m. David took himself off. I returned to Pins Lane. Aby and I had been apart for over six weeks. My eager anticipation changed to joy, seeing Aby in our little house. At first she was not aware of my arrival. Then, turning, she saw me, and radiance transformed her face. She reached for me.

"Hello, husband mine."

Then her eyes traveled 'round my face, to my slung arm. They opened wider, still wider as she took in the mess. Her fingers touched each wound, now healing rapidly. She looked back into my eyes, still swollen and bruised. She slowly shook her head. I could see the thought in her mind. Her request for me to be careful. But, bless her, she moved on.

"Isaac, Isaac, my darling man. You are like a schoolboy coming home after a fight, proudly bearing your scars. What am I to do with you?"

We were in each other's arms. After a long, long embrace, we sat together, and she told me her adventures. Most important, she gets on well with Lady Ann. They spent an exhausting week visiting the palatial mansion of an entertainment-mad cousin, married to a wealthy, well-connected landowner in Essex, every night a party, somewhere, of some kind, and every day riding or visiting other stately mansions. Aby was included with Lady Ann's entourage because Lady Ann wanted her close and she had become quite indispensable. When Aby arrived back in Plymouth, there were a few days of gentle duty, then they were off to Wraxall to spend a long weekend with Sir Edward, whom Aby found charming, and back to Plymouth to work, helping Lady Ann with a number of charitable projects among the indigent of Plymouth. She said, with everything else, she still had time to scrub, paint, and redecorate our home. With that, we walked hand-in-hand throughout the house for me to admire her handiwork. I was very proud of her.

We turned to my adventures. Soon told, as most of the time we were at sea. I didn't dwell on the beating, but Aby asked about each cut and bruise. Luckily, I couldn't remember. We laughed about the ambush in the alley with the donkeys. An embellishment or two made it sound much funnier than it had been.

Then she asked a strange question. "How is your relationship with David Tremaine?"

I was surprised. "Why do you ask?"

"The way you didn't talk about him as you have in the past. You used to speak of him as a hero. Now you don't."

"It's difficult to describe, but I think David saw me as a protégé," I said. "He was, I believe, disconcerted that he had to depend on me in Malaga. He was even more upset when I took a beating to protect him. He became more distant on our trip back to London, and was quick to leave me after we went to Sir F.'s office, with an almost perfunctory goodbye."

"But you like him still?"

"Of course."

"Then, you should reach out to him. Invite him back here for supper. I think he sees in you a young David Tremaine. He is trying to work out how to deal with the change in your relationship."

Late to sleep, early to rise, we were off on our duties on time the next morning.

Journal entry—*6 December to 8 January 1616*

Mr. Bushrode was with Sir F. when David and I arrived in his office. After introducing David to Mr. Bushrode, Sir F. turned to me. He said he had thought my trip to Malaga would be a simple one, without danger, but he could see from my appearance that his idea had proven not to be the case. David reported on his time in Spain with the pirate network, now closed to him, and I described my trip. Sir F. complimented us both on a job well done. I told Sir F. about my conversations with Tisquantum. Putting together what I had heard from him and Captain Smith, I provided a description of the New England coastline with its key points of interest.

"What has become clear to me in those conversations is the extraordinary opportunity that exists for settlement by whole communities of English people," I observed.

Sir F. responded that he and Mr. Bushrode had been discussing the subject of New England and its potential, prior to our arrival.

Mr. Bushrode spoke of a worsening picture he saw for our countrymen who do not have land or wealth. "England's population is increasing and we aren't growing enough food, meaning more hungry people," he said. "The woolen industry is finding it hard to export its goods to the continent, due to massive inflation there, making life even harder. But the government continues to favor that industry by enclosing open arable land to raise more sheep. That means more people on farms are put out of work, and less food is grown."

Mr. Bushrode became quite agitated as he continued. "They who cannot get relief from their local parishes gravitate to the towns, greatly expanding the pool of beggars. And now with the peace treaties being signed, England's armies are back to England. They are either disbanded or billeted with private citizens who have to pay the associated costs. The extraordinary natural wealth and availability of land in New England to own and farm could help these people—could be a godsend. In New England, people could find a healthy climate to raise families. They would still be Englishmen, subjects of the king, with all those responsibilities and privileges, but they would also have gained the freedom to govern themselves."

I said his comments reminded me of my conversations with the Reverend John White back in Dorchester. Mr. Bushrode said he and Mr. White had had many conversations on the subject and were of like mind.

Sir F. turned to me. "Now tell me, would you and Aby leave everything to risk your lives setting up home in such a foreign land? I can bribe men to go by paying them. But, as you know, they don't stay."

Once again, I was hearing this idea broached—initially by P., now by Sir F. I surprised him by responding, "I've had the same question put to me before. I didn't take it seriously then. Perhaps I should have. I need to talk to Aby. Are there circumstances that would persuade us to leave England and settle in New England? I really don't know."

David and I were dismissed. As we left, I asked him to come and have supper with us in our new home. He was surprised. He stopped, looked at me for a moment, then smiled and said he would be honored to. I suggested the following night.

The following evening, we entertained our first guest, the three of us talking comfortably throughout the evening. Aby wanted to know about David's life, asking what I thought were probing and possibly overstepping questions, such as "Why haven't you married?" David seemed easy in his answers. I asked him what was in store for him now that his Spanish job was finished. He said he didn't know but was sure he would soon be off on some project or other for Sir

F. David asked about the missing three months in my life. I told him what I had deduced after finding my wedding ring in the pawn shop. The best thing was to see if the pawn shop proprietor had been able to identify the man who sold him the ring. I'd asked Will to keep in touch with the proprietor and let me know of any developments. One thing David did say was that there had been heavy snow during that period. If I had been taken to an outlying farm, it would have been cut off for a long time. Aby agreed. She said that Will had been searching for me up till Christmas, but he had had to stop because of the amount of snow on the ground. The evening ended well, happy in each other's company.

Following on from the meeting we had with Sir F. and Mr. Bushrode, and in subsequent meetings, it was clear that Sir F. was keen to build local support for further trips to New England. It was one thing to find the right ingredients of settlers, leadership, and local Indian support, but trade was also vitally important. Sir F.'s model assumed settlers would be funded by backers to pay travel and living expenses, plus paying each settler a wage. Those backers would be looking for a good return on their investment from trade. Reports coming back, especially those from Captain Smith, clearly identified the cornucopia of trade goods available. These products would come directly to England's West Country seaports, bypassing the former intermediary and expensive French ports. The next trip planned by Sir F. was to be under the command of his good friend Dr. Richard Vines. Much emphasis had been placed on settlements east of Sagadahoc, specifically a location below a promontory named by Captain Smith as Cape Elizabeth. It was to this bay that Dr. Vines was to proceed, with the intent to establish a settlement. Of special interest to me was the fact that David Thomson was determined to go on the trip.

I kept thinking about the idea of Aby and me going to New England. We had talked about it, knew about the other attempts and their failures. We agreed with P.'s assessment as to what kind of settlement would be the most likely to work. Up to now, no families—no women for that matter—had been asked or induced to go there. It seemed to me that before we could think seriously about moving to New England, I'd need to find out for myself what it was like to live there, especially over the dreaded winter months. Truth be told, I felt my previous journey there had left a void, incomplete and with it a sense of failure. With David going, it might be opportune for me to go as well. Amyes and Aby could live together while we were away. They could provide mutual support to each other. I needed to talk further with Aby.

Christmas was fast approaching and Aby wanted her father to spend it with us. She had been in touch with him, and he was happy to send his love but felt he needed to stay with his invalid sister in Devizes. Aby had established herself as a regular member of the congregation of St. Andrews. It's a fine church, the largest in Devon, in the center of Plymouth, a short walk from Pins Lane. I joined her every Sunday on my return to Plymouth to attend Matins. We had developed a circle of friends, including Annie with her network through the Minerva, David and Amyes Thomson's friends, as well as Vivienne and her Huguenot circle. Christmas was about sharing, bringing the community together. We, therefore, brought our Dorchester Christmas celebrations to Plymouth. The twelve days were spent with much merriment or huddling round roaring fires, keeping the bitter cold away. It had snowed over Christmas, continuing for a week. The removal of snow became a symptom of the wide-ranging and regular community effort. By the end of Christmas, Aby and I felt so much basic decency had been shown in such a short period of time that we were saddened to think of the inevitable reaction to that euphoria, with the darker side of people's characters likely to become more evident.

When alone, we talked more about the idea of going to New England. Aby said my life was her life. Where I went, she would go. She wanted me to make sure I had fully explored the risks and opportunities. To those ends, she agreed that I needed to go back to New England to find out. Monday, 8 January, after the meeting, I asked for a few minutes of Sir F.'s time. I said that I had been thinking a great deal about the upcoming Vines voyage to New England. I said that Aby and I had discussed the conditions under which we would consider settling in New England. We'd concluded that without first-hand knowledge, especially of the winter there, it would be difficult to form a reasonable opinion. It seemed therefore, subject to Sir F.'s approval, that I should join the Vines voyage to gain that knowledge. Sir F. agreed. With the information that I had already gathered, plus my direct earlier experience, I would make an ideal companion for Dr. Vines. He remarked, with a smile, that, given my propensity for escapades with injuries resulting, Dr. Vines, a physician, could be useful to me as well.

CHAPTER 25

Journal entry—*9 to 31 January 1616*

Events moved quickly, once Sir F. had arranged a meeting with Dr. Vines, a slim man of medium height, with graying hair, but youthful looking, age about thirty. His gray eyes were deep and penetrating. He was thoughtful, listened well, and spoke quietly but with conviction. He told me his plans were to sail with a select group of men under contract to spend up to twelve months in New England, for which they would be paid handsomely. It was Sir Ferdinando's desire to prove that, despite the Popham failure and Captain Smith's misadventures, it was feasible for English settlers to live comfortably through a New England winter. Or, if not comfortably, then at least without excessive hardship. He planned to leave Plymouth in April, returning by the following April of 1617. His destination would likely be Saco, as both Champlain and Smith had written enthusiastically about it. We also had a map of Saco drawn by Champlain. He asked me what I thought.

"Well, sir, I have some personal knowledge of the coastline and the Indians, but further east around Monhegan. The local people, having had the bad experience of the capture of their people, are—or certainly were—much incensed by the English. Farther south, for the same reason, they are equally so. Therefore, finding a location somewhere between the two, where the local inhabitants might not be so inflamed, could make sense."

He said that Sir Ferdinando was in the process of obtaining a vessel to carry his party over there. He understood a fishing boat called the *Sweet Rose* might be available. Did I know it?

"Aye, sir. I know it well, although it would be better described as a merchant vessel."

I was surprised and pleased at the thought of rejoining my old shipmates.

They were tried, trustworthy, and highly competent. With the opportunity to fill their holds with New England furs, beaver pelts, dried fish, and timber, they had added incentive. I would trust the boat and its crew with my life. I said as much. I also realized Mr. Bushrode, *Rosie's* co-owner, had been more deeply involved in the planning than I had thought. Dr. Vines was pleased. He had put together a team of eight, with two soldiers, two farmers, two fishermen, David Thomson, and himself. I would be the ninth. With David's help, he was preparing an inventory of supplies needed for the voyage.

Later, at home with Aby, I told her what had transpired with Sir F. and what I'd learned about the planned Vines voyage. We talked well into the evening about what the trip would mean for us. I would be away for a year. Aby, with her head, understood the importance of the trip to our future—but that future was a long way off. Her heart had trouble with the fact that I would be leaving her in three months.

"I didn't know before where you were or whether you were alive or dead," she said. "Now, I do know where you'll be, but I still won't know whether you are alive or dead."

I was miserable to be the cause of her tears. We went to bed emotionally exhausted. Aby clung to me. I didn't sleep, my mind churning. Next morning, still fatigued, I crawled out of bed. Aby was already up preparing breakfast. I slouched into the kitchen, dreading a continuation of the previous night's discussion. Aby greeted me with a cheerful smile and gave me a warm hug as if everything were right with the world.

"I've worked it all out in my mind. I have plans to make to fill the year. I will be very busy. You must make the trip if we are to ever decide to settle in New England. Come, have your breakfast."

She leaned over, gave me a kiss, and apologized for causing a scene last night. It was all a part of the process of her coming to terms with the situation. Bewildered, relieved, and thankful, I gave her a hug, and we went off to our separate duties. Over the following days we planned how we would deal together with the next three months before my departure. We talked about what Aby had planned for the time while I was away, having mostly ideas that would become more realistic in the future. We tried not to view April as some dreadful termination point in our life together. It would be more a leave of absence, like attending a year-long study at a college at Oxford or Cambridge. We agreed that I was going to spend a year studying at the University of New England. Viewing the matter that way eased our emotions greatly.

The following week, *Rosie* came to port. With excitement, I went down to the dockside in Sutton Pool to find her alongside, discharging cargo. Obi, now a seaman, was the first to see and greet me, expressing surprise and great gladness. I also got a warm welcome from J.B., now promoted to bosun. Dusty came out of his lair when he heard the greetings, waving his hand in salute, a cloud of flour blown away in the wind. Peg was the watch officer. He invited me onto the quarterdeck, shaking my hand with vigor. He sent a seaman below to inform the skipper. While I had not seen *Rosie*'s crew for nine months, I had not forgotten that, when last we had traveled together, I suffered a capture that had wrenched me from them and them from me. Not knowing if I were alive or dead, they felt they had abandoned me in New England. They obviously knew I had turned up eventually, but seeing me back on *Rosie* was like the closing of an unhappy chapter in their lives.

Soon after I went on board, I was called to the skipper's cabin. As I entered, he stood looking out the stern windows. He turned and looked at me, but his thoughts seemed somewhere else. He pulled himself together and told me to sit.

"So, you are a married man at last. I'm glad."

His greeting implied more than that. I remembered the sad tale of his lost love. We sat for a while, both with our own thoughts. Then he asked for a recap of all that had happened since I had disappeared that night on Monhegan. I told him.

"I know Morris. A good man. I will thank him myself, when I next see him."

I broached the subject of Dr. Vines' planned voyage. I said that I had volunteered to accompany that trip and explained why. He nodded, saying he thought that one day I might settle over there. I understood that it was possible that the *Sweet Rose* might be transporting us. He said that was likely. Mr. Bushrode had the final say, but there was great potential for substantial commerce, especially if there was a permanent English settlement there. Helping confirm the feasibility of such a settlement was merely a sound business investment. I hadn't thought of it in those terms before. It made great sense. He ended the conversation by saying it gave him great pleasure to have me back on *Rosie* again, even if it was as a guest rather than a crewman. I was welcome back on board whenever convenient to me. He added that they had at least one more trip to make to Honfleur. Mr. Bushrode had established a new working relationship with M. Giradeau. Honfleur was becoming almost another home port for *Rosie*. I would be welcome on board if I had reason to go there. I thanked him and said it would be up to my new employer Sir F. but I would be happy to take him up on the offer. It would help me get my sea legs back before the transatlantic voyage.

I went to see Dusty next and told him what I knew of Johnny Dawkins. He was pleased. He felt Johnny should never have been sent to sea, and that he'd make a good vicar. He asked me if I had my memory back fully. I said I was missing three months still. He said that I had worried them. When I disappeared on Monhegan, they feared I might have wandered off, even fallen into the sea. It was only when they found my cap, with blood on an adjacent tree, that they realized I'd probably been taken, which might also have meant death. It was an unhappy ship that left those waters without me. I might not know it, he said, but I had become a kind of lucky charm. Much liked, sorely missed. J.B. said that Obi had become hysterical when *Rosie* left Monhegan. He attempted to throw himself overboard and swim back to the island to wait, or be captured and reunited in Indian captivity. Dusty had worked his healing magic on him. Dusty told him that I'd want him to take up the great adventure Isaac had been on. That meant he had to make sure *Rosie* got back to England safely. After a week Obi recovered. Seems he preferred that I handle the great adventures. He would be happy to watch, albeit from as close a proximity as possible without there being too much danger. As I disembarked, J.B. handed me a packet. He said he had kept it in the hope he would be able to return it to me. Inside, my missing journal entries, the ones the Skipper told me to write to help me regain my memory.

I returned to Aby with a glow. She remarked on it. I told her of the reception I'd had.

"Well, why not? You are extraordinary, and they aboard *Rosie* know that fact better than most. Now, before all this praise goes to your head, come, build up the fire, while I cook us supper."

Journal entry—*1 to 21 February 1616*

I made the passage with *Rosie* to Honfleur, a seven-day trip. Sir F. thought it a good idea for me to meet some of Champlain's companions that M. Medec had promised to introduce me to, if they were around, to learn firsthand about the coast around Saco. In Honfleur, I met with M. Medec, who remembered me. After inquiring after each other's health, I reminded him of his offer to introduce me to some of his seamen friends. Happy to oblige, he closed his shop and we went to a local bar. A few minutes later, I was seated at a table with M. Medec and three Breton seamen. He acted as translator, as my fractured French was broken completely by their patois.

One of them had traveled with Champlain on his trip down the coast of

New England. They had explored the inlet south of Cape Elizabeth. This seaman told me that we needed to be careful with the entrance to the inlet. Two islands and a good channel have a bearing southwest between them that opens up into a protected mooring, but the holding ground is bad with kelp covering the seabed. A narrow passage leads to an inner pool, fine for a smaller boat, of maybe fifty tons, holding ground good. A long rocky peninsula protects the pool from the Atlantic to the east and the prevailing late year winds from the northeast. Beyond the pool, a long spit of land joins the peninsula to the mainland. It is marshy, mud filled at low water on the land side of the spit. The Saco River is due west of the islands with a narrow entrance, needing constant soundings, opening up into a sheltered natural harbor. The mainland is low lying and heavily wooded, where it hasn't been cleared for cultivation.

Many Indians live in what look like permanent houses, not tents or wigwams. This seaman and others in his party had rowed up the river and seen many encampments of Indians who'd been friendly once they'd overcome their fear of strangers. They were keen to barter anything for the trinkets Champlain's men had. They were a peaceable tribe, but always worried about occasional attacks from more warlike neighbors to the north. The fishing was good, especially a bit farther out to sea. In the Bretons' opinion, it would make a fine place to establish a settlement. They had spent time at Port Royal in New France. Winters there were terrible, but Saco was much farther south. It might not be as bad. Anyway, one of them said, pointing with his chin in my direction, I came from England, where everyone knows the weather is always bad. Why should I care?

We spent a happy two hours in conversation. M. Medec and I then returned to his shop and toasted each other with a fine glass of brandy. I stumbled back to *Rosie*, semi-oblivious from the alcohol consumed.

Journal entry—*22 February to 8 April 1616*

Back in Plymouth, Saturday evening, 24 February, I hurried back home to Aby. I brought her some lace and three bottles of wine. In the ten days I had been away she had been spending the time with Lady Ann, who was reorganizing her household ahead of a summer to be spent away from Plymouth. In the evenings Aby was with Amyse, who was not well and needed help. Apparently, she was pregnant again, the baby due in October. Aby was beginning to appreciate the idea of having children of her own. As we viewed pregnancy more as a blessing from God, rather than something we scrupulously avoided in our lovemaking, Aby was comfortable with God's timetable. I, personally, would prefer God to delay his blessings until I had returned from New England. Aware of the speed with which time flew and my fast-approaching departure on my "university course," we spent every moment together that we could. We loved taking Maddie and Tess on long rides onto the moors. We welcomed the sudden downpours that forced us to find a rocky overhang where we sheltered in the lee of the storm, horses hobbled to crop with backs to the weather. We talked about everything and nothing, with the peace of two happy people, content in each other's arms.

By March, all was set between Mr. Bushrode and Sir F. regarding the chartering of *Rosie*. P. was much interested in the Vines expedition. Mr. Bushrode had kept him up to date. Aby packed my chest. She had made or acquired heavy winter clothing and sturdy weatherproof oilskins. She packed my sword, too. As a present, she packed a silver flask, which she said I could use for any "medicinal" purposes. It was a family heirloom, which her father had passed on to her. On 7 April, the eve of my departure, she and I spent a clear spring day riding our favorite trails. We had a simple lunch on top of Great Mis Tor, leaving the horses at the foot of the final scramble up the rocks. We settled with backs against a rock, protected from the wind, looking northeast over Dartmoor. Lines of many-toned, green-clad ridges, the colors fading as they stretched away to the horizon, interspersed with gray rocky outcrops. With Dartmoor at its most benign, we were loath to leave it. Even as we descended to the horses, we felt the process of our separation had begun. It was dusk when we arrived back at the Minerva's stable. I said a sad farewell to Maddie, who caught my mood. She gave me a gentle nuzzle, nibbling at my collar. We slipped into the snug bar. Over a drink and a meal, I said my goodbyes to Annie. She promised to look after Aby and gave us both a big hug before we went home to bed. What started as a desperate need to build memories that would sustain us over the next year settled into a gentle and continuous congress of mind and body till we drifted off to sleep in each other's arms, limbs entwined.

CHAPTER 26

Journal entry—*9 April to 2 June 1616*

By seven a.m., 9 April, six bells in the morning watch, I was aboard *Rosie*. My chest had been delivered the day before. Dr. Vines, whom I now referred to as Doc, and his party had come aboard the day before. I was the last arrival. Hands were set to prepare for warping out of Sutton Pool. By seven bells, we were underway. As we passed out of the pool, I saw Aby waving. We were close to the pier she was on, and I was tempted to jump ship. We waved to each other till *Rosie* moved out into the sound and we could no longer see each other. With favorable winds and strong current, we moved quickly down the sound, past St. Nicholas Island, heading for the open sea. J.B. slapped me on the shoulder. He told me we were already a day closer to our return.

"By the way, the skipper has invited you to join him in his cabin."

Dusty had prepared a wonderful breakfast, laid out in the great cabin. Doc was there.

Over the meal, the skipper discussed the voyage. As with his last trip, he would sail round the Lizard, off Cornwall, then head up to the southwest coast of Ireland. He advised us that the weather would be changeable, and we should expect storms with generally bad weather south of Iceland—late spring icebergs between Iceland and Newfoundland, and thick fog over the grand banks as we closed Newfoundland. Thereafter, a strong current would drive us southwest down the North American coast to Monhegan. From there was a short, comfortable passage to Saco. Back topside, I had the chance to meet up with my old crewmates. I talked to J.B. about the several new faces. I had noticed, fairly quickly, that one of them looked like trouble—a surly brute named Crabtree. Long-term crew members were reserved in their interactions with him, while the younger ones were inclined to pay him more attention and court his favor.

The knowledge that I was a former crew member had this seaman in a quandary about me. He decided that I had ideas above my station and was deserving of rough treatment. J.B. advised me to watch my back. He said that they'd been shorthanded over the winter. A transatlantic voyage required a full complement, and they had to take whoever they could find. There were two others, strong of body but weak of character, who came with Crabtree. He treated them as his minions. The minions were split between watches, which reduced tension a little. But, as J.B. confided, Crabtree's presence was beginning to cause issues among the crew. The skipper had been able to build a crew over a long period into an excellent team that was capable, disciplined, and loyal. He treated them well because they earned his respect and he earned theirs. So far, Crabtree was cunning enough to keep his head down for a while. Soon however, he started making waves, as was inevitable given his nature.

Rosie was a small boat. Nothing untoward should be able to take place unnoticed, but Crabtree would make a remark to one of his minions as I passed, greeted by a snigger. I ignored it. Unfortunately, Obi, when he witnessed it, became riled. I had to calm him down. After several similar episodes over the first week, with some of the younger crew enjoying it all, Crabtree had worked himself into a position where he needed to show his supporters some action. He was tired of my lack of reaction. Next time I passed, he stuck his foot out. I easily avoided the trip but gave his exposed ankle a hard rap with the toe of my boot. He grunted, jumped to his feet, arm raised, ham-sized fists clenched. Obi leapt to my defense. Crabtree swept him aside with a raised arm swinging across, knocking him over a table. Off-watch crew, all lounging on the lower deck with mess tables rigged, jumped back to make room. Obi, unhurt and embarrassed, was helped to his feet. I stood easy, waiting for Crabtree to move. Being the bully he was, he was surprised that his much smaller opponent hadn't backed off. He realized he couldn't back off either or he would lose face. He raised his arms.

"Come here, you little runt."

He reached for me. I ducked under his arms, hit him hard twice in his belly, and jumped back before he could react. Angered and winded, he lumbered toward me. Not watching his feet, he tripped over a crewman's leg that somehow had found its way in his path. As he stumbled, I hit him on his nose, flattened and bloody. J.B., who'd come down from topside, was watching. He called on two crewmen to seize Crabtree and bind his wrists.

"What do you think you are doing?"

"He attacked me, bosun."

"No, he didn't. You knocked down one seaman. You threatened Mr. Stan-field, a passenger half your size, and he defended himself. You are a disgrace. Take him to the holding cage in the for'ard hold. You will be up before the captain first thing tomorrow."

Crabtree was taken away, dripping blood. I followed J.B. to the main deck.

"You all right?" he asked. "You handled that well. Couldn't have asked better. I have been waiting to throw the book at Crabtree. Trouble is he has been doing his duty, just. No complaints sufficient to justify action. I warned Peg that something was brewing between the two of you. I told him I had no worries about you. He advised me to keep a close watch, not to let anything get out of hand."

Next morning, Crabtree was paraded before the captain, attended by the first mate, Peg; quartermaster, Mr. Lee; and the bosun, J.B. I was not called, as J.B. had seen much of what had gone before. Sentence, Crabtree to be flogged, tied to the gratings before the ship's company—a dozen lashes at noon. The captain warned him that any further incitement to riot or other mayhem would result in him being hanged from the yardarm. J.B. reported back to me that Crabtree went ashen. Somehow in his career he had avoided a flogging. The sentence was carried out before the ship's company. Crabtree took it badly, to the contempt of the crew. Howling at the first lash, administered by the bosun. He was cut down at the end of the punishment and crumpled to the deck. His back red, not very bloody. A bucket of seawater was thrown over him. He screamed as the salt cleansed the wounds. He was removed back to the hold. Dusty was detailed to see to his needs. Doc, used to corporal punishment, attended with his party. Of the party, only David Thomson seemed in any way disturbed. Doc said that, in his capacity as a doctor, he could visit the punished man, but the skipper turned down his offer. Crabtree was a member of his crew. He would be dealt with by a member of the crew.

There was a general sense of shock at Crabtree's display of cowardice. Obi had difficulty watching it, but he was repelled by the man's behavior. Crabtree was finished as a working member of the crew. He appeared a broken man and became a galley steward, largely ignored by the crew. He was an embarrass-ment to them. Crabtree's two erstwhile minions were taken in hand by J.B. Two stable, reliable seamen shepherded them toward a more productive future as *Rosie* crewmen.

We continued to head northwest, aiming to head west and turning west southwest when we were south of Greenland. A significant amount of ocean remained for us to traverse before we got to that point. As we headed farther out into the Atlantic, three weeks out of Plymouth, winds from the southwest picked up. The seas began to build. Heavy clouds on the horizon expanded to thunderheads. We were in for a storm, and it came soon enough. Fore tops'l and sprits'l were furled, bonnets doused, and courses braced spilling wind. Relieving tackle on helm. Pumps already manned. *Rosie* drove on. As the wind continued to rise, the whistle through the rigging increased in sound, becoming a howl. The sound of the sea was a continuous roar, making it difficult to hear. Communication was by hand signals. Rain started, being driven horizontally. *Rosie's* bow began pitching deeper into the oncoming waves. As she came up out of the wave's trough, the wind tried to drag her to leeward, which caused her to roll with scuppers under water. Lifelines were rigged, all hands called. Passengers except myself were sent below. Pumps were double-manned, and helm likewise. Fore course furled, which eased the bow's motion. Wind increased. The skipper, shouting to make himself heard, issued orders for *Rosie* to lie to. We had to ride out the storm and had plenty of sea room. *Rosie* rounded to lie five points off the wind, under reefed, hard-braced main tops'l, fore stays'l, main and mizzen courses furled. Fore topmast spars sent down. Mast wedges secured. Sprits'l yard swung, lashed to the bowsprit. Hatches double battened. Guns secured, anchors catted and fished, chains unshackled, hawseholes plugged. All drain holes cleared, including pump limber holes in hold.

Rosie met the oncoming waves. They surged occasionally over but now, more often, under her port bow, beaten down, rising up, shaking away the sea like a dog coming out of water. Wind pressure on the main tops'l caused *Rosie* to heel to leeward easing the motion, allowing more waves to slide under the bows. The storm continued through the night and into the next day. I stayed on the quarterdeck for most of the storm. I wanted to be there, a part of *Rosie*. She battled and was winning. I was willing her on, exhilarated by the elemental struggle to defeat the constant attempts of the mighty ocean to overwhelm us.

The storm left us tossing in its wake, and the crew assessed the damage. Some spars had been damaged, some lines broken. Mizzen course tack had come away, and the flogging sail badly torn before it could be brought under control. One crew member had a broken arm, others had banged heads. Dr. Vine insisted on providing assistance, which was gratefully received. The lower deck accommodation was a sodden, confused mess, but once the crew replaced or mended sails, we continued on our way. Within twenty-four hours on larboard tack we were heading west southwest, sailing full and by, off the wind. Everything was soon shipshape and drying out. After the storm cleared, we had excellent sailing weather that lasted a week. We saw no icebergs, but the water was cold. Deep gray-blue seas with white crests and wind-blown spume. *Rosie* loved it. We did too. Then, a morning dawned with a bank of gray fog lying ahead of us. We were approaching the Grand Banks. We now saw other vessels, fishing boats converging on the fishing grounds.

The voyage gave me time to talk to David about his experiences with the Popham expedition to Sagadahoc in 1607. He went as a nineteen-year-old, full of daring, keen to experience a great adventure, but with no idea what was to come. The one thing he learned was the importance of having an Indian as a guide, intermediary, and translator. Skicowarres, one of the Indians captured by Captain Weymouth, had been an important member of the team. What was a most pleasant surprise was the appearance of Tahanedo, the Pemaquid sachem, returned from England with Captain Pring a year or so previously, who had come to meet the English again. Between them, they advised the leaders on the local conditions, the weather patterns, the Indians who were friendly, those who were less so, and what to plant and where to plant it.

"When we get to Saco, we have to establish a strong, trusting relationship with the local people," David said. "We are a small group with a specific goal. We need to build on what was learned at Sagadahoc. I am sure that permanent settlements will come. We are pioneers leading the way and, through these collective experiences, we will make it more certain that future settlements will be successful. We will lead a tidal flow of families moving to this incredible land of opportunity."

He said he was determined to move his family here one day. We entered the fog bank. The wind dropped. We crept forward, went to double-lookouts. No rain, but every line dripped water, and sails flapped, showering anyone unfortunate enough to be beneath. Ghost ships would appear ahead, greetings called, and slip away astern. After a further two days of slow progress, the current off Newfoundland bore us southwest, carried us out of the fog banks, and into gray, heavy weather. Contrary winds slowed us, but increasing numbers of seabirds, floating clumps of seaweed, and the occasional tree limb heralded land ahead. We sighted land after nearly six weeks at sea: the southeast tip of Newfoundland. A tremendous cheer from the crew at the masthead lookout's cry.

"Land ho, two points off starboard bow."

The wind from the north, with the favorable current, now pushed us quickly down the coast, across the great estuary of the St. Lawrence, inside Sable Island, along the coast of Acadia. Weather cleared, and the wind settled from the southeast. We sighted Monhegan a fortnight later. We made the harbor there the morning of 1 June. We had been at sea fifty-four days.

Journal entry—*3 June to 1 November 1616*

We stayed at Monhegan two days. The skipper moved *Rosie* to our previous anchorage, north of the island, more protected with more room. The off-watch crew were allowed ashore to replenish water casks and to hunt for fruit and game to refresh our stores. The on-watch crew worked on maintenance, repairs, and cleaning. When I had the chance, I went ashore to retrace my steps to the point I had been captured by the Indians, following the path down to the water's edge. I looked north to the two islands guarding the entrance to the St. George's River. No signs, no smoke.

On 5 June, with wind continuing from the southeast, we left Monhegan to head down the coast, passing Pemaquid, between low-lying islands and the mainland. Damariscove harbor was busy, with many masts poking over the land. We passed the wide mouth of the Sheepscot River, heading southwest to skirt Seguin Island, leaving it to starboard with Sagadahoc visible beyond. We made for Cape Elizabeth and Saco, which we reached late afternoon, anchoring in the bay in the lee of the two islands, east of the river entrance, which had been described to me in Honfleur. Doc, David Thomson, and I were rowed in *Rosie's* boat to the rivermouth. Peg accompanied us with two crew rowing, one sounding as we entered. We had a copy of the chart made by Champlain, which showed his soundings.

They proved accurate. A sandbar lay across the mouth, a possible problem only at low water. Once over the bar, the river widened into a pleasant, well-protected natural harbor. Further soundings showed there was plenty of room for *Rosie* to anchor and swing with the tides and wind. We noticed a small number of Indians watching from the shore with numerous dogs that barked at us. Champlain had talked of large numbers of local, friendly inhabitants. Where was everyone else? There was a village there, cultivated land and living abodes, scattered about. It all seemed peaceful. We returned to *Rosie*. With the favorable wind, now a gentle breeze, we sailed into the river and anchored. Double watch was kept that night. Regardless of Champlain's description, the skipper was a cautious man. We were not disturbed, although the village dogs barked at any movement or noise on our part.

Next morning, Doc, David, and I were rowed upriver to the west bank near a fort-like structure. Watchers on shore approached as we landed. A group of four of the villagers greeted us most cordially, and by their gestures invited us to accompany them to the fort. Dogs sniffed at our legs, others accompanied us at a distance. The stockade of the fort consisted of a ring of tree trunks, bound together about eight feet high. The trunks, sharpened on top, were embedded vertically in a bank with a ditch in front, encompassing a round area of about seventy-five feet in diameter. A large hut raised on a stage occupied the center of the stockade, with other smaller huts close to the wall. The wall had a raised walkway that ran around the inside about three feet above the ground. There were narrow gaps at regular intervals in the wall, through which to look and shoot arrows. Two stout gates were open, one on each end of the stockade.

My immediate reaction was one of surprise. I expected more people, more activity, but it seemed quiet—too quiet. I told Doc that according to Champlain, in 1605 the sagamore here was a young man called Honemechin. Could be he was still here. A villager invited Doc, our obvious leader, to the main hut. After a moment's hesitation he mounted the steps and entered. He was gone for some thirty minutes. David and I spent the time looking around, attempting to interact with the two villagers with us. An air of stoic sadness hung about them. I remarked on the fact to David, who had noticed the same almost fatalist attitude. Doc came out. He joined us with a serious look on his face.

"We have a problem. Six people in the hut are very sick. It seems that the sagamore is the person Champlain met. Although his mind is distracted, he appears to have some memory of the meeting. With the help of an old woman, he is attempting to aid the sick, but they indicate that none of their medicines are effective. Ten have already died, including two children. Others are sick in their own huts outside the fort. I have attempted an initial diagnosis. David, I would be grateful if you would do the same."

David entered the hut. Doc looked worried.

"I want David to confirm my own findings," he said. "It seems they have caught some kind of virulent disease. The symptoms remind me of a kind of plague, which used to occur frequently throughout the continent and England. It's like a fever. Over the years, our people have become immune to it. From what I understood from the sagamore, people started getting sick some months ago. They sought help from other tribes in the area but, apparently, they too are suffering the same sickness."

David came out and conferred with Doc. They had come to the same conclusion, that something like this disease, alien to the Indians, might well have come from foreign visitors, such as English or French fishermen. They needed to fetch the medicines they had onboard to see if we could remedy or alleviate the sickness in any way. We indicated to our Indian hosts that we were returning to *Rosie* but would be back soon. Back onboard, we talked to the skipper. His responsibility was to protect the crew from contagion. It was possible we were all immune to the disease, but the skipper was taking no chances. While we returned to the village, his crew would offload all our possessions on the riverbank. He did not want us back on board *Rosie*. The rest of our shore party would either stay on board and return to England, or disembark, not being allowed to re-board. The skipper took me aside. He apologized, but he said his duty was to his crew. He'd delivered us to our destination, and would remain for one week in case of emergencies, after which he would leave. More formally, he told Doc of his decision. Doc understood, accepting it.

It was agreed that the *Sweet Rose* or, failing her, another vessel would return next April to pick us up and return us to Plymouth. Doc talked to his people, all of whom agreed to go ashore. The skipper wished us well as we were ferried ashore. Our two doctors went with their medicines to the fort. I followed and was quickly joined by the two Indian villagers. I indicated that our small group, now all ashore, would be staying there for the passing of many moons. Our supplies started coming ashore. Other Indians began to appear, and the young ones, especially, became inquisitive. Somehow, I made it plain to our two villagers that nothing should be touched, and they ordered the older children to take responsibility for guarding our possessions, which they proceeded to do with great success. Our doctors came back, not particularly sanguine about the efficacy of their medicines, but they had done and would continue to do their best.

Meantime, we needed to organize ourselves. We had to build four huts to house the nine of us and our supplies while close to but not a part of the village, preferably with our own fresh water supply, by the river. Our shallop, in two pieces with attendant spars, sails, cordage, and so on, needed to be assembled. Work details were organized. I undertook to work with our two Indian friends, Mingan and Kitchi, to find the right location and report back. By diagrams drawn in the dirt, I told them what we were after. They talked together for a moment, then led me downriver toward the mouth, walking through fields of maize, beans, and squash. On a bluff, an empty hut sat with cultivated land around it, now uncared for. I understood that the inhabitants had died some months previously and no one wanted to live there now. Would we like it? I looked around. It seemed ideal. We were close to the river, the bay, and a freshwater spring. We were within a short distance of the fort, on the perimeter of the village, which already had the basis for our own vegetable garden and room to plant more. There was land to add additional huts. I nodded, smiled, and shook their hands.

I informed Doc, and after his inspection, he called us all together. We laid out the lines for the three additional huts. The existing hut we used as the model for the others, but we planned one larger structure for storage. Mingan and Kitchi helped us as we started building. We cut down thirty strong saplings, ten feet long, and dug them in the ground, twelve inches apart in a circle about ten feet in diameter. The saplings were bent inward to form a round domelike structure, leaving a hole about twelve inches in diameter in the center. We bound them together with hemp cords and strips of walnut bark, providing a strong frame which was covered with long pieces of bark stretching the length of the saplings, which we sewed together and to the frame. Afterward, the whole was covered with thatching from marsh grass and maize stalks. Inside, a fire pit was made, surrounded by smooth river rocks, under the hole in the roof. An animal skin covered an entranceway. We were told that when winter came, matting, woven from sedge and reed, was added to the inside walls. Another replaced the animal skin door, to make a snug, secure dwelling place. Within a week, we had our four huts. We had weeded and watered our vegetable patch. The soil was fertile and was quick to respond with new seedlings. We were shown the manner in which they farmed and the vegetables they grew, which were maize, beans, squash, and big orange pumpkins. They would pile small heaps of soil a few feet apart, plant a small number of seeds in the center of each heap with a large, dead fish buried beneath to fertilize the seeds. One quickly got used to the smell of rotten fish. The village dogs had to be chased away, as the smell was irresistible to them.

The one thing we could not get used to was the flying insects, mosquitos, flies large and small, tiny ones you could hardly see. The villagers boiled the bark of a shrub and added some plant leaves. The smell was pungent, and the flying insects didn't like it. In the evenings, when they were at their worst, pots of the liquid were placed upwind and kept simmering, helping drive them off. I tried smearing the liquid on my exposed skin, arms, and face. The soldiers in our band peed into a pot and smeared the pee on themselves, which worked well enough to keep us all away from them. By September, the temperature was much cooler, and the insects less bothersome. Any breeze tended to keep them away as well. But from June till the end of August, they were with us in clouds.

The sick people did not improve. The villagers saw the care and attention our doctors were giving to their people and were grateful, but the deaths continued. Doc described the progress of the illness. The lungs became badly affected, breathing increasingly difficult, and the heart strained. The old and the young died sooner. The more active among the young men, the hunters, the young women, the farmers, seemed better able to fend off the disease. They were outside more and were much fitter to begin with.

Our first objectives were to become self-sufficient and to develop a strong, dependable relationship with our villagers. We wanted to grow food, but we had to ensure that what we required beyond what we were able to grow would be available in an emergency from our Indian friends. In order to achieve the latter, we needed to work hard to build our relations with the tribe. We had brought with us our own tools for hunting, farming, and cooking, and had made sure we'd enough to barter or give away. They were amazed at what we showed them. They had heard of the stick that explodes with a terrifying bang and kills from a distance. They saw it demonstrated. I used a fowling piece to bring down duck on the wing. They were astounded. Their hunting dogs barked furiously, then followed their masters as they ran into the marshes whooping with excitement and retrieved the downed birds.

They taught us to hunt their way, having a huge advantage, in the same way that Epenow had taught me at Wraxall. They could walk through the thickest forest without a sound. They had hunting bows with beautifully made arrows, which they prized. Not wanting to lose any, they were very accurate. They knew the ways of the animals they hunted, and it seemed as if they could read the animals' minds. We had little chance to emulate those skills, but there was plenty of game. We could, in our own blundering way, bring down bucks, even the occasional moose, as well as trap rabbits.

The metal tools we had—the spades, forks, hoes, rakes, and scythes—were what most attracted the Indians. Their tools, which they had used for as far back as their history recorded, were made of worked stone lashed to wooden handles, or large clamshells used as scoops or for cutting. We had brought many spares, and they were overwhelmed to receive them as gifts. Funny though, tradition was hard to break. The women, who did all the cultivation, had a long-accustomed rhythm to their work, but those who adopted our tools, once they became adept, were able to do more faster and with less effort. With the sickness reducing the number of workers, this ability proved beneficial to the village. We won over the women with our cooking pots, pans, and ladles. Again, the metal utensils amazed them. They made cooking and storage pots from clay and the most intricate baskets of all sizes, from thin strips of wood or bark, or woven with hemp. They made much use of wooden and stone mortars and pestles. They had personal ones, small enough to hold in their laps, and larger community ones, their bases buried in the ground, allowing a number of people to grind the grain at the same time. We learned and borrowed from them, and they did likewise from us. There was one significant difference in our cultures. The women shrieked with laughter when they saw us doing our own cooking and gardening.

With our small shallop fully seaworthy, we had a good platform for our fishing and were able to catch more fish than we could hope to eat. We shared our catches with the villagers and they, in turn, provided us with meat. We developed a taste for shellfish, oysters, mussels, clams, and lobsters larger and more abundant than anything we had seen before. We also began fishing in earnest to build a store of fish to be dried and salted for shipment back to England. We built fishing stages (flakes). The salt we brought with us needed to be replenished. Our needs being relatively minor, we were able to obtain sufficient from Damariscove.

Our next objective, dependent on achieving the first two, was to be able to prepare for the winter. We needed not only to survive but to overcome the fear of that unknown. For an English settlement to succeed, winter had to be reduced to being merely one of the four seasons, each one with its own challenges and opportunities. We learned from our Indians how to store our harvests, the clay pots making excellent storage containers; how to keep fruit such as apples, pumpkins, and all kinds of berries; how to store salted grain, meat, and undried fish in underground shelters; and how to track game to hunt. We had to cut firewood and learn to tack the wood in round piles, five feet high and six across, covered on top with matting. We began to wear the clothes they wore in winter, at least to accumulate wardrobes for use once the snows came. Animal skins we sized and sewed into leggings and boots. We were shown snowshoes, how to make and mend them. We began to look forward to winter, with all the preparations we had undergone.

Doc and David realized they were battling a plague-like disease that they did not have the wherewithal to combat. As with the plagues back home, fresh air, clean surroundings, and prayer seemed to be all we could do. Indian travelers came by and told of serious loss of life along the coast. The inland tribes were less affected, which tended to prove Doc's theory that the infection resulted from contact with foreign fishermen. The fact that none of us went sick further supported that contention that we carried the disease with us but were immune. We worried that winter would accelerate the death rate. The villagers already knew that loss would happen. Their burial pits were prepared before the ground froze. Doc established a weekly Sunday service, the Book of Common Prayer's order of service for each Sunday with a reading from the Bible. We prayed for the poor villagers bewildered, frightened, and dying of some unknown, unseen scourge. We had no serious intent to introduce our Indian friends to our form of worship and to the Christian creed, but being highly intelligent and inexhaustibly curious, plus learning some English, they asked questions. At the same time, we, especially David, were able to speak to them increasingly in their language. They were touched when told we were praying to our God for their deliverance from their dreadful predicament. Some would come to our services. They seemed fascinated by the idea that there was but one God who made everything. They talked about such a concept among themselves. They found it logical.

We explored the Saco River and the coastline to the north and south. Of most interest were our explorations south. Captain Smith explored the river where the Piscataqua tribe of Abenaki Indians lived. It provided us with weeks of fascinating journeys. A few hours, sail from Saco, we took the shallop and spent days at a time exploring miles of river with its inlets, bays, and creeks. We stayed on the water. We did not, initially, make contact with the Piscataqua people. We visited Captain Smith's isles, a few miles out to sea, east of the Piscataqua River. Our shallop was small, eighteen feet long, lighter than normal with a shallower draft. A party of four of us could row or sail over considerable distances. As autumn came, the leaves of the trees exploded into color—reds, yellows, and oranges. I would sit on the riverbank and gaze around me. I was in another world and wished Aby were with me.

David and I spent much time talking about home and our respective families. We discussed a settlement such as we now had, but with our families with us. Until now, life had been hard but almost idyllic. What would winter bring? We both hoped our ladies would be strong, capable of learning the skills the Indian women here possessed. When we could see well Indians among the sick, they were remarkably healthy. The young were of good complexion, sturdy, upright, and taller than us on average. They had the most amazingly perfect teeth, their diet perhaps. When they smiled it was like a flash of white light brightening their faces. There was no comparison in terms of the healthy life they led here to what now seemed to be a dark, dank, pestilent place back home. And yet, we were in the middle of a terrible plague in this New World.

We made contact with Indians upriver. We put together a bartering process whereby we were able to acquire skins of beaver, wolf, fox, bear, and deer in exchange for tools and trinkets. We gathered sassafras roots, which we used for our own purposes to make medicinal teas but added to the collection of produce to be shipped back to England. We were able to harvest the wild grape that grew in profusion and made a sweet wine from it. Doc stored a large amount of the wine in jars and added them to his medicine supplies—to counter scurvy, he said. With Mingan and Kitchi, we journeyed inland to the forests that covered the land and hills. The Indians kept the undergrowth clear under the trees by regularly burning it, and we were able to walk for miles along open trails through the forests. Under their guidance we steered clear of unwelcoming tribes. We saw every kind of tree known to us and many unknown. Trees were tall, straight, ideal for ship building, with rivers nearby to float them down to the sea, to be carried home. The occasional visiting fishing boats came by with letters received, answered, and with our reports sent back. We shipped back the produce we had collected for delivery to Sir F. in Plymouth.

CHAPTER 27

Journal entry—*2 November 1616 to 6 January 1617*

The days grew shorter, darker, the weather colder, the winds stronger and more bone chilling. In late November, we had a three-day storm when the winds howled down on us from the northeast. We had difficulty standing. The rain was torrential and horizontal. Our huts trembled but stayed strong and warm. We installed the extra matting inside them. The animal-skin clothes we wore proved warm and waterproof. The storm was a good test for the even worse weather ahead.

One cold morning, as dawn broke, we heard shouting from the fort. We left our huts as Kitchi ran down to us. A villager from an outlying hut upriver had come to the fort, wounded, when his family had been attacked by a band of Mohawk from farther inland. They were after harvested produce and women. They must've heard of the loss of life and saw an opportunity to make a profitable incursion. We grabbed our weapons and ran to the fort.

We were just in time. Some twenty Mohawks, armed with bows, arrows, and clubs, with faces colored in black paint, were fast approaching from the shelter of the woods about 100 yards away. Their surprise attack had been thwarted, but they still were confident of overcoming a weakened defense. They ran for the fort with three ladders, the ladder bearers protected by carrying shields of thick leather, which the defenders' arrows couldn't penetrate. Our two soldiers were quick to load, aim, and fire at the attacking group, now only twenty yards away. Two ladder carriers fell. The noise and smoke added to the shock and horror. The attackers stopped. Picking up their fallen, they ran back to the safety of the trees. After a short break, reappearing on the edge of the tree line, they started shouting abuse at the fort. Sadly, they thought they were out of range of our guns. Muskets reloaded, the soldiers fired again. Two more were hit, and again they disappeared among the trees. They must have thought the risks too high to continue because nothing more was seen or heard. A scouting party was sent out, which I accompanied, sword in hand. Evidence was there: blood on the ground, a trail leading west.

We found the family they'd first attacked. Two men lay dead, scalped, something I had heard about but never seen before. The two daughters were gone, and the old woman, untouched, was mourning her family. Their storage of winter food had been taken. We brought the old woman back to the fort, after burying her two sons. One of the daughters who had been taken had started to sicken, she told us. The raiders had captured more than they had bargained for.

In early December it started to snow. We learned the art of snowshoeing so we could continue to hunt deer and moose. I had surreptitiously kept Aby's small flask filled with "medicine." It held about a half pint. I had brought a bottle of brandy, which I kept hidden—my own medicine supply—and carried the flask with me whenever I went out. It was a part of Aby. I only took an occasional nip, to ward off extreme cold, when I was alone or out of sight. I found the immediate effect was good, but the aftereffect made me feel colder. It became a toast to Aby. A full flask lasted a month or more. We fished, pulling plentiful, enormous cod, salmon, and other types not known to me from the river and sea. Our villagers continued to die. Doc and David took each death personally. They grieved with the families. Christmas was recognized by a short service and no celebration.

So many were now sick that Doc roped the rest of us in to providing care and assistance. The sagamore died and was honored in a long ceremony. Sagamores from local tribes came to honor him. It was a solemn process, with music and slow, almost hypnotic dancing, and the cries of the mourners. Smoke from torches and fires created an almost mystical or dreamlike atmosphere, especially at night, mingling with the falling snow. Eventually, the guests left, the mourning ended, and the sagamore was buried. The remaining elders met to elect the successor: a younger man, a strong leader, much respected by the whole tribe. His name was Askuwheteau, *the watch-keeper*.

Journal entry—*7 to 30 January 1617*

By early January, we had, for the most part, become used to the cold and the living conditions. David and I discussed how we would establish our own settlement. We were living three to a hut, on top of one another. The huts had become fetid, unwholesome habitations. We had become inured to the nightly belching, snoring, and farting, and were used to the shared latrines. But to bring our families, we needed our own housing. For the families to be part of a community, we needed a community house, a church, and a stockade to protect us. We needed land of our own to farm. The coastal Indian tribes had shown how important they were to our survival. Living in harmony with them was not only necessary but satisfying. Winter continued on, snowing every day, deep drifts piling up on the leeward side of any obstacle to the wind. Doors in the lee were blocked by up to six feet of snow while on the windward side, usually north or northeast, the wind scrubbed the ground clear of snow, carrying it all round to the sheltered side. The ground was rock hard, making digging impossible. Our pre-dug graves now full, the Indian dead—men, women, and children—were wrapped and kept in a hut in the fort, waiting for spring. The cold froze the bodies. The loss of so many capable Indian hunters, including the sick who were in many cases too weak, meant that our roles had reversed. At the start of the winter, we were dependent on our Indian hosts to teach us about hunting in the snow, the trails, the likely spots, the traps to set, the use of snowshoes. Now, we had to do the hunting for meat ourselves to provide for everyone's needs.

I organized a small team, the two soldiers and the two farmers, on daily hunting trips. Normally two of us went out at a time. While we were successful early on staying close to the village, our quarry became more wary and moved farther into the forests. Our hunting trips became longer, more arduous. We had a musket and a bow between us. The density of the trees meant that we had to track and wait, thankfully with little or no undergrowth. We learned where deer and moose would gather or which paths they used at what times of day. Constant snowfall quickly covered tracks, so we also had to learn how to navigate our way home. Apart from the skill necessary, it required great patience. We had to learn to deal with the cold during those long, silent waits. When we made a kill, we used a travois, two poles lashed at the top end with a third shorter pole lashed near the base to form a letter "A." A rope harness was tied to the top end. The carcass was tied on to the travois and hauled back to the village. We could have made life easier for ourselves by butchering it immediately, but we worried about attracting wolves. We set traps for rabbits. Our fishermen worked the river and the bay. The river being tidal, there was open water but the ice, stretching from the shore to the open stretches, was unsafe. The shallop was used. We kept it free of the ice, close to the river mouth where the current and the saltwater kept the ice away. We had learned to use the Indian canoes, but they seemed fragile to us in the ice-filled river. They were unstable the way we used them. We didn't want to be tipped into the freezing water.

On a particularly dreary morning, against the rules I had set with my team, I went out alone to check the traps. It was cold and dark. Heavy clouds amassed, promising serious snow. The wind had died, almost as if it were drawing breath before it let loose. Well into the forest, clumping along on my snowshoes, I saw a dark shape moving through the trees. I stopped. The shape stopped. I moved. It moved. I had a musket but couldn't make out what the shape was. It was too big; I wouldn't be able to bring it back. It couldn't be a bear, I thought, knowing that they would all be in hibernation. Slowly, it seemed as if we were converging. I lost sight of it behind a thicket of tightly packed trees. As I worked my way 'round, and before I had time to react, a large bear hit me and sent me sprawling. I lost my musket. I rolled and it clawed my back and bit into my arm. I was able to free my knife and lunged at the bear's throat. The knife went in up to the hilt. The bear let go of me, and I let go the knife, too weak to pull it out. The bear shambled off snarling, clawing at the wound I had caused.

I was in a bad way, my left side a bloody mess. The bear's claw had ripped through my clothing and torn great furrows on my side and back. My arm was useless. Blood flowing, I wadded up snow and pressed it to the wounds I was able to reach. I had lost one snowshoe and was unable to get to my feet, so I dragged myself to a tree and used it to hoist myself up. I could see the adrift snowshoe out of reach, and the stock of the musket sticking out of a snowbank. I was growing cold, and I'd started shaking from the aftereffects of the attack. What to do? I had a nip from Aby's flask, making a major, if temporary improvement. I couldn't move on one snowshoe. The shoeless leg just sank to my thigh, and I had a devil of a job extricating myself. Eventually, in my befuddled state, I took my snowshoe off and, lying on my front, I slid across the snow using my right hand as a paddle to fetch the other one. Another problem, I only had one arm useable. I threw the snowshoe toward my tree and paddled to the snowshoe and repeated the action, until I was back at the tree.

Trying to attach the snowshoes with one hand was almost impossible. It was cold; I wasn't thinking clearly, and it was dark. Finally I realized that by placing the snowshoes flat on the snow and hauling myself upright with my good arm holding a branch, I could stand on the snowshoes, then wrap the leather straps around my boots and hitch them somewhat securely. I left the musket and started slowly back toward the village, a mile away. After about a hundred yards I was beginning to black out, leaving a trail of blood in the snow behind me. I rested and tried again, wanting to lie down, desperate to sleep, but knowing that would be the end. One step, followed by another, with the goal of fifty steps. Then, when reached, I would retighten the straps and set a new goal. My left side screamed in complaint.

A wolf called away behind me and another answered, closer. I had no weapons to defend myself, and their calls woke me up. I had another nip and struggled on. More wolf calls. It was no use—try as I might, my body started closing down. The last I remembered was a feeling of surprise that I was dying, something entirely unexpected. I passed out, smelling the smoke from the village.

Next thing I knew, I was in my hut, wounds bandaged, warm, wrapped in animal skins. The sound of the wolves had alerted Kitchi, who was sick. I had dropped in to check on him before I left on my hunting trip. He, with another less sick Indian, had gone out for me. They found me just inside the tree line and brought me back. I've been laid up for several days.

A few of the Indians, including Mingan and Kitchii, seem to be recovering. At first, it had seemed as if the illness was always fatal once it struck, but now people saw hope and struggled harder. Askuwheteau had not been affected. He was a tower of strength. Powerful magic obviously surrounded him.

It is Thursday, 30 January 1617. As I complete this entry, I realize I have missed my twentieth birthday.

Journal entry—*31 January to 28 February 1617*

On Friday, 31 January, early morning, Doc came to see how I was doing, bringing Askuwheteau, who told me that after his people had rescued me, he had gone back with two others to track my wounded bear. They followed my bloody trail to the point of attack, found the gun, which they retrieved, and the bear's equally bloody trail. Luckily the promised snowfall had yet to start. I had done serious damage to it with that knife thrust because about a mile farther into the forest, they found it dead, bled dry. They retrieved my knife. Doc said they have it as a trophy with the skin of the bear. When I was able to move, Askuwheteau invited me to inspect the bearskin. I was puzzled about the bear, as I thought they all hibernated in winter. Askuwheteau said no, that single male bears, such as this one, close to good feeding, with copious amounts of fish in the river, sometimes don't hibernate at all. I had obviously surprised it. Normally, it would have avoided contact with man. Anyway, they brought the bear back. They considered its meat, especially the internal organs, a huge treat, and used it to make the broth I have been fed these past few days. They now consider me a true Indian brave for single-handedly slaying such a big bear, and they call me Machk—*the bear*. Askuwheteau wished me well and left. It seems I have broken through the barrier that separated us. Doc said that the Indians had taken note of my track back. I'd stopped many times. They were amazed I'd made it back as far as I had. I said I didn't remember the number of times, but when I did stop, I was able to start again, thanks to Aby.

"Aby?"

"Yes, she gave me a small hip flask as a present. When I go hunting in the snow, I take it with me. It has brandy in it. When in serious difficulties, I toast Aby by taking a nip."

"That explains it. When we got you back, stripped you, cleaned, repaired, and put to bed, you smelt of alcohol. I was concerned that you had gone off on your trip in an alcoholic haze. That it was your condition that had nearly killed you."

"Where is my flask?" I asked. "I wonder how much is left inside. It only holds a half pint."

"I have it. David found it while we were stripping you. It's empty. It must have helped save your life. Forgive me for doubting you. I'll return it."

"Thank you," I said.

After an uncomfortable pause, Doc continued, "I am not happy with you having your own supply of alcohol. I am not against it in the right place at the right time, but we are in a difficult situation here. We survive through strong discipline with our ability to trust and support each other. Alcohol is a threat to that good order. Do you have any brandy left?"

"It is in my chest over there."

Doc rummaged through my clothes. He found the bottle. It was about half full.

"If you don't mind, I will add this to my medicine dispensary."

I was in no position to argue. He made good sense. He was our leader and had proven a good one, but I was a little upset. I had been reprimanded, which I didn't much like. I said no more. I was hurting. No bones broken. Doc looked at me quizzically, nodded, and told me to sleep. My body needed rest. It was another three days before I could stand for any length of time. One of my first walks, mandated by the good Doc, was on a better day. Clear sky, low wind, snow crusted, easy to walk along the beaten path to the stockade. I approached the fort slowly, favoring my stiff left arm. The scabs on my shoulder and chest pulling as my muscles worked. I was sweating with the effort and out of sorts by the time I arrived.

I was greeted by a shout, rather like: "Aieeeeee, Ma Chick, Ma Chick."

I had forgotten I'd been given a new name. People came out and surrounded me, laughing and clapping. Askuwheteau came to the door of the central hut.

He stood looking down at me. He raised his hand high in greeting. I did likewise as I approached him. He came down the steps, put his arms on my shoulders, not too gently, and led me up the steps into his hut. There at one end, spread over the wall, was the skin of a huge black bear, my *machk*. It had been fleshed, but tanning would have to wait till the weather turned warmer. My knife was there, too. He made to present it to me, but I smiled and told him it had serious magic, and to keep it. He was appreciative. The next day, 5 February, I felt much better but was still very sore. I was keen to get out. Weather cold and clear. I had been thinking about the increasingly calamitous situation with our Indian villagers. The winter continued to take its toll. For every Indian who recovered or showed signs of recovering, five died, with barely fifteen left standing. It was not possible for this wonderful community, people who had embraced us and become our friends, to survive by itself.

I found David and Doc sitting on a log outside their hut, smoking pipes. They welcomed me and pulled up another log. I raised my worry with them. They said they had been talking about it. David had spent the winter learning their language while he cared for the sick. He had been able to talk to Askuwheteau about how he saw the future. He had been philosophical: What will be will be. But when pressed about the continuing deaths and their effect on the ability of the village to survive, he said that he'd already had meetings with his fellow sagamores. Once the winter was over, they planned to have a great powwow to negotiate a combining of three local tribes into one. Until then, they did not know how many would survive, nor did they know where the tribe would be located. The feeling was that they should move away from the coast. There were tribes inland that were hostile to them, but everyone was suffering from this terrible plague. They recognized that it had to be fought together—they were all Algonquin. It seemed that the same conversations were going on all along the coastal regions. Tribes were being decimated. The remnants were pulling away from the coast, avoiding contact with foreigners who'd brought this plague to them. We thought about what David had told us. I felt a sense of incredible sadness wash over me. We had come to what seemed like a utopia. Gentle, hospitable people who had welcomed us unreservedly. We were a terrible scourge that was destroying them.

I brought another matter to Doc. I had, over the past few years, been gathering a history of the voyages to New England, many of the trips organized by Sir F. Considering all the other issues with which he was dealing, how was it possible that he could spend all that time, effort, and money without achieving lasting success? Why was there not more support for him and for the vision he had for settlement in New England? Wasn't he working with Sir John Popham? Doc, with great patience, started to explain.

"Sir John Popham, at that time the Lord Chief Justice, persuaded King Charles to issue letters-patent dividing Virginia, which was bounded by the 34th and 45th latitudes, into two companies—the Northern and Southern Virginia Companies—with an overlap."

"Why was Sir John interested?" I asked.

"He saw the transfer of the destitute and criminals out of England to the new lands being opened up as a way to ease the chronic social problems in England. Prior to this point, Sir F. had worked closely with Sir John and other interested people to fund and organize voyages to prove the concept of settlements. But merchants in the West Country would only be persuaded to invest in such voyages if the king would grant them exclusive rights to exploit these new lands for commercial gain. Thus, their priorities drove the issuing of the letters-patent."

"What about the overlap?

"The overlapping land between the thirty-eighth and the forty-first latitudes was open to the company first occupying it. There was a stipulation that neither company could make a settlement within one hundred miles of any previous settlement of the other company. A first settlement in the Cape Cod area by the Northern Virginia Company would prevent the Southern Virginia Company from establishing one of their settlements within a hundred miles, which would take them almost back to the thirty-eighth latitude, around the Hudson River. Sir Ferdinando was well aware of this stipulation."

"How are the two companies managed?"

"They were to be controlled by a Royal Council for Virginia, the members of which would be the representatives of those wishing to engage directly in the settlement process. Sir F. was an original member of that Royal Council representing Northern Virginia interests. The council's membership was weighted heavily toward London-based interests in Southern Virginia. After protests and discussion, the council was changed to represent each of the two companies, separately—six members elected for each. What it did was to get the Southern Virginia supporters out of the hair of Northern Virginia, without offering practical or financial support to Sir F."

I thought for a moment, then asked, "So the 1607 Sagadahoc settlement was Sir F.'s attempt to establish ownership of Northern Virginia?"

"Actually, although supported by Sir F., it was driven by Sir John Popham. Unfortunately, Sir John died, leading the settlement to fail. It also meant that Sir F. was left to run the Northern Virginia Company, largely on his own."

It was too much to take in for someone in my state. I found exercise and fresh air the best healer. I wanted to explore the neck of land just to the south of our encampment. At low water, wearing snowshoes, I could walk over the marshland, across the ice onto the neck. It was almost an island, connected by a sandbar stretching southwest toward the mainland. The tree-covered neck was largely free of snow, blown clear by the prevailing nor'easters. Much evidence of Indian activity—large heaps of clamshells close by fire pits. It seemed it was a favored place for celebrations and feasting. To that extent it reminded me of Monhegan. There were pleasant views from the northeast tip of the neck with water or the open sea on all sides. With strong winds, the waves crashing against the rocks made a splendid if noisy sight. I found the place to be a refuge, a balm to the soul. The sickness pervading the village and the sense of foreboding and unease it gave to our settlement was dispiriting. The winter, the cold, the loneliness away from Aby all contributed to the need I had to find a place where I could set my mind to pleasant thoughts.

February seemed a very long month, with its frequent snowstorms. The constant hunt for food, with the depleted stock of fruit and vegetables, was exhausting. It would still be two months before *Rosie* returned, making the days drag by. Doc had us meet as a group to discuss how we each saw a permanent settlement could overcome the winter challenges. The general feeling, something we kept coming back to, was that it would only work if the settlement consisted of a community of families, supporting themselves and the community as a whole. Each family needed its own workable land. The wider community would have the necessary skilled artisans to enable it to be self-sustaining. The community would need carpenters, stone masons, builders, weavers, leatherworkers, blacksmiths, metal workers, farmers, and fishermen, and a church, minister, and doctor, too. Those of us married would never stay long away from our wives. Those not married missed the company of women. We weren't particularly religious, apart from Doc. Even so, we missed the comfort of religious service, with the binding of the community around the church and its minister.

An important point was raised. Back in England, land was owned by the gentry. Therefore, the community was dependent on the landowner. The people saw him as their master. A settlement, where each man (and family) owned his own land, eliminated that dependence. It would allow the community to elect its own leadership. This set of circumstances raised the question of ultimate authority. The king grants land rights. How would his authority be maintained, that far away? The question was left unanswered, but I thought back to my question to Doc about Sir F. being the sole promoter and organizer of the Northern

Virginia Company. He, presumably, was the governor, the representative of the king, over the lands granted. As yet, we had no settlements to govern, but what would happen when we did? I had read Captain Smith's account of the James-town settlements and the problems that had resulted, the near-fatal calamities that had befallen them. In those cases, the inexperienced gentry, incapable of leading, and the dregs of society, unaccustomed to discipline or working hard, had both been inadequate. Together, they were unable and unwilling to grow their own food or develop reasonable relationships with the Indians, who might have supported them in other circumstances. Pioneers were needed, with the fortitude and moral fiber to brave the first year, the first winter, and the absence of sufficient food, clothing, and habitation. They would work to grow their own food, develop mutually beneficial relations with their neighbors, and make a settlement. But how would they keep what they had striven so hard for, if late-comers poured in, overwhelming them?

Journal entry—*1 to 31 March 1617*

March brought warmer days. Snowfall lessened. It rained. The wind blew. The land cleared of snow and the ground frost melted. We were able to dig graves to bury those who had died over the winter. There were many—too many. I was amazed and touched by the stoicism of the Indians. There were few left. I felt they only stayed because we were there. Some, in fact, had slipped away. Doc organized us to build new huts. The old were too fetid to clean. We dismantled or burned them. Our Indians were amused. They kept themselves a hell of a lot cleaner than we did by washing themselves and their clothes frequently. They spent more time outside, part of nature itself. With that in mind, Doc ordered us all to strip off and swim in the freezing water. No brave men here. We jumped in screaming and jumped right out again. Soon we grown men were playing like children. It was a lesson learned. It showed the respect we had for Doc as a leader. Mind you, he was first in and last out. It became a regular event. I took to shaving occasionally as well.

One morning we were surprised by two visitors—Skicowarres and Tahanedo. They had come from their tribal homes at Sagadahoc and Pemaquid. They had been talking to other sachems and sagamores along the coast to reach some con-clusion about the terrible depredations over the winter. They had heard of our arrival and the work we had done to help the Saco Indians. David was especially pleased to meet up with them again, and they felt likewise about seeing him. They met separately with Askuwheteau. We spent an evening with them and the Saco villagers in the fort—we prepared a feast in their honor. It was sad how few villagers were left. The next day, the visitors were gone, continuing their mission south to the farther reaches of the Abenaki territory.

Before they left, I asked after Samoset. They said that he had been on a journey of his own. The name he now had was in recognition of the long and strange journeys he had had while captured by the English. He had suffered far longer than the other captives, in addition to having been a slave of the Pemaquids. Tahanedo had released him from that captivity, because of his long, bitter exile from his home. The knowledge gained of foreign lands and people made him a leader. They noted his natural grace. He was made a sagamore before he left, not only as an acknowledgment, but a status that would help him as he continued his wanderings along the coast. I asked Tahanedo if he had been aware of my captivity. He smiled. Malian is his daughter. He was the sachem to whom Samoset had spoken to save my life. Tahanedo said he was sorry for the way his young Indian warriors had treated me. He was only aware of my enforced removal when Malian had come to him, grievously upset. He had dealt with the warriors. He told Malian that it had been for the best. I was not a suitable husband for his daughter. Laughing, I agreed.

Two weeks later, we had another visitor—Samoset. He had met Tahanedo farther south, who told him of my presence. I was touched and pleased to see him. He spent two days at Saco. He confirmed that the plague had affected the whole coastline. Some villages were well on the way to being eradicated. He said that in the history of his people never had there been such a disaster. While he was pleased to see me, he saw the plague as being the result of English explorers and fishermen coming into direct contact with his people, unintended though it might have been. He assumed that his time in England had enabled him to withstand the disease, which was, perhaps, one of the two good things to have happened to him. Kindly, he said the other was the time he spent with me at Wraxall. In spite of his longing for his homeland, he had found a degree of peace there. I asked him what he was planning to do now. He said he was a traveler, and felt he was in some in-between state. He was not quite an Indian anymore, nor was he an Englishman. He had tried to banish his English experience, refused to talk or think about it. He had gone to the extent of trying to eradicate his knowledge of the English language—not totally successful, as we were able to converse. He traveled to where he wasn't known, to provide support and counsel to the people. When they no longer needed him, he moved on. He had learned the medicines and healing plants. He was always welcomed. His name went before him. His knowledge didn't cover this plague. In his travels he had learned a little about what appeared to help people fight the disease, but it wasn't much. As with the others, he was stoic in his attitude to what his gods had thrown at his people. It was not for him, he felt, to question too deeply. When he left, I felt a pang of real regret and hoped our paths would cross again. It reinforced the huge sense of guilt I had that we English had, unwittingly, destroyed an innocent people.

We had visits from fishermen who had wintered in Damariscove and Monhegan. They had had a rough winter and were grateful for provisions we had available to give them, especially meat and the dried fruit. The scurvy had been kept at bay while they had fish, but even so, they suffered from it. Doc had made juices which were kept in his cold store and gave some to them.

March closed with the promise of spring. Wind and rain continued. Our farmers had prepared the land. Spring growing season had begun. Green shoots already appearing. We all took our turn both on our plots and the villagers' land. There were too few women to cultivate the fields, and the able men were hunting and fishing. There were mouths to feed.

CHAPTER 28

Journal entry—*1 April to 3 June 1617*

We anxiously awaited the arrival of *Rosie*. We assumed it would be April, but it depended on weather conditions back home, as much as in the mid-Atlantic. Contrary winds in England's southwest approaches could hold up any departure for months. Allowing a conservative eight weeks, they would have had to leave in February. Not a good time of year for sailing. We needed to keep our hopes down and focus on completing the tasks we had ahead of us before we could leave. We had written our reports, stored away the maps and charts we had been preparing since we arrived last June. We had a large store of produce—dried, salted fish, samples of the timber available, pelts of all sorts but especially many beaver pelts which we had bartered for over the winter. We had a collection of Indian hunting, farming, and cooking implements and clothing made of skins to take back with us as an exhibition of Indian life, including a beautiful soft doeskin cloak for Aby. Our time was spent with our Indian friends, the poor remnants.

The fort was the last remaining occupied dwelling place. The outlying habitations had either been dismantled or abandoned. The burial ground was carefully marked out. It had become a sacred place. Askuwheteau, Kitchi, and Mingan had stayed, but most of their surviving people had already moved inland. The sadness, deep, almost paralyzing in its intensity, remained. The three of them, each on their own at different times, could often be found on some high ground, still and tall, eyes distant, minds on what had been. They were there for us but wished to hold on to what they'd once had. Indian warriors don't cry. They don't show pain. We wept for them.

On the nineteenth, I sighted a sail far to the northeast—a white dot. For the past two weeks, I had canoed across to "my" neck for several hours for time alone with my thoughts of Aby and home, while keeping a lookout. We had had fishing vessels visit earlier in the month. I was prepared to receive another. After an hour, I recognized the unmistakable outline of *Rosie*. I hurried back to advise the others. Two hours later, *Rosie* sailed into the bay and anchored off the mouth of the river. The long boat was manned, and the skipper was rowed across and up the river to our landing area, rowers under the command of J.B. We were all of us at the water's edge to greet them. Once convinced that we were not con-taminated or contagious, the skipper suggested Doc return with him to *Rosie* to report. It seemed that the skipper was ready for a quick turn 'round. But after six weeks at sea, his crew needed to stretch their legs, clean ship, refill water casks, and take on whatever edibles remaining from our winter storage and the bar-tered goods we had acquired from our Indian friends. We had much to provide and much to load. Back with the crew of *Rosie*, it was like coming home—the simple pleasures of meeting up with old friends like J.B. and Obi, hearing about their adventures as well as talking about ours. On our trip back to England we would have plenty of time for all that.

The day came for our departure: 26 April. Askuwheteau brought me a large bundle: the bearskin with my knife. I asked him if he would like to keep them both as a good memory of our visit. He smiled and bowed his head. He would be honored to do so. We parted with sorrow and firm handshakes from our three Indian friends. We wished them well. *Rosie* had been brought into the river to aid the loading. As we warped our way out of the river, we saw the three of them standing, like statues, watching. What were they thinking? On the quarterdeck, looking over the stern rail, I saw them still. I raised an arm. One of them, Kitchi, raised his. They turned and were gone.

David and I were in some state of agitation and impatience on our trip back to Plymouth. We wanted to go home: me to my wife, and David to his family. Did he have a son or a daughter? Was Amyse well? How was the childbirth? I wondered again how Aby felt about having a child. I questioned why I was wondering, too. I chose not to pursue that thought, preferring to wait for Aby. I hoped I'd be back for her birthday. We talked much during the voyage about our impressions. What we had learned, what it meant to us, how it might shape our future. During those conversations, it was clear that David had become entranced by New England. The tragedy we had lived through, if anything, had made him love the people and the country even more. He really couldn't wait to return there with his family.

England appeared on the horizon five weeks out of Saco. We are alongside in the Pool, two bells first dog watch, Tuesday, 3 June. It is very good to be home.

I am completing this entry as we work our way into port, having gathered my possessions, shaved, washed, and clothed myself in clean apparel, ready to disembark. I am ready to go to my wife and wish her happy birthday.

Journal entry—*Tuesday, June 3, 1617*

I returned to Pins Lane, anxious, excited like a schoolboy, a huge knot of anticipation in my stomach. Climbing the steps to the front door, I stopped as I heard the soft singing from within. A sad song, but beautiful. I hesitated to enter and knocked gently. The singing died away, light footsteps came to the door. It opened. Aby. She had a sweet smile on her lips—me with a huge foolish grin all over mine. She slowly raised her hand. We touched fingers and came together, hands clasped at each other's breast. Inside, door closed, we clung to each other, eyes shut, still not a word spoken between us. We stepped back and looked at each other. I've grown up as well as out. I am now about five foot seven inches tall, and Aby can rest her head comfortably on my shoulder. I am broader, large-chested but not barrel-shaped like my father. Aby looks taller also, with long legs and slim hips. My own face is now scarred and lined, darkened by the sun and wind. Her face, slightly tanned, a lovely oval, her cheekbones less pronounced. Her brown eyes are deep and wide. I pulled the cap off her head. Her long, golden brown hair fell over her shoulders, framing her beautiful face. Then she led me to our bedroom and gently started undressing me. As the bear damage revealed itself, Aby stopped. She touched each furrow, now healed, thanks to Doc's sewing and the Indian medicine, just five thin purple lines. She looked up at me, shaking her head.

"Isaac Stanfield. You must stop coming home with more and more bits missing or damaged. Soon there will be nothing left of you."

For a long time we lay facing each other, gazing deep, deep into each other's souls, ridding the distance, the time that had separated us, the tips of our fingers gently exploring. Much later, Aby arose, dressed, and went to the kitchen to prepare a late meal, leaving me asleep. I got up to join her, and in front of the fire Aby had me tell her in much detail all that had happened. She wept at the desperate plight of the Indians. She shed tears to think of the bear alone, bleeding to death. She laughed, sighed, exclaimed, and tut-tutted at all the right moments. I remembered finally that today was Aby's birthday. I went to my baggage and brought out the doeskin cloak, presented it to her with a hug and a happy birthday greeting. She loved the cloak and wore it for the rest of the evening. Aby told me all that she had been doing to keep herself busy.

First, Amyse had had a difficult but successful childbirth in the middle of last October. They now have a little girl, called Priscilla. Lady Ann had given Aby plenty of free time to help Amyse through Priscilla's birth. Aby and Amyse had become like sisters. I mentioned that David appeared totally captivated by New England. I was sure he would want to return there with his family as soon as possible. She gazed at me.

"What about, you, my love? Where are your heart and head?"

"I'm sure, one day, I will want to return, but only with you by my side. As long as Sir F. continues to send men under contract, I don't believe any settlement will survive, let alone prosper. David agrees with me, but he is much more willing to give it a go on any basis."

Aby described her year with me away. It had been an extraordinary time for her, with Amyse's childbirth and helping with baby Priscilla on the one hand, and the hard work and a busy social life on the other. Lady Ann had become like a loving aunt to Aby, and it seemed as though she'd been adopted by the Gorges. Being a part of their household, her wardrobe was now filled with the finest costumes and clothing in keeping with her position. She was engaged with the whole experience and all that she was learning and doing. I felt a brief worry but dismissed it as Aby told me my absence had been a huge shadow hanging over everything she did. It was clear to me, as it had always been to Aby, that I should never leave her for such an extended period again. We talked about how she felt about children. She loved them but saw how totally absorbing they were. We agreed that, while we hadn't been too careful about avoiding pregnancy, it would be better to wait until we were a little older and more settled. But God would ultimately determine that event. In the back of my mind, I wondered if her mother dying in childbirth had anything to do with her feelings.

Journal entry—*4 to 9 June 1617*

A message was delivered early the following morning, Wednesday, 4 June, requesting my presence at Sir F.'s office at half past eight a.m. Doc and David Thomson were present. While we still had to complete our detailed reports, much had been written on the voyage back which had been delivered to Sir F. the evening before. He had read them overnight. He was anxious to question us on their content. He wanted to learn directly from us what we had learned from our trip. Much of what we covered I had copied from what I had written in my journal to provide a written report for Sir F. But we spent some time discussing the plague that had decimated the Indians. Sir F. asked whether it could have been smallpox. Doc said no, he was experienced with that disease, and none of the Indians he treated had the symptoms. He was certain it was a respiratory affliction. Sir F. had heard from returning fishermen that there would soon be few Indians living along the coastline from Penobscot to Cape Cod, possibly as far as Capawak. Sir F., somewhat unfeelingly, stated that while it was a disaster for the Indians, it left the way clear for settlements to be established without the fear of Indian hostility.

I agreed with the fact but suggested that to the Indians it would look like yet another devastating affliction visited on them by the hated English, since there had not been a similar plague among the Indians in Acadia and Canada. We would need to do much, with great patience and understanding, to correct the reputation we now had. It provided us with an opportunity to reach out to the remaining coastal tribes, as well as to those apparently less affected inland. I referred to Champlain's efforts to build good long-term relations. How important they were to establishing secure settlements. David, who'd immersed himself in the culture and language of the Algonquin, spoke movingly of the need to return as soon as possible, both to help the Indians and, more importantly, to establish a permanent settlement. He said we had to demonstrate to the Indians by our constant presence that we were a force for good and advantageous to them. The meeting lasted several hours, with each of us given the opportunity to describe our impressions, feelings, and concerns about the expedition.

At the end of the meeting, I stayed behind. I asked Sir F. if it was possible for Aby and me to return to Dorchester. We would be away about two weeks. Sir F. said that Lady Ann would be unhappy to lose Aby, but as July would be a busy month for her, he suggested we plan to leave as soon as possible in order to return before the end of June. We agreed to be back on Monday, 23 June. I sent a note to Will that we hoped to be in Dorchester for a week by Monday, 9 June. I asked him to please reserve us a room at the Sun. That evening, we went over to the Minerva. Annie gave us each a big hug. She and Aby had been in frequent contact, if for no other reason than to exercise Maddie and Tess. In fact, they'd become good friends. Annie's social life was different from that which Aby experienced with Lady Ann. I wondered how Aby felt about that. I was cautious about asking.

We left Plymouth on horseback, saddlebags full, early Saturday morning, June 7. It was a lovely day, with blue sky and a light breeze, cool with the promise of warmth as the sun rose. Every shade of green sparkled from the overnight dew. We followed the same paths we had ridden before. We had allowed two nights on the journey and chose our inns well, arriving in

Dorchester in the late afternoon on Monday. The Sun welcomed us in the shape of Mr. Jeremiah Gosling.

"Good afternoon, Mr. Gosling."

"Good afternoon to you both, Mr. and Mrs. Stanfield. Now if I may be so bold, I have known Abigail here since she was a wee one in the arms of her father. I would take it as a privilege, indeed an honor, to have you use my first name and, at that same time, counting you as my friends, allow me to use yours."

"Why, Jeremiah, I would be content on both counts, as I'm sure would Aby."

Jeremiah beamed. He responded, "Well now, Isaac, Abigail, thrice welcome. Please consider the Sun to be your home away from home. We will always have a room available for you. Come, some refreshment to quench your thirst and food to settle your stomachs."

With that we entered the inn. Aby slipped away to change, and I accompanied our most genial host to the barroom. There was a note waiting for us from Will, who had invited us back to his parents' house for supper. Aby sent a note to him, thanking him and saying we would be pleased to attend at seven o'clock that evening. We washed, dressed, and walked to the Whiteways' house by way of the west gate. Colliton Row is now deemed unsafe for women to walk down in the evening, which is a sad reflection on the rising number of destitute and desperate people gravitating to Dorchester from the countryside. We were fondly greeted by the whole Whiteway family. It was a lively evening. Reverend John White and his wife had been invited.

P. did not push me too hard for information. Early in the evening, we agreed to meet the following morning in his study for a detailed discussion on New England. Everyone paid critical attention as I described the general situation there. I noticed that P.'s reaction to hearing the plight of the Indians was far more thoughtful than the others. For the most part they had no comprehension of the Indians' human condition, since to most people, they were almost exotics. Their reaction was not surprising, as they had had no contact with any Indian. They had heard only the occasional lurid stories. But, even making those allowances, I was disturbed and wondered what the consequences of such seeming indifference might have on future settlements. P. said that he had been in regular touch with the Separatist community that had fled to Leiden in Holland in 1607 to avoid persecution in England. It appeared that trouble was brewing. The community was generally unhappy with their condition, even though they had been left to worship as they desired. One of their leaders, William Brewster, had become a printer in Leiden. He had started to print and distribute articles and books which were considered highly critical of the Church in England—therefore, by association, critical of His Majesty, King James.

Pressure was being brought to bear. P. felt it was only a question of time before something happened. He was sure they would have to leave Leiden—but whither? I looked forward to my meeting the next day with P. The conversation at the table alluded to factions in Dorchester, which seemed to have become more delineated. The evening ended with humor and good fellowship. We were both pleased to have been welcomed back with such affection.

Journal entry—*10 to 22 June 1617*

Next day, I had arranged to meet with P. Aby had plans to meet up with a number of old friends. Messages had been sent, enthusiastic replies received. We went our separate ways with a kiss.

P. welcomed me into his study. Throughout the next hour, I recounted in detail my sojourn in Saco. He asked me penetrating questions about it, about what I'd learned and what I thought about future settlements. He said that the news from Leiden was not good. In addition to Mr. Brewster's activities, it seemed the community there had become isolated from the wider Dutch community within which they lived. With that isolation came a more constrained view of their faith. They had become intolerant of the laxer views of their Dutch neighbors with respect to adherence to Calvinist dogma. They feared their children were being influenced in ungodly ways. Those children were becoming more Dutch than English. They lived in a cramped, unhealthy, and urban setting. They worked in foul factories making woolen garments. They longed for the rural life they had left behind in England, with countryside, fresh air, farming. According to P., they'd decided to leave Leiden. Brewster and the Reverend John Robinson, the father of the Leiden community, had put out inquiries to the London Company regarding immigration to Southern Virginia. New England was a possibility too, but, it seemed, Southern Virginia was preferred.

I asked P. about what I'd sensed at last night's dinner. The schism that has begun to make itself evident in the affairs of Dorchester. P. was thoughtful. He said that when he came to Dorchester in 1607, he had been concerned about the level of turpitude here. He had worked hard to improve the morality of its citizens. The great fire of 1613 could have been sent from heaven. P. used it as a godly sign to further that improvement. He said he was a faithful and practicing member of the Church of England. However, he saw laxness in the "Elizabethan" approach to worship. As a result, he had become moderately Puritan in outlook, as he sought, within his own parish, to purify his beloved Church. People of similar outlook had been attracted to come to Dorchester around the time of P.'s appointment to Trinity, the Bushrode and Whiteway families being just two examples. This development had resulted in a reaction from the longer-standing families who were comfortable in their religious and social mores, a faction that viewed P. as the instigator of the change of which they greatly disapproved. P. believes that there is a strong movement away from the laxness of old. He believes that the inherent conflict between Calvinism and Catholicism has continued with the Church of England. P. tried explaining it to me, but I'm not a theologian. Calvinism upholds a belief called predestination, which states that God's grace is preordained. Therefore, God has already determined who will be saved. I was shocked.

"But surely, sir, the Lord Jesus says in the Gospels that anyone who believes in him will be saved."

"Isaac, God has already ensured that only the preordained really believe."

"So, assuming I have not been preordained, something I won't know till I die, I can live a pure, godly life, even become a monk or a minister, devoting myself to God, but it will do me no good?"

"God knows you wouldn't do that if you haven't been preordained."

"Conversely, if I have been preordained, but live a dissolute life, you are saying that God would prevent me from leading that dissolute life?"

"Isaac, your questions are too simplistic."

"Sir, I worry that my life is not mine to live as I want. You say I don't have freedom of choice, and that ultimately, everything is preordained. You make it sound like we are puppets."

This exchange was perhaps the only time when I had a serious disagreement or lack of understanding with P.

He held his hands up, saying, "We should come back to this another time. But, Isaac, you should think about what we have been talking about. Just remember, God is omniscient. Surely, it is not beyond our comprehension, therefore, to think that he knows all there is to know about us, including our ultimate salvation or damnation."

Mrs. White had made lunch for us, which we ate in good fellowship. Afterward I left to find Will, who was at home buried in books. He has a voracious appetite for learning. His study is expanding. He too is growing up. His trip to France had greatly expanded his outlook. He said for the first time he could feel what he had learned through study, touching the walls of ancient Paris, walking the streets made famous in history books, seeing the tombs of kings and princes of centuries past. "Thrilling," he proclaimed.

I gave him the latest entries to my journal. He said he was so taken with it that he's planning to start his own diary. It would not be a personal journal like mine but a compendium of the remarkable events that occurred locally or distantly. He would send me a copy from time to time. He said that he didn't think it would be about him. His life was much too sedentary. He's much more interested in recording what's going on around him. For example, he said his hero Will Shakespeare had died in April of last year. He'd only heard about it some months later. Something he had recorded and brooded over. We talked about marriage and women. Poor Will, he finds them frightening, leaving him tongue-tied. He was brought up in the knowledge that procreation was a necessary duty and, therefore, marriage a requirement, but he has difficulty in imagining such a happy state. He's intrigued by the descriptions of intimacy in my entries but considers my behavior to be part of my essentially country stock.

"Will, may you be forgiven. Are you calling me base, of animal instinct, following the example of the animal kingdom?"

"No, no. I meant you are less inhibited as a man of the country. You are a man of action."

"Will. Fear not. It is inevitable that you will become attracted to one, maybe more, ladies, sooner rather than later. I wager that you will be married, probably by the time you are twenty."

Will blushed. He admitted that he had started noticing a young lady but was too shy to do anything about it. He wouldn't divulge who it was. We talked about my conversation with P. I asked him what he, Will, saw that was different in Dorchester. He felt, in his bones, that Dorchester was going through a process of change that was reflected throughout England. Being a student of history, he saw the possibilities for serious unrest. The changes in religious attitude that P. had discussed had to be put into context. There was the gap in living standards between rich and poor that created destructive envy; political dissention; abject poverty; the feudal system still manifest, with people toiling for their masters with no chance of advancement. According to Will, the reason P. was interested in my experiences in New England was that he saw the crushing pressure of economic, political, and religious oppression being mitigated by immigration to new and bountiful lands, where the immigrants could establish their own political and religious structures, build their own communities, and establish and develop their own farmland.

Will suddenly exclaimed that he had entirely forgotten to pass on to me something he'd found out ages ago. Back in September last year, he had received a note from Mr. Tatler.

"Who?"

"Mr. Tatler owns the pawn shop where you bought back your wedding ring. He asked me to come to his shop, at my convenience, which I did. Remember, you told him to contact me if he had anything to report about the man who had sold him your ring? Apparently, the man came into his shop with something else to sell. Mr. Tatler, with great presence of mind, recognized the man and told him the present item needed careful evaluation, which required his partner's attention, due back shortly. Would he be prepared to leave the item and return in perhaps two hours? The man was agreeable. Mr. Tatler gave him a receipt for the item, which required, for Mr. Tatler's records, the name and address of the gentleman. Two hours later the man came back and received payment for the item. Mr. Tatler gave me the man's name and address. I forgot to give it to you. Let me get it now."

I had forgotten about that incident. It seemed a long time ago. Will came back with a piece of paper. The name was Mr. Thurrock, and the given address was near Duntish. Will had ridden to Duntish to look for a likely farm or other habitation, but no trace of Mr. Thurrock. He went to Cerne Abbas and asked for directions to Mr. Thurrock's farm. The people he asked did not know that name. I thanked Will. Intrigued, I decided that Aby and I would go for a ride on the morrow. Will was eager to accompany us.

Next morning, Wednesday, 11 June, the three of us rode north. Enjoying a warm, gentle breeze, we followed the route I would have taken from the Sun, a path I had ridden several times before. We rode on into Cerne Abbas. Will said he had stopped at the local inns. I thought it more likely that Mr. Thurrock would frequent a shop for provisions or even the local church. So, hitching our mounts, we walked down the main road in Cerne Abbas, looking for likely shops. Aby had a positive response to her inquiry about Mrs. Thurrock at one. She comes to town once a week, driven by her husband in a cart. They are quite old and not very nimble. In fact, they have not been regular this year. Last time she was seen was about three weeks ago. The shopkeeper hoped they were all right.

"Where do they live? Perhaps we should go to see if they are in trouble."

"They have a small farm north of Church Hill. Take the road to Alton Pancras. Church Hill is a ridge a short distance beyond to the northeast. Follow the track round the ridge to the west. The farm lies just beyond."

Thanking the shopkeeper, we rode as directed. We rounded Church Hill and continued to follow the track, coming to a path leading through a field toward some trees, with signs of habitation. We dismounted and walked up the path, leading the horses into a small farmyard with some scrawny chickens pecking at the ground. An inquisitive, bedraggled, unkempt horse looked out at us from a stable door. The yard was untidy, badly cared for, and the water trough foul. The low thatched cottage to the side looked empty. Aby started, saying she saw movement. I went to the door and knocked. I heard slow, tentative movement. A querulous, old woman's voice asked what we wanted.

"Mrs. Thurrock. We have come from Cerne Abbas. People are worried about you. You have not been seen for several weeks. Are you all right?"

The door opened, and a little old lady peered out from behind it. She saw Aby and came out. She wagered a woman being present among our party meant less risk.

"It's Mr. Thurrock. He fell and damaged his leg. He can't move. I am too old to manage the horse and cart."

I asked whether I might be permitted to enter to see her husband. She stepped aside, moving toward Aby seeking reassurance. Aby put her arm round Mrs. Thurrock's painfully thin shoulders, and the old lady almost collapsed with relief at the promise of help. It looked like she had not eaten much for a while. I went in passing directly into their one combined living room and kitchen. It was a small version of our Pins Lane house. It appeared to be their bedroom as well. Mr. Thurrock was lying on the bed. He glared at me as I came in, demanding to know what the hell I was doing trespassing on his property. I made soothing noises and asked to see his wounded leg. He pulled the blanket away, uncovering a mess. He had broken the lower part of his right leg. A crude splint had been applied but seemed not to be effective. The bandages were old, not really covering the wound, which was encrusted with dried blood and flies. It looked badly infected. I asked him if he would allow my wife to come in to clean the wound. He grunted in the affirmative. I went to the door, sent Mrs. Thurrock for a pan of heated water, and told Aby what the situation was. She immediately came into the room. With the hot water, Aby gently removed the bandage and splint, then attempted to clean the wound. As gentle as she was, the pain must still have been excruciating. Mr. Thurrock was a tough old bird. He just grunted occasionally. I left Aby to it, suggesting to Mrs. Thurrock that we go out to have a chat. I had no memory of the Thurrocks or the farm.

There was a bench by the front door, where we sat in the sun. I asked how long ago the accident had happened. Slowly she started talking and the dam burst—a torrent of words and tears came out. It seemed they were just about on their last legs. The owner of the farm wanted them out. They had not been able to pay the rent for months. They were too old to work the land and had no children close by to look after them.

"Do you have any family?"

"Yes, but they are a long way from here. We don't write. We don't know how. My son and his wife farm in Herefordshire, near the Welsh border."

"Give me their address. I will see that they find out about your condition. Your husband needs proper attention on his leg. We need to get him to a doctor."

"I don't think it possible to move him. He is in too much pain," Mrs. Thurrock whispered, tearful again.

"Do you know anyone locally who has the medical knowledge and would come here?"

"Yes, there is a horse doctor that lives the other side of Cerne Abbas."

Better than nothing, I thought. She gave me his name. A little while later Aby came out, looking pale.

"He's in a bad way. We need to get him help. He might lose his leg. I have cleaned the wound, bandaged, and adjusted the splint. He is an incredibly tough old man. I would have been screaming."

"Well done, my love. You did well."

I asked Mrs. Thurrock what essential supplies she needed which we would fetch for her. By now she thought we were administering angels. She identified her immediate needs, which Will noted down. I asked her whether she had any friends locally. She shook her head, but she said the local rector's wife was kind. Mrs. Thurrock had helped her with the church flowers on occasion. We left having told her that we or someone would be back shortly. We rode back to Cerne Abbas, Will to find the rector's wife, Aby to buy supplies, me to find the horse doctor. An hour later, we met at the church. The rector's wife was on her way to the Thurrocks. I had found the horse doctor, and he promised that he would make a call there later in the afternoon. He had known the couple for years. They'd never been more than a coat of whitewash above the poverty line, but they were stubborn and proud. Aby had baskets full of supplies. Dividing the baskets between us, we rode back to the Thurrocks.

The rector's wife was there—an earnest woman, efficient, quick to take charge. She welcomed the supplies and had us take them into the kitchen and living room. It was already a much tidier, cleaner place. Mr. Thurrock had been given some strong broth the rector's wife had brought with her. He was sitting up and looked almost human. His wife looked better, too, less alone. Aby took her outside for a chat. With the help of the rector's wife, we stored the supplies we had brought. I asked her whether she knew of the distant son. She did not. The Thurrocks were private. Mrs. Thurrock helped with the flowers in the church, but they were not seen much. Later, I told Mrs. Thurrock I would send a message to their son, as soon as I got back to Dorchester. She gave me the name of the Herefordshire town where he lived, Ross-on-Wye. With the Thurrocks about to be evicted, the son needed to fetch his parents as soon as Mr. Thurrock could be moved.

Meantime, Aby, who, later, gave me a full account of her conversation with Mrs. Thurrock, sitting with an arm 'round Mrs. Thurrock's shoulders, had started to chat with her. How had they coped? A long story that stretched back several years about the help they occasionally had. Then, quietly, Aby asked about Christmas times. What did they do? Last Christmas wasn't too bad. They had visited their son the Christmas before, 1615. They had a guest the Christmas before that.

"A guest?"

"Someone we found on the road."

"That sounds intriguing."

With little prompting, the story came out. They had found this young man, lying on the road, with a terrible wound on the side of his head. He had been lying there for some time because there was a thin cover of snow on him. Mr. Thurrock thought he was dead or dying. But she said they couldn't leave him. They loaded the man onto their cart and in the gathering darkness drove home. The man remained unconscious for several days. Mrs. Thurrock had undressed him, cleaned him with warm water, and put him to bed, with a bandage round his head. When he woke up, he couldn't speak. He seemed confused at first. After several more days, he regained his voice. By this time the farm was snowed in. They were closed off from the world. By Christmas he had recovered enough to get around but had no memory of anything. He was a willing helper. Once recovered, he was strong. For the next month or two, he worked around the farm, doing whatever was asked of him.

Aby asked, "Was there no indication on him of who he might be and where he had come from? What sort of clothes was he wearing? Was he rich or poor? Had you thought how he came to be there? This all sounds most mysterious."

Aby's interest, seemingly without any ulterior motive, kept the flow going. Mr. Thurrock had decided that the man must have been knocked from his horse by a low-hanging branch. There was a big one over the path close to where they'd found him. He was well dressed, was probably gentry, but no one came looking. No one seemed interested. Perhaps, Aby suggested, the weather didn't permit it.

"What happened to the clothes?"

"We have them still. They were too fine to be worn while working round the farm. We gave him some of ours."

"Why didn't he take them when he left?"

"Well, this is the most mysterious part of it all. Toward the end of February, the man was becoming agitated. He kept saying he had to be somewhere on a specific date. It was all he could remember. We put it down to his head wound and didn't think much of it. Around the beginning of March, he disappeared. The road was open. We went looking for him, but not a sign."

"How extraordinary."

"I have often thought of him. I became fond of him, almost like another son. Mr. Thurrock treated him roughly, but the man—as he became more familiar, we saw he was more of a boy than a man—didn't seem to mind. I wondered what happened to him. I worried that he had eventually been found dead in a ditch somewhere."

"How would you recognize him, if you saw him again?"

"He had the most wonderful smile."

At that moment I came back out. I approached them both. Aby stood and came up to me.

"Dearest, I want you to go over to Mrs. Thurrock, bend down, and give her your best smile."

Puzzled, I complied. Mrs. Thurrock looked up at me, stared into my eyes. Hers slowly opened wide. She reached up to my face and stroked my cheek.

"It's you!" she said.

She began to cry, overcome to recognize me. While not fully knowing what was going on, I reached down and gave her a long hug. She demanded to know what had happened to me. I gave her a summary. I looked at Aby, confused. She quickly told me what Mrs. Thurrock had told her. I turned back to Mrs. Thurrock, still not recognizing her. She asked why I had appeared not to know her when we came that morning. She was assuming now that we had come back especially to see her. I said that I still had no memory of the time I was there. It had been a strange coincidence that we had come to Cerne Abbas and heard that she and her husband were in trouble. I thanked her for saving my life. She said, in turn, she couldn't thank us enough for coming to help her and her husband. She felt we had saved their lives, too. I reassured her that we would make sure that her son in Hereford would come to take them back home with him.

Until he did so, we would arrange for someone to come out to help them. Most importantly Mr. Thurrock's leg needed to be mended. The horse doctor would be arriving shortly. The rector's wife, much taken with the reunion, said that she would wait for him. I gave her money to pay the doctor and to cover the cost of someone to come regularly to help them. Mrs. Thurrock came out with a bundle of clothes I recognized. I thanked her and put them in my saddlebag.

I went in to see Mr. Thurrock. His wife had told him I was the prodigal returned. He acknowledged me, gruffly, thanking me for our help. He was clearly embarrassed. I assumed it was because of the ring he had stolen. I made no mention of it. I had retrieved it, the money had helped him, and it had brought us here, resolving a mystery. I shook his hand and went out, giving Mrs. Thurrock another hug before we left. Back in Dorchester, I sent a message to Herefordshire, with no idea how long it would take to reach the son and for the son to get to his parents. Will promised that he would ride to check on them over the next few weeks. He would let me know what happened.

The rest of our stay in Dorchester flew by. We walked through the newly built town. Work was still in progress but everything seemed to be bustling, at least on the surface. Friends entertained us to dinner or we hosted our own dinners at the Sun, most evenings. We had both reconnected with all our old friends. Mr. Baker rode down from Devizes to see us. We exchanged news on what we had all been doing. Aby said little but had missed him terribly. Afterward, she spent some time alone with him. They agreed that they would arrange to get together on a regular basis either in Plymouth or in Devizes.

We rode back to Plymouth leaving Dorchester Thursday, 19 June, a day that was windy with heavy rain. We traveled in the lee of high ground and through sheltering woods as much as possible. We frequently interrupted our journey to seek dry shelter in accommodating inns. We were on the road four days, arriving home on the afternoon of Sunday, 22 June. After seeing to Maddie and Tess at the Minerva stables, we had a chat over a hot drink in the bar with Annie. There really is something heartwarming about being greeted with boundless affection and a huge, welcoming smile. Annie does it every time and it is impossible not to respond in like manner. We walked home to Pins Lane. I built a roaring fire. We filled pans with water to heat for our bath. Aby had found the tub on one of her shopping expeditions. It was a large metal trough with a high back. One person could sit in it with legs dangling over the side. Somehow, Aby and I were able to share it. Sometime later, clean, deeply content, in fresh dry clothes, we returned to the Minerva for a meal and back home to bed, ready to report for work the following morning.

CHAPTER 29

Journal entry—*23 June to 1 August 1617*

At the regular meeting in Sir F.'s office, first thing Monday morning, David Tremaine was there. He had been absent two weeks earlier. It was good to see him. He had just returned from Ireland on a secret mission for Sir F., involving Sir Walter Raleigh, Sir F.'s cousin. According to Sir F., Sir Walter had many enemies in Court, his brilliant successes matched by his errors and lack of diplomatic skills. King James was not well disposed toward him. Sir F. felt protection was needed to the extent he was capable of giving it. Nothing was said about the secret mission. Before his Irish trip, Sir F. had sent David to Gravesend to meet with Captain Samuel Argall, who was about to set sail for Southern Virginia. Sir F. was concerned about Argall. He had shown interest in New England, seemingly representing the interests of Southern Virginia. He had already made himself useful a few years back in ridding New England of French presence, something which worried Sir F. as to Southern Virginia's intentions. David reported back that Argall had told him that the Southern Virginians had no interest in New England, other than to fish for their own consumption.

A report was given on the current situation with piracy and the threat to England's West Country. Sir F. was worried enough that in April he had written to London, yet again, seeking help. He had met with the mayor of Plymouth, from which a meeting was organized in Exeter with West Country ship owners to establish cooperation with the ship owners in London. The intent was to extinguish this threat of piracy at sea, which had deprived England of three hundred ships, their crew, and cargo. Actions were planned, but the key agreement was for information to be passed back to Sir F.'s office on pirate activity. This strategy greatly increased the intelligence gathering that Sir F.'s office had put in place over three years ago.

I was asked detailed questions on what I called my Saco adventure, which I answered from my experience. Was it possible to survive without Indian help in winter? With experience, yes. How much of a menace were the bears? Manageable. If the Indian population was decimated, how would such wild animals be kept in check? Settlers would learn to deal with them. How practical were snowshoes? Very. How viable were the Indian huts for long-term habitation? Settlers would want to build permanent housing of the type and design they were used to. Wood is available in abundance. What were the best modes of river transport for the English? Shallop. Could we make the Indian canoe without Indian help? Yes. Sir F., having been advised that English settlements would only survive with Indian help, was concerned about the probable absence of that help in the future.

I said that we had learned a great deal about every aspect of Indian life. We had learned how and what they grew, how the food was stored over the winter, how they fished and hunted for game. We learned how they defended themselves from hostile enemies. Added to that, the Indian was wary of our guns. They wanted to have us as friends, not enemies. By our attempted care of the sick in Saco, we had shown that we could be good, useful, and loyal friends. I added that we were beginning to understand the tribal system in America, as divided into large groups or nations, such as the Algonquin. The Algonquin had numerous different tribes, including the Abenaki, Wabanaki, Wampanoag, and Mohegans. They shared a language with regional differences. They fought among themselves. Those tribes were further separated into villages or nomadic bands, each with their own differences. I said that reading Champlain's accounts of his interaction with the Indians in New France indicated that the English would need to develop a keen insight into tribal politics and treat all groups with diplomacy. The final item of interest was the news that Tisquantum, whom I had left with Mr. Slaney in London at the end of 1615, had stayed in London until recently. While I had been in Saco, Sir F. had met Tisquantum and was most impressed with him. I wondered when we would meet next. He was now in Newfoundland.

My new duties were to act as Sir F.'s eyes and ears among the fishing vessels that Sir F. was chartering to rebuild his fortunes. It meant I was spending a lot of time meeting with ships' masters, assessing their capabilities and knowledge of New England waters. I worried that my little practical knowledge might be a dangerous basis for any judgment, but I enjoyed reasonable interaction with the people I met. My experiences intrigued them. My history was known enough for them to ask me my opinion, as often as not. Sir F. invited me to become an investor in his commercial ventures. I discussed this idea with Aby, cautious but excited. A successful investment would help us accumulate financial resources. If we lost that investment, we would be not substantially worse off than before. Being an investor would raise our status in the community. It could, therefore, give us entree into the merchant community in Plymouth. We were already on the fringes with our working relationships and friendships with the Giradeaus, Bushrodes, and the Gorges. We could, eventually, have our own trading business, being employers rather than employees. So, after this discussion with Aby and with her agreement, I let Sir F. know I would be pleased to make a £100 investment. He was gratified. We completed the paperwork to make me a junior partner in the enterprise.

Aby went back to work organizing Lady Ann's social and domestic life, leaving me at the end of June to accompany Lady Ann for a week in Clerkenwell before the summer heat made the smells of London unbearable. That trip was followed by an extended tour of southern England to stay with Lady Ann's family and friends. Aby was due back in Plymouth sometime in August. I had mixed feelings. The Aby of my youth was changing. So now it was I who had to stay at home. In Aby's absence, I did some research on acquiring a larger home. I checked with M. Giradeau and others of my contacts who were house owners. He said he would put out feelers. I sought out people who might act as sellers' representatives. I had no idea how one went about the process of renting, leasing, or buying a house. Sir F. gave me the name of a lawyer who might help. It all seemed risky and complicated. I decided to wait for Aby.

After my encounter with the highwayman Jack Melrose back in '14, and his admonishment that I needed to improve my skills, I had promised myself I would find a suitable fencing master in Plymouth. I had met with one or two, but they hadn't been adequate. Being away frequently, and then injured, I had not yet satisfied my promise. Now, I was determined. David Tremaine suggested Stephen Rockwell and introduced us. Stephen had been a student of George Silver, the fencing master supreme in London, and had spent time in Italy learning the Italian style. We immediately established a good relationship. I preferred to use my sword, a military version of the rapier. For instruction, Stephen had me use the standard rapier, which he called an epee. It had a thinner blade, lighter than mine. He taught me the Italian style, more graceful, with different footwork than the English style. We met daily through July. Much of the existing technique I had to unlearn before I could rebuild on a much sounder basis. After two weeks of intensive effort, I felt I had at least returned to my previous proficiency. Now came the hard part. Stephen gave me exercises to strengthen my legs and arms. My left side was still weak, which was not of immediate concern, but Stephen said my whole body had to be in harmony and supple. We also worked on my mind, since fencing requires a complete mental focus. Through exercises for improving concentration, my mind developed so I could control action and reaction without my ponderous thought and decision processes getting in the way. I both worked with Stephen and practiced his drills and exercises on my own. By the end of July, after just a month, I felt more alert and more fit.

No matter how well I fenced, however, Stephen Rockwell was always better. If I got too cocky, a simple flick of his wrist and my sword would be wrenched from my grasp and sent in a whirling, whistling arc to clatter to the ground some distance away. He taught me many of his tricks and skills, but I could never catch him. He said I needed to practice my skills every day for hours at a time. Maybe in a few years' time, he might recognize me as a swordsman.

I spent time with David Tremaine whenever he was in town. We occasionally fenced together, but he felt clumsy with a rapier, much preferring a cutlass. I taught him the rapier while he taught me the cutlass. Different weapons, using very different muscles. We would spend evenings at the Minerva. Annie was always pleased to see us. She looked after us well. I wondered to David at one point why Annie, attractive, engaging, and accomplished, was not married with bouncing babies to take care of. She had occasionally helped Amyse with her baby and clearly adored doing so. David shook his head and changed the subject.

On 1 August, Friday, I received a note via Captain Turner from Sir F., who was at Avebury Manor in Wiltshire. Sir F. was awaiting dispatches. As soon as they arrived at his office in Plymouth, I would be told by Captain Turner to deliver them to him at Avebury. Directions would be provided to me. Sir F. said that Lady Ann and her staff were there. They would be extending their time away from Plymouth by several weeks. I was surprised to find no note from Aby enclosed, as I usually did.

Journal entry—*2 to 12 August 1617*

It was the following Thursday, 7 August, that Captain Turner came to the house with the dispatches and directions for their delivery. By nine o'clock in the morning, I was on Maddie heading north. My mind was full of doubts. I was not used to being left at home. Aby had become accomplished at it. I still had to learn. Why hadn't Aby written? Her last note had been two weeks ago. I had responded. Our promises of regular correspondence had not materialized, by either of us to be honest. Was she becoming used to the social life of which she was now so much a part? Were we living a lifestyle that had consequences beyond our intentions? With all these thoughts running through my mind, I was barely aware of my journey. I stayed at a coaching inn, outside a village, the name of which I don't remember, near Yeovil. It had been a long ride. Next morning we set off early on a sticky day that promised to be hot, heading for Marlborough, and arrived, tired, at Avebury Manor late afternoon on Friday. As I rode up the long driveway toward the manor's front door, I arrived at the same time as two other horsemen. I swung down from Maddie and, to my surprise, I was hailed by one of the horsemen, dismounting.

"You! Take my horse."

I looked at the man, startled. My appearance was not that of gentry, but nor did I look like a groom. I glanced at the other horseman. It was Robert Gorges, behind his rude companion. He recognized me, smiled, and shrugged his shoulders. Not wishing to cause a scene, I walked over, leading Maddie, and took the bridle of the man's horse. At that moment, some ladies came out of the front door, including Aby. She was a vision.

Before I could say anything, Aby called out: "Richard. We've been waiting for you. You have taken an age. Come, we must prepare."

With that, Richard, the man whose horse I held, leapt to her side and, offering her his arm, they went together into the house with the other ladies following. I had been hidden by the horses. I looked over at Robert, still on his horse.

"Sorry, Isaac. Welcome to Avebury. That is Sir Richard Rumsey, scion of a local landowner. Full of himself, a bully, fancies himself as a lady's man, considers himself a good swordsman, but he is undisciplined."

"Hello, Robert. How's life in the army?"

He shrugged.

"Isaac. Don't draw wrong conclusions. Sir Richard has recently inherited his title after his father's death. He is the nephew of an important man. My father needs to maintain good relations with the uncle. Aby is required to be nice to the nephew, and so are you."

I shook my head. Robert dismounted.

"Come, I'll show you to the stables."

We led the three horses around the house and entered an adjoining stable block through an archway into an enclosed, cobbled stable yard. To distract me, Robert was talking about his experience overseas in the army. He summarized it as mostly boredom and occasionally stark terror. As we talked, Sir Richard came from a door connecting the stable block to the main house.

He ignored Robert. "Hey, you!" he shouted at me. "Why haven't you stabled my horse, yet? I'll have your hide, you churl."

He came up to his horse, reaching to take something out of his saddlebag. I was on the other side, between his horse and Maddie. I took a deep dislike to the man. I dug two fingers into the neck of his horse. The horse shied, knocking Sir Richard off his feet into a patch of manure. With an oath, he sprang to his feet and swatted his horse out of the way. He drew his sword. Mine was still strapped to my saddlebag. I swung Maddie round to be between Sir Richard and me, drew my sword, released Maddie's bridle, and slapped her on the rump. She moved away. We faced each other, surrounded by a gathering of stable hands. He lunged at me, which I parried, and we engaged. He attacked. I defended. I had Robert's warning in my mind, and yet I'd foolishly goaded him. He was now bent on punishing me for my temerity. I stayed ahead of him. He was competent but not very good, flashy but wasteful. We moved about enough for the circle of spectators to widen and flow round us.

After a minute or two, I heard ladies' voices coming from the same door that Sir Richard had used. I needed to bring this encounter to a swift conclusion. A quick twist and flick, and Sir Richard's sword spiraled away over the ring of spectators, landing in front of the ladies, with Aby in their midst. I went to Maddie and led her into the stable. Behind me, a furious and embarrassed Sir Richard went to retrieve his sword. His mood was made worse by a laughing Robert Gorges, who was clapping. I heard Aby's voice.

"La, Richard. You are filthy. What have you been doing? You really must come in. It is late."

With bad grace, he left with the others, Aby still unaware of my presence. Robert came into the stable and congratulated me.

"Serves the bastard right. But, Isaac, he is a dangerous man with a vile temper. He must feel that you, in his mind a peasant, have made a fool of him."

I said that I had dispatches to deliver to his father. He showed me into the house, to an anteroom, and told me to wait while he fetched him. He was gone a while before Sir F. appeared. He thanked me for the quick delivery of the package. He said that Robert had given him an account of what had happened with Sir Richard. He apologized but said that I needed to steer clear of him, as he didn't want an altercation to come to the ears of his uncle, who might misconstrue the circumstances. He said that Abigail was doing what she was told. I shouldn't worry. There was a dinner party tonight. Aby would be a guest, but not me. He wanted me to have an early night and return to Plymouth the following morning.

"Am I not to see my wife, sir? Our separation has been a month and more, sir."
Sir F. heard my suppressed anger. He frowned.

"Isaac. There are matters that are more important than a minor inconvenience to two people in my employ. I understand that your hackles are raised over someone paying attention to your wife. She is looked after and deserves a lot more trust than you appear to be showing. Now be off with you. We will be back in Plymouth in two weeks or so."

I left without another word, angry at myself, the situation I found myself in, Sir F., Rumsey, and Aby. I went to the kitchen. The steward, already informed of the stable yard incident, greeted me, shook my hand, and had me eat a good meal with a flagon of beer. Feeling more comfortable after my first meal since breakfast, I went to a tiny bedroom that I had been allotted. It had everything necessary. Most important, the bed was comfortable. I slept soundly. By six o'clock the next morning, I was back in the kitchen for a good breakfast and headed out to the stables. I tacked up Maddie and led her out into the stable yard. A groom held Maddie while I mounted. I reset my saddlebag with sword in its scabbard re-strapped. Just as I was riding off, there was a shout. An order to the groom to stop me. It was Sir Richard. The groom reached for Maddie's bridle and looked at me, grimacing. He was on the right, the far side of Maddie from Sir Richard. I leaned over and whispered

"When I say 'now,' pull the bridle down, let go, move away."

Sir Richard was approaching fast with drawn sword, screaming abuse. He could have awakened the dead. "Now," I said. With my right foot, I kicked Maddie hard in the ribs. With her head pulled down and me kicking her, she shied and spun to the left, knocking into Sir Richard, sending him flying. I was off and armed in a trice. Now, the duel was in earnest. I faced an angry man who wanted retribution. I needed to end this engagement quickly, without harming the man. Within a minute or two, I had knocked his cap off, sliced the sleeves on both his arms, and cut his scabbard away from his belt, which fell and tangled itself between his legs. Then we heard a sharp, commanding voice. I remembered that voice. We stepped back. The same old gentleman who had witnessed my fight with the highwayman was watching us from his horse. He must have seen it all.

"Richard, you are a disgrace. Leave immediately. I will talk to your uncle."
Sir Richard left, chastened and flustered.

"Mr. Stanfield. We meet again. Your swordsmanship has improved. Thank you for not harming Richard. He needs to be taught discipline. Your lesson this morning is something we might build on. You may be about your business."

"Thank you, sir."

I left and headed home with much to ponder. I rued my childish behavior over Aby. Was Sir F. right? Had I drawn the wrong conclusion? Or was Aby changing? Was I jealous? If so, I would need to get that dangerous emotion under control. On the bright side, it was good to see her. Actually, thinking back, it was lovely being able to see her without her knowing. Then, I realized that Aby was Aby. A natural leader, calm, self-confident, and open. I wished I had not held back, but had called to her. Somehow, I didn't want Sir Richard to know about us. My natural inclination was to give nothing away—to control any situation that might become contentious or worse.

Maddie and I journeyed back at a much more sedate pace. The weather stayed good. The countryside we passed through was redolent with summer and harvest. I reflected with amazement that it had been four years since the great fire. Four years since Aby and I came to understand how much we loved each other. Who was I fooling? Aby had decided we would be married a year before that, even before she first hit me over the head with her skillet, or whatever it was. She remembered the moment. Amazing. She said that she had to wait patiently for me to know, too. She never doubted it would happen. I thought remorsefully of my straying, regardless of the circumstances. But the somber mood soon passed. Maddie and I continued our slow journey back to Plymouth. We arrived on the evening of Tuesday, 12 August.

CHAPTER 30

Journal entry—*13 August to 14 December 1617*

With Aby away till the end of the month, I spent my evenings thinking about what we would want as an ideal home. I drew the layout of our current accommodation at Pins Lane to scale, measuring the dimensions of each room. I considered the likelihood that our next home would probably need room for children. We did not have internal running water, currently. Instead we used a common pump outside in the lane. We'd want our own pump in our kitchen. Night soil was accumulated in a barrel in the storeroom, and removed by the town gong farmer weekly. Either Aby or I would take our chamber pots down to the storeroom every morning and empty them into the barrel, shoveling soil over the layer to eliminate the smell. Newer townhouses boasted a small hut outside, called a privie, built against the back wall of the property. Inside was a seat over a pit, and a hatch door in the alleyway on the other side of the wall allowed the gong farmer to empty the pit. It was a much better, more wholesome design. It would also be nice to have a central fireplace accessible from two rooms, enabling the heat to be dispersed throughout the house from both the hearth and the chimney upstairs. Having a house on two floors meant we could have two bedrooms with closets for clothes and bedding and another room for storage. On the ground floor, we'd have a kitchen with a separate pantry, a withdrawing room, and a dining room. The front door would have an entry porch to keep dirt and weather at bay.

I wondered what Aby would think of my plans. It was then that I realized I'd gone too far in my enthusiasm without consulting her. After all, Aby was the mistress of our home.

I worked on my fencing exercises provided by Stephen Rockwell. I hung an apple on a thread from the ceiling in the kitchen, moved the furniture out of the way, and practiced fast-paced movements back and forward, left and right, constantly thrusting the blade to peel the apple, which swung every which way, its movements difficult to anticipate. Practice improved my technique and accuracy. Another exercise was to fence against myself using a mirror. I could only find a cracked, half-size mirror with the reflective backing in bad repair. It was like fencing in fog. Another technique was to practice with my back to the wall, or even better, in a corner. Thus restricted in movement, I doubled the speed of my swordplay. The exercises made me fitter and improved my technique. Stephen noted the improvement when I met him for our weekly sessions back in Plymouth.

Work continued, monitoring Sir F.'s commercial fishing and trading enterprises. Over the next few months, the fishing fleets would return from New England. Sir F. had negotiated several commercially successful trading trips to France. While he had others keeping financial accounts of all these activities, I would be busy for the rest of the year ensuring everything ran smoothly. Having made an investment of my own in Sir F.'s trading helped my motivation. I had maintained my original investment of £100, reinvesting the return. Now I waited to see what that compounded return would produce by the end of the year.

Aby returned on Wednesday, 27 August, to much mutual joy. She had written me a note to say when she would be back. She said she had much to talk about, which raised a number of questions in my mind. She had written after my visit there, so I imagined what one of the subject matters would be. I had written to her on my return, but didn't mention the visit. So, that evening, nestled once more in front of the kitchen fire, watching the pots simmering in preparation for supper, Aby told me that she'd been informed of my short visit the day after I left. At first, she'd been shocked that I hadn't gone to her, but Robert told her what had happened. She had been surprised on the morning after I left. Sir Richard came to breakfast as if he'd been whipped. It seems he got a tongue-lashing from his uncle about his rude and bullying behavior. If I'd been still there, he would have been required to apologize to me in person. As it was, all they knew about me was that I'd been there as a courier for Sir F., and had departed within twelve hours of arriving. Only later had it come out that Sir Richard should count himself lucky not to have been seriously damaged.

Initially, Aby had been angry, then surprised, shocked, and proud of her man. She desperately wanted to get back to me. She said she found Sir Richard's attentions uncomfortable, but he'd such an immature approach to women that Aby felt sorry for him. I asked why she'd kept telling him that he needed to get ready. Ready for what? She laughed. His uncle had told her that Sir Richard was a terrible timekeeper who was late for everything, and not only was he a bad timekeeper, he was vain and slow in dressing. The older gentleman had asked the ladies of the house to keep chivying his nephew to meet his appointments. It had become a game. That night, their hosts expected them at a big dinner with many guests. So, my causing him to fall into the muck had caused merriment, knowing it would require more delays.

Over supper and for several days thereafter, we went through the plans I had prepared of our model house. She liked my ideas, but had many practical changes. Our talks gradually resulted in a detailed description of the house we'd want to move to, when propitious.

We talked again about children. I had the definite sense that Aby was frightened. She couldn't let go of her mother's death giving birth. We agreed, once more, that God would decide. Funny, after reaching that conclusion our lovemaking became more abandoned than ever. Aby had a deep sense of God's protective hand.

The Gorgeses were fine employers but kept us very busy. Lady Ann was away again in October, up to Clerkenwell. Aby accompanied her. *Rosie* was in Sutton Pool in November, picking up a cargo for M. Giradeau to take to Honfleur, with a return cargo to Plymouth. I had a small investment in that trip, as had Sir F., who suggested I accompany *Rosie* for the experience of learning the way my investment was handled. I was pleased to do it. We'd be away two weeks, overlapping the time Aby was away in London. It was good to be at sea with my old shipmates again. This time I saw only a few new faces. Obi was a full-fledged seaman and had lost much of his awkwardness. He was now a full member of the crew. The two new ship's boys looked terribly young.

Once we arrived in Honfleur, I hoped to see M. Medec. I had much to tell him about Saco. The voyage to Honfleur was straightforward—southerly fresh breeze with light airs in the afternoon filled in during the evening, with a strong breeze through the night. We were dockside Honfleur two days out from Plymouth. I oversaw the unloading and followed the carts to the warehouse. Such items had to be bonded until the duties were paid, which was not something I had paid much attention to before. I returned to *Rosie* to find the carts filled with merchandise being driven down to the dock to be loaded. All seemed efficient. The wines and brandy would be bonded in Plymouth, as considerable duty needed to be paid for their import. I was beginning to learn a little about the intricacies of the import/export business. I went in search of M. Medec. He was in his shop and welcomed me like a prodigal son, kissing both my cheeks. I had to bend a long way down for him to do so. He asked me if I had made the trip to Saco. I nodded. We happily agreed it would be a good time to pay a visit to our old friends at the local bar, so he grabbed his hat, put a *Fermé* sign on the door, and off we went.

My Saco friends were there. I wondered whether they had left the bar since I was last with them, and said as much to M. Medec. He replied that it was fortuitous I'd arrived on a Wednesday. I wondered if he would have said the same thing if I'd happened to arrive on a Thursday, or any other day for that matter. We spent an hour or so there together, talking about my adventures. They were shocked to hear about the terrible plague of sickness and death that had affected the Indians. After our visit, I returned with M. Medec to his shop, where he said he had something for me. He disappeared, returning with a package. It was a damaged, scorched copy of M. Champlain's logs of his more recent trips to New France, after those narrated in his book from 1613. I was astonished to see this book and glad to pay him its price. I asked how on earth he'd managed to get hold of it. He said he'd been asked by Champlain's Rouen representative to review it prior to publication. Unfortunately, when he had held the pages too close to a candle, they'd caught fire. In a panic, M. Medoc had thrown water over them to extinguish the flames. The book had been badly damaged, although it was still readable. He'd already admitted the mishap to the representative, saying the copy had been destroyed. He was being sent another copy, which he was required to pay for. So my reimbursing him for this copy was a boon to him. I was grateful, as these logs seemed to be the basis for a book that would be published by Champlain sometime in the next year. My journey was doubly fruitful.

When I returned to *Rosie*, I was met by an anxious skipper. The weather was turning nasty, and we needed to get out of the Seine or we might be trapped. They had a full cargo battened down. We sailed as soon as I was aboard. Clouds were towering to the southwest as we worked our way into and down the river, passing Le Havre on our way out to the estuary. Wind was building from the east, and we sailed west, heading toward Barfleur, making as much westerly distance as we could. The skipper was certain the wind would fill in from the south, then shift to the southwest. If we were lucky, we would make enough way west that as the wind changed direction, we could head up with the wind to sail full and by to Plymouth.

He got it mostly right. We were able to follow the wind 'round. Our track became more northerly through the day and into the night as the wind remained on our port beam. By the time we were well southwest of the Isle of Wight, we were sailing jammed, heading for Plymouth. Unfortunately, the wind continued to shift. We were forced farther north of our intended track and fought our way toward Salcombe. A full gale, wind four points off port bow, bonnets down, fore course, and sprits'l furled. We eventually found shelter in Starehole Bay. The skipper thought the wind direction would continue to change, filling to the North overnight. We anchored rather than slip into Salcombe. Next morning, the Skipper proved right. We were able to complete our journey to Plymouth by four bells in forenoon watch.

I spent time with the skipper and J.B., separately. It was good to talk to them. The skipper had continued to take a fatherly interest in Aby and me. He let his guard down around me when no one else was around in a way that revealed a vulnerable side seldom seen. J.B. never tired of asking me to describe my adventures, said they gave him a window into a life entirely foreign to him. A seaman's lot was mostly humdrum—not a word I knew. He said he had heard it used in London recently. It meant boring. I liked it and stored it away for future use. I added the latest Champlain logs to the library of documents about North America that I had been collecting for Sir F. and asked M. Giradeau if his translator might work his magic on this book, as he had on the previous one. I said that we, meaning Sir F., would be happy to pay for it. Again, he insisted that it was a small price to pay and would be pleased to do so. I gave the charred logs to him, apologizing for their condition.

Aby returned in early November, glad to be home. She'd longed for a normal life with me. Soon after her return, Sir F. and I met to talk business, together with Mr. Ebenezer Scroud, the business manager Sir F. had found for me to arrange my financial assets. My investments combined with the payments made over the past few years, it seemed my account now held over £300, with more to come from the Honfleur trip just completed. We agreed that I should leave twenty percent of the balance in the investment account I had with Sir F. I talked about our interest in moving to a larger house, describing what we were looking for. Mr. Scroud said he'd make the necessary inquiries.

Aby and I continued to work hard during the day, enjoying each other's company in the evening. Aby had continued her regular membership of the congregation of St. Andrews, and I joined her when in Plymouth. Our social life was as busy as we wanted it.

Journal entry—*15 December 1617 to 10 January 1618*

We had yet to decide how and where we would celebrate Christmas. We'd not had Christmas in Dorchester for three years. The Gorgeses would be spending Christmas at Wraxall Court with Sir Edward. We were invited to join them, but if we wished otherwise, they would give us the twelve days plus travel time. We'd spent two weeks in Dorchester earlier in the year. We felt comfortable that the Gorgeses' invitation to us was genuine and heartfelt, so we informed them we'd be honored to accept their kindness. We had warm regard for Wraxall Court. The staff there had looked after us well, and we looked forward to the comfort of their welcoming embrace. Sir F. and Lady Ann were pleased, as our acceptance meant they would not lose our services, though they were quick to add that they very much enjoyed our company. Two people in love, they said, made everyone else happy. They intended to travel to Wraxall on Monday, 22 December, and suggested that we join them.

A significant piece of news: A message came back from Captain Dermer. He'd arrived in Newfoundland and had bumped into Tisquantum, who had arrived on one of John Slaney's fishing boats earlier in the year. The message said that he, Dermer, would continue to New England in 1618 with Tisquantum, using him to build relations with the local people.

The day 22 December dawned, a clear brisk morning. Light snow had fallen overnight. Aby, given her many visits among the landed gentry, had become accomplished at riding side-saddle. Mounted on Maddie and Tess, we were well bundled, our breath misting around our heads. The Gorgeses' coach left New Street with us following, heading north toward Bristol. We stopped frequently at local inns to warm ourselves with hot drinks and food, taking the journey in easy stages. It was the afternoon of Christmas Eve before we arrived. Sir Edward was there to greet us. We left the Gorgeses to enter by the front door while we followed the coach round to the stables and were given a warm welcome by the stable lads.

After seeing to Maddie and Tess's needs, we walked through to the kitchen to another warm welcome, especially from Mary. Mr. Wellings came into the kitchen, gave me a hearty handshake, and Aby a chaste kiss on the cheek. He welcomed us to Wraxall Court and told us he'd been sent to fetch us. We were to join the family in the drawing room. Wraxall Court was wreathed in decorations of holly, ivy, laurel, and mistletoe, with a huge yule log in the hearth ready to light the next morning. Robert and his elder brother John were there, and many other Gorges relatives. I felt awkward, while Aby was totally at ease. She knew them all. It was obvious she was well liked by everyone. I was uncomfortable and felt out of place, much happier in the kitchen or out with the grooms in the stables. So, despite the friendly reception, I tried to keep in the background. I was happy to observe the scene from a corner of the room. The door opened and an older man came in; I recognized him immediately. Everyone stopped talking and turned to greet him, clearly a much-loved member of the family. He went to Sir Edward and Lady Gorges to greet them, as our hosts, and received a glass from Mr. Wellings. He looked around the room, saw me in my corner, and immediately came over.

"Why, Mr. Stanfield. It is indeed my joy to see you. Even more with you unarmed and me dismounted."

His voice carried, catching the attention of everyone in the room. Aby came to my side.

"Ah. The lovely Abigail. Greetings, my dear."

His kissed her hand, obviously a friend as Aby grinned at him.

"So good to see you again, Sir Teddy. It seems you know my husband."

"I do indeed."

Turning to the watching family, Sir Teddy announced: "Some of you might know about this young man and his escapades. Ferdinando, of course, has a complete compendium of them, but I personally witnessed two, which I will now describe."

Sir Teddy was the family raconteur, a gifted storyteller who could mesmerize with his words. The family came closer, making a tight ring round him. Sir Teddy laid a hand on my shoulder and Aby nestled close, an arm through mine. To my acute embarrassment, Sir Teddy launched into the stories of my capturing Jack Melrose, followed by an account of the comeuppance of Sir Richard Rumsey. The Melrose story had become closer to the adventures of a knight errant. I hoped the family recognized the exaggerations, but they were generous in their applause. The latter tale was introduced by Robert Gorges, who provided the eyewitness account of the start of the whole thing. Robert's laughter kept engulfing him as he told his part of the story, and he soon had everyone else laughing. By the time Sir Teddy had finished, the younger members of the family were cheering.

Apparently, Sir Richard was known. The way Sir Teddy told of what he had witnessed, I barely recognized the scene. At the end, everyone clapped enthusiastically. Aby's eyes were shining with pride, happy that I was being drawn into the bosom of the family she liked so much. I was brought to the fireplace, surrounded, and peppered with questions. At one point I caught Sir F.'s eye. He raised his glass to me and winked. "Teddy," so named to distinguish him from the other Edwards in the family, including Sir F.'s brother, had broken the ice. He had been to Virginia in the 1580s. While fighting as a soldier in France he'd been captured and held prisoner for some time. Never married, he now lived in London but spent much time traveling through England visiting the wide-ranging Gorges family members. He enjoyed the role of adored uncle to all his nephews and nieces.

Sir Edward insisted we attend the three services on Christmas Day. Our exercise consisted of the walk down the driveway to All Saints Church, nestled at the corner of the estate, for each of the services. There was a small choir that sang the psalms beautifully. Aby was quite overcome. Although we were dressed warmly, the walks were cold and the church colder. Snow lay on the ground, since large flakes had been drifting down all day, and some snowballs flew. That evening, dressed in our finery, we all assembled in the drawing room, where we were offered drinks from the wassail punch bowl. We were led into the dining room to our assigned seating. The main course featured a remarkable culinary feat called the Coffin. A huge pastry pie, somewhat in the shape of a coffin. Inside, an enormous, roasted, deboned turkey, inside of which was a deboned goose. Inside the goose, a deboned chicken, then a partridge, and finally a pigeon. The whole dinner was a wonderful, convivial celebration. No one behaved out of keeping. Aby and I were incredibly fortunate to be allowed to participate as members of the family. I could see why Aby liked them all so much. Sir Teddy, sitting next to Aby, took it upon himself to throw questions at me about New England, about my time at Wraxall with the Indians, and other episodes that he must have learned about from Sir F. The evening went well, and we went to our bed happy, replete, and tired.

Up early the following morning, we attended a full breakfast, followed by a riding party and lunch at a neighbor's estate, which lasted into the early evening. On our return, we readied ourselves for another dinner, which continued late into the night with many guests. This intense social engagement went on throughout the twelve days, with all in the party entertained at Wraxall or at sumptuous dinners elsewhere. We played indoor games with enthusiastic merriment and all kinds of sporting activities outside. Sir Edward had even arranged a jousting tournament. The padded lances were shortened, and our lack of skill meant little damage done, though those who participated had sore muscles and bones from being knocked off our mounts. A company of players came to the house. They performed Mr. Shakespeare's *Twelfth Night*. Teddy, of course—who else?—raised a toast to the passing of the bard, which had occurred some months previously. I thought of Will and his love for the bard's work. The play was funny. Poor Malvolio.

By 6 January, much of the family had left Wraxall. John with his family returned to London, Robert left to join the Venetian armies as a mercenary officer, and Sir Teddy was off to who knows where. We had a wonderful last evening before riding back to Plymouth behind the Gorges coach on Wednesday, the seventh, arriving late on Saturday the tenth.

CHAPTER 31

Journal entry—*11 January to 29 March 1618*

We were soon back in our respective employments. We had little time to seek new accommodation. I had to advise Mr. Scroud that further activity on our part would have to wait till the spring. Through March, we had only two weeks in total at home, despite the winter weather. Heavy snow delayed our travel, Aby's more than mine, as Lady Ann traveled by coach. Maddie and I had become adept at finding ways sufficiently to travel in all but the worst weather. Occasionally, we were holed up in a convivial inn for a few days. Aby was with Lady Ann. Sometimes, I would accompany Sir F. when visiting his wife, but as often as not, I was off on some errand or other, pursuing Sir F.'s wide-ranging interests. The fishing fleets were not expected back until beginning of April. I was directed elsewhere.

Piracy was getting worse. David Tremaine continued to gather information in various guises down to Cornwall and on the south coast of Ireland. I found he had an amazing gift for mimicry. His Cork brogue seemed to my untrained ear entirely authentic, as was his Cornish dialect. My role in the anti-piracy activities was to gather information and to distribute it among the key merchants in the West Country. This information was coordinated with the news we received from the London merchants which was passed on to Sir F.'s office. A clerk there recorded the information. On a regular basis it was passed on to shipping captains as well as the Navy. Sir F. had tried repeatedly to obtain financial support from the king through the privy council, but the king seemed distracted by other matters. It meant that I was frequently on the move. When I attended meetings in London or Bristol, I was able to stay at the Gorgeses' residences at Clerkenwell or Wraxall. Aby was there occasionally, to our mutual delight. By the end of March, spring was very much in evidence.

Journal entry—*30 March to 29 June 1618*

On 3 April, Captain Dermer arrived back from Newfoundland. He had brought Tisquantum with him, unable to find a vessel to take him down to New England. I was pleased to see Tisquantum again. But, perhaps the most enthusiastic was David Thomson. David had already begun to seek support from merchants in London and the Plymouth area to go on a trading voyage to New England. He'd become like a man possessed in his desire to go back. With Tisquantum keen to complete his journey home, the pressure on Sir F. to sanction such a voyage was immense. Unknown to David, while he was away in London seeking commercial backing, Sir F. had already agreed to support a voyage by Captain Rocroft, who'd been on Captain Smith's voyage with Dermer in 1615. Rocroft had sailed earlier this year to meet up with Dermer at Monhegan, unsuccessfully, as Dermer was still stuck in Newfoundland. Rocroft had come across a French fishing boat off Monhegan and had captured it, transferred the French crew to his own ship, and sent it back to Plymouth under the command of Rocroft's first mate. He retained the smaller French vessel to continue his voyage to Southern Virginia, shorthanded. Sir F. was significantly chagrined to learn that the crew turned out to be Huguenots. After intercessions from M. Giradeau, as well as other representatives of the Huguenot community in Plymouth, he released and paid the crew compensation before returning them to France.

Sir F. had been somewhat loath to underwrite yet another voyage. He was still busy in financial recovery operations. He was doing well, but not that well. However, in conversations with David and Tisquantum, Sir F.'s own overwhelming interest in New England couldn't be suppressed. Having Tisquantum there satisfied a prerequisite condition. No further voyages would be made without the means to interact with the local inhabitants by having an Indian guide on board. It seemed definite that a new voyage was being planned for early next year in which David Thomson and Tisquantum would participate. In the intervening months, both Sir F. and I, separately, had plenty of time to spend with Tisquantum, which was always enjoyable. Tisquantum was housed for a while at 32 New St. I also had the chance to visit with him at Wraxall and accompany him on a trip back to London to meet with Mr. Slaney and Captain Smith. It was difficult, however, to have to describe what we had found at Saco. Tisquantum had heard about the plague and was deeply concerned. He was doubly anxious to return to his homeland. Perhaps the disease had not penetrated as far south as Patuxet. He expressed worry about how it'd come about.

Aby and I were able to spend much more time together. Lady Ann spent May and June in Plymouth. After the travel of the first months of the year, we were able to settle down once more. Not only were we hopelessly in love with each other, we were our favorite companions. Mr. Scroud was able to show us some larger houses that fit our stipulations for rents that were acceptable. We decided on a house in the Huguenot quarter of Plymouth, 15 Whimple Street. It was close to St. Andrew's Church, which had offered Huguenots a special welcome for a long time. As a result, they tended to gather nearby to buy or rent homes there, and the Giradeaus lived close by. By the end of June we were close to completing the move. We were down the road from 1 Whimple St., the guild hall. Our front door, which was directly on the street, opened into a hallway with stairs to the first floor. To the right of the stairs, a door led to a large kitchen with an enormous open fire hearth, a passage to the left past the chimney to a living room, the hearth open between the two rooms. In the living room, a large window next to a door on the back wall looked out onto a modest, walled garden. In the garden, we had our own privie against the wall at the rear of the garden. Upstairs, a small hall with a sewing room to the left, and to the right a door to a bedroom. There was a connecting door between the first bedroom and a second, larger bedroom with a fireplace, which would be ours. The house felt enormous after Pins Lane.

We were invited to a dinner hosted by Sir F. and Lady Ann on Saturday, 27 June. We were escorted by watchmen, sent by Sir F. There were many guests, including some of our new Huguenot neighbors. M. and Mme. Giradeau were there, with Vivienne and her fiancé. We met new people as well as old friends. Dinner was lavish. At the end of the evening, however, there was an unfortunate misunderstanding. The Giradeaus had offered to have their watchmen take us back to Whimple St. The hour being late, all considered it inadvisable to walk unaccompanied through the streets of Plymouth. Vivienne's fiancé mentioned the offer to me, so I told Sir F. that his offer of an escort back to our house was not needed now. Meantime, unbeknownst to me, Aby had told M. Giradeau that we were using the escort provided by Sir Ferdinando. By the time we were ready to leave, both escorts were gone. It was a pleasant moonlit evening and, recklessly, I decided that it was a short and safe walk for us both. We left, having retrieved my weapons—deposited when we arrived—and walked up New St. and onto Looe St. A man appeared from an alleyway; two others joined him. They spread out in front of us.

"Going for a stroll on such a lovely evening?" asked one.

"That's a fine lady you have with you," said another.

"What say you just leave her with us and be on your way?" said the third.

I loosened my sword, which was hidden under my cloak. I slipped my dirk into my left hand and whispered, "Aby, love, stay behind me." I moved left toward a wall buttress that gave me protection and cover for Aby. "If anyone grabs you, start screaming as loud as you can and fight with everything you've got—nails, teeth, everything. When I shout 'now,' go limp, play dead."

The footpads moved forward, baiting me, but clearly more circumspect, as I wasn't reacting the way they expected. One raised a sword, the others had knives. The swordsman lunged. I parried with my dirk and whipped out my sword. A hasty parry and we were at it. I stayed close in front of Aby. A lunge and a back step. Needing to finish quickly, I picked up the tempo, and the swordsman started to retreat. I couldn't go after him. Realizing this, he was able to dictate the pace, moving out of range and bringing his fellows into attack, and then, with my attention diverted, lunging forward again. I had to eliminate him. Next time he lunged I went after him. He stumbled back under my attack, given no chance to attack me, as he was busy defending himself frantically. My sword was too quick for him. With a thrust, I took him through his right shoulder, and as he dropped his sword arm, he swung at me with the dagger in his left hand. I parried with my dirk and the follow-through bit deep into his stomach. I heard a cry behind me and I saw that Aby had been grabbed. She fought like a wildcat, raking her attacker's cheeks. He swore and swung her 'round and held her from behind to avoid those claws. He was waving a knife and had his arm 'round her chest, tearing at her dress and clutching her breast. Aby screamed and, bless her, continued to struggle, stamping his foot, elbowing and continuing to scream as loud as she could. I advanced and shouted, "Now!" She dropped. The man, surprised, bent forward to catch her. That was my Aby! I went cold and stuck him through the neck. I turned and the third man fled. Aby staggered to her feet, bruised and bloody from her assailant. She wrapped her torn dress around herself, sobbing. Two men lay groaning at her feet. She stepped over them, and we flung our arms around each other and held on for dear life. With the pounding of feet, the night guard arrived. We were escorted home while my two victims were dealt with.

That night we loved and clung together in bed till daybreak. Aby had recovered her spirits, though she was still sore. We washed, dressed, and went to Church to give thanks for our escape. Word was already out. Sir F. and Lady Ann, after the service, came to us in shock and horror. Sir F. looked at me and shook his head. An officer from the night guard came early on Monday to hear me explain what happened. The man I'd stuck in the neck had died during the night. The other man had been persuaded to describe the incident, the description generally matching mine. He had died while still being questioned, having been persuaded to name the third accomplice, who was currently being sought. The officer was followed by a visit from Captain Turner. He wanted to check on us.

"You really are getting quite a reputation. Word will be out before tomorrow that the captor of Jack Melrose was challenged and beat off three assailants, killing two and chasing away another."

The reaction set in. I had not knowingly killed two people face-to-face before. Shooting at pirates was something altogether different. I held myself together till Captain Turner left. Then, I started shaking. Aby, who'd been tending the fire, turned to look at me, a worried look on her face. She didn't approach me immediately.

"It is hitting you, too, isn't it?" I asked.

"What do you mean?"

"I killed two men on Saturday night."

"I know."

"I'm not sure they would have been killed if I had been by myself. In protecting you, I felt myself go cold as ice."

She came to me and put her arms 'round me. My shaking eased.

"You are a man. You have experienced something that has marked you, deep down. I must recognize this and accept the change. You are my man. My own. My love. Forever."

Letter to Isaac—*30 June 1618*

Dear Isaac,

I can't believe it has been a year since you and Aby were last in Dorchester. We have both been remiss in writing to each other. More to the point, I eagerly await the next installments of your journal. I have to tell you that I am now committed to starting the diary I mentioned to you when we last met. I have numerous distractions to get out of the way. First, I will establish a discipline to write a brief summary of happenings locally, nationally, and internationally every month. If nothing else, it will be fun to refer to it in later years. Once the summer is over, I will organize myself.

I have to tell you that I have settled into a happy relationship with Elenor Parkins. Surprise, surprise. You probably don't remember her; she was but twelve years old at the time of the Great Fire and your abrupt departure from Dorchester. I think Aby knows her quite well. We have not talked of marriage, but I get the impression that the idea has been mooted by our respective parents. It seems they feel it would have all the makings of a satisfactory arrangement. Thanks to God, we love each other. Still, there is a rebellious thought that surfaces occasionally. I wouldn't dream of admitting it to Elenor.

P. is becoming increasingly concerned about our Leiden friends. He mentioned to me that he would welcome the opportunity to send someone he trusts over there to get a better idea of exactly what they plan to do and when. There are all sorts of rumors. It does seem they or at least some of them are desperate to leave. But with no New England settlements, they worry about the risks. They fear the unknown. They appear to be leaning toward Southern Virginia but are worried about the lack of religious beliefs there, according to P. I have to say, from reading your account of your Saco adventure—you would be an ideal person to further P.'s interest.

That's that for the time being. Please do write and send me your journal entries.

Will

Journal entry—*30 June to 10 July 1618*

When I received Will's letter, I shared it with Aby. She said she knew Elenor well and was joyful they were together. I told her that I would talk to Sir F. about the suggestion Will had made. I was certain that Sir F. would welcome the Leiden people establishing a settlement in New England.

Sir F. had heard nothing, but said he would make discreet inquiries. His son, John, is close to a daughter of the earl of Lincoln, who is supportive of the Leiden Separatists. He said that if passage could be found for me to make the trip to Leiden, he would find it useful. He said he was in a quandary with respect to the Separatists. He felt he hadn't sufficient legal authority to offer them the right to settle without that offer being challenged by the Southern Virginia Company, now called the Virginia Company. Sir F. needed to replace the original 1606 charter establishing Northern Virginia, its terms largely made irrelevant by additional charters obtained by the Virginia Company. Without a new charter, New England would be in danger of serious encroachment by the Virginia Company. Not just their use of New England waters to fish for their own sustenance, but more importantly, they could stifle settlements in New England. Sir F. needed to establish a new council with a new charter to replace the Northern Virginia charter, sanctioned by King James to provide Sir F. with direct or delegated governance over all new settlements in New England. Even in the absence of this new charter, he said a Separatists settlement, under the auspices of Northern Virginia, would be a major step forward in both protecting and furthering the development of New England.

I needed to meet with P. If he really did support me going to Leiden, it should be seen to be happening on his behalf with a letter of introduction to his friend Pastor John Robinson, and there needed to be a commercial reason to sail to Leiden. Perhaps P. could persuade Mr. Bushrode to send *Rosie* there. Who knows, if the trip was commercially viable, I might even make a small investment. I will write to Will and suggest a meeting with P.

Letter to Will—*10 July 1618*

Dear Will,

Thank you for your letter of 30 June. I must apologize for my not having written to you for a long time. I enclose my journal entries for you to catch up on what I have been doing. Congratulations to you and Elenor. Of course, we both remember her, Aby much more than me. She sends her love to you both. I look forward to receiving your diary, once you start. You are being methodical, but that's you.

I talked to Sir F. about your Leiden suggestion. If there were enough commercial reason to send a boat to Leiden, he would be happy to have me go there. He has as much interest in knowing what's transpiring as P. does, albeit for different reasons. I thought P. might persuade Mr. Bushrode to send *Rosie*. More importantly, I need to meet with P. to discuss this matter further. Please find out when would be a good time for me to come to Dorchester to meet with him. Who knows, I might be able to bring Aby.

Isaac

Letter to Isaac—*15 July 1618*

Dear Isaac,

P. says come as soon as you can. Bring Aby.

Will

Journal entry—*11 to 22 July 1618*

Aby and I talked about going to Dorchester. After the attack on us both 27 June, we had been hard at work, but it seemed we should ask for some time to recover finally from the horror of the attack. Lady Ann was due to leave Plymouth at any moment, going to the Isle of Wight to visit relations. It seemed opportune for Aby to come with me to Dorchester. While I went to Leiden, Aby could go on to be with Lady Ann, if it could be arranged. We went separately to our employers to ask for leave to go to Dorchester, which was readily given. We planned to have a leisurely ride along our normal route to Dorchester, taking three days. We decided to leave Monday, 20 July, arriving Dorchester late on the twenty-second.

CHAPTER 32

Journal entry—*23 July to 1 August 1618*

We arrived at the Sun on Wednesday evening to a warm welcome from Jeremiah and his staff. I sent a note to P. saying I hoped to see him on Thursday morning. I received an immediate response that he looked forward to seeing me at ten a.m. on the morrow. I sent a note to Will that we'd arrived. I said that Aby looked forward to meeting him and his lady whilst I was with P. A welcoming note came back asking me to deliver Aby to the Whiteway household by nine a.m., which I did. We were received with the warmest of greetings. I left, promising to return after my meeting with P., which turned out to be a long one.

He first wanted to know how my life had gone this last twelve months, asking the most pertinent questions. He extracted from me a description of the attack of 27 June. He dug deep, as only a pastor can, into my mental state. He probed my conscience. While he recognized my instinct to protect Aby, he was concerned by the single-minded ferocity with which I had attacked the two men. He dwelt on my subsequent reaction, which he considered healthy. We prayed together for God's guidance and support to help me deal with that ferocity.

"God has given you that instinct," he said. "In spite of my concerns—use it well."

I was startled. He laughed. We proceeded on to other matters, talking about Leiden. He said he'd been in touch with Mr. Bushrode. Being the astute businessman that he is, Bushrode saw the value in establishing direct contact with the Separatists before they left for America, as well as persuading them to settle in New England. He felt, said P., that there could be excellent trade with them both ways. He had an opportunity to ship merchandise to Holland with a business agent in Rotterdam who would find a return cargo. *Rosie* was due back into

Weymouth in about a week. Perhaps a voyage to Holland could be arranged in about a fortnight. *Rosie* would need to go via Gravesend, as additional merchandise needed to be shipped from there.

P. gave me a description of the situation as he knew it from correspondence with Pastor Robinson, their leader. It seemed dire. A combination of their faith and fear of retribution if they returned to England had kept them there in spite of poor, squalid living conditions, hard, unrewarding work, and a sense they were foreigners living their lives as disrespected immigrants—without the full rights of citizens. Their children were becoming strangers to them, picking up the behavioral habits of their peers. Once grown, they left to find their fortunes elsewhere. Their numbers weren't reducing, but they weren't increasing either. More Separatists continued to join them, but left once they found the conditions unacceptable. As a result, the core group were not being leavened by younger additions. They were aging and weary.

Some had determined they must leave. Their London contacts had suggested they obtain land held by the Virginia Company. P. gave them an alternative option: New England. We discussed my role, and P. said they'd benefit from learning about my experiences in Saco, as they'd had no contact with people who had such experience. Given my position as a confidant of Sir Ferdinando, I would be able to advise them of his interest in supporting their move to New England. As for P., I would be able to represent his interests in helping them. He said he would write an introductory letter to Pastor Robinson, advising him of my planned visit to Holland.

After that meeting I returned to the Whiteways' house. I told Aby that I needed to ride down to Weymouth to organize her journey to the Isle of Wight. In Weymouth, I found a coastal trader that was due out of Weymouth, eight a.m., Thursday, 30 July. They planned, weather permitting, to arrive in Southampton by late afternoon, same day. A note was sent to Lady Ann informing her of our intended arrival on the thirty-first. I returned to Dorchester. All too soon and very early, we left Dorchester once more, laden with several saddlebags, all containing Aby's wardrobe. My few possessions remained with Maddie and Tess, stabled at the King's Arms. On my return from my trip to Leiden, I would take both horses back to Plymouth.

The trip to Southampton was most pleasant. The captain gave us use of his cabin whenever we wished, but spent much of the day sharing his quarterdeck. We entered the Solent with a following breeze in bright afternoon sun. We disembarked with the best wishes of the crew. Aby had been much admired. At the harbor master's office, we were told we had missed the last ferry that day. We found a convenient inn for the night, and the next morning we were at the ferry dock in plenty of time to be in Cowes by midday. A boy was sent to the residence where Lady Ann was staying, and returned excitedly an hour later, riding on the back of a carriage. We climbed in, the boy was paid off, and we were taken to the residence. Aby was happily reunited with Lady Ann. I left her after a long embrace and the promise to be together again by the end of the summer in Plymouth. We had become used to parting, but it was still painful for both of us. We lived at a much higher level when we were together, and felt a continuing sense of emptiness when we were apart. But such was our chosen life. The coming together again was always joyous, making it almost worth the pain of the separation. I was back in Weymouth the following afternoon, 1 August.

Journal entry—*2 to 31 August 1618*

Rosie had returned in my absence. I went to see the skipper. Mr. Bushrode had informed him of the trip to Holland, and we checked the charts. Delfshaven on the river Nieuwe Maas, close to Rotterdam, was the likely port, but would require a ride of twenty miles for me to get to Leiden. The alternative was Amsterdam, which was a much longer journey by sea. He needed a week for Bushrode's business agents to find enough freight for Rotterdam. Bushrode's Weymouth and London agents were busy finding freight to ship out and bring back. It seemed that the best plan would be to sail to London, either Gravesend or Rotherhithe, to fill *Rosie*'s holds, as Weymouth was short of exportable merchandise to meet Holland's exacting requirements. With Spain throwing its weight around, the skipper said weapons—component parts of guns for reassembly by the Dutch, made of iron, steel, and wood, as well as body armor—were always welcome. Those we would pick up in London. Five days later, we sailed, making Gravesend on 12 August. Bushrode's agents had been busy. Added to the fine-weave woolens and sacks of carded wool loaded in Weymouth, the boxes of weapons material at Gravesend completely filled the holds. We had been lucky, last-minute arrangements had netted a full cargo. By 17 August we were in Delfshaven. I left the skipper to argue with customs officials while I went to the livery stables. I hired a fine-looking black horse with a hard mouth for the ride to Leiden, rather than going by boat along the River Schie and the Vliet canal.

Leiden is a large, walled city with a population of over forty thousand, compared to Plymouth's five thousand. It is surrounded by a moat, the River Rhine flowing through the center with numerous connecting canals. Pastor Robinson lives in a house close to St. Peter's Church. I had the address, but that landmark made it easy. I left the horse at a livery near the South Gate and entered the city. A short walk through the teeming citizenry brought me to the Church, which is an impressively large building. Apparently, it used to have a massive tower with a wooden spire, but the tower collapsed a hundred years ago. The church bell survived and is housed in a smaller wooden structure, a freestanding belfry beside the church. I have to say it looked odd but was a testament to the practical, not to say frugal, minds of the Dutch. By the southwest corner of the church is a tall house on Green Close, the home of Pastor Robinson. The Close was originally an open area, but it has been built on to form dwellings for some of the Separatists, a tight little community. There are several hundred Separatists living in Leiden, most of them living close to the church.

I was met by Mrs. Robinson, who advised me that her husband was at the university. She explained to me that he has become something of a celebrated theologian arguing the cause of Calvinism against the current Dutch Reformed Church dogma of Arminianism, to the great interest of the faculty, students, and citizens of Leiden. She is clearly concerned. I asked her why. She said that the arguments between the Calvinists and Arminianists are much more than just a university debate. Factions in the city on both sides have resorted to violence. But the good pastor sees only the intellectual aspects of the debate. His wife feels he is too unworldly on this matter. She is worried about his safety. I asked her what she understood Arminianism to be, to which she said it is named for Jacob Arminius, a Dutch theologian who died about ten years ago. He espoused the doctrine that man's salvation is possible to all through the grace of God. I imagined there was more to it than that, but I thought back to my conversation with P. on the subject of Calvinism. On his return, Pastor Robinson introduced himself to me with great charm. He had received a letter from his friend John White, who had introduced me in glowing terms, such that he'd been greatly looking forward to my visit. They invited me to sup with them and stay the night.

At the supper, there were five of his Separatist colleagues: Mr. Brewster, Mr. Carver, Mr. Allerton, Mr. Bradford, and Mr. Winslow. It seemed from the conversation 'round the table that the last two—younger men—were most likely to be the leaders of any voyage they might make to America, which was why the pastor had asked them to hear about my adventures. They expressed concern for Mr. Brewster, the deputy leader of the Separatist group in Leiden and the presumed leader of a voyage to America. He was a printer by trade, and, at some risk to himself, had printed articles that were not complimentary about the religious situation in Scotland. King James was displeased. The English ambassador to Holland had been asked to find Mr. Brewster and he had attempted to get the Dutch authorities to help, though they were proceeding slowly. The Separatists planned to make Mr. Brewster disappear before the authorities were stirred into more precipitous action, and they didn't know what effect his disappearance would have on their plans to go to America.

Prior to further discussion, Pastor Robinson asked me to describe my experiences. I gave a thorough account of my time at Saco. They asked about the voyage across the Atlantic and expressed grave concern about the Indians—not, as I first thought, about their parlous condition but about their savagery. They had received stories from Jamestown about the horrors of the battles the settlers had waged with the local tribes. How settlers, men, women, and children had been captured, tortured in the most unspeakable ways, and killed. From my experience, what I had read and heard directly from Captain Smith, I told them that there were two sides to every story, and numerous causes and effects. It was vital in my experience, as well as the experience of those Sir Ferdinando had sent to New England, that new settlers had to have with them, or establish as soon as they arrived, a native guide. There needed to be a local Indian they could trust, who could interpret for them and establish clear understanding and friendship between the local Indians and the settlers. I talked about the time I had spent in England with men like Samoset, Tisquantum, and Epenow. These were proud men, highly intelligent, but they were fearful of us and what we were bringing to their shores. They had had bitter experience of the Englishman's capacity for depravity through men like Captain Hunt. They were suffering an epidemic that had already killed a large proportion of their people and were convinced it had come from the English, yet they saw how our use of metal could help them to farm, hunt, and defend themselves. The women saw the marvels of our domestic tools and utensils. They were beginning to see the need to trade their seemingly limitless resources and understood the inevitability of people leaving the crowded shores of England to find space in their land. I added that in my own experience, they were curious about the God we worshipped.

This point caused a strong, positive reaction from everyone round the table. I'm afraid I was not subtle. I said that my experience in New England was different, much more positive than the experiences they had read about of the settlers in Virginia. Sir Ferdinando Gorges and Rector John White had both made it clear to me that they'd welcome and support the Separatists' move to New England, rather than Virginia. Furthermore, they shared the religious feelings of the Separatists to a greater extent than did the merchant adventurers of the Virginia

Company. My dinner companions listened to what I had to say, after which there was much discussion. They worried that there was a risk that the persecution they faced in England could follow them to Virginia, which had maintained a strongly royalist attitude to the established church. They were excited about the opportunity to bring heathens into the embrace of their faith.

I felt an affinity for the two younger men, William Bradford and Edward Winslow, being closer to my age. Mr. Bradford was in his late twenties, a silk weaver by trade. He did not speak a great deal, but when he did, he was listened to with respect. He appeared to have great depth of character. He was thoughtful. The few questions he asked were pertinent. Mr. Winslow most interested me, being the nearest to my age. Born in 1595, he had come to Leiden in 1617 and recently married. A printer by training, he had been apprenticed to a printer in London. He was intelligent and inquisitive, maybe a little impulsive. I felt he would make a good leader. He certainly seemed to have the character for it.

"We need money, land, and a ship—possibly two," he said. "Tell us how you will support our needs."

"The money should come from investors who see commercial gain from providing you with financial support," I responded. "I, myself, am a small investor. I would need to see your plans to exploit the commercial opportunity that readily exists in New England. What skills, in addition to building a permanent community, do you have? Will you be able to sustain yourselves? Can you fish, cut timber, trap animals for their fur, negotiate with the Indians?"

I went on. "I came by boat from Weymouth. The boat's owners have made it available to me to begin the process of developing a commercial relationship between West Country merchants and you when you get to New England. The land we could provide through the form of a patent or contract. As for ships, Sir Ferdinando has them making voyages to New England every year. The next trip is planned for the spring of 1619, and I understand it will be carrying out further exploration in southern New England from Cape Ann round the Massachusetts Bay to Cape Cod, which should provide important information for any settlers wishing to make a home in that area."

My intent was to provide them with an alternative opportunity. Unfortunately, I was coming late to the table. Mr. Winslow told me that one of their number, Mr. Cushman, was already in London talking to the Virginia Company representatives. Mr. Carver was due to leave Leiden within a few days to join him in those discussions. In addition, the Dutch had been talking to them about making land available in the territory they had started to settle along the Hudson River. This development interested me. Both the Virginia Company and Sir Ferdinando's Council believed they controlled that land. I was left with the feeling that those round the table, excepting Pastor Robinson, were determined to go, but they were stressed. There were so many unknowns, and they would have to depend on people they didn't know. They still had to find out how many of their group were prepared to go, perhaps no more than about a hundred. While they had relative freedom to worship the way they wanted, there was increasing concern whether they would be allowed to continue to do so.

The Spanish threat to Holland's sovereignty was becoming a serious worry. Under Spanish control, they'd no longer have that religious freedom. They mentioned that of the several Separatist churches in Amsterdam, a group under the leadership of Reverend Blackwell had already contracted with the Virginia Company. They sailed with 180 people earlier this year, headed for Virginia. The Blackwell group admitted to an unquenchable compulsion to propagate the gospel to the heathen, in parallel with their desire, ironically, to pursue their own religious freedom, both of which the Leiden group shared. While they had yet to hear from the Reverend Blackwell, it gave them much encouragement to continue to pursue their interests in London.

I sensed they did not see the inherent conflict between wanting freedom to worship their way and seeking to enforce that form of worship on other people, but perhaps I was being cynical. I did understand how much pressure they were under. I felt it, and it was uncomfortable—an explosion waiting to happen. Pastor Robinson, an oasis of calm, was their continuing comfort and shepherd. It was a long evening with much lively discussion. I had the sense that I was somehow tied up in their future. I knew that they needed help, and I was determined to provide it. Their future should be in New England. I had an absolute conviction that the Leiden company would be much better off going there, quite apart from the obvious benefit to Sir F. I bade farewell and left the next morning with Pastor Robinson's thanks ringing in my ears.

I was soon back in Delfshaven. *Rosie* was still loading the freight to be carried back to London and Weymouth. It seemed the business agent for the importer of the armaments had not pre-cleared his order with the customs officials, which was hardly surprising, given how hastily the trip had been put together. It had taken a day to convince the authorities that the armaments were for the benefit of the state, given their concerns over Spain's intentions. The importer had been acting for the local militia, who had to be brought in to confirm that everything was aboveboard. Barrels of sugar and tobacco were being swung aboard, along with casks of gin, crates of silks, and other Dutch East Indies produce, including spices. As an investor, I was keenly interested.

So back to the Thames, where we were able to make our way upriver as far as Rotherhithe. Once there, we had more problems, this time with the English customs and excise. Apparently, they were worried about the casks of gin we had on board—more than the manifest said we should've had. This seemed like it was going to take a while, so I went ashore with Obi, who was off watch. We went to the nearby Shippe Inn, a convivial place, full of seafarers. I found space at a table in a spare corner in the taproom.

"Obi, you've become an accomplished sailor. Congratulations. Tell me about it."

"After I thought you had died some years back, Bosun Braddock . . ."

Obi paused as my eyes widened. Who was Bosun Braddock? I realized—J.B.

"He told me that you were bound to turn up one day," Obi continued. "He said you had magical properties. But until then, he said, you'd want me to become an accomplished seaman. Who knows, I might even be the skipper of a ship sailing Isaac Stanfield on one of his many trips to New England. That gave me the goal and the focus. Sure enough, your magic worked. Mr. Braddock was right."

I laughed. "So, you see your future as a seaman, do you?"

"Absolutely. Mr. Braddock has kind of adopted me. He is making me learn the duties of every crew position. Currently, I am a main top man. But I expect he will have me somewhere else soon. I'm still young, but can fend for myself with any of the crew. I think he sees me as a future bosun's mate."

I agreed. J.B. was looking out for him, and in a year or two he would be ready for promotion, but he needed to study navigation and seamanship and spend time with Mr. Babbs and his guns. Then there was the need to develop his hand-to-hand fighting skills. We returned to *Rosie*. Everything had been squared away with the customs people, the necessary duty had been paid, and the London freight was being offloaded. The skipper wanted to make the start of the ebb tide early the next morning. Everyone sprang to action to make it happen. With no additional freight to be loaded, we were back on the river the next morning, just before dawn. London, behind us upriver, was lit by the rosy pink of the early sun as it appeared over the horizon. The sun was in our eyes as we moved downstream. It had been a quick turnaround and profitable. It was Friday, 21 August.

As we left the Thames estuary moving east, then south along the east coast of Kent toward the white cliffs, the wind started to die. The skipper managed to make Dover before we would have been taken by the tidal currents onto the Goodwin sands, whence lay disaster. In the harbor we stayed, the calm preceding a storm, a real sou'wester, which was awe-inspiring from behind the breakwater. It would have been tough to manage in the limited sea room of the English Channel. We were there for a week. I took a room at the Cock on Strond St., close to the harbor. J.B. and I had a pleasant meal together, and I mentioned my conversation with Obi. He said he would make sure Obi continued his progress in mastering all aspects of being a seaman. The problem was, he said, that Obi couldn't read. Without that skill, he didn't have much chance of advancement.

"Is there anyone aboard with the time and inclination to teach him?"

"Well, there aren't many that have the knowledge to be able to," he said. "As for inclination, a few bob would help with that." He thought for a moment. "Mr. Babbs has time on his hands. He isn't exercising the guns on these coastal passages we've been doing the last several months. He is an avid reader, too. Seen him in a corner reading a dog-eared tome."

I made a mental note to talk to Mr. Babbs.

"Why are you interested in Obi?" J.B. asked.

"He reminds me of myself. I have it in my bones that we are destined for adventures together. If that is the case, I want him to be ready. Apart from that, he needs to be able to fight pirates and defend himself, come what may."

J.B. laughed. He said as we parted, somewhat wistfully: "Keep me in mind, when you go a-venturing."

Eventually, the storm passed. The wind backed to the south and east. There had been much damage caused in and around Dover—roofs coming off houses that had been exposed to the wind, trees down blocking roads, and unfortunate ships driven ashore. The Goodwin Sands had netted two more. There but for the grace of God, I thought. We had passed the sands just north of Dover the day before the storm hit.

Two days later, Sunday, 30 August, we were in Weymouth. I had a chance to talk to Mr. Babbs. He said he looked forward to teaching Obi to read and write. I persuaded Obi that he should take advantage of Mr. Babbs' kind offer and apply himself. Obi was eager to start. *Rosie* was going on to Plymouth after offloading cargo and taking on more local produce. I hadn't heard from Aby but expected her back in Plymouth by the beginning of September. I had a few days spare, and I wanted to report on my Leiden trip to P. I rode Maddie to Dorchester and was lucky to catch P. between services.

In his study, I gave him a detailed description of my meeting with Pastor Robinson and his people. P. asked his usual probing questions. At the end of my account, he sat back, steepled his hands together, elbows on the armrests of his chair, and thought about what I had said.

"It seems we are late and ill-prepared to offer them a viable alternative business proposition to that offered by London or the Dutch. I don't have a group of merchant investors to provide them with the financial support they must have. It's clear that I need to establish a group of investors here in Dorchester if I am to be of any real help and influence on people wishing to settle in New England. Sir Ferdinando has barely the means to provide assured patents to settlers though the Plymouth Council, which he really must re-establish. It needs to have the same authority and legal standing as the Virginia Company, otherwise he will have no chance of competing with them or protecting his own territory in New England."

I agreed that depending on how long it took them to get organized, it didn't seem we would be of much use to the Separatists. On the face of it we were without the means to persuade them to settle in New England. *Other than by guile.* I didn't say anything to P., but it set my mind thinking.

CHAPTER 33

Journal entry—*1 September to 31 October 1618*

I returned to Weymouth. I had a good night's sleep at the King's Arms. Next morning, bright and early, Maddie and I rode out along the coast road, leading Tess. The weather was glorious. I kept close to the coast on the uplands. I remembered the last ride I had taken from Weymouth to Plymouth, under different circumstances and temper. I made good time. I alternated riding the two horses so they stayed relatively fresh. Riding one while leading the other was awkward, but we did well to average thirty miles per day.

My second evening on the road, I chose to stay at the King John's Tavern on South Street in Exmouth. I was seeking to use the Exmouth ferry across the Exe to Starcross the following morning. I had just arrived and was settling the horses into their stalls in the inn's stables when I was accosted. I had removed my saddlebags; my cloak was covering them and my sword on the ground. I had no idea what caused the aggression, but a tall man with a long moustache and military bearing started shouting in my direction. I looked round, as I assumed he was addressing someone else. There wasn't anyone. An ominous sign, the ostlers had backed off in the stable yard to watch the proceedings. The gentleman by this time was very angry—in fact, he was so enraged that, combined with his patrician accent, I couldn't understand him. It sounded like he had swallowed his moustache. He was in the yard with a horse close by held by an anxious-looking groom. The horse was beginning to fret, ears back, whites of eyes beginning to show, tossing his head and pawing. The groom backed him away. I eventually understood that he was commanding me to approach him. I bent down to retrieve my sheathed sword. Carrying it, I walked out into the yard toward him. He proceeded to call me names, some of which I had not come across before. I said nothing but was fascinated by the spittle that had appeared on his moustache. I stopped listening to him to look around the yard, where knots of people were watching, waiting for something to happen. This outburst, it seemed, was not an entirely unusual occurrence.

Without warning, the enraged man struck me across the face with the back of his left hand. I had not been paying attention. He tried again. This time I was. I grabbed his wrist with my left hand, pulling his arm hard across his body. With the momentum of the intended strike, he spun round. I struck him hard across his buttocks with my sheathed sword. This action was greeted by a cheer and applause from the crowd. I stepped back, drew my sword, tossed my scabbard aside, and waited. The man drew his sword and lunged, attempting to skewer me through the throat. A simple parry, a twist, a flick of my wrist at his second lunge, and he was without sword. More applause. I waited as he stumbled to retrieve his sword, now quiet and worried.

He picked it up, visibly quivering. "Who are you?"

"Isaac Stanfield."

He stepped back, went white, and almost dropped his sword. He clumsily put it away, cutting his guiding fingers in the process. With fingers in mouth quenching the trickle of blood he spluttered, "*The* Isaac Stanfield?"

"I don't know of any others."

He turned. Without another word, he went into the inn. More applause. A groom approached. I asked him what that was all about. He said it was a local gentry, an ex-army captain. Perchance, I had used a stall that he normally used, although he had no special right to it.

"Begging your pardon, sir, but your appearance might have given him to understand that you were someone's groom."

I laughed.

"Are you really Isaac Stanfield, who captured Jack Melrose?"

"Afraid so."

"And killed those men in Plymouth."

"Enough."

I collected my bags and entered the inn. The crowd broke up, speaking of what had happened. I supposed the incident enlivened an otherwise boring day. I was met at the door by the landlord, who had been alerted and heard the last questions. He apologized profusely for his other guest's behavior and informed me the man was drunk. He'd gone to his room in a state of shock. I was treated well and pleased to be on the ferry early the following morning with my two faithful mounts. I decided to keep to the coast. What followed was the most pleasant ride, interspersed by ferries at Teignmouth and at Dartmouth by way of Kingswear. I decided to stay the night at the Cherub Inn, which was surely a place to come back to with Aby.

The following morning, Thursday, 3 September, I continued my ride, still swapping my mounts at regular intervals. We rode along the coast, adding other ferry rides on the way to Plymouth: at Portlemouth to Salcombe across Salcombe Harbor; on to the River Avon at Bantham. Aby was much in my thoughts. With the traveling I had done over the past few years, I had seen some extraordinary countries, each exciting and incredibly attractive in their own ways. While Aby hadn't been beside me, she had, for the most part, been with me in spirit. This most beautiful countryside, Dorset and Devon, was unbeatable. New England beckoned—high adventure. But . . .

We arrived in Plymouth late afternoon on the third. To the Minerva to stable the horses and a quick hug with Annie. She was keen to catch up, but I was in a rush to get home and she noticed my impatience. Annie smiled—a little sadly, I realized too late.

"Aby's not yet back," she said. "She and Lady Ann are due back Saturday, according to the Thomsons."

I grimaced. I had been rude and unthinking. Annie deserved better, even if Aby had been home. I apologized most sincerely, and we went to a corner space in the barroom. I sat, and she brought me a tankard with a steaming plate of stew. We caught up amid frequent interruptions, as she had her duties. Annie was sparkly and animated, a joy to be with. At length, I returned to Whimple St. We had arranged with Annie for her to keep an eye on the place whenever we were away. Everything was clean and tidy, with a smell of furniture polish.

Next morning, shaved, washed, and dressed well, I presented myself at Sir F.'s office. Captain Turner greeted me as a friend. Sir F. was due back with his wife the next day from the Isle of Wight, together with their staff, which included Aby—my heart surged at Captain Turner's mention of her name. Sir F. would not be long in Plymouth. He would be returning to London as he was in negotiations to establish a new charter to replace the Northern Virginia Charter of 1606. I went in search of David Thomson. David had been working with Captain Dermer on the final details of their planned voyage back to New England. His anticipation of that trip had become overwhelming. I suggested he might need to rest his mind a little. Otherwise, the strain could be injurious to his health, not to say of concern to his wife. He was a bit taken back by my implied criticism. He frowned, then ruefully nodded.

"My fascination, no, my besottedness with New England is all-consuming," he said. "I want to go back as a settler, taking my family there. After our Saco trip, I have been barely able to think of much else. Poor Amyse. I know she feels my lack of attention to my family."

He paused for a moment.

"This voyage with Captain Dermer and Tisquantum next spring has, for me, the single objective of finding the most suitable location for a settlement. We will cover much the same ground starting from Monhegan, working our way along the coast to Saco and on from there. Do you remember our exploration of the Piscataqua River? It is something I have never forgotten. I have every expectation that we will find the location for my settlement there."

We talked further about his intended trip and how he was progressing with Tisquantum. He said it was going well. Tisquantum had become a good friend, eager to participate in David's adventure, especially as it would return him home.

Saturday, I spent the morning wandering around our clean home, preparing for the arrival of my wife. The Gorgeses arrived by boat in the late afternoon. I was on the quay and saluted them as their party disembarked. Sir F. shook my hand and told me he hoped to see me first thing on Monday in his office. Aby, the soul of discretion, detached herself from the party, and with a kiss and a quick hug, took my arm. We walked to Whimple St. Back home, behind the shut front door, all pretense gone, she sank into her favorite chair, exhausted. I carried her to her bed, where she immediately fell into a deep sleep till evening. When she woke, I had our bath ready with hot water in front of a roaring fire. As she soaked, I gently washed her, massaging her tired limbs, neck, and back, marveling at her alabaster beauty. Then, stepping from the bath, she allowed me to dry her.

"Enough, you lovely man."

Putting on a robe, she stripped me, ordered me into her bath, and did much the same for me, and then we were abed very quickly. We were back as one. Aby described her time on the Isle of Wight. She loved Lady Ann dearly and was pleased to be the recipient of her affection. The management of Lady Ann's life was fascinating and rewarding, too. Ensuring everything ran smoothly and, clearly, being held in high regard, in a position of responsibility were gratifying. I could sense some reservation, though. It seemed that the constant round of social whirl had become something to endure. The dressing up, the constant, empty small talk, the necessity of entertaining boring or boorish dinner companions, of being a cheerful presence, the constant demand on the dance floor, no matter how the feet hurt—all were barely endurable. It was all exhausting.

"What are you going to do about it?"

Aby looked startled for a moment.

"I honestly don't know. I'm sure there is a compromise here. With your absence for long periods, it has become normal for me to be included in the whole round of Lady Ann's world. It has become an expectation. I need to talk to her to see if we can come to another arrangement. I enjoy the organizational aspect of my employment. I cherish the friendship with Lady Ann. I am devoted to her. So, I am very fortunate, really."

We were silent with our thoughts for a while. I told her all I had been doing. At the end, she asked me what I had meant by "guile" to get the Separatists to settle in New England. That's why I love Aby—well, one reason, anyway—she gets right to the core. I said I didn't know, but I was determined to keep a close eye on their efforts to obtain passage across the Atlantic. Until I knew who the players were, there wasn't much I could do. I was to have a meeting with Sir F. in the morning. I would discuss it further with him then.

Monday, I reported for duty. All of Sir F.'s aides were there, too. It was good to see Tremaine. We agreed to get together after the meeting. We all gave reports and talked over whatever matters pertained to them. Sir F. said that he would defer discussion on my report until after the meeting. He said he would be returning to London within the week to continue to build support for his petition to the king's privy council for, as he called it, a charter of New England by the Northern Company of Adventurers. The Virginia Company, headquartered in London, had got wind of Sir F.'s attempts to strengthen his authority over New England. They had begun to express concern. That concern seemed primarily to lie in the protection of their freedom to fish in New England waters. Sir F.'s concern was to ensure there was no encroachment by the Virginia Company. They should be given no opportunity to take *de facto* control of New England territory through a gradual process of annexation. Then, without a clear-cut declaration by King James, the Dutch to the south and the French to the north would feel free to nibble at the edges of New England territory.

From the report that I had brought back from Leiden, it was clear that without that charter, it would be impossible for Sir F. to attract settlement groups to New England with the existing Plymouth Company. Sir F. asked me about Rev. John White's position. I had already described in my report my meeting with P. I reiterated his opinion that we were late getting organized. He was much less able to provide meaningful, collective support for New England settlements than Sir F., but he remained absolutely committed in his approach to attracting communities to emigrate, such as the Separatists. P. was still in the throes of building broad support for Dorchester. The destruction caused by the 1613 fire was well on the way to being repaired. He needed to galvanize financial support from the wealthy for the benefit of the citizens of Dorchester, who were living through hard times, and even more, for those forced off the land who were moving to Dorchester with absolutely nothing. In desperation, and with no other means at their disposal, they were resorting to crime. Once he felt he could justify turning the attention of the wealthy away from Dorchester, he would find the means to concentrate their attention on the "godly development" of New England. Sir F. pondered the issue.

"So, we have a community of settlers, of the exact requirements that both Rector White and I need, to whom we are currently unable to provide practical inducement for them to settle in New England. Isaac, in your report, you mentioned 'guile.' What do you mean by that?"

"Well, sir. If we had the ships they require to transport them, we could take them wherever we wanted. But we don't, at least, I don't believe so, at this stage. Therefore, if we don't have the ships, but the captain was our man, it would come to the same thing. At the same time, it would be difficult for us to appoint one of our captains to a ship belonging to someone else."

"Go on."

I glanced at the two Davids. David Thomson was looking at me blankly, but David Tremaine was nodding, a grin spreading across his face. He was, after all, a master of intrigue. He couldn't contain himself.

"Isaac, you dog. You are suggesting we bribe the captain chosen to transport the settlers."

He laughed with glee at the thought. David Thomson looked shocked.

Sir F. was thoughtful. After a moment, he said, "Isaac, go on."

"We have no idea how Mr. Cushman and Mr. Carver are coping in London. We know their needs; land, financial support, and ships. Seems like the first thing we need to do is get close to them. We must keep abreast of their activities and understand better the schedule they are working within. We should carve out time to come up with legitimate and acceptable alternative inducements. At least, the knowledge we obtain will allow us to scheme how we might intercept or influence their plans."

Sir F. looked at me. He slowly shook his head.

"I've said it before. I'm sure I will continue to say it. You amaze me. So, we need a spy. I am shortly back to London. I will be able to monitor what the Virginia Company is doing. Sir Edwin Sandys has just been made the treasurer of the company. He is its main proponent. I know him and can speak with him, although he is worried about the effect my actions might have on the long-term sustainability of his Virginian settlements. By seeking to reassure him, I can probably pick his brains about the Leiden group, which I believe is somewhat inconsequential to his broader aims. I also need to talk to him about the Somers Isles Company."

David Tremaine and I looked at each other, eyebrows raised.

"I beg your pardon, sir, the Somers Isles Company?" I asked.

"Yes, the Virginia Company spawned another company with much the same investors, also with Sir Edwin its treasurer.

"We hear terrible things about the costs of survival in Virginia, the loss of life, and the poor financial returns. We hear little about this other company that has established a settlement in Bermuda. Apparently, it is thriving, with many settlers and profitable tobacco harvests, among other things. Perhaps we should be paying more attention to Bermuda. I understand it has even supplied Virginia with meat, fish, homegrown wheat, and maize."

I had heard about Bermuda. I remember Will mentioning something about it when he went to see the play, *The Tempest*, by Mr. Shakespeare. I was amazed. I thought it had a reputation to be avoided at all costs. Returning to the matter in hand, Sir F. looked at Tremaine.

"David, I believe the job of spying is yours. You have all the attributes. What do you say?"

"Fascinated, sir. I know London well. I can be taken for a Londoner, of differing backgrounds, as the need arises. I believe I can get close enough to offer my services to the Leiden representatives. I suspect they are floundering a little, as devoted men of God, suspect because of their beliefs. Their association with proscribed Separatists can't be helping them. They are like trout negotiating their survival in a lake of pike."

Sir F. turned to David Thomson.

"Mr. Thomson, your thoughts."

"Shocked, sir. But I admit to a somewhat stultifying morality. Leaving that aside, I have to say that we need to build the right settlements in New England, quickly. As you know, I want to be a part of that process. The more settlements we have, the better I am able to satisfy my ambitions. So, yes, you have my support."

I looked at him. I wanted to feel comfortable with what he had just said, his level of commitment. "David, let us assume that for whatever reasons, the Leiden group find themselves in New England," I said. "We have previously agreed that for a settlement to succeed it has to have the support of local Indians.

That support best comes from having an Indian ready to interpret, guide, and be their intermediary."

David Thomson's face went through a range of expressions—confused, thoughtful, shocked, and enlightened—all in a matter of a moment. It was fascinating to see the outward manifestation of someone's thought processes.

"You mean Tisquantum. We will be in New England next year, so you are saying that we need to make sure Tisquantum is in the right place to be prepared to support them, wherever and whenever they land. It would be best if we had advance knowledge of their destination, but from what you are saying we might not be in a position to do so. It would help if our 'bribed' captain could be persuaded to accept a destination, at least a general area, of our choosing. That way we could ensure that Tisquantum would be there to greet them."

I asked Sir F. if we could look at the map of New England I had drawn. He nodded and sent Captain Turner to fetch it. When he returned, I laid it on Sir F.'s desk.

"I think their destination will not be a major problem. Tisquantum told me that he hopes to return to his homeland in southern New England—Patuxet. If we do manage to persuade the captain to change course, he would need a reason to do so. Wind and weather or minor error in navigation should be enough."

On the map, I showed the probable track of a ship making for, or south of, the Hudson River.

"The track would take them south of Cape Cod," I explained. "With a small navigational change, which the captain could explain away to landlubbers as being due to adverse winds that pushed them farther north, they could end up at, or even a little north of, Cape Cod. After a long and uncomfortable voyage, the passengers would be looking for any opportunity to land. If the captain came close to Cape Cod, the decision to land there would be an easy one to make. Once the ship was out of the Atlantic, protected by Cape Cod, by moving southwest from there they'd end up close to Patuxet. Otherwise, they might make landfall on the inside in the hook of Cape Cod."

I showed them where on the map. I also showed them Champlain's 1605 map of a natural harbor near Patauxet which he called Port St. Louis, which seemed ideal.

"If he moved south along the Atlantic coast of Cape Cod, he would come to Capawack. I'm not sure that would be good news, as that is where Epenow is. He is anti-English at the moment. We would want to warn the captain accordingly, as a real inducement for him to stay farther north."

"Another thing," I added. "Based on the exploration notes I have accumulated from the likes of Smith and Champlain, the area to the immediate south of Cape Cod is a dangerous area for navigation, with many shoals. Our captain, presumably experienced, would not want to venture in those waters. Even if, once inside the bay, he sailed due west, he would make landfall not too far north of Patuxet. If alerted, the coastal Indians would soon inform Tisquantum where they were."

Sir F. studied the map which showed the preferred area.

"Somehow, we need to get the captain to sail into Massachusetts Bay," he said. "Gentlemen, we have many 'ifs' and 'buts' here, but we have a plan. We can deal with problems as they occur. I will return to London to keep abreast of the Virginia Company's activities. David Tremaine will establish himself in the confidences of Cushman and Carver from Leiden. David Thomson will work with Tisquantum so he will be ready to offer his services to the Leiden group when they get to New England. Isaac, you will be the spider, controlling the web back here in Plymouth."

With that we broke up the meeting. I returned with David Tremaine to Whimple St. Aby was still at New St. with Lady Ann. So, David and I settled down for a chat. First, I wanted to know what he had been doing. Why the secrecy of his report to Sir F.? David chuckled at my inquisitiveness.

"Because it was secret. Sir F. is worried about confidentiality. He keeps stumbling over highly confidential matters somehow getting to the wrong ears, says some of his aides are as leaky as the walls of the castle. I'm sure your lovely house is secure. I have been in north Devon, where a pirate lair has been established on Lundy Island, off Bideford. No serious attempts have been made to eradicate them, apart from the occasional local effort, which has had minimal long-term effect. They are associated with the pirates in the Scillies. At last, the various coastal commanders, including Sir Ferdinando, have come together to do something about it. I represented Sir F. at a meeting in Bideford to coordinate action against them."

"How did it go?"

"Not well. As always, fingers were pointed, demands made for action, but no one was prepared to lead. I offered, but Sir F. is not favored because he comes from South Devon. It should really be led from Bristol, but they keep prevaricating. Anyway, while in Bideford, I was spotted by an old pirate acquaintance who was pretending to be a local fisherman. With Lundy just a few miles from Bideford, it is bound to be a hotbed of pirate spies and sympathizers. Crazy place to hold the meeting. Anyone would think the organizers were sympathizers themselves."

"So what happened?"

"My cover was uncovered, I thought it best to leave before they found out why I was down there."

"No wonder Sir F. didn't want to talk about it," I said.

We talked about his new assignment. He was most excited to be on home territory, London, which he loved, in a new role away from anything to do with piracy and its increasing risks. I described Mr. Carver and gave him what information I had on Mr. Cushman. I suggested I contact Leiden for more, but David said no, much better for him to do his own infiltration. Sir F. traveled back to London. David Tremaine prepared to follow suit once he had his plans in order. I spent time thinking about my role as the spider. It would be a while before any meaningful information came in. I would need to sort through that information. It had to be kept confidential, passing on only that which had value to a particular recipient. David Thomson spent much of his time with or close to Tisquantum. I was comfortable that by the time they got to New England, Tisquantum would be in a good position to prepare for the Separatists' arrival.

I suggested to Aby that while the weather remained good she should ask Lady Ann for a few days off duty so we could ride the coastal route I had promised to show her. Lady Ann thought it very romantic. She was pleased to see us spend such time together. So, mid-September, with the promise of a lovely late summer, we rode east, crossing the River Plym, and continuing along the coast at a gentle walk, with the occasional canter as much for the horses' benefit as ours. Aby delighted to be able to revert to riding straddle. We savored the little world that we had created for ourselves—balmy weather, glorious views, alone together. By the time we reached the Cherub Inn in Dartmouth, we were tired but at peace. Next morning, the weather continued as before. As we rode along the coast, I noticed that Aby was looking thoughtful.

"Aby, my love, what are you thinking?"

Stopping Tess, she turned from gazing along the coastline to look at me. She smiled, reached over, and took my hand.

"There surely can be few places on earth that can match the beauty of what we are now part of here. Wherever we go, for however long, we will always have this memory to come back to."

I must have looked surprised.

"My darling boy. I know you have been worrying about taking me away from England to places unknown, to adventures beyond imagining. I go where you go. With you the world is a beautiful place; without you it is drear. I could not have more a secure companion to share our adventures."

She was way ahead of me, as always. We kissed. Maddie and Tessie shook their heads in agreement. Aby had taken a huge weight off my mind. We turned, rode back through Dartmouth, to home.

In the latter part of September the weather changed, turning blustery. Aby worked with Lady Ann as she decided her activities for the rest of the year. While Sir F. planned to stay in London until he had achieved success with his new Charter, Lady Ann preferred to stay in Devon. Her work with the poor and destitute in Plymouth and the surrounding rural areas took a great deal of her time. Aby was pleased to help her; it meant that their social life was much curtailed. In October, Sir F. had begun sending me letters every week summarizing his discussions with his backers and the king's privy council. Of more importance, he was keeping me abreast of the discussions that Sir Edwin Sandys, representing the Virginia Company, was having with the Separatists, Mr. Cushman and Mr. Carver.

Matters were proceeding slowly. There were differences of opinion regarding the levels of support for the Separatists within the Virginia Company hierarchy. Sir Edwin was pitted against Sir John Wolstenholme, who was a strong proponent for the Separatists. Even Sir Robert Naunton, King James's secretary of state, had become involved. He was negatively disposed, proving to be intransigent. Opposition from the Archbishop of Canterbury was a stumbling block. With the strength of the opposition, it seemed that while King James was in favor of a land patent being granted to the Separatists, he wouldn't make any public statement of support. His support was better than nothing, but not much to build a future on. The fact that Mr. Brewster was being sought by the authorities was a problem which affected their credibility. The availability of land was tied to finances. Investors or sponsors were needed to cover the £10 per head it cost to get the settlers there. Ship and crew needed to be chartered, provisions and stores for passengers and crew paid for. Land needed to be productive so settlers could pay for that land by providing a return to the investors. The same or more investors had to be found to cover their initial living expenses and the means to repay that investment. It was all complicated. I felt sorry for Mr. Carver and Mr. Cushman. David Tremaine had disappeared. He was presumably in London. He would be preparing his ground carefully.

CHAPTER 34

Journal entry—*1 to 29 November 1618*

I received a note via Captain Turner from David Tremaine. He had established contact with Mr. Cushman. While they were engaged in discussions with the Virginia Company, there was little for David to do. He had "bumped into" Cushman after following him to a religious meeting. He had established a casual but friendly relationship based on a shared belief in the gospel, as David put it. Cushman appeared to be the businessman, Carver, the idealist.

Aby and I talked about Christmas. Lady Ann would be traveling to Clerkenwell. She invited us to accompany her, but we decided we'd prefer to spend the Christmas period at home in Plymouth. Lady Ann was graciously acquiescent to our plans. Aby invited her father and Aunt Hilda to spend Christmas with us. Sadly, Aunt Hilda was too frail to make the journey. Mr. Baker would not leave her by herself. We promised to visit them in the new year. With our widening circle of friends, we expected to celebrate the twelve days in the Dorchester manner. The Thomsons would spend Christmas and Boxing Day with us. Amyse was pregnant again and slowing down. Annie reduced her time at the Minerva to become a regular support for the Thomsons. She adores children and is good with little Priscilla. Annie is a wonderful housekeeper, which allows Amyse the rest she needs. Annie has also been retained by Aby to help keep our house clean. They are fast friends. When they are together, ostensibly cleaning, the house is filled with chatter and laughter. In fact, Aby has persuaded Annie to learn to read and write and has been busy teaching her. So, Annie will be here too, both as guest and helper. We sent an invitation to David Tremaine, who indicated that if he could get away from London, he would be delighted to join us. Aby has a secret plan to matchmake, bringing David and Annie together. They would make a lovely couple, Aby says. I'm not sure, but I keep my own counsel. I took the opportunity to meet with Mr. Scroud. Under his watchful eye, my investment in Sir F.'s commercial activities had continued to do well. With Sir F. still aggressively rebuilding his financial resources, it seemed wise for me to continue with the same arrangement. Mr. Scroud suggested that my running account within Sir F.'s investments should be diversified somewhat.

Sir F. is focusing a great deal on the North America market. He has a merchant vessel trading with Jamestown in Southern Virginia, for example. He suggested I look to investing more in the continental trade, through M. Giradeau, Mr. Bushrode, and the like. I agreed. I received a healthy return from the small investment I made in the trip that took me to Leiden, thanks to Mr. Bushrode. I left him to make the necessary arrangements.

Journal entry—*30 November 1618 to 6 January 1619*

I continued to receive messages from London. Not much progress was being made by the Separatists. It seemed lack of sponsors, or investors, was the major problem. It was clear the Separatists were not excited about settling in or near Jamestown, but a group of them had such a strong desire to leave Leiden that there was a sense they'd be prepared to go anywhere. The Hudson had become the destination of choice, as we had surmised. The days shortened. The winter solstice was fast approaching. Aby was preparing for Christmas, cooking and planning a whole round of entertainments with our friends. The twelve days would be full of religious observance and merrymaking. We went to find our yule log together and brought it back on Christmas Eve. We decorated our house till we were living in a green forest glade, with holly, mistletoe, and ivy festooned everywhere. The red berries on the holly, which were in profusion this year, added to the colors of the oranges, apples, and other exotic fruit that Aby had found. We had candles on every horizontal surface. Aby had found sconces at her favorite furniture shop that I had fixed to the walls in the downstairs rooms. All in all, the house was a grand sight.

Christmas Day we spent at several services at St. Andrews, and between them, home in quiet contemplation. Boxing Day, we attended the opening and sharing of the church's alms box among the needy of the parish. Lady Ann had asked Aby to be her official representative. She had provided Aby with additional contributions to which we added our own. We had our guests, including David Tremaine, for games and a feast that evening. Aby tried every subtle ploy she could think of to bring David Tremaine and Annie as close together as possible. It was fairly easy, as they were the only two there unaccompanied, and were paired off for party games and at dinner. I don't know what Aby expected. Presumably some spark that her woman's intuition would have divined as a match in the making, but it seemed the two were happy together as friends, with no discernable stress of an intimate relationship forming.

John Thomson was born one day before my birthday, on January 5, with Amyse and the baby doing well. David was beside himself at having a son. Annie attended the birth. In addition to her other accomplishments, she is becoming a fine midwife. She looked after Priscilla while Amyse remained confined to her bed. Aby assisted in the birth. She came from that experience very thoughtful. It had been an easy birth. The sight of a newborn baby had a powerful positive affect on her.

We celebrated the feast of epiphany, going to the early service at St. Andrew's to mark the end of the twelve days of Christmas. We had a quiet evening celebrating my twenty-second birthday.

Journal entry—*7 January to 28 February 1619*

Through February, not much additional information came down from London. Captain Dermer with his crew were getting ready for their voyage to New England. David Thomson remained in a high state of eager anticipation. I met with Dermer on several occasions. Sir F. was keen for him to prove or otherwise disprove the existence of mineable ore, in addition to filling his vessel with fish and other produce he might come across. He wanted the income to pay for the voyage. He planned to have a pinnace—a small, shallow-drafted, single-decked sailing vessel—sail with him, to use for further exploration with a small crew, sending back his primary vessel with what he hoped would be a full load of produce. Sir F. was keen for Captain Dermer to continue his coastal exploration farther south of Capawak Island, as far as the mouth of the Hudson River. He had many concerns: What are the Dutch doing there? Has the epidemic in New England abated? What is the condition of the Indian population? Has their hatred of the English been in any way assuaged?

It was of special concern when Sir F. found out that the Virginia Company was offering land to the Separatists around the Hudson River. I remembered from what Doc Vines had told me in Saco, that if the settlers acquired that land from the Virginia Company, it would control the whole of the overlapping territory, from the thirty-eighth to forty-first latitudes, under the terms of the 1606 charter. Doc had emphasized the point that the charter stipulated that any new settlement by one company in that area had to be a hundred miles away from any previously established settlement by the other company. Conversely, if Sir F., representing the Plymouth Company, provided the land patent, that territory would be controlled by Sir F., but until Sir F.'s new charter was approved by the king's privy council, he did not have the legal authority to offer that patent. Anyway, he did not want to have to deal with the Dutch. Therefore, he really didn't want to provide the Separatists with land that far south, which would mean being at the doorstep of the Dutch.

Journal entry—*1 March to 30 April 1619*

Lady Ann asked Aby to join her at Clerkenwell. Lady Ann had been ill over Christmas, and was only recently well enough to continue her social and charitable activities. It meant that we'd had a wonderful few months together in Plymouth, a married couple enjoying our own tightly intertwined life, becoming used to living together. So, it was a real wrench to think that this happy period was being interrupted. Although the weather looked blustery, the winds promised to remain from the southwest. The most convenient way to travel to London was by sea. I thought it useful, in addition to escorting Aby, to go to London to meet with Sir F. and David Tremaine to discuss progress on the various New England activities. A captain I knew was leaving for Rotherhithe and was happy for us to sail with him, leaving Wednesday, 3 March. We were at the Gorges residence in Clerkenwell by late afternoon on 7 March, where we were well received. Lady Ann was quick to whisk Aby away. Sir F. was home. He sent a note to David Tremaine that I was in town. A note came back, suggesting I meet David at the Devil's Tavern on the river at Wapping the following midday. I wouldn't recognize him. I should not be surprised at being accosted.

Sir F. brought me up to date. His petition to the privy council, for a charter for the Council for New England, was accepted on 3 March, but not yet approved, as it must go through the judicial process with full debate. Unfortunately, the Virginia Company formally oppose the creation of the Council. They insist that it would limit their ability to sustain their settlers by restricting their right to fish in New England waters. They have petitioned the Privy Council and are forcing long debates. Referrals keep being made to special subcommittees. It seems like they hope to wear down the privy council by a continuous process of obfuscation. Such is the fervor of the debate that Sir F. has had to attend all sessions of the privy council and relevant subcommittees. He has some knights and noble lords supporting him, but Sir Edwin Sandys' backing is as substantial as that of Sir F. More to the point, large numbers of settlers continue to immigrate to Virginia, totaling over three thousand to date. They need to be supported by whatever means possible. New England, on the other hand, is essentially deserted of settlements. It is a tough argument to make that New England's fishing grounds need to be protected. Sir F.'s counterargument, that those fishing grounds provide and would continue to provide revenue to the Crown, has been received favorably. The debate continues.

I met with David at the Devil's Tavern. I'd heard many stories about the pub, but had never been there before. David advised me to go in seaman's clothes. Previously called the Pelican, it was at least a hundred years old and perched by the river, rough made with timbers from old ships, with stone floors and low, blackened ceilings. The clientele were as rough, looking like a mix of foot pads and smugglers. But the ale was good. It would need to be. The landlord would probably have his throat cut if it wasn't. No wonder David was disguised. I did not recognize him or his strong riverside London brogue. In fact, even when he sat beside me I had no idea. He passed comment on the day's news, the view of the Thames. We entered into casual conversation over several minutes. Still, nothing. Eventually, bored of the subterfuge, under his breath, he said—"remember Agincourt." I started with surprise, laughing.

He said that he continued to strengthen the relationship he'd established with the Separatists Cushman and Carver as an interested fellow traveler. He professed to them that he was not yet ready to commit to leaving England, but wanted to know more. He told me that from his recent conversation with Mr. Cushman, the Separatists had heard about the unfortunate Rev. Blackwell. Apparently, Rev. Blackwell's voyage to Jamestown had been a disastrous one. He, along with 130 of the 180 souls aboard, died on the voyage—including the ship's captain and many of his crew. The poor passengers were packed into a ship too small, and once dysentery took hold it decimated the huddled masses below deck, living in filth and squalor. Scurvy was a terrible problem too. Blame was laid squarely on the shoulders of the now deceased Rev. Blackwell. Only God knows what Pastor Robinson must be thinking about his plans to go to America.

Apparently, Blackwell had left Amsterdam under something of a cloud. He had managed to get the blessing for his voyage from the religious hierarchy in London, including the archbishop, apparently by lying about his intentions and denying his Separatist beliefs. Divine retribution appears to have been visited upon him and his unfortunate followers. The Virginia Company continues to promote settlement in their territory, but they are unable to provide the financial sponsorship or ships that the Separatists require. The company appears to be strapped for resources, which makes their almost desperate insistence on access to the New England fishing grounds more understandable. I asked him about Bermuda. Didn't they have resources to provision Virginia?

David shook his head. "There appears to be an unfortunate schism between the Virginia Company and the Somers Isles Company. Notwithstanding the common stockholders there appears to be little mutual support or interest."

Back to the Separatists, David said that a man by the name of Thomas Weston had appeared on the scene. According to Mr. Cushman, Weston was promising all sorts of inducements. He had even been to Leiden to talk directly to Pastor Robinson. Cushman didn't trust the man, but he didn't have other options available. David said that he had done some investigation of his own. Weston is a leading light of an organization that calls itself the Merchant Adventurers of London. It seems there are such groups in different major ports in England and on the continent. They are composed of a group of like-minded merchants keen on making investments in overseas trade. They look for short-term gain. They have little or no interest in ideological inducements, although they're quick to embrace a cause if they think it gives them a negotiating advantage. The Leiden Separatists, to Weston, are an exploitable opportunity, seen as a ready-made community easily persuaded to settle in a favored location and provide a flow of highly profitable produce back to the Merchant Adventurers. This approach is different from Sir F.'s efforts to build long-term, sustainable, permanent settlements to protect the land from incursion by others. The Merchant Adventurers aim to promote, entice, or otherwise persuade gullible people to accept barely sufficient loans or be bound by a joint stock ownership plan that has onerous penalty clauses to the short-term commercial benefit of the Merchant Adventurers. The one advantage, as far as we have determined, is that Mr. Weston has promoted New England as their favored location. David will continue to watch, reporting back as necessary. At this stage, there appears little that he can do to influence the thought processes of Mr. Cushman and Mr. Carver. David and I wished each other good fortune in our respective endeavors and he relapsed into his disguise while I went about my business.

Sir F. asked me to return to Plymouth expeditiously, as Captain Dermer was about to leave for New England, and he wanted me there to make sure everything was in order for their departure. So, Aby and I had a last night together. The Gorgeses were away for the night. They kindly left us to the care of their household staff. We were well fed and wined and withdrew to our bedchamber early, with its roaring fire and four-poster bed. We loved the night long and slept intermittently.

At dawn, I was away to Rotherhithe to catch a boat heading south and west. I took a coastal trader to Dover, another to Portsmouth, a Bristol merchantman that was prepared to stop in Weymouth for me, and another coastal trader to Plymouth. With good weather, it took me a week. I was back home by the sixteenth. Dermer, with David Thomson and Tisquantum aboard, sailed for New England a fortnight after my return in a merchant vessel, accompanied by a pinnace. Dermer is a fine sailor, a consummate, experienced explorer, and a charismatic leader. David thinks the world of him. Detailed planning has gone into the voyage. They are well organized, well prepared, and fully provisioned with a small but experienced crew. It is their intention to use Tisquantum's skills and knowledge to continue their exploration into Massachusetts Bay down to Tisquantum's homeland, Patuxet, and to leave him there, returning to Monhegan. David will return to England in the merchant vessel under the command of Captain Dermer's first mate. Captain Dermer will sail via Cape Cod to the south in the pinnace with a small exploration party. They expect to arrive at Monhegan in May to begin their exploration.

I was kept busy during April, helping Captain Turner look after Sir F.'s affairs in Plymouth. Sir F., while distracted with what was going on in London, still had many irons in the fire. Captain Turner was a typical soldier, able to focus on only a single matter at a time. It was important that I defer to him, being the responsible adjutant, but the many, sometimes conflicting activities requiring constant attention needed a slightly less rigid approach. Luckily, I got on well with him. He was happy to have my help.

CHAPTER 35

Journal entry—*1 May to 30 June 1619*

Early May, the Gorgeses came back to Plymouth. Sir F. had left his petition in the hands of his supporters. He felt comfortable, if impatient, that progress was being made. With the Gorgeses, Aby returned. On the evening of her return, Friday, 7 May, we were back at home. Aby settled me down with a glass of wine in front of the kitchen fire. She came to sit on a stool at my feet, her arms resting on my knees. She took both my hands in hers.

"My dear, I have something to tell you."

She was wide eyed, solemn. My heart sank. Doom in its many guises flashed across my mind. I tensed. She felt it, shook my hands gently, and smiled.

"My darling, I'm pregnant."

I was stunned. We had left it to God. I had not thought deeply about it as a result. Aby's sober demeanor brought back to me the worries she had expressed about her mother dying giving birth to her.

I took her hands in mine. "How do you feel about that?"

She looked down. After a long pause she slowly raised her head. She had tears in her eyes. "We are blessed, and I am deeply, deeply content."

"Then, so am I."

I knelt down beside her. We embraced. For a long time, we said nothing, just feeling each other's beating hearts, beginning to think of the changes this new person would make to our lives, but just letting those thoughts evolve, solidify, drift away, to be overtaken by others.

"How many months pregnant are you?"

"Two."

I thought back. That last night at Clerkenwell.

"Do the Gorgeses know?"

"Yes, Lady Ann guessed. They are very happy for us."

"Have they worked out the dates?"

"Yes. They say they are the godparents of the child, as they were accessories to the conception."

We both laughed. We spent the rest of the evening voicing the many thoughts we had had, without reaching any conclusions. The following days we found our relationship had started to change. It was no longer just the two of us, but a vitally important third presence had appeared. We weren't thinking as two relatively independent people, making our own plans, following our own careers. We had begun thinking as a family. It bound the marriage more closely. I wouldn't have thought it possible, but somehow the line that marked our separation as two people had dissipated like a line in the sand washed by the incoming tide. Aby realized that the freedom she had to build a working life with Lady Ann would have to be curtailed. My thoughts about New England were no longer well defined. Obviously, as we grew used to this new circumstance, we'd be better able to reset our priorities. But we couldn't believe as we discussed it that we'd have any real idea how our life would change until the child was born. One thing we did realize—we had each matured, both on our own and as a married couple. Yes, we still loved each other with a passion, but now something much deeper bound us together. We had a shared responsibility, an obligation that we hadn't had before. We talked about names. If it was a girl, Aby said she wanted to name her for her late mother—Elizabeth. If a boy, she asked me what I thought.

"What about James, in honor of your father. It's a grand name. He would be pleased."

Aby hugged me.

"Thank you, my dearest, sweet Isaac. He would be overjoyed."

It looks like it had better be a boy, I thought, seeing her reaction. May and June passed like a dream. Aby had some sickness, and her birthday was not a happy one as she was confined to bed. She found it difficult to get used to the changes happening to her body, but by the end of June, she was fully recovered—with a perfect little bump, though hidden under her clothes. She was still working with Lady Ann, who was being most solicitous of her, insisting that Aby should only work a few hours a day. Aby was training another girl to help take over more of her responsibilities the closer she came to her confinement.

Journal entry—*1 to 31 July 1619*

David Thomson arrived back with a ship load of fish, sassafras, and some pelts. He had left Captain Dermer with a small, intrepid band at Monhegan, as planned. The captain, having dropped David off at Monhegan, turned 'round to head back south in his pinnace around Cape Cod, making for Capawak, thence down the coast as far as Virginia. At a meeting with Sir F., David gave us an account.

They arrived at Monhegan in May. A small party under Captain Dermer, together with Tisquantum and David, left in the pinnace. The remaining crew with the fishermen, brought from England for that purpose, would stay in the vicinity of Monhegan to fish. It took Captain Dermer's party about a fortnight to work their way along the coast. They visited Saco and found it largely deserted. David was sad to see it. He and Tisquantum talked to an Indian there. They were surprised and gratified to find that there were plans for the tribe to return. By coincidence, the Indian had been on a scouting trip for his sachem. David's party heard no mention of our Indian friends from our previous trip. As they moved down the coast, they saw nothing but empty villages. In some cases, the dead had been left, partially consumed by wild animals, with large numbers of human bones broken and scattered. Tisquantum became very quiet. It was a chilling sight. David was the only one of the party to have seen the onset of this terrible epidemic. He was able to provide the context to his companions. They were all shocked and horrified. It was a slow, sad process as they explored the coast.

When they ventured farther inland, they found the same eerie emptiness everywhere. They spent some time, at David's insistence, exploring the Piscataqua River. At its mouth is a large natural harbor. The many islands, fresh water, and good agricultural land, which seemed to stretch away into the distance on either side of the river, confirmed to David that it would make an ideal location for permanent settlement. Leaving Piscataqua, they continued along the coast passing the mouth of another mighty river. The entrance was tricky. As with the Saco, there was a sandbar across the entrance. With the outflow of the river, an incoming tide, and adverse winds, the water would be unsettled enough at the mouth to capsize a boat. Once in the river, while its course was wide and strong from the west, it opened up to the south into a huge marshland with other rivers meandering through to disappear inland. Tisquantum said it was the land of the Merrimac people. They sailed on round Cape Ann, into the large harbor that Champlain had called Beauport. After exploring that well-protected harbor, they moved on along the coastline west. They came to another river mouth protected by many islands. They ventured into an enormous natural harbor. Tisquantum said the Shawmut people lived there. They would need more time than they had available to explore, but from the little they saw, it would make yet another ideal place to build one or more settlements.

They continued south. As they approached Patuxet, they had seen few if any Indians. Tisquantum was becoming increasingly withdrawn. His stillness became more marked the nearer they came to his homeland. David said that in anyone else, one would see the agitation. The stoicism of the Indians was such that it seemed to work in reverse—the more concerned, the quieter they became. At one point, they were together on the foredeck leaning over the larboard rails watching the coastline roll past. Tisquantum expressed his deep concern for his people. All the evidence pointed to the heavy loss of life all the way down the coast. David asked him what he intended to do. He answered it had been several years, and he had suffered many strange adventures far, far away since he last was home. He had spent those years treasuring the faces, voices of his family, the presence of his friends in his heart. He had started the return journey with the happy expectation that he would be reunited with them soon. Now he feared that they would be gone from him.

When they arrived at Patuxet, Tisquantum went ashore by himself. He disappeared on his own awful journey of discovery. David said it was the same there as everywhere else. Tisquantum came back, unable to find anyone alive, though he'd found many burial mounds. He said he would go farther inland to search for the living to find out what had happened. Captain Dermer accompanied him with David and his crew. After a day's march they came to the village of Namasket. Tisquantum found his tribe had been badly decimated—his immediate family all dead. He had been able to find some surviving members who described the terrible suffering that had occurred in his absence. He told David he must go away. He needed to allow his natural world to embrace, soothe, and gently return him to the land of the living, for surely he was torn to follow those who had gone before him.

Such a healing had to be postponed, as there was an immediate problem: The village was filled with Indians angered by the sight of English people. David said it was entirely understandable. We'd been lucky in Saco because we had been able to help and build trust. Here, they saw Englishmen who they believed were the cause of all their misery. Tisquantum came to their defense. He was able to calm everyone down. David said he was able to make himself understood enough to describe the winter we had spent at Saco. The Indians at Namasket had heard that story. Once they understood David was a part of that company of Englishmen, they became appreciative. At one point they asked David if he was Machk. David laughed. No, he wasn't. That was a brave and good friend of his who was now back in England, but he said Machk loved the Indians and wanted to return. A message was sent to the sachems of two major Abenaki tribes farther south. They arrived with a large bodyguard. With Tisquantum's help, as the returning prodigal son who was held in the highest regard, they were able to restore some of the good relations of years past. Tisquantum was keen to go to the village of the chief sagamore of all the local tribes, Massasoit, there being no one and nothing left for him at Patuxet. He wanted to go there to begin his lonely journey of healing with people who were part of his larger community. He said it was important that Massasoit be persuaded to look on the English with favor. He needed to counter the antagonism of local sagamores like Epenow. He said it would be a renewal for him. He no longer had his own family and tribe.

David had told Tisquantum and Captain Dermer on the voyage from Plymouth that it was Sir Ferdinando's intention to send a large group of settlers to New England. Sir Ferdinando, who was respected by Tisquantum, had an important role for him to play to look after those settlers. It was not known exactly where they would land, but it was Sir Ferdinando's hope and expectation to have them settle somewhere near Patuxet on the coast in Massachusetts Bay. Tisquantum promised to keep an eye out for them. They also talked about Samoset, whose life now consisted of travel along the coast of New England. Tisquantum should attempt to make contact with him. Samoset would be as likely as anyone to find out if, when, and where the Separatists landed. Tisquantum said that he would inform the coastal Abenaki. They would tell him when the settlers arrived. He promised that he would go to the Separatists and provide assistance.

Captain Dermer and company continued to explore the coastline north from Patuxet to Cape Ann, onward back to Saco, thence to Monhegan. He sent the now fully loaded ship back to Plymouth with David Thomson while he, intrepid explorer that he was, set off in the pinnace once more with his equally brave party, heading south.

Sir F. thanked David for his efforts. He discussed the current status of the Separatists. They were clearly becoming anxious. David Tremaine, still in London, reported that Messrs Cushman and Carver were under enormous pressure from Leiden to complete negotiations for a ship and financing. They'd assumed that land would be available from the Virginia Company, in the same way it had been made available to Rev. Blackwell's settlers. Now, the signs were that, once again, they were going to have to depend on the Dutch to find land near the Hudson River. There seemed no possibility of those negotiations reaching fruition in time for them to set sail this year. To the Leiden Separatists, this was an almost unbearable disappointment. Given that pressure, Sir F. was concerned the Separatists might be persuaded to make the wrong decision too quickly. He'd told David Tremaine to act the wise counselor and dissuade them from making a rash decision. He had been successful, but for how much longer? Sir F. considered the options available to ensure the Separatists settled in New England. It looked, increasingly, that the Council for New England would not have its charter ratified until 1620, by which time the Separatists would, presumably, be on their way. Looking at me, he said guile seemed the only option. We needed to help them find a ship, the captain of which could be persuaded to make for New England.

I nodded. "That persuasion will be an interesting exercise, sir. If you will allow me to speak my thoughts."

Sir F. nodded.

"We need to leave Tremaine as our sole contact with Cushman and Carver. I have numerous contacts in the maritime world, and I suggest I begin the process of working those connections to come up with some likely options. I must be circumspect. Any potential captain, at this stage, should not be aware of our specific interest. I will keep Tremaine apprised of my activity. He will need to be the judge of when to insinuate our choice of captain into the Separatists' thought processes."

Sir F. pondered for a while, and then said, "Thomas Weston is known to be an unprincipled promoter. He's likely to offer a boat, possibly even before he has reached agreement with the boat owner or captain. Tremaine needs to confound Weston sufficiently to allow us to help the Separatists find their own vessel."

Sir F. told me to travel to London and discuss our plans with Tremaine. I had to make sure he understood his role. With that he closed the meeting.

I returned home to Aby. I told her I had to go to London. Now that she was feeling better, still fully mobile, I said it would be the best time for me to leave her. I would be gone for at most a fortnight—back, I hoped, by the end of July. Aby's mind was on starting a family. She had been introduced to Amyse's midwife, Sarah Winstanley, who was a plump, cheery middle-aged woman, taught by her mother. She had delivered hundreds of babies and would be pleased to deliver Aby's. Aby had talked to Doc Vines, who'd made a study of childbirth and was considered something of an expert. He promised to provide whatever medical assistance was required. Sarah described the birthing scene—a birthing stool, which she would provide, the birth to take place in the kitchen in front of the fire with plenty of clean, hot water available. Straw on the floor to make cleanup from the birth simple. All seemed straightforward, if one didn't dwell on the process itself. Aby was both excited to be a mother and quietly terrified of having a baby. The sooner I left, the sooner I would return. She would need my emotional support, if nothing else, increasingly as her time for confinement approached. Sarah was able to give Aby a good idea of what to expect after the birth. Breastfeeding—would Aby be feeding the child herself or would she like Sarah to find a wet nurse? Sarah pointed out that sometimes a mother was unable to breastfeed, which meant a wet nurse would be necessary. That wouldn't be known until the baby was born, so it would be best to have a wet nurse available in case. Aby insisted it was not a question to be asked; she would be breastfeeding her baby, come what may.

Aby would be expected to remain in bed for several weeks after the birth. Did she have someone who would act as nurse and housekeeper? If not, Sarah said she would be able to find one, possibly the wet nurse herself. Aby said that she had already talked to Annie Potts, from the Minerva Inn. Annie had been adamant she'd be available as soon as Aby needed her and would remain as long as she was required. Her uncle, Alfred, was aware and had been told he had no say in the matter. Knowing Alfred, I thought he would probably welcome a respite from Annie, at least for the first day or two until he realized how much he depended on her. Sarah knew her from Amyse's delivery and was pleased. I made my escape. Aby was otherwise engaged. She wanted to organize the changes to the house to be suitable for a baby, to talk with Amyse and learn everything she could about the experience that lay ahead. How would her wardrobe change? She was already thinking about when it would become difficult to wear some of her existing clothes. I had commented that surely that would be a while yet. My comment was not well received. I would not be missed.

I decided to ride Maddie to London. I needed the fresh air; Maddie needed the exercise. I made the most of it, taking four days to get there, arriving Wednesday, 18 July. I stayed at the Old Mitre Inn in Ely Place, Clerkenwell. I didn't want to bother the staff at the Gorges residence, even though Sir F. suggested I stay there, but the inn was close by in case of an unforeseen emergency. David Tremaine met me at the Mitre the next day. I updated him on our meeting with Sir F. and the expanded role we had for him. He didn't blink. In fact, he had been thinking along those lines already. He really didn't have much good to say about Weston. Cushman was inclined to act without too much forethought, but Carver was much more cautious. They both had come to rely on David's disinterested, objective advice. Weston had been forced to be honest. Cushman was eager but held back by Carver. It was going to be a delicate task to foil his attempts to find a vessel for the Separatists.

"Until we have found a skipper and boat for the Separatists, we don't want to stop Weston from finding one," David told me. "We might not do any better. In which case, we would need to come up with a plan to persuade the skipper of that boat where he, in fact, should be landing his passengers."

I promised to begin my search immediately. In fact, I had possibilities that I needed to follow up on in Rotherhithe and Gravesend. David said he had contacts too, which he would pursue. He said he would give me anything useful that arose. We had a pleasant evening. After a meal and into our third tankard, we got to talking about more personal matters. He wanted to know about how married life suited Aby and me. I gave him a description but, though sorely tempted, refrained from mentioning Aby's pregnancy. I said that Annie had become a close companion to Aby. David nodded slowly and looked at me. He had done that before when Annie had been mentioned. Remembering that Aby wanted to play matchmaker, I asked him what he thought about Annie.

"I like her. She is a good woman."

"To my knowledge, she is not spoken for. She certainly doesn't seem to be interested in anyone. Have you thought of getting to know her better?"

David laughed. "I'm not ready to hang a matrimonial millwheel round my neck. I enjoy women. I have had dalliances with many a pretty wench, in many different towns here in England and on the continent. Annie is not for me. She wants to marry and wants children of her own."

"You are betraying yourself," I said, smiling. "So, you have spent time with her. You know the way she is feeling, what she wants. To get that far, you must have done some wooing."

David smiled, somewhat sheepishly. "No matter, that is all past. She wasn't interested. Her mind is set elsewhere."

"Really," I said. "That sounds intriguing. I didn't know."

David shook his head. He said it was time to move on to other things. Later, I made a note to tell Aby that her matchmaking had come to naught before she had even begun. I spent the next three days mostly riding Maddie around London and the surrounding villages, or by wherry on the Thames following my leads and, in the guise of an investor looking for likely ship charters for the Americas, talking to a number of skippers, whose names I had received previously. They led me to others. On the plus side, I built my network substantially. I had skippers who appeared reliable, others not. Skippers who traded only in coastal British waters; those who knew the continental trade and the main ports; those who knew Newfoundland waters; none of whom had been to New England but some who knew Virginia, even Bermuda. It had been a useful few days. I had a final meeting with David. He had nothing to report back to me but would let me know when he did. Maddie and I returned to Plymouth, arriving Saturday, 31 July.

Journal entry—*1 August to 6 December 1619*

I arrived back to a transformed house, though I had only been away a few weeks. The house had been repainted, the floors re-stained, the kitchen reorganized, and re-furnished. The furniture brought from Dorchester had been replaced for the most part with new pieces. A handsome, sturdy, ornate, highly polished table with a set of six tall backed, upholstered chairs. The sideboard was gone, replaced by a dresser, equally ornate. We still had our easy chairs and large couch. Our bedroom was also changed. A large four-poster with curtains and a crib had been added, with a dresser to be used just for the baby's clothes and whatnot. There was a double washstand with matching jugs and basins. One, presumably, for the baby. Heavy drapes in colorful, pleasing shades for the windows. Any chance of cold drafts was largely eliminated. A larger reflector plate had been installed at the back of the fireplace to increase the amount of heat reflected into the room. Aby had thought of everything, and had proceeded to accomplish it all while she was well, fit, and strong. The second bedroom had been made into living quarters for Annie, who was to be nurse and housekeeper. She had been asked to advise what she would like to have done to the room to make it as comfortable as possible. She had been touched at Aby's thoughtfulness and had been happy to help Aby prepare the room to her absolute liking.

The next few months went quickly. I had to make a brief trip to Bristol to meet with Captain Morris. He was not available for or interested in voyages to New England. He had become active in the import of wines; madeira, alicante, burgundy, and brandy, with the result that his voyages were confined to France and Spain, in spite of the poor relations those countries had with England. Politics was one thing but trade something altogether different. He would keep his ears open for any likely captain who was interested in going to New England. But he did seem willing to have me become a small investor in his commercial enterprise. With little happening in London, my attention, increasingly, was drawn to Aby with her pregnancy. I had thought that a husband at such times was a somewhat useless appendage. Surprisingly, I found I had an essential role to play. As Aby grew heavier with child, she became less active, needing more rest. Lady Ann had now taken on the assistant Aby had trained full-time. It took Aby time to accept that she was no longer the person helping Lady Ann, but the fatigue made the change seem sensible and necessary.

Aby developed aches in her limbs and her back. I became, with experience, an expert massager. With the summer coming to an end, autumn weather brought cold winds. Attendant drafts we thought we had excluded had to be blocked. Aby now was beginning to suffer from her lack of activity. She found she had both hot and cold spells. Midwife Sarah had become an increasingly frequent visitor. Rather belatedly, I understood from her that she was a bit worried about Aby's skeletal structure. I looked stupid when told this. I had no idea what that meant. It seems she has narrow hips, her pelvis not being an ideal shape to bear babies. The remedy was for Aby to be given exercises to make her nether regions as flexible as possible. Ointments were used to massage those muscles to keep them loose. Sarah suggested I might like to be responsible for that ministration, which both Aby and I were happy for me to take on. Doc visited us as well, but he said that Sarah seemed to have everything under control at this stage. Aby was due the first week of December. By the end of November, Annie came to stay. Thereafter, Sarah and Annie took over control. It was suggested that I find alternative accommodation. I was no longer deemed a satisfactory massager or general errand boy. I was disconcerted, but realized I was in no position to provide any help at this stage. So, I moved to the Minerva. Alfred Potts suggested, as Annie had taken over my house, perhaps I might like to take over her job. I could visit Aby for short visits every morning and afternoon. At a point, on 4 December, Sarah advised me to wait to be called before visiting again. Alfred became my companion. I did not dare leave the inn, as that's where I would receive any message from Whimple St.

David Thomson came by and shared a tankard with me, full of commiseration about the wait for something to happen. He had been away for the birth of his two surviving children. He had little in the way of practical advice to give me. I'm not sure he was even around for the birth of their first child, who had died shortly after childbirth, but he was company. Then on 6 December, I was told to come to Whimple St. I ran the whole way there. I was met by an anxious Annie. Apparently, it was a difficult birth, Aby was having a very bad time of it and had pleaded for me to come. I went to her. She was on the birthing stool, legs bent and raised, feet on two steps. A large sheet covered her from the waist down. Sarah was under the sheet, working to release the baby. Aby was in agony, crying hysterically. I had never seen her like this and wrapped my arms round her, whispering my love for her. She clutched me and stopped crying, but moaned piteously. Sarah appeared from under the sheet and called to Annie.

"Get Doctor Vines."

I hadn't realized, but he was waiting close by. He came immediately and told me to leave. Doc gave my shoulder a quick, reassuring squeeze as I left. What was happening? What could I do? Where should I go? I was distraught. Time passed. I sat, stood, paced outside the house. What seemed like several hours went by, the weather had been cold, cloudy, no snow. As the afternoon became dusk, it started to snow.

Doc appeared, tired and troubled. He found me.

"Aby is not well, but the baby is born. A boy. Congratulations."

"What do you mean, not well?'

"She has lost a lot of blood," he said. "The baby got stuck. There was some damage to Aby as the birth passage was forced open to allow the baby to be born. There are some muscles down there that are very strong and prevented the passage from opening. Those muscles have been damaged and, as a result, caused terrible pain." Doc paused, then went on. "The tear caused much blood loss, too much. I closed it, and the blood has now been stanched, but she is very weak. She's asleep and being looked after by Annie. Sarah is taking care of the baby. You should come in to meet your son, but let Aby sleep."

I went in, followed by Doc. The kitchen had been tidied. The straw had been swept from the floor. It was wrapped in a large, bloody sheet—Aby's blood. Tearing my eyes away from that horror, I looked at Sarah. She was cuddling my son, James. She looked harassed, worried, tired, and maternal as she gazed down at little James. She looked up at me and smiled, passing him over to me.

"Your son. Perfectly formed and healthy."

I looked down at this little bundle, fast asleep, pink with a thatch of dark hair. I bent down and kissed his head, noticing his sweet smell. He stirred, settling once more. I handed him back to Sarah with a smile, a thank-you, and asked to see my wife. She nodded, pointing with her chin to the door to the bedroom. I entered to be met by Annie, round eyes red from weeping. Doc followed me into the room.

"She is asleep," he said. "Be gentle, very quiet."

I knelt down beside the bed and gazed at my darling wife and dearest friend. She was white and drawn. Lines etched into her face. She was barely breathing, her breast hardly moving. A while later, I got up. Doc and I left the room.

"What is wrong with her? When will she recover?"

Doc sat me down. "I can't tell you if she will recover," he said gently. "Her body has to rebuild the blood she had lost. We won't know whether she will be able to do that for another forty-eight hours. Keep her warm, wipe her face occasionally with a damp warm cloth. Try to get liquid into her. I have had Annie boil some water that is now cool in the jug on the table beside her. Use that to moisten her lips. If she is responsive, lift her with Annie's help, gently, and try to get her to sip the water from a cup, but regardless, moisten her lips. She needs to eat something. There is a bowl of broth that Annie made, but at this stage I doubt you will get any of that into her. You must be patient and wait."

The next twenty-four hours were the worst of my life. I was helpless, sitting in a chair next to the bed. I held her hand, soft and unresponsive, massaging it gently with my thumb. Occasionally, I would lean over and lightly brush my lips over her damp forehead. Annie sat at the other side of the bed, gazing with love and sorrow at us both. She smiled when I looked up at her, a comfort more than she could know. We were able to get a little water into Aby and keep her lips moistened. Doc had left me. He returned the next morning. I had hardly moved during the night. Annie had gone to her room to sleep for a few hours just before dawn. He asked me to go to the kitchen while he and Sarah examined Aby. James was in his crib. In the kitchen, another lady sat by the fire—Beth Webster, a wet nurse. She'd been here every few hours since the birth to feed James. She had come through the night and again this morning several hours earlier and had continued to provide James his feed, obviously satisfying as he was fast asleep. Apparently, Beth had one of her own children breastfeeding and was capable of producing the milk that James needed as well. Doc came out and beckoned me to come into the bedroom. Aby was awake. I knelt and enfolded her in my arms. She was very weak, hardly able to speak. We whispered a few sweet words to each other, and she went back to sleep. Doc said that Aby was still not out of danger, but improving. He advised me to get some sleep. By the time I came back, he hoped Aby would be on the way to recovery. I went back to the Minerva to my room and fell onto my bed. The tension slowly released and I slept. It was afternoon before I returned to Aby.

She awoke late in the afternoon. Baby James, all swaddled, had been placed on a pillow next to her, and she was able to turn her head and kiss him. Annie was with her, beaming. Doc had been in. He had pronounced Aby much better. She had eaten the bowl of broth, thanks to Annie's administrations. Annie left us and we spent a happy, happy ten minutes holding hands in companionable silence. Aby was still too weak to move or talk, the pain still intense. I gently wiped her forehead and her cheeks with a damp cloth which seemed to ease her a little. She, poor love, was suffering, and I could do nothing. Annie came back in and shooed me out. Aby needed to sleep. Beth was a regular visitor in the kitchen. James was a loud, demanding feeder, and she seemed hard put to keep him satisfied.

--- CHAPTER 36 ---

Journal entry—*8 December 1619 to 28 January 1620*

I found out subsequently, talking to Alfred Potts, as well as other husbands and fathers, just how significantly convention had been overturned in Aby's delivery. The idea of any man being present at a birth is most unusual. Thank God Doc had been there. He'd been able to complete the delivery and repair the damage to Aby. She continued to progress but slowly, unable to breastfeed for a fortnight, too weak, which was distressing for her. I was reduced to holding Aby's hands and soothing her brow whenever I was allowed to visit her. Christmas was largely overlooked as Aby was unable to participate. I wasn't interested in anything except supporting Aby and holding James. Annie was an absolute godsend. Thursday, 23 December, was a red-letter day. Aby, now sitting up in bed, was able to hold James and start the process of feeding him herself. At first, she produced little milk, but Beth advised patience. After several weeks, Aby was able to keep up with James' demands. A wonderful change came over her as she took to full-time feeding duties. She had her baby, and glowed. With the pain largely gone, helped by Annie, she began to practice walking again. Whenever I could, mostly in the early evenings, I sat holding James, still swaddled, while Annie slowly walked Aby round the room. All I could do was massage her poor, tired muscles.

Meantime, back in the world outside I had work to do. A report from David Tremaine described the business arrangement that Weston had negotiated with the Separatists to enable them to obtain the financial backing they needed. The arrangement seemed onerous to me, but the terms had been accepted by the Separatists. Although the colonizing enterprise was established as a joint stock undertaking, with investors, including settlers, each having stock ownership, in essence they would be required to work four days a week to acquire or produce fish, pelts, timber, and other goods to be sent back to London, for the benefit of the stockholders. With a day off for worship, they'd only two days a week left to build their own self-sufficiency. Weston had promised them that investors were available on these terms. He had still not found a ship. David told me that he was in touch, through a friend, with a possible candidate. Until he had a better idea of the Separatists' timetable and the reality of Weston's grandiose statements, he preferred to keep quiet. According to Carver, his Leiden people were still trying to reach agreement on the number of settlers who would be going. There were about four hundred Separatists living in Leiden. A manageable number to travel at one time was thought to be about a third of that number. Who would be the first to go, and under whose leadership, Robinson or Brewster? David said that he had been talking to Weston about the possibility of land being made available in New England, through the newly formed Council for New England. By dropping that choice morsel in Weston's ear, he hoped to have Weston act as unwitting agent for Sir F.'s design. It seemed to be working, as Weston had gone to Carver and Cushman to warn them about the risks of doing business with the Dutch or the Virginia Company. This warning fell on ready ears, as the Virginia Company was still in a state of confusion and penury. The Dutch were beginning to make noises in Holland that perhaps they weren't quite so keen to offer English settlers land in their Dutch enclave between English Virginia and English New England.

Journal entry—*29 January to 1 May 1620*

James was growing rapidly. Aby continued to make progress. I was worried about her. It was taking her a long time to regain her strength and mobility. Annie told me to be patient, but she, too, showed signs of being concerned. I talked to Doc. He told me that what Aby had been through was beyond anything I could possibly imagine. She was lucky to be alive. I had tried talking to her about what I was doing with the Separatists, but whereas she had been fascinated and engaged before, now she showed no interest. Her life was James, pure and simple.

David reported that Weston was beginning to lose some of his investors. At least, that was what Weston was saying. Based on Weston's reputation David believed he probably had never completed an agreement with them. Time was approaching when Weston had to make good on his promises and was having difficulty doing so. Then another blow to Weston's credibility. He had persuaded Cushman that to ensure there were enough investors he had to change the negotiated agreement they had. The investors were now demanding that the settlers, admittedly small stockholders themselves, would have to work full-time for the benefit of all the stockholders for the first seven years. No more would they be able to work the two days a week for their own particular salvation. Unbelievably, Cushman had agreed to the new terms without involving Carver or checking back with Leiden. Then worse news came. Weston had been unable to find a ship to take them on their voyage. What must the people back in Leiden be thinking? Pastor Robinson must be having a terrible time keeping his group together. Meeting with Sir F., we agreed it was time we stepped in with some help. A message was sent to David to ask about the ship's captain he had identified. A message came back suggesting I come to London to meet with this captain. Leaving Aby was hard, but she was in her own world and well looked after. I would not be missed, sad thought though it was. I rode Maddie up to London. At David's suggestion I stayed at the Shippe, as his contact lived in Rotherhithe.

David introduced me to a Captain Christopher Jones, part-owner and skipper of a merchant trader, the *Mayflower*. While he hadn't sailed to Virginia before, he'd been to Newfoundland, while his navigator, Mr. Coppin, had been to Virginia several times under different captains. I explained that we were attempting to assist a group of settlers in their desire to move to America. They had tentatively reached agreement with the Virginia Company to settle on land they would provide, but it was unlikely that would happen, based on the information we had. I represented Sir Ferdinando Gorges of the Plymouth Company, now being reconstituted as the Council for New England. We were concerned to support the Separatists for a number of religious and commercial reasons but wanted to stay in the background. Would he be interested in transporting the settlers to New England this summer?

"As long as we can agree to terms, I would be prepared to do so," Captain Jones answered.

I told him we would like to keep knowledge of our involvement unknown to the settlers, so would prefer it if we gave his name to Thomas Weston, the gentleman responsible to the settlers for arranging their transport and settlement, and a member of the Merchant Adventurers of London. Captain Jones was, of course, entirely free to negotiate with Mr. Weston whatever terms were mutually agreeable. But, if there were any further details he wished to discuss with us, we would be grateful if he would contact us through Mr. Tremaine. We covered a number of matters. In the course of our conversation, I came to understand the man. With the right inducement, I felt he could be trusted. He had a strong character and was self-assured. I believed that when the time came and the circumstances dictated, he would do whatever he'd agreed to accomplish. Afterward, David said he would advise Weston to make contact with Captain Jones and watch progress. We talked about the moral advisability of introducing a man such as Jones who we were persuading to follow our plan, unbeknownst to the Separatists, to someone seemingly devoid of integrity himself. We convinced ourselves it was for the ultimate good of the settlers. We shared a twinge of conscience about the guile with which we were seeking our own ends. We were able to convince ourselves that the end justified the means. The Separatists wished to settle in America. I was convinced New England was the best place for them, even if they did not yet know that.

I rode back to Plymouth, having been away ten days. On my return, Aby was most welcoming. She apologized for being disengaged when I left. She was still in recovery but much better. She admitted she was totally captivated by our gorgeous young son. Lady Ann had written to ask how Aby was. The Gorgeses had now returned to Clerkenwell. Lady Ann was anxious for Aby to return to her service. The replacement had not been a success. The request from Lady Ann had given Aby pause. Was it possible that, with James now part of her life, she would consider going back to work? We talked about it. Annie was devoted to James and had become a full-time nursemaid for him. If Aby was of a mind to, she should be able to return to at least some part of her past employment, but not for a couple of months, until she was fully recovered. She wrote to tell Lady Ann.

Journal entry—*2 May to 15 July 1620*

Sir F. was now in serious debate and bitter dispute with Sir Edwin Sandys of the Virginia Company. They had issued instructions to their people in Jamestown authorizing them to fish in New England waters, regardless of the restrictions on that fishing being covered in Sir F.'s charter, currently before the privy council. Meantime, the Leiden Separatists, tired of the delays and dubious about Weston's ability to ever deliver a boat to them, had chartered a small vessel—the *Speedwell*—in Holland. As it happened, Weston had reached agreement with Cushman and Carver to charter the *Mayflower*. Now having the two ships originally planned for, their intent was for some of the Separatists to sail in the *Speedwell* to meet the *Mayflower* in Southampton. The number that had decided to make this first trip was insufficient to fill the *Mayflower* and the *Speedwell*, even though several England-based Separatists had agreed to join the Leiden group in their move to New England. Weston, therefore, had recruited non-Separatists, or "Strangers," who wanted to immigrate for economic reasons, to make up numbers. Weston had insisted that one of these Strangers should be the leader of both the Separatists and the Strangers. This leader was Christopher Martin. Reports coming back from David Tremaine suggested Martin was not an easy man to deal with. It'd taken considerable forbearance on David's part not to have a serious argument with him. After all, David said he wasn't involved. But heaven help the people under Martin's command.

After inordinate delay, the enterprise slowly began to move. Investors were found, but only after Weston changed the agreement he'd negotiated with the settlers to greatly advantage the investors, to the settlers' detriment. The *Mayflower* took on supplies and passengers, and the *Speedwell* filled with Leiden Separatists. Both vessels proceeded to Southampton, the former from London, the latter from Delfthaven. They were tired of dealing with the Virginia Company, who had still not confirmed the availability of a land grant. There was no confirmation of land available in New England, either. As a result, they had set their sights on the Dutch on the Hudson. The whole expedition seemed doomed from the start. Weston, at best unreliable, was seriously underfunded. His change in the agreement with the settlers was rejected out of hand once the Leiden group understood the impact of the change. Weston, angry, departed Southampton, where he'd gone to wish the settlers bon voyage. Martin was proving impossible—entrusted with the task of ensuring the settlers were properly provisioned for the voyage, they suspected him of dishonesty, and when they confronted him he reacted with rage. He was contemptuous of the settlers and treated them very badly. Above it all stood Captain Jones, calm and measured as he attempted to keep everything on track. By this time, David had come down from London and based himself in Southampton to watch over the proceedings. He told me Captain Jones was aware the settlers were under the impression they were heading for the Hudson River. Captain Jones told Mr. Martin that he saw their logic. It was the land common to all three of the parties with whom the Separatists had been in negotiation—the Virginia Company, the Council for New England, and the Dutch. It seemed that one of them should be able to confirm their right to settle there. They had no control of the political machinations among the three parties; they put their trust in God that it would be resolved to their advantage in the fullness of time. Irrespective of the Separatists' desires, David had convinced Captain Jones to agree it would be to the advantage of all concerned if somehow he contrived to land the settlers farther north, preferably in Massachusetts Bay. Captain Jones himself was unhappy about venturing his boat into territory the Dutch considered their own. Their privateering tendencies might get the better of them. Mr. Brewster, who had appeared from hiding, had expressed his view, out of Mr. Martin's hearing, that the Separatists were not keen to find that, after escaping the Dutch way of life in Leiden, they were returning to something similar in America.

CHAPTER 37

Journal entry—*16 July to 8 August 1620*

Lady Ann had sent a note pressing Aby to come up to Clerkenwell. She would be honored to welcome the whole Stanfield family. If Aby decided she'd be unable to continue in Lady Ann's service, the lady wanted to know so she could plan accordingly. Although the departure of the settlers from Southampton was imminent, I was able to accompany my family and Annie up to London. I'd made sure *Rosie* was available not only to take us up to London, but to get me back to Southampton by the end of July. Luckily, it fitted into the skipper's plans reasonably well. Not only was I a favored friend, I was becoming an important business partner, given the investments I was making in the import and export of goods by way of the *Sweet Rose*. We went aboard. The ladies and James were settled in the embrace of a devoted crew, prepared to take us on a five-day sea voyage under gentle breezes on calm seas to London. We left Plymouth on 21 July. We docked in Rotherhithe on the twenty-sixth.

The voyage was an opportunity for Aby and me to spend time together as we'd been unable to do since James' birth. Annie continued her devoted care of James, which allowed us three to spend much of every day together. We talked about all that had happened to us, how it had affected us, and what we hoped for in the future. It enabled us to regain some of the closeness we'd had before, but it was clear things were different. I now shared Aby with James. The future, as far as Aby was concerned, meant the care and protection of our son. She used to have ideas of having a number of children. The horror of the birth and her close brush with the hereafter convinced her that she would have no more. Not wishing to trust to God's determination concerning future pregnancies, she said that once we settled back home and we returned to our previous intimacy, we would need to be mindful that she did not wish to become pregnant again. I wasn't sure what that meant. Neither of us did, but it was yet another indication that the life we had led previously seemed to have gone forever.

We talked about going to New England. Aby remembered the words she'd spoken to me before about going wherever I went. She was sad to feel she was disappointing me, but admitted that until James was old enough, she could not imagine risking his life to the dangers and discomfort of a settler's life in a hostile country. Her vehemence set me back, but through the words there shone her love. I realized that it was not *my* life, it was not what *I* wanted, but *our* life and what was right for us as a family. By the time *Rosie* arrived in Rotherhithe, we were in complete agreement that our life for the foreseeable future centered on Plymouth. I would look to continue to work with Sir F. If that was no longer feasible, I was beginning to establish myself as a merchant trader. Being in that line would require frequent trips in the furtherance of that trade, but I would be away for no more than a week or two at a time. What was important was the fact that we saw ourselves as an inseparable partnership for life. We were, and always would be, each other's constant companion.

When we arrived at the Clerkenwell residence, we found that John Gorges, Sir F.'s eldest son, was to be married to Lady Frances Fynes, daughter of the earl of Lincoln, on 31 July at St. James, Clerkenwell. Neither Aby nor I had been made aware of the intended nuptials, but I could understand why Lady Ann wanted Aby with her. I was certainly in the way. It was as well that there was a quick turnaround for *Rosie*. I'd barely enough time to see my family safely settled at the Gorges residence in Clerkenwell before I was back on board *Rosie* for the return trip to Southampton. Before I left, I could see with pride that James had become the apple of everyone's eye in the Gorges household. I left, happy that he and Aby were safe and secure in a loving home.

I was in Southampton by the thirty-first. *Rosie* was making another quick turnaround with freight for Gravesend. She expected to be back in London by 3 August. The *Mayflower* and *Speedwell* were in harbor. David Tremaine was there. I stayed in the background as much as possible but began to see signs that there was some serious dissent among the settlers. Weston had left to return to London. Martin was being dictatorial. I briefly met with the *Speedwell*'s Captain Reynolds at a tavern. David introduced me as a possible investor. I did not take to Captain Reynolds, who seemed concerned about the risks he would be taking in a small boat across the Atlantic, and said the *Speedwell* was not a tight ship—it was inclined to leak in heavy seas. It was almost as if he were looking for a reason not to make the trip. I'd heard that she had originally been built as a naval vessel, albeit small, called the *Swiftsure*. While she was old, I would have thought her sound enough—but I wasn't the captain. David told me that Weston's departure was due to the Separatists from Leiden repudiating the revised agreement that Cushman had accepted on their behalf. As he was the person upon whom the Separatists relied for continued financing, his departure had put them into a financial bind. Delays in Southampton was costing them money. They had debts that needed to be paid before their departure. To pay the debts, they had to sell some of their essential provisions, provisions they were carrying with them to help them survive that first winter. David Tremaine and I went by boat to board the *Mayflower*. Before we were both properly aboard, I was checked by a scowling, dark-faced man. David was still boarding from the boat below.

"Who the hell are you? What are you doing on my ship?"

Taken aback, I stared back at him. He grabbed me. Instinctively, I spun him round and with a leg block had him on his knees with his right arm hard pressed up his back.

"And who are you, sir?" I demanded.

Furious and in pain, he admitted to being Mr. Martin. David arrived to intercede. I let him go, stepped back, and told him we were here to see the captain of the *Mayflower*. At that point, Captain Jones came to the quarterdeck rail. He looked down at us and ordered Mr. Martin below, detailing two sailors to ensure that happened. He invited us to join him. He apologized and admitted having a problem keeping the Separatists, the Strangers, and the crew from each other's throats. Mr. Martin was, by his attitude, an instigator of a lot of the foment. We went to Captain Jones' cabin, where we were able to have a quiet word with him. He said he was comfortable with the agreement he'd struck with Mr. Tremaine. It was his intent to make for Cape Cod. He'd instructed his navigator, Mr. Coppin, accordingly. We sympathized with his issues with Mr. Martin. He smiled, saying he'd known much worse. We left him to return to shore. On 5 August, we watched as the *Mayflower* and *Speedwell* departed. Two unhappy ships it seemed to me, but they were on their way. Everyone aboard seemed prepared and willing to make the journey. We returned to Plymouth.

On 8 August, I received a brief note from Sir F., by way of Captain Turner, that Lady Ann had died after a brief illness on 5 August. What could have happened? Six days after her eldest son's wedding. The *Sweet Rose* was bringing Aby and James back to Plymouth. At the onset of Lady Ann's illness, Sir F. had arranged for their immediate departure. They should be back in Plymouth by the ninth or tenth. I was shocked and confused, as was Captain Turner. We had no other information. I could only await the return of *Rosie* and her precious cargo.

Journal entry—*9 to 17 August 1620*

I arranged with a young lad to organize his fellow scamps to keep watch from the Hoe for sign of *Rosie*. I provided a detailed description and was to be informed as soon as she was sighted. I would be at the fort. Captain Turner and I sought refuge in Sir F.'s study. The note from Sir F. had been followed by a further note. We talked about the ramifications of the news. After the wedding party had left and the house was again quiet, Lady Ann had been visiting a destitute area bringing food, clothing, and alms, presumably some things left over from the wedding, as well. She had been struck down with a fever shortly afterward. There was no mention of whether Aby had been with her. I could only imagine the worst. Had Sir F. sent her back because she'd caught the same fever, or was it to protect her and the baby from harm? It was no use speculating. After a while, Captain Turner had to leave to attend his duties. He invited me to stay there as long as I liked and said he'd come back whenever he could. He was unable to speak much comfort, but was a friendly presence. Before he returned, a message was delivered. *Rosie* was in sight. I left word for Captain Turner and walked down to the Barbican quayside on the pool. It was a while before *Rosie* arrived. She came straight to the quayside. As she docked, I went aboard and was greeted by the skipper looking grave.

"Abigail is in my cabin, lying down. She is not well, not at all well. Annie is with her. Young James is being looked after by Dusty."

I went straight down to see Aby, my heart in my mouth. Annie was standing by the berth with a towel and a basin of cold water, bathing Aby's face. She was unconscious, with shallow breath, looking desperately ill. Annie reached out to hold my arm, her eyes brimming with tears.

"It hit her two days out from London. She's been getting steadily worse."

I knelt down beside my dear, sweet wife. This could not be happening again. It was too soon. She'd barely recovered.

"We need to move her back home," I said. "We need to get Doc to see her. Do you think she can be moved?"

Annie agreed. "This boat is no place for her, cramped, smelly, and dirty. We have to move her."

I went back to the quarterdeck to tell the skipper, who barked his instructions. Obi was sent at a run to find Doc, and a messenger went over the side to the fort to fetch an enclosed litter. Within fifteen minutes it was alongside. Next with four seamen, the skipper's berth was raised, eased out of the cabin, up to the waist, and over the side. Aby was gently lifted into the litter and we set off for home. Annie followed with James in her arms. It made a sorry sight. Passersby not knowing the situation but seeing the grim faces assumed the worst and stepped aside. The men doffed their caps and the ladies curtseyed. By the time we arrived home, Doc was waiting for us. We lay Aby on the bed. The sailors, whispering their condolences, left us. Annie went to her room with James, who was by now awake, hungry, and noisy. Dusty had prepared some baby food, somehow, on the trip down. Annie still had some, but barely enough. Doc had us all leave while he examined Aby. I found a lad to go to Beth with the message to come when she could.

Ten minutes of agonized waiting until Doc came back. He sat me down and said there was little he could do. The fever had taken hold and was destroying her ability to breathe. She was fighting it, but the crisis point had not been reached. Past the crisis point she would recover, but things looked bleak. We could do no more than bathe her face and cool the heat radiating from her forehead. He would be back in a few hours. Beth came. She took care of James in the kitchen. Annie and I sat by the bed doing what we could, which was little enough. Doc came back. He checked her heart and breathing, shaking his head. It was becoming more labored. He stayed, sitting on a chair at the foot of the bed. At a certain point, Aby opened her eyes and whispered my name. I knelt beside her, my hands over hers on her breast. She looked at me and smiled the sweetest smile. She started whispering. I leaned over, my ear to her mouth.

"I love you, my dearest. Look after James. Till we meet again."

And she left me.

I couldn't move. I wouldn't move. Her lips were still against my cheek. I was frozen. Oh no, this was not happening. Annie started sobbing and my tears came, too. I buried my head in Aby's soft, still bosom. Gently, Doc took me by the shoulder and slowly lifted me up and away. I stood, turned clinging to him, incoherent. He beckoned to Annie to take me to the other bedroom.

Annie led me away while I had one last desperate look at my wife.

The next few days were a blur. Aby's body was removed. People came and went. I was in a daze. David Tremaine and Annie became my minders. They told me what to do, when to do it. Beth took over caring for James. As long as he was fed regularly, he remained blissfully unaware of the tragedy around him.

I hardly remember Aby's funeral. I embraced many men and women who shared their sorrows with me. Will and Elenor came, Elenor inconsolable. She had regained a dear friend who'd now been lost to her again. The Giradeaus came, both in tears. David Thomson arrived with Amyse, heavily pregnant again. Aby's father came and shook my hand. We wept together. He was bowed,

broken as only a father burying his only daughter could be. No one from *Rosie*—
they had left a day or two earlier back to France. At a certain point I realized
how selfish, how self-involved I was. Grief was destroying her memory. She
was loved by many. James *needed* me. I had to snap out of my misery. I took her
father to meet his namesake. There was an instant bonding. James reached out
to the old man from Beth's arms and clasped his grandfather 'round the neck.
Grandfather Baker straightened and smiled for the first time. He laughed, a
peal of laughter, as James pulled at the old man's beard with a big grin.

"He has her eyes. The same eyes as my wife," he said, his eyes shining.

Mr. Baker stayed till the seventeenth, inseparable from his grandson. Annie
reorganized my life and home. It was no longer proper for her to be living there.
She cleaned the house from top to bottom, and took on housekeeping duties, coming two hours every morning to clean and cook meals for the day. She arranged
for Beth to continue as wet nurse on a permanent basis. As she lived just around
the corner, she was able to come for the day to feed and care for James. Only when
I returned in the evening did she leave. I asked about her own children.

"Nothing to worry about, sir. I have weaned my youngest. My oldest girl of
fourteen years looks after the five surviving children."

Now I am a widower with a baby to look after through the evening and
night. Beth returns to feed James as necessary, but it is a new adventure for
me. James is a nine-month-old bundle of mischief. He is not yet walking,
but able to crawl incredibly swiftly. A moment's lack of attention on my
part, and he would be into something. He was fascinated by the hearth, the
embers, the soot, especially the ash. Occasionally he became so filthy I put
him under the kitchen pump to sluice him down. He hoisted himself upright
using any furniture available. Anything loose he would grab, either put it in
his mouth or throw it away. If breakable, it broke. Once I was prepared to
accept that this exploring was both a game and a learning process for James,
I entered into the spirit with much greater patience. But it was hard work.
James was talkative. He had a range of expressive sounds, including his own
words—well, noises really—for most items he came across. It would have been
easier to interpret them if he was consistent.

I was grateful when Annie came and cooked me a meal. The real reason she
came, she said, was to have time to spend with James, her little darling. I coun-
tered by saying the best reason for her to come was to deal with the accumulated
piss and poop in James's clout, not for the faint-hearted. There were times I
would leave him in his long shirt, unclouted. I preferred to deal with the mess
he deposited on the floor by throwing ash over the piles and puddles, sweeping

them up to throw in the fire. Each morning, Annie would arrive before I left to clean the house and eliminate the smells. Beth would come in time for James' first feed. With her vast experience bringing up children, she managed to keep everything under control during the day. When I arrived back home, I was handed a clean, sweet-smelling baby in a clean, sweet-smelling house. At night, before James' time for sleep, I would wash and swaddle him, then rock him to sleep in my arms, sitting in front of the fire. Before he was rocked to sleep, he would look up at me with Aby's eyes and the little wrinkle Aby had between her eyebrows when she was thinking about something. He would smile, close his eyes, and go to sleep. These were the times I felt the desperate loss, the unbearable loneliness. I tried to imagine Aby sitting with me, sleeping beside me. I had long conversations with her. I was told it would ease the loss. We would still be each other's constant companion, as we had promised each other only a short time ago. Sometimes, especially late at night in bed, I was certain they were wrong. It made the sense of loss worse. A phantom Aby was no Aby. I had to deal with the cold fact that Aby was gone from me, forever. But in the morning, with James playing happily at my feet looking up at me, Aby's eyes were there, full of wonder. I would remember the happy times, and there were so many. Aby would be with me once more.

Journal entry—*Friday, 18 August, to Wednesday, 6 September 1620*

We heard that the *Mayflower* and *Speedwell* had returned to Dartmouth after the *Speedwell* had sprung a leak off Cornwall. Since Aby's death on the ninth, I had become more obviously cynical, a trait I needed to deal with. But I wondered about Reynolds, whether the leaking had been manufactured by him in some way. Seemingly, the leak was soon repaired but contrary winds kept them from leaving. It seemed the poor passengers were not allowed to disembark the week they spent there. Strange. Apparently, the orders came from Mr. Martin. The weather improved. Once more they were off. Again, *Speedwell* proved unseaworthy. They returned, this time to Plymouth. We watched as passengers were rearranged because Captain Reynolds had deemed the *Speedwell* to be unfit to continue. Some of the passengers decided to take heed of the omens. They returned whence they had come, while the rest somehow found room on the *Mayflower*. It was getting late in the year to make the Atlantic crossing. But Captain Jones, true to his word, committed to make the journey. Again, the *Mayflower*, now alone, prepared to set off. This time on 6 September.

Letter to Will—*6 September 1620*

Dear Will,

Thank you and Elenor for coming down to Aby's funeral. Your support meant the world to me. Please thank Elenor for her sweet words. I know how the loss of Aby must be hard for you both. We must keep thinking of all the wonderful moments. When I do, Aby is right with me, as she will be always. Once more, I congratulate you both on your wedding. I said in my last letter we hoped to come to Dorchester at the end of the summer. How unutterably sad that Aby now won't be there—but I hope to come myself. The future is looking bleak right now, but when my mind settles, I will decide what I want to do. Please advise P. that the settlers are on their way. He will be pleased.

I have no energy or appetite to continue my journal. I enclose everything I have written since I gave you my last installment.

I had a sorrowful meeting with Sir F. on his return. He and Lady Ann had been married thirty years and, as Sir F. said, they had been each other's closest companions and friends for their whole marriage. He was destroyed by her death. Her funeral took place at their parish church in Clerkenwell, St. James, where her body was laid to rest. Sir F. was also distraught about the loss of Aby, saying she had become family, not only to him and Lady Ann, but to the wider Gorges family. Another among the heartbroken was Sir Teddy, who sent me a sad note by way of Sir F.

I went out to the Hoe as the *Mayflower* left. I stood brooding, watching as she slowly receded, to disappear behind the headland. A sense of overwhelming loss washed through me. We had agreed that our life together would be centered on Plymouth, but Aby has left me to go on her own journey. It almost seems that she is a part of *Mayflower*'s leaving. I have a desperate, if irrational, desire to follow her.

Isaac

Appendix

—— MAIN CHARACTERS ——

Assacomet	Native American captured by Capt. Weymouth
Baker, Abigail ("Aby")	Daughter of James Baker, born June 3, 1597
Baker, James	Tallow-maker and chandler
Beale, Silas	Ostler at the George Inn
Braddock, James ("J.B.")	Able seaman aboard the *Sweet Rose*
Brown, Isaiah	Captain aboard the *Sweet Rose*
Burch, Obediah ("Obi")	Ship's boy aboard the *Sweet Rose*
Bushrode, Richard	Merchant friend of Rev. White
Cattigan, Dusty	Cook aboard the *Sweet Rose*
Cheeke, Robert	Schoolmaster in Dorchester
Dawkins, Johnny	Ship's boy aboard the *Sweet Rose*
Epenow	Native American captured by Capt. Harlow
Giradeau, Henri	Merchant in La Rochelle

Giradeau, Vivienne	Daughter of Henri
Gorges, Robert	Second son of Sir Ferdinando
Gorges, Sir Ferdinando ("Sir F.")	Governor of Plymouth Fort
Gorges, Sir Teddy	Cousin of Sir Ferdinando
Gosling, Jeremiah	Landlord of the Sun in Lower Barton
Gunt, Tred	Second mate of the *Sweet Rose*
Hadfield, Tiny	Able seaman aboard the *Sweet Rose*
Jones, Andrew ("Peg")	First mate aboard the *Sweet Rose*
Potts, Alfred	Landlord of the Minerva Inn in Plymouth
Potts, Annie	Niece of Alfred, barmaid at the Minerva Inn
Robinson, John	Leader of the Separatists in Leiden
Scroud, Ebenezer	Isaac's business manager
Stanfield, Isaac	Narrator, born January 6, 1597
Stanfield, James	Son of Isaac and Aby, born December 6, 1619
Swain, Charlie	Friend of Isaac
Thomson, Amyse	Wife of David Thomson
Thomson, David	Apothecary's assistant and settler

Tisquantum	Native American captured by Capt. Hunt
Tremaine, David	Secret agent of Sir Ferdinando
Trescothick, Adam	Groom at the King's Arms
Turner (Capt)	Sir Ferdinando's staff officer
Vines, Richard (Doc)	Doctor and settler
Wellings	Steward to Sir Edward Gorges at Wraxall Court
Weston, Thomas	London merchant adventurer
White, John ("Patriarch" or "P.")	Rector of Holy Trinity Church
Whiteway, Will	Friend of Isaac

Southwest England

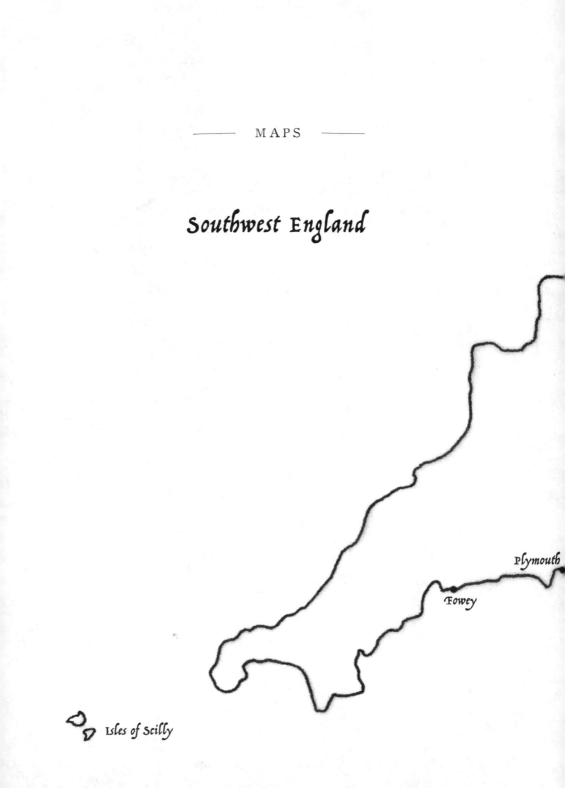

Plymouth

Fowey

Isles of Scilly

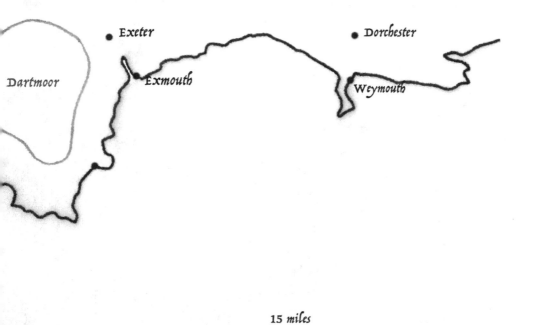

15 miles

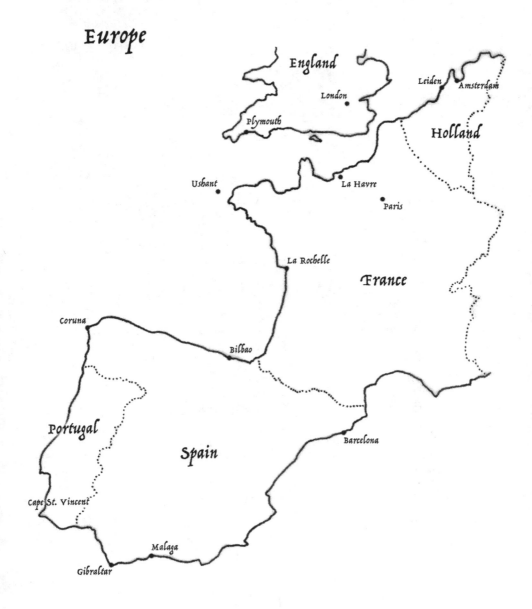

Europe

England

London

Plymouth

Leiden   Amsterdam

Holland

Ushant

La Havre

Paris

La Rochelle

France

Coruna

Bilbao

Barcelona

Portugal

Spain

Cape St. Vincent

Malaga

Gibraltar

200 miles

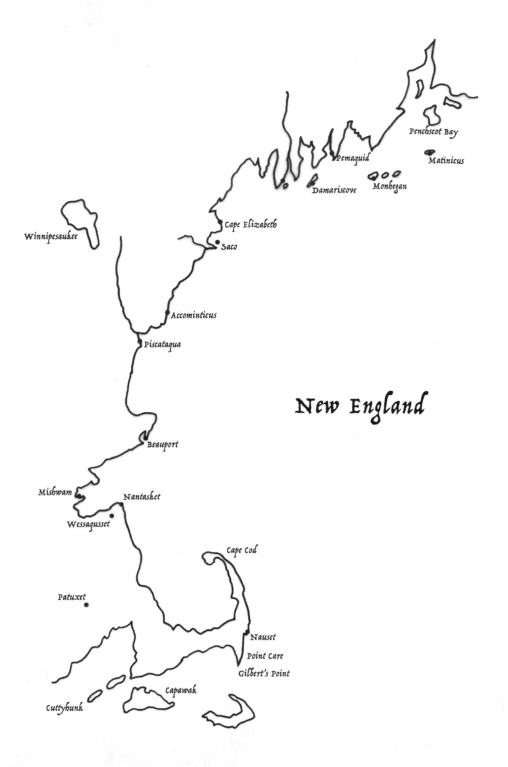

Penchscot Bay

Matinicus

Pemaquid

Monhegan

Damariscove

Cape Elizabeth

Winnipesaukee

Saco

Accominticus

Piscataqua

New England

Beauport

Mishwam

Nantasket

Wessagusset

Cape Cod

Patuxet

Nauset

Point Care

Gilbert's Point

Capawak

Cuttyhunk

Long before documented explorations were made of the North American coastline, fishermen from Portugal, Spain, and France were harvesting the cod off Newfoundland. Basque fishing fleets were almost permanent visitors before Christopher Columbus "discovered" America.

Read Mark Kurlansky's *Cod*, published by Walker Publishing Company in 1997, to learn more.

It was only later that English fishermen sailed to Newfoundland, as they found their fishing grounds in the North Sea and around Iceland to be less productive. Perhaps of more importance, they did not have such ready access to salt to preserve the fish as their continental rivals. When they did venture farther west, they had established some sources for salt but they saw the need to dry the fish on land prior to shipment home.

Accounts of many of the explorations listed below can be found in the following book, published in two volumes:

Forerunners of the Pilgrims. Ed. Livermore, Charles Herbert (The New England Society of Brooklyn, 1912).

1524 GIOVANNI DA VERRAZZANO

Explored the North American coastline north from Cape Fear, North Carolina. He was the first European to land in Cape Cod, and continued north up the Maine coast.

1525 ESTEVAN GOMEZ

Explored the North American coastline south from Nova Scotia. He charted the Maine coastline in his search for the fabled northern passage to China.

1580 JOHN WALKER

Explored Penobscot Bay, Maine, under the direction of Sir Humphrey Gilbert. He was searching for silver mines rumored to be abundant in Norumbega.

1602 BARTHOLOMEW GOSNOLD

Explored coastline from Cape Elizabeth to Martha's Vineyard and Cuttyhunk. Sir Walter Raleigh was the patentee but did not sanction the voyage.

1603 MARTIN PRING

Explored the Maine coast and Cape Cod Bay, including Plymouth harbor. Sent by Sir Walter Raleigh June 1603, arrived in Penobscot Bay at Fox Island, which he named. (It is now called Vinalhaven.) Then he traveled along the Maine coast exploring the Saco, Kennebunk, York, and Piscataqua rivers. He named Savage Rock, now Cape Neddick. He sailed around Cape Ann into Massachusetts Bay and spent seven or eight weeks in what he called Whitson Bay (now New Plymouth Harbor) exploring and gathering sassafras. He sailed back to Cape Cod Harbor and returned to England in October 1603.

1604 SAMUEL DE CHAMPLAIN

Explored the whole Maine coast, including Mount Desert, Penobscot Bay, and Penobscot River to Castine. Frenchman's Bay is named for him. He was part of a French expedition under de Monts.

1605 GEORGE WEYMOUTH

Explored the coastline from Nantucket to Monhegan and St. Georges River to Thomaston. Sent by the earl of Southampton and Lord Arundell.

1606 HENRY CHALLONS, THOMAS HANHAM, AND MARTIN PRING

Sent by Sir Ferdinando Gorges to survey the coastline around Sagadahoc, ahead of the Popham expedition.

Challons' voyage was a disaster. He disobeyed instructions as to the route to be taken, and after a number of misadventures was captured by a Spanish ship and carried off to Spain, including the two Indians Gorges had sent back with Challons, one of them Assacomet.

Hanham and Pring arrived and in Challons' absence further explored the Kennebec and earmarked the Sagadahoc site for future settlement. They returned at the end of the year to Bristol. They too had taken an Indian, Tahanedo, captured the previous year by Weymouth, back to New England and left him there.

1607 SAMUEL DE CHAMPLAIN—SECOND VOYAGE

Explored the coast of Maine and Massachusetts around Cape Ann to Glouces-
ter (Beauport), Cape Cod, and Martha's Vineyard.

1607 GEORGE POPHAM AND RALEIGH GILBERT

They were sent by Sir Ferdinando Gorges and the Plymouth Company to settle
at Sagadahoc, at the mouth of the Kennebec. This expedition was spurred by the
positive report brought back by the Hanham and Pring voyage.

They built a fort that they called St. Georges at Sagadahoc but ill-equipped,
late arriving, poor leadership, exacerbated by George Popham's death and
Raleigh Gilbert returning to England to take up his inheritance from his dead
brother, resulted in the settlement being abandoned and all returned to England
in 1608.

1608 DAMARISCOVE FISHING SETTLEMENT

Island at the entrance to Boothbay, Maine. Named for Humphrey Damarill,
resident entrepreneur. Year-round fishing settlement by 1620. In 1622 Edward
Winslow sailed from Plymouth seeking food for the starving Plymouth colony.

1609 HENRY HUDSON

Explored the coastline from Newfoundland to the Delaware Bay, via Penobscot Bay and Cape Cod. (Check account of Robert Jewett in *Forerunners of the
Pilgrims.*)

1610 SAMUEL ARGALL

Sailed the coastline from Newfoundland to the Penobscot and Cape Cod on
his way to Jamestown. (Check Argall's account in *Forerunners of the Pilgrims.*)

1611 EDWARD HARLOW AND NICHOLAS HOBSON

Sailed the coastline from the Kennebec River in Maine to Cape Cod and on to
Martha's Vineyard.

1613 SAMUEL ARGALL

Traveling from Jamestown, destroys French settlements on Mount Desert, as
well as St. Croix and Port Royal in French Canada.

1614 CAPT. JOHN SMITH

Explored and charted Maine coast. Johns Bay named for him. Isle of Shoals he named *Smith's Isles*.

1614 CAPT. THOMAS HUNT

After Smith left for England in one bark, Hunt sailed south in the other to catch fish and barter with the natives that Smith had met in the month or so previously. At Nauset and Accomack, he captured twenty-seven Native Americans altogether, including Tisquantum, to be sold as slaves in Spain on his return.

1614 CAPT. NICHOLAS HOBSON

Sent by Sir Ferdinando Gorges to Martha's Vineyard (the island of Capawak), Massachusetts, to establish settlement. The Native Americans, angry at Hunt's exploit, wouldn't allow it, and he returned to England.

1615 CAPTS. JOHN SMITH AND THOMAS DERMER

Sent by Sir Ferdinando Gorges. Capts. Smith and Dermer sailed in two ships to attempt to establish settlement in Pemaquid area, but Capt. Smith was captured at sea by the Spanish. Dermer sailed on to Newfoundland.

1615 SIR RICHARD HAWKINS

Sent by Sir Ferdinando Gorges to seek Capt. Smith and gather produce for sale. He wintered in the Pemaquid area and then sailed to Jamestown and thence to Spain to sell his produce.

1616–17 RICHARD VINES

Established a settlement at Biddeford Pool at mouth of the Saco River. Sent by Sir Ferdinando Gorges.

1618 CAPT. ROCROFT

Explored coastline from Monhegan, Maine, to Virginia. Sent by Sir Ferdinando Gorges.

1618–19 CAPT. THOMAS DERMER

Explores coastline from Monhegan, Maine, to Plymouth Harbor and back. Sir Ferdinando Gorges' agent.

1620 PLYMOUTH COLONY

Mayflower takes Pilgrims to found colony.

1621 CAPT. THOMAS DERMER

From Virginia to Cape Cod.

1622 DAVID THOMSON

From Plymouth, Devon, to Piscataqua to establish a settlement.

1622 THOMAS WESTON

Establishes a settlement at Wessagussett (Weymouth), Massachusetts.

1623–24 CHRISTOPHER LEVETT

Explored the Maine coastline: Cape Harbor, Cape Newagen, Boothbay, Sheepscot River, and south. In 1624, he noted that York Harbor would be a good place for a settlement. Levett was an agent of Sir Ferdinando Gorges.

1623 CAPE ANN SETTLEMENT, MASSACHUSETTS

Sent by Rev. John White and the Dorchester Company in Dorchester, Dorset.

1623 PISCATAQUA SETTLEMENT, MAINE

David Thompson settled at Pannaway, at the mouth of the Piscataqua.

1623 ROBERT GORGES

Sent by his father, Sir Ferdinando Gorges, accompanied by colonists to establish a New England government at Wessagusset. Robert returned to England within six months.

NATIVE AMERICANS
BROUGHT TO ENGLAND

Five Native Americans were brought back to England by Captain Weymouth from the Monhegan area in 1605, according to James Rosier, who accompanied Weymouth to record a full account of the voyage.

Tahanedo, Amoret, Skicowarres, Maneddo, and Assacomet

- Sir Ferdinando Gorges arranged for Maneddo and Assacomet to return to Northern Virginia on Challons' ill-fated voyage in 1605. Challons' ship was captured by the Spanish and taken to Spain. The crew were held prisoners in Seville until handed over to the English and returned to England. Maneddo died in Spain before he could be rescued.

- Assacomet returned to England and Sir Ferdinando Gorges.

- Skicowarres went with the Popham settlement expedition in 1607. When that failed, he stayed with his people in Sagadahoc.

- Amoret and Tahanedo went with the Capt. Pring voyage in 1606. They were left at Pemaquid by Pring.

Capt. Harlow captured Epenow, Manawet (also known as Monope), Sakaweston, Pekenimme, and Coneconam, primarily from the Monhegan and Capawack areas, in 1611. Epenow was handed over to Sir Ferdinando Gorges. Only Epenow is known to have been returned to New England.

Capt. Hunt captured Tisquantum and numerous other Native Americans in 1614. Tisquantum after many adventures returned to New England in 1618.

FOR AN EXCLUSIVE PREVIEW OF
THE NEXT EPIC CHAPTER
IN DAVID TORY'S

The Stanfield Chronicles,

TURN TO THE NEXT PAGE.

CHAPTER 1 ————

September 1620

I went out to the Hoe to watch the departure of the *Mayflower*. As it receded and disappeared behind the headland a sense of loss overwhelmed me. Aby and I had agreed that our life would always be together, centered on Plymouth, but she has left me to go on her own journey, it seemed, a part of the *Mayflower*'s leaving. I had a desperate if irrational desire to follow her. Long after the *Mayflower* had gone, I stood staring out to sea, my mind a turmoil, and it was late evening before I wended my way back home to Annie and James. I was so caught up with my grief I didn't notice the worried look on Annie's face when I came in, not knowing where I had been and concerned about my state of mind. She, too, was dealing with Aby's death in her own way. At the same time she had become, of necessity, James' parent as I had effectively abrogated my responsibility. I slumped into a chair and Annie, saying nothing, put a bowl of hot broth in front of me. I stared at it and then looked up at her, seeing her sorrow and concern.

"Dear Annie. I'm so sorry. I feel wretched. Thinking I had dealt with Aby's death, I went to the Hoe to watch the *Mayflower* sail and a great wave of anguish washed over me, imagining Aby on the boat leaving me."

She put a hand on my shoulder and shook her head. James was asleep in his crib and Annie's duties for the day were done. She lingered.

"Isaac, are you able to fend for yourself? It's time I left."

I nodded, thanked her, and saw her to the door. She gave me a hug, a quick kiss on the cheek, and left while I returned to my chair. The momentary lifting of my spirits passed and in my reverie it took a while for me to recognize James' crying, the sound acting like sharp nudges into my subconscious. Aroused, I moved quickly to his crib and lifted him into my arms wrapped in his bedclothes.

It was a timely reminder and we sat in front of the fire, his little body breathing life into me as I rocked him gently, hanging on to him long after he had gone back to sleep. It was late when I put him back with a soft kiss on his forehead and went to my own bed.

November 1620

Over the following weeks my depressed state became worse. During the day I continued to work on Sir Ferdinando's collection of maps and reports on New England. I received a letter from Will Whiteway in Dorchester, asking after me, James, and Annie, pleading with me to continue writing my journal and to send the entries to him as before. After much deliberation I realized that continuing my journal might help me sort myself out, but was still reluctant. Also, a letter from the Patriarch, Reverend John White, in Dorchester, which I replied to perfunctorily. Returning home from the Fort, James was my solace but, once he was abed, I found the nights long and unremitting and almost welcomed the moments when his disturbed sleeping called me to him. I also went for long rides on my faithful and constant Maddie. She understood my moods and accommodated her behavior accordingly. I thought occasionally about the *Sweet Rose*. She was berthed in Weymouth over the winter. In Plymouth, her crew might have raised my spirits. I didn't eat properly despite Annie's attempts. One night I drank too heavily. Annie saw the results when she arrived early the next morning and found me in the kitchen, snoring with my head on the table and an empty bottle on the floor. She sprang into action before the wet nurse, Beth, arrived and James was up. She lifted my head by the hair and slapped me hard across the face, dragged me to my feet, and shoved my head under the water pump.

"Isaac Stanfield! Don't you ever do that again. You are a disgrace with so much to live for yet you seem to want to throw your life away. Aby has gone. You have James. Who knows what might have happened if he had needed you during the night. You have people who love and depend on you, but you have become totally wrapped up in yourself. Now stop it."

I said nothing. I had a splitting headache and was horrified at losing control, especially when James was in my care, and went to my room to clean up. Returning downstairs, with a curt apology, said I was going for a walk to clear my head, after which I had a meeting at the Fort with Sir Ferdinando. With that I left her, mortified, and Annie angry, pink of face with her fists tightly clenched on her hips.

At the Fort, I met with Sir F. and David Thomson. The meeting was to discuss the impending departure of David for New England and Sir F. had asked me to attend. I was surprised to see David and commiserated with him, as Amyse had recently given birth to a daughter who had died a few days later. He thanked me and was quick to change the subject. David had been gathering financial support among merchant adventurers in London, since his return from New England in July of 1619. He wanted to establish a permanent settlement on the Piscataqua River, suggesting that Smith's Isles, close by, could be a shore base for fishing fleets and an alternative to Monhegan. He was going back to find a suitable location, build a fortified house, then return to England to find and take settlers back, including his family. Sir F. was supportive as he was anxious to establish another settlement in New England. It was not known what had happened to the Leiden Separatist Pilgrims on the *Mayflower* and, with the Council for New England now established, it was important to start the colonization process. He had agreed to grant David a large tract of land as well as to support his Piscataqua venture. David needed to determine for himself the land he wanted so that he could establish the patent for it on his return. Sir F. had gone as far as to help organize a construction crew to go with David on this trip.

Sir F. was still recovering from the loss of his wife and smiled ruefully.

"The three of us share much sorrow. Isaac, perhaps you should follow David's example and take your mind off your loss. Why don't you accompany him to New England?"

I couldn't believe what I heard. Of course, I could escape this mental morass I was in, find myself and, by following Aby or the thought of her, put her to rest. I said that I would be happy to go. Sir F. said he wanted me to continue to evaluate opportunities for further settlement, provide advice and assistance to David but, most importantly, find out what was happening with the Separatists. I returned home with a plan which gave me focus, becoming all-consuming in the few weeks before leaving. I was so caught up in that excitement I did not pay due attention to my family. God bless Annie, who was pleased that I was re-animated but deeply saddened that I was leaving for New England. I explained that Sir F. needed me to go, not telling her it had been a suggestion not an order, and tried to convince her that it was also for my own peace of mind. Seeing and accepting the inevitability of my departure, she agreed to take on full responsibility for James while I was away and to move into 15 Whimple Street. I arranged with my business manager, Mr. Scroud, to provide her with the financial support and whatever else she needed. I convinced myself that Annie would ensure that James had a secure, comfortable, and loving life while I was away. But James sensed my imminent departure and reached out to me. 6th day of December, his first birthday, I went for a long walk to the Hoe with